I0746300

SERIOUS BUSINESS

A Harry Becker Mystery

GORDON REID

 A catalogue record for this book is available from the National Library of Australia

Copyright © 2025 by Gordon Reid

All rights reserved, including the right to reproduce this book or portions thereof in any form whatsoever.

This book is, of course, fiction.

Publisher:
Australian Self Publishing Group, Pty. Ltd. / Inspiring Publishers
PO Box 159, Calwell, ACT 2905, Australia.
Phone: 61-(0) 2 6291-2904
http://australianselfpublishinggroup.com

National Library of Australia Prepublication Data Service

Author: Gordon Reid

Title: **SERIOUS BUSINESS**

ISBN: 978-1-923250-91-8 (print)
ISBN: 978-1-923250-92-5 (ePub2)

CHAPTER 1

The black car was there again today. She parked the Nissan outside the school and walked over—not directly to the car, but toward the shop. It was parked in the free space beside the shop, facing the school. As soon as she was out of sight, she changed course, walking around the corner and up to the black car. It was an old Ford Fairlane, in fairly good condition, with tinted windows so no-one could see who was sitting in it day after day.

Chook rapped on the glass. It rolled down slowly, evenly. Obviously electric.

The smoke hit her. It smelt Turkish, but could have been something else just as heavy. The man cleared his throat lightly, more a subtle cough. Squinted up at her. Small eyes—old, tired, reddish, inconsequential. Thick eyebrows, large nose, aquiline. Harry Becker had once described a man like this—a man who'd sat beside him and Evelyn Crowley at a table outside a cafe in Canberra, years ago. She'd asked him to find out who was blackmailing her. Of course, there was no blackmail. She had conned him into a little scheme she had to kill her husband, a big man in a big bank.

'What are you doing here?' Chook asked.

He screwed up his face and smiled—a polite smirk, almost.

'What I do here, lady?'

'Why park here every day?'

'Every day, you say?' He shrugged. 'That my business, I think.'

'Yeah? Well, it's my business too.'

He stared at her, not liking her tone. Very few people did. She had a menacing manner, like a Mafia boss—soft and slow and deadly.

'I wait somebody.'

'You wait somebody?'

'Yairs.'

'Every day?'

'I just sit here, wait somebody.'

'You told the lady at the school you're waiting for a boy, your son?'

'Yairs, my son.'

'A boy? On a bus?' The interstates did stop at the shop if they had to.

He glanced around. 'I wait him. He no come.'

'By bus?'

'Pardon, lady?'

'You expect him to come by bus?'

'By bus? Oh...' He shrugged again, one hand on the steering wheel, the other held the cigarette. 'No on bus.'

'How then?'

'How?' He shrugged. 'Maybe he come on bike.'

'A bike? What kind of bike?'

'You know, big bike. For mountain, I think.'

'A mountain bike? A dirt bike?'

'Yairs, I think you say dirt bike.' He drew on the cigarette, let the smoke drift out again. 'Get plenty dirt, that bike.'

'What make of bike?'

Chook was leaning on the old Ford now, a hand on top, bending down. Watching him closely. She didn't like what she saw. This man was lying, anyone could see that. Why would a kid turn up on a bus seven years later? More likely, he was scouting around, hoping to meet someone who knew what happened.

'I don' know, you know?' He waved the cigarette. It was well down now, close to his fingers. They were small fat fingers, brown. Not exactly dirty, but brown with age or hard work. Or bad blood supply. He looked like he'd been a labouring man all his life, maybe now retired. Maybe looking for his son. The son she'd killed seven years ago.

'What colour was the bike?'

Immediately she realised her mistake. She should have asked, What colour *is* the bike? as though the kid were still alive.

'What colour? Maybe it red.'

'A red motor bike? A dirt bike?'

He nodded. 'I think.'

'You don't sound too sure.'

The old man shrugged.

'What make was it?'

'Make? I dunno. Maybe Honda, I dunno, you know?'

'Where did he live?'

'He used live by me his father and family, you know? Then he take off. On this bike. He say he not gonna work no more for me. He hate concrete, hate that work, form work. He not gonna be like his father anymore, makin' footpaths, makin' foundations, you know? He gonna make some money. You know? These kids, they want' everything. Never think for to work hard. Have good time, you know? I say him, You got steady job. You got money every Friday.'

'What did he say?'

'He just laugh. He say he got plenty money now. He got bike, big bike. He ride off. That what you say? Ride off?'

'Did he say anything else?'

'He just say, Hi-ho! Silver.'

'Hi-ho, Silver? When was this?'

'Six year, maybe seven. I don't know now. I old man now. I look for him.'

'Why're you looking here?'

'Here? New South Wales? I ask friends, they say he gone Griffith. They say he got special job. I ask them, What job? They just laugh, you know? He follow man name Scarafini, Italian name. Why he follow, they don' know. So I go Griffith. I ask 'round, I ask police. They never see him, they say. Not in Griffith now. Maybe go to Wagga.'

Chook knew that name. It had been Evelyn Crowley's maiden name, Evalina Scarafini.

'You went to Wagga?'

'Yairs, I go there. Nobody know him. So, I come back. I come this place. Ask in shop here. They say never see him, long time ago.'

She patted the roof.

'What's your name?'

'My name? My name Medich.'

'Medich?'

He nodded. 'Yairs.'

'And the name of your son?'

'Branko.'

'Branko Medich?'

'Branko, yairs.'

Chook straightened up.

She felt bad in her guts. This was the father of the kid, as they called him. When she'd seen the red bike by Harry Becker's gate, she'd crept up using the old pepper tree as cover. She'd slipped to a window. The kid was talking, giggling. He sounded happy—like he got fun out of killing people. Then he'd shot Alfredo Scarafini, shot him dead. Was about to shoot Harry Becker, but she'd walked in and shot the kid, straight through the head. Very neat, not much blood. She'd been about to phone in and report what she'd done, but had looked out a back window. Had seen Robyn and her kids playing with a dog, a crazy dog chasing a ball, barking. It went into a beautiful creek. Dog went in after it. Boy in after the dog. Got sopping wet, Robyn hauling him out. Laughing and scolding and cuddling him. Chook had not been able to make the call. If she had, the farm would soon have been swarming with cops. This happy family would have been devastated. So, she'd put both bodies in the boot of her car and driven south, across the border. To her father, who worked nights at a crematorium. Everything was taken care of.

Until now.

She stood back. 'If I hear anything, Mr Medich—'

'Thank you, lady. I thank you.'

He started the engine. Just a light jolt then a purr. She waited for him to drive off. But he paused, the window still down. No longer he held a cigarette. A tidy man, you could see. He was old and tired after decades of shovelling cement to make paths and garage floors and foundations for houses. Looked worn out.

'You name?' he asked.

'My name?'

'You talk me. I feel more better now.'

'My name? It's Becker.'

'Becker?'

'I am Mrs Becker.'

'You Mrs Becker?'

'Anna Becker.' She said it seriously, like saying: Yes, your son killed my partner, Polly Politis, so I killed your son. He was going to kill Harry Becker, but I arrived in time. You will never find your son, nor will the police. And another thing: If you touch my girl, I will kill you too. Understand?

She didn't say those words. She looked them at him.

He seemed to understand. Looked away at the little school across the road, at the passing traffic, at the store and a few of the houses of this little town called Old Man Creek. A bell rang at the school. Children would be coming out soon.

'You know that name? Old Man Creek?'

'Yairs,' he said. He seemed surprised, as though he'd heard about her. Heard certain things. That she was a dangerous woman. Carried a weapon most of the time. No-one ever gave her any cheek. She was a cop. Or, she was not a cop, but behaved like one.

Everyone in the Wagga Wagga district knew her name.

Back when she was a Federal Police officer, she'd killed a man in a shootout in a hotel on the main street. Later, she'd shot a fellow police officer in an office on Morrow Street because he'd pulled a gun on her—or had not pulled a gun on her. It was not clear. Then, those two hicks had put two bullets in her, one passing through her side. She'd survived, quit the force with a large pension, and married Harry Becker. Now, she was a grazier's wife and a legend in her own time. The fastest gun in the west, so the local paper called her.

Medich was still squinting.

'You police lady?'

Chook still carried a weapon, slung under her left shoulder. Under her jacket. She leaned down again, pulling back the jacket. Revealing the butt of the Colt. She had a licence to carry it. The local police had tried to stop her, but she'd appealed to a court and won.

'What do you think?'

His eyes closed. He tried to smile politely, but could not.

'Good day, lady,' he said.

She slapped the roof hard this time.

'On your way, Mr Medich.'

He drove off. Not to Wagga, but along the Lockhart Road a few yards, then turned left onto the back road to Henty. Then, presumably, back to Melbourne. Was this the real Fat Man and not the old man in Melbourne she'd choked to death? Medich was not an Italian name. Nor did he sound Italian. Maybe had nothing to do with the Mafia. She did not know.

But why was he nosing around now?

Children began to come out, cars waiting to pick them up. Roberta appeared on the verge, calling, 'Mummy! Pick me up?'

'Yes,' she said, more to herself than to her daughter.

Then walked back across the road. As she did, she noticed the teacher.

Nerida Larkin saw her approaching and faltered, as if shocked, scared, or uncertain. Perhaps afraid that this formidable woman might set upon her. Chastise her, lodge a complaint.

Chook took her daughter's hand and turned her around.

The teacher had frozen, waiting, a satchel under her arm.

An ordinary sort of young woman in her late twenties. Slim but not tall, long dark hair. In the afternoon sunlight, her skin glowed like polished stone—a Mediterranean sort of complexion. She tried to smile but failed. Her eyes looked afraid.

'Hullo,' she said.

'Has that man been annoying you?' Chook asked. 'The one in the black car?'

She jumped.

'Him? Oh, I don't know who he is.'

'I didn't say you did.'

'Oh, he—that man is a nuisance. I mean, he just sits there day after day and…'

'You drew the curtain?'

'The curtain?'

'Robbie said you drew the curtain yesterday.'

'Oh, yes, I had to. I mean, all the children could see.'

'See him? His windows are tinted. I could not see him until he rolled his window down.'

'Couldn't you? Oh, well, it is so distracting for them, isn't it? Parking there every day?'

'Do you know him, Nerida?'

She jumped again. 'Know him? Oh, no, I've never seen him in my…'

'He told me he is waiting for his son.'

'His son? Did he?'

'His son was Branko Medich.'

'Medich?'

'Do you know that name?'

'Medich?'

Her eyes darted, looking for somewhere to hide.

'If you will excuse me—'

She lived in a cottage around the corner on Lockhart Road. She was a good teacher. It was a small school, only sixty pupils in three classes. Roberta was only five and yet already in second grade. Loved school. Loved her teacher.

'You are fond of my little girl?'

'Fond? Of Roberta? Of course, yes. But one has to avoid showing affection, you know.'

'In that case, why were you hugging and kissing her behind the weather shed?'

'Was I?'

'A few days ago, Nora Hopkins said.'

'Was I? Oh, she must have been crying.'

'Not according to someone who saw you.'

'Well, I—' She didn't know what to say. She was caught.

'I can understand,' Chook said. 'She is a prize girl. Everyone loves a prize.'

'A prize?' The teacher seemed dismayed. 'Please—' she said.
'Have you ever had a child, Nerida?'
'What? Oh, no, no—'
She was lying through her teeth, anyone could see that.
'It's all right,' Chook said. 'I know how you feel.'

CHAPTER 2

They were having a beer at the William Hovell when she walked in. Anastacia was still working, though only two days a week at the gym just around the corner on Morgan Street. Her partners covered the other days. Normally, she never went into the pub—fame and infamy kept her away—but today, she walked in looking for Jack Jackson. She must have been thirty-eight by now, but didn't look a day older. And not as heavy also. She was a big woman, over six-feet tall and heavy, but mostly muscle. Lost a bit of weight too. Walked in wearing her usual working gear—loose blue sweatshirt and tight blue pants, trainers on her feet—with an easy swing in her step and all the confidence in the world.

She'd gotten back to gym work after taking two bullets from those two hicks from down Henty way. One bullet had gone right through and out the other side, so she had three holes in her body. Not natural orifices, as she liked to point out. Making everyone laugh, especially the cops. She knew most of them.

Breezed up and said, 'Heard you might be here, Jack.'

'Yeah?' he said. 'Trouble?'

He was a senior sergeant now, generally running things at the Wagga Wagga police centre. But the day shift had ended for him, Max Kruger, and a couple of other guys. Max was now a senior constable, not on the road so much now. There was a new guy standing beside him.

'This is Dex,' Max said.

The stranger's eyes lit up. 'Howdy, ma'am?'

He put up a hand to raise his hat, which was not there—a reflex on meeting a lady. Otherwise, he stood with both hands on his hips, like someone in a publicity shot for an old Hollywood western.

'Tex?' she said.

'No, Dex. For Dexter.'

'Dexter from Texas?'

'No, ma'am, Oklahoma.'

'Oklahoma?'

'That's right, ma'am.'

'Where the sun comes sweepin' down the plain?'

'Hey, you know that song?'

'I think I saw the movie when I was a kid.'

Max said, 'We were just talking about you.'

'No doubt about my notoriety.'

'Dexter wanted to know what the cuttings were all about.'

The press cuttings were still in a frame on the wall behind them, next to the portrait of William Hovell. In case you don't know of William Hovell, he was a surveyor who went overland with Hamilton Hume from Yass—where Hume had a property—down to Port Phillip Bay, crossing the Murrumbidgee near where Wagga Wagga is today. That was in 1824. They weren't overlanding sheep or anything like that, just exploring. Wanted to know whether there was a safe and secure route to the south coast. And there was, if you didn't mind occasionally getting lost or dealing with attacks by the Aborigines.

These days, no-one looks at Hovell's portrait; they look at the cuttings about the day Anastacia Babchuck killed that smelly piece of crap, Gregory Shafter, whose one claim to fame was, as he put it, shafting women, whether they liked it or not. He'd walked in with a sawn-off shot gun, declaring that he was gonna kill her for putting him away for sixteen years. Actually, he'd got out after thirteen and was looking to 'spread her guts around.' Anastacia, or Stacey, or Chook as she was sometimes called, was so fast that old-timers in the bar that day swear they heard only one shot—though Shafter, on examination, had three messy holes in him. He was bleeding like a stuck pig, as they say.

That's how fast she was when she was in the Federal Police. How fast she was with a Glock 22. You've probably heard this story a million times, but the tourists love it. So does the hotel's management.

'I'm gonna tear those pictures down one day,' she said.

'Still drinking Jack Daniels?' Jackson asked.

'I'll have one with you,' she said.

Jackson's real name is Cecil. At school years ago, all the kids used to laugh at him, so he told them to call him Jack. Or else.

Bettina was behind the bar. 'Stacey,' she said. 'Is that you?'

'More or less.'

'Welcome back,' Bettina said.

You might remember her as Bruce. She'd been Bettina since she made the big decision five years ago. Everyone was fascinated, not sure whether they cut off a dick or bored a hole or both. Anyway, it took some time for most regulars at the Hovell, as it was known, to get over the shock. Bettina and a friend have a small place overlooking Lake Albert. No-one is sure whether the friend is a man or a woman. It's hard to tell these days.

'Cheers,' Chook said.

'Cheers,' they said.

'When did you start, Dexter?' she asked.

'Just last week, didn't I, Sarge?'

'Yeah,' Jack said. He was a man of few words.

'He's doing my old run,' Max said, trying to help. 'So you might see a bit of him.'

Everyone could see that Dexter was dying to ask her directly about the shoot-out she never wanted to talk about. She was a farmer's wife now and she never gave interviews.

'How's Harry?' Jackson asked.

'He's all right, but trying to make a decision. Whether to plant or not to plant.'

'Plant what?'

'Maize.'

'Isn't it a bit early for planting maize? As I understand it, the ground temperature has to be at least twelve degrees Celsius before it's wise to plant.'

'He fears this dry spell will continue. It'll be worse this summer.'

'So he wants to get it in early and out to market early?'

'If we get a good season, he'll do that. If it's a bad, he'll cut in November and use it for stock feed.'

'Guarding against all eventualities?'

'He's a very guarded man.'

'Otherwise, how is he?'

'Complaining about his shoulder. It's hurting badly now and he's thinking of having a reconstruction.'

'Excuse me, ma'am, what happened?' Dexter asked.

'Well,' she said, putting down her glass and signalling to Bettina. 'Someone shot him one evening.'

'Yeah?'

'At his home in Sydney, years ago.'

'Yeah?'

Bettina came back with the order. Chook waited until she was out of earshot.

'Something's happened,' she said.

Jackson was surprised. 'What is it?'

'I think the Fat Man is back.'

The others raised their eyebrows, except the new guy. He didn't know who the Fat Man was, nor did the others. But they knew he was bad news, whoever he was. Becker had thought the farmhouse explosion back in 1996 had been an effort to kill him, following on what had happened in Sydney. But Chook was pretty sure that *she* had been the target. That was years ago. Two hicks who had tried to kill her had told the police a fat man from Melbourne had paid them. Now, a fat man turns up in a black car from Melbourne and watches a little country school. And Harry's daughter is a little kid at that school.

'What makes you think that?'

'He could be anyone, Stacey.'

'I had a few words with him. He's fat and he smokes stinking cigarettes and he stares at you as if he is thinking bad things.'

'You've seen him?'

'Not much of him, a few inches when he rolls down the window.'

'Yeah?'

'A tinted window,' she added. 'His name is Medich.'

'Medich?'

'You think he is the Fat Man?'

'I'm not sure.'

'Did he say why he is there? At the school?'

'Waiting for his son.'

'Does anyone turn up?'

'No.'

'Medich, eh?'

'Same name as the young creep who disappeared out this way seven years ago.'

'His bike was found in Wybilonga.'

'But the kids who'd pinched it said they found it outside our place.'

'Got a number for this car?'

'Yeah.' She handed him a piece of paper.

'A Victorian number?'

'Yeah.'

'I'll have it checked out.'

'That would be appreciated, Jack.'

'No-one seen getting in or out?'

'No, I checked at the local store. Several people have noticed the car—a Ford Fairlane. Could be ten years old, maybe more. Shiny black, in good condition.'

'No-one gets out? Or in?'

'No, never.'

'Why would they be interested in you?'

'I'm not sure they are interested in me, but Robbie.'

'You mean he may be checking your daily movements?'

'Yeah.'

Jack raised his eyebrows; that's about as expressive as he ever got. But he held his breath for a second longer than normal. They were all ears, intrigued. Max placed a hand on his hip as if reaching for his sidearm.

Jack asked Dexter, 'Have you noticed him?'

The new man looked blank. Then shook his head.

'Check it first thing tomorrow morning.'

'Yes, sir.'

'You checked with the storekeeper?' Jack asked Chook.

'Yeah, he doesn't know the car.'

'Is the car parked directly outside the school?'

'No, opposite the school, in the car park beside the store. Facing the school.'

'But it is there when school lets out?'

'Yeah, sometimes.'

'What does Harry think?'

'Anyone planning harm is not likely to drive an easily identifiable vehicle and appear at least three times before doing it.'

Jackson sighed.

'What makes you think he could be the Fat Man?'

'Just a feeling.'

This talk occurred back in 2002.

Things were not going too well for the man on the land back then. For the woman too.

The place is called Old Man Creek, simply because there is a creek of that name. Actually it is not a creek at all. It's an an anabranch of the Murrumbidgee, which means that the water flows out of the river upstream and flows back downstream.

It is a small village. There is a general store with three fuel pumps out front. Also, a pub and church and a community hall and a handful of houses. Agricultural workers live there in a few behind and beside, but not in front of, the little school. Workers who don't own land. Or, might own a few acres here and there. Some of them had owned big blocks at one time, mainly wheat blocks, but had been forced to walk away. Usually, because of the drought or the market or the banks or just bad luck. People who tried and failed. Others who did not try but still failed. Some on a pension. Others not on anything, except their memories and a bottle each day.

That being the way things were in the second year of the new century.

▲

CHAPTER 3

Anastacia went home dissatisfied, grumpy when she got out of the B.M.W. Nutty danced around, but she was in no mood for pats and kind words. She found Harry Becker in the kitchen, drinking water. It had been a hot day, and he was trying to follow her advice: Drink water, Harry. You lose a lot of water every day, working out there in the sun. If you don't, don't blame me when you fall down in a stupor. He worked hard to drought-proof this farm. It was called *Nil Desperandum.*

He put down the glass and turned to her.

'What's happened?'

She told him. 'Jack says he'll get someone to talk to him.'

'That's all he can do.'

'If that man is thinking of abducting Robbie—'

'You don't know that, Anna.'

'If he is, I'll kill him.'

He slid off the kitchen bench and went over to her.

'Listen, you can't threaten to kill someone. That's a crime in itself.'

'I'm going to find out where he lives.'

'You said the car has a Victorian plate.'

'I'll find him.'

'He has committed no crime.'

'Loitering with intent is a crime.'

17

'What crime? You don't know why he waits there each day.'

'He's not waiting for his son. Why is he lying? His son died seven years ago. You know that. I killed him, right here in this house.'

It was not in the present house. The original house had been blown up on Becker's birthday, during a luncheon party. His wife, Robyn, had been killed. Their unborn daughter, Roberta, had survived. Old Bert Henscke, who'd had the farm next door, had seen a man standing in the trees along the creek. The man had a phone in his hand. Had he pressed a button, detonating the bomb? No-one knew. The police had searched but never found the Fat Man.

Was there really a Fat Man?

A man who solved problems for certain people at a good price?

She relaxed. 'Where's Robbie?'

'In her room.'

'I don't hear her.'

'She was singing to herself before you came in.'

Chook listened. 'She's talking to someone now.'

She went to Robbie's room and shouted, 'Get out! You bad dog, get out of the house!'

She chased Nutty through the back door.

'Where was he?'

'On her bed with her, licking her face. She was giggling. Had her arms around him.'

'He loves her.'

'He's filthy. He lies in the dirt all day.'

'Ah, don't be harsh on him. He's a good dog, a good guard dog. No-one can get into this place without him knowing.'

The girl came in. 'Hullo, Mummy.'

'Hullo, darling.'

She went to Chook, put an arm about her legs, kissed her hand. 'You smell, Mummy.'

'I know I smell. You'd smell too if you had to jump around all day, trying to whip up action among a lot of giggling Gerties trying to lose weight. I'm gonna have a shower and then a long glass of beer.'

When she came back, as fresh as a daisy, she said, 'Now, where's my drink?'

Becker passed her a beer in a long glass—a middy, or half a pint in the old measures. The girl cuddled up beside her on the divan. She said nothing, but simply looked up at her mother. Anastacia had changed into a loose dress with bare arms. Open sandals on her feet, with clunky heels. She never wore high heels, certainly not spiky ones. She'd wobble too much. From her point of view, the only value of high heels would be to fight with them. Swinging them viciously, going for the eyes with the heels. If it came to that.

'You smell lovely, Mummy.'

'Do I, Chicken Lickin'?' She kissed the girl on her nose. Roberta did not know that Anastacia was not her birth mother. 'How was school?'

'All right.'

'Just all right?'

'Uh hum.'

'Did you do anything interesting?'

'No, not much today.'

'Did you get another gold star?'

She shook her head, curls flying.

'Nothing happened at all?'

'Mrs Hopkins went across and spoke to the man.'

'What man?'

Chook was surprised. She looked at Becker, asking without words: Do you know about this? He could only shake his head.

'What man, darling?'

'The man in the car.'

'What car?'

'Across the road, by the shop.'
'Was it a big, black car?'
Roberta nodded.
'And what did Mrs Hopkins say? To the man?'
'I don't know.'
No, of course, the headmistress would not tell the children.
'Did the man get out of the car?'
She paused. 'No—'
'You can see the store quite clearly from your window, can't you?'
'Nerida said, "Eyes front."'
'So you had to get on with your lesson?'
'Yes.'
'Was the man there when Daddy picked you up?'
Roberta shook her head. Anastacia changed the subject.
'What was the lesson?'
'All about the world.'
'Oh, geography?'
The girl nodded.
'And what did you learn?'
'I know where you came from.'
Chook was surprised. 'Where I came from?'
'Yes.'
'How do you mean?'
'On the round map.'
'Oh, the globe? The big round globe on Nerida's desk?'
Roberta nodded.
'And where do I come from?'
'Ukraine.'
Chook was impressed. 'How did you know that?'
'I heard you telling Daddy one day.'
'You have good ears. Pretty ears, they hear everything. Nearly as good as Nutty's. He can hear things we cannot.'

She was running fingers over the girl's head. 'Would you like soup before dinner? We could have mushroom soup? Have you ever had that? With Nanna, perhaps?'

'What does it taste like?'

'Mushy mushrooms.'

'Did you make it in Ukraine?'

'I don't come from the Ukraine. I was born in Melbourne. But my mother and father did.'

'Did they come in a boat?'

'Yes, they did.'

'Where are they now?'

'My mother died a long time ago.'

'And your daddy?'

'He went back to the Ukraine.'

'What happened to him? In Ukraine?'

'I don't know, darling? I don't know.'

'Doesn't he send you any letters?'

'No, nothing.'

Chook looked at her watch. 'Oh, gosh, it's gone six! We must do something about food. What would you like, Robbie?'

Roberta shook her head. 'I don't know.'

'I know, pancakes! Ukrainian pancakes!'

'Are they yummy?'

'Oh, yes, they are. I once cooked them for Daddy.'

'Did he like them?'

'Yes, he did. Then he kissed me.'

'Was that the first time he kissed you?'

'Yes, it was.'

The girl collapsed against her. 'I love you, Mummy.'

'I love you too, darling.'

They sat like that for some time, the woman sitting cross-legged in a light pink and green summery frock. It was not officially spring, but it felt like it—a warm, dry spring. A long, hot, dry spell was coming. You could feel it.

'Did the man come?' she asked Becker.

'The agronomist? Yeah, he came.'

'What did he say?'

'He went all over the paddock, testing. There's still some moisture in it. Most of it.'

'How long will it last?'

'If it doesn't rain? Two or three weeks.'

'Is that long enough to get a good crop?'

'Nope, not long enough at all.'

'Will it be worth cutting?'

'Oh, yeah, it can go into the bin. The stock will eat it. They'll have to eat it.'

'It looks so sad now. It's going dry, isn't it?'

'Yeah, bone dry.'

He was in the kitchen, checking the recipe book, then making sure they had the ingredients. They didn't have everything for Ukie pancakes, but they could compromise with ham instead of red meat. They did have some sour cream, plenty of fresh herbs, eggs and flour. He often cooked when she'd had a heavy day at the gym. The gym was not open on Sundays, nor at night. Some city gyms allowed patrons to use the equipment without staff present, but Wagga Wagga was not ready for that yet.

Roberta came out of her room. She'd been watching the six o'clock news on her own small television. There were terrible pictures from Iraq. Tanks and guns and people lying in the streets. A dog was sniffing one of the bodies. It was a child.

'Mummy?'

'Yes?'

'Is the man in the black car going to hurt us?'

CHAPTER 4

The next day, they hadn't been home long when someone knocked on the front door. A tentative knock, perhaps by a boy, a small man, or a stranger asking for water or to make a phone call. That happened sometimes; after all, they lived by a highway and all sorts of things happened to travellers. When Becker opened the door, he saw a policeman—not too young, but a bit older than Max Kruger, who used to patrol the highway all the way to Narrandera, depending on who or what he encountered. Now and then, he called in to say goodday. More than once he'd had a quick cup of tea and a chat. A friendly cop, Max—the type you could depend on, come rain or shine. This man was different—and diffident. Becker had never met a more diffident cop. He had taken off his cap and was holding it in two hands, respectfully.

'Ah, hi,' he said. On his hip sat the usual equipment, including a Glock pistol. At the gate was the big red Holden with a blue and white stripe along the side and Highway Patrol across the back. Antennas and lights were mounted importantly on top.

'Hi,' Becker said.

'Hi there. Dexter Grass,' he said. 'Sorry if I'm disturbin' you folks any.'

'Not at all. You've taken over from Max?'

'Officer Kruger? Yeah, sure thang. We was havin' a beer with Sergeant Jackson yesterday, and she came in— Your lady wife, I mean. And said there was this guy.'

'In a black car?'

'Yeah, sure. And Sergeant Jackson— He's my boss. He said for me to check it out first thang today.'

'He did?'

'And I did just that.'

'You did?'

'Yes, sir, I squatted myself down first thang today— In my waggon, of course. That's the one right there by your gate. Outside that perty little school this mornin' and waited. But no show. Not this mornin' anyway. So I called again just now and the lady in charge said that dammed black car hadn't showed itself all day. All the kids had gone and the kids had gone home and she was just about to lock her door.'

'And she said my wife had spoken to him?'

'Yes, sir, sure thang. She said that your lady wife had a great gift for frightening people she did not like?' He made it a question.

'Yeah, she's a bit like that.'

The American leaned forward, as if short-sighted.

'You're Mr Becker?'

'I think so.'

'Mr Henry Becker?

'I think so.'

The American laughed—a short-sharp laugh, much like a pistol shot.

'Hey there, is she at home right now?'

'I think so.'

He laughed, like another pistol.

'Could I—hey, I don't want to disturb you folks any, but could I have a word with her? I mean, you ain't preparin' to set down to supper or anythang like that?'

'At four o'clock? I don't think so.'

Becker looked back.

Anastacia was right behind him, peeping. She stepped out. Roberta tried to follow, but Becker nudged her back inside and closed the door.

She studied him.

Dexter Grass was a lean man, lean to the point of looking half-starved. Not an ounce of fat on him. Skin stretched tight on his face, like saddle-worn leather. Looked like a farm boy, raised on pork, grits, and corn dogs. Hair cut was cut close but ragged, like a crew-cut that hadn't seen a barber in a while. His eyes weren't quite blue nor brown but reminded her of dusty roads and parched fields and dole queues. He seemed to hop as he spoke, like a square dancer—one foot out, then the next, taking a step back, always ending up where he started. He was chewing gum. Could have been where he got his energy.

He told it all again.

'The lady in charge—'

'Nora Hopkins.'

'Sayed you spoke to him.'

'I did.'

'You did?'

'Yesterday afternoon.'

'Ah, right, yeah.' He stopped dancing. 'Yeah, well, ma'am, we done checked his number.'

'You did? His registration number?'

She meant the vehicle's registration number. He nodded victoriously. 'Yayer, ma'am.'

'And?'

'His name is Medich.'

'Medich?'

She knew that, but played dumb.

'He lives in Melbourne.'

'Melbourne, eh?'

'Seems to be perfectly legit. A retired builder sort of guy, although they say down thayre he still does a bit of work, mainly paths and raynderin'.'

'Reigndeering?'

He laughed. 'Cementin' on walls. Maybe you folks call it stucco.'

'Oh, yeah. And why is he up here?'

'We don't know. The school lady, Mrs Hopkins, she says he is not welcome 'round her school.'

'Strange men who hang around kids, you know.'

He'd begun square dancing again. She waited patiently, half-smiling, amused by his accent—pure hillbilly out of the Ozarks.

'Thought you might have got some details out of him.'

'Details?'

'Yes, ma'am, like why he was thayer?'

'Oh, sure. He said he was waiting for his son.'

'His son?'

'His son.'

'He was waitin' for his son thayer, day after day?'

'Yes, but his son didn't turn up.'

'He was comin' on a bus, maybe?'

'No, his son was travelling along this road seven years ago and disappeared.'

'Disappeared? Where exactly?'

'Somewhere along this road.'

'At that spot? At the old store? At the school?'

'He didn't say exactly where.'

'Seven years ago? Hell, that's a long time to wait. I mean, why now? Why is he lookin' now?'

It had been obvious why the old man had been there. He knew or had a reasonable suspicion that she was in some way connected with his son's death. Now, why would he know that? Who would have told him?

'I don't know. Perhaps he's very old. You know how people get funny ideas when they're old. Some leave home and go off to some distant place they knew as a child. And disappear. The police have to locate them.'

'You think maybe he's a kook? I mean, strange? In the hayd?'

'Could be.'

'Gee, that's amazin'.'

'What's amazing?'

'According to the Melbourne police, he did have a son.'

'He did?'

'Branko? Branko? Yeah, Branko Medich. And his bike was found hayer on this road sayven years ago.'

'I did hear that.'

'And no-one ever claimed the bike. Looks like he just disappeared.'

'It happens.'

She was becoming tired of his buffoonery.

'Oh yeah, sure. Hell, I wonder what happened to him?'

'No idea. I've been here only five years.'

'Yeah, well, I gayss we'll never know.' He began to move off the verandah. 'Hey, I heard the bike was found here, on the roadside.'

'Yes, I heard that too. Some Aboriginal kids pinched it. Went for a joy ride.'

'Yeah?'

She waited. 'Was there anything else?'

'Oh, hell, no, I don't thank. Hey, if he turns up again—'

'I'll give you a call, Tex.'

He grinned. 'Ah, hell, I ain't from Texas, no, sir, ma'am. I'm an Okie.'

'An Okie, eh? I'm a Ukie,' she said.

'Excuse me?'

'From Ukraine.'

'Ukraine? Hell, is that in the States?'

'Not yet.'

'What?' He paused, possibly hoping to carry on like this.

'Nice to meet you, Tex.'

'Hey, it's Dex, short for Dexter.'

'So long, Dexter.'

'Yeah, sure, great. Great to meet you, ma'am—'

Yet he lingered. 'Jack said you was a derned cop yourself.'

'I don't know about derned.'

He laughed. 'Heard you were with the Federal Police?'

'That's right.'

'They reckon you're great with a Glock.'

'What are you getting at, Dexter?'

'Oh, nothin', ma'am. I, well, I was just wonderin'. Ah, hell, I'm bein' nosy, I gayss. Thought maybe we could talk sometime. They reckon you know this area better'n anybody. Who's who, that kinda thang.'

'I'm always too busy for talking.'

He was disappointed, given the brush-off.

'Oh, yeah, sure, I gayss that's orright.'

'Nice of you to call, Dexter.'

'Yes, ma'am. Well, so long then.'

He began to walk off. She had an idea. He could be useful.

'Dexter—'

'Yes, ma'am?'

'I told that old guy that, if I ever heard anything, I'd contact him.'

'Yeah?'

'I don't have his address.'

'His address?' He flipped through his notes. 'Oh, hell, I thought I had it. Yayer, sure, I've got it back at the station. I can gayt that for you, no swayt.'

'You could?'

'No problem.'

She smiled. 'I'd appreciate it.'

'Yayer, sure, I'll call you. As soon as I git back.'

He could have called in on his intercom and got it, but was too excited to think straight.

'I'd be grateful,' she said.

'Okay, ma'am, you've got it.'

He walked back to his vehicle, shaking his head. As if he'd just met the fastest gun in the whole world.

'Fucking idiot,' she said to herself.

They had dinner and talked about everything else, mindful of Roberta. She was a sensitive child, attuned to what others felt. Even what they were thinking. Not attuned to their actual words, but attuned to the sense of what was being said. As if she could read your mind.

Half an hour later, Dexter phoned. He was excited.

'Hey there, it's Dexter! I got that aydress for you!'

'You have?'

'Yeah, sure thang.'

'Just a moment while I get a pen. Okay, what is it?'

He gave her an address, a place in Cremorne, Melbourne.

She knew it. She'd lived nearby in Burnley until she was eighteen, when she'd lit out on her own. 'Thank you, Dexter.'

'No trouble, ma'am. Say—'

He was going to chat, but she cut him off. 'I won't forget this.'

That night, they talked about it in bed.

'So?' she said, leaning on an elbow. 'You think Medich knows?'

'I'm sure he does. He was not looking for his son; that was a cover. He was looking for us. Parking opposite the school was his way of drawing us out. So he could have a good look at us—with subtle menace.'

'Menace?'

'Parking outside the school—that's a menace in itself.'

'You mean he's trying to install fear?'

'That's the first step.'

'And the next?'

'Direct menace.'

'How?'

'Perhaps something in the post. Or someone watching this house. Or, more likely, someone talking to Robbie—making sure we see it, so that we fear she's about to be kidnapped.'

'What does he want of us?'

'Revenge.'

Becker lay there, a hand behind his head, staring at the ceiling.

The side-table lamp was full on her face. Her hair hung down. She always unrolled it out of a knot or a ponytail or whatever she did to keep it out of her face when working at the gym. Or working around the house. It had been pale golden hair when Becker first laid eyes on her. Now it was slowly losing colour. Before long it would be as white as the Siberian snow.

'What can we do?'

'Play the same game.'

'Retaliate? Threaten him?'

'Why not?'

'You mean go to Melbourne, threaten him?'

'It wouldn't be hard. He probably knows me by reputation. A Federal cop, the one who was with Salvatore Pisano, when he died.'

'Medich is not Italian. He's a Croat. My guess is he's just a guy who arranges things, no matter what you are.'

'So, what do you propose?'

'I go to Melbourne, have a word with him.'

He didn't ask her what she'd do. He knew what she'd do—frighten the shit out of Medich. She'd already said so. She'd mentioned that if she'd encountered him outside the school, she would have dragged him out of his car, stood him against it, and beaten him.

'No,' he said.

'No?'

'It's wrong, Chook.'

She did not respond to the nickname. 'What's the alternative?'

'Go to the police. Tell 'em we think he's going to hurt us, perhaps take Robbie, perhaps kill her—for revenge.'

'Revenge for what?'

He knew what she was saying. They'd have to tell the police why they thought Medich was seeking revenge. Revenge for what? they would ask.

They could not say. They couldn't confess that Chook had killed the Medich kid and disposed of the body—along with the one the kid had killed.

Becker lay there, thinking.

'What if we're wrong? What if old Medich is innocent? We can't assume he knew what his son was doing.'

'He knew, I'm sure.'

'Why would he know? You assume he sent his own son to Canberra to kill Evelyn. What is the evidence?'

'We don't need evidence.'

'What?'

'If he's the one we think he is, we have to act. If he is not, no harm done. All he gets is a big fright. If he falls dead with shock, too bad.'

He took his arm down; it was beginning to ache.

'Oh, Christ, Chook—'

He waited for her chastisement, but it did not come.

'We can't do such a thing,' he said. 'Revenge leads to revenge. There is no winner, and the losses are awful.'

'Losing Robbie would be more awful.'

'If you'd not done it,' he said. 'If you'd not taken the bodies, if you'd made that call reporting in—'

'I did it for you,' she said.

'Yes, I know, I know.'

She leaned down and kissed him on the mouth, a quick peck.

'Think about it,' she said.

He tried to think about it, even when she turned out the lamp.

He was still thinking two hours later.

A huge truck went by on the highway. It sounded like a giant with two big trailers up back. It howled. The night was perfectly still, not even a bird. But the howling went on and on. Fading, fading away into the unending night. Even when the howling stopped, he could still hear it.

The inevitability of it.

▲

CHAPTER 5

She sat in the park and watched the house. The sun had set, and, as the sky darkened, she could see more clearly who was where. The house was one of those old houses in a middle-class suburb that you saw everywhere in Melbourne in those days. Brown brick, double-bricked, which you don't see these days. Very solid, cool in summer and warm in winter. A narrow frontage, a bay window on one side, a small verandah stretching from the front door to the other side, probably tiled. Almost hidden behind a bushy sort of tree, not big or dense—perhaps a *Pittosporum*. The bay window would likely be part of the living room, but no lights had come on inside it. Was no-one at home?

She'd seen a young man come home—a late teenager, she thought, maybe older, wearing a suit. Obviously not a tradesman. Quite slim. And a woman in a taxi, old enough to be his mother. He held the gate open for her, helped her up the steps with a hand. They'd gone inside. But the bay window remained dark. They must be in another room.

She could imagine the layout.

Behind the living room would be a dining room. Beyond that would be a kitchen and possibly another room beyond the kitchen. Maybe a laundry.

On the left side, behind the verandah, would be the main bedroom; it was always at the front in such houses. Behind that, two more bedrooms and maybe a bathroom. Perhaps another room added at the back, similar to the laundry, with a corrugated roof. Then, a small backyard, a clothesline, and a plum tree. And a back lane, cobblestoned, where tradesmen used to come in the old days. Where they would park the Fairlane, where there might be a garage or there might not.

A light came on in the front bedroom. A shadow moved on the curtains—old voile curtains, cotton. Then the light went out.

Still, the living room did not come on.

Chook checked her watch. Almost six-thirty.

These people would eat by six-thirty, working class. Then watch the television news at seven. Perhaps they were waiting for someone. Another member of the family?

Street lights flickered on. Lit up the road, the passing traffic. Not much in this street, which seemed to lead nowhere except to the river. Shadows deepened in the park. A little park, just big enough to kick around a football, but not much else. A few seats, and a fountain. Not much of a fountain. And a statue to a man with an arm raised. Probably no-one remembered him to this day. Some official, perhaps a municipal mayor now covered with pigeon crap. Homegoers went past. No-one would have cared if they noticed her sitting quietly on a bench.

Then the bay window lit up.

Someone moved about in the main front room, pacing back and forth, like setting a table. But they wouldn't eat in the living room. Maybe they did, ate off their laps while watching the news. That did not seem like old Medich— a man with a well-kept car like the Fairlane. Not a squeak when it had driven off. Probably meticulous in all he did now that he was retired.

Chook knew this part of Melbourne well.

In her lonely days, she'd wandered these streets. This was called Cremorne, an old-fashioned name for a small suburb, tucked in by the winding river. Hemmed in by the Rosella pickle factory and the endlessly rumbling trains crossing the river and across Swan Street, creeping into Richmond station. Ten tracks wide, running all day long and well into the night. Looking for a job, but no-one would have her. Too tall and skinny and ugly. A motherless child with no prospects. Until she'd encountered Stumpy Watson one day outside the White Swan in Swan Street. He'd greeted her with, 'G'day, Lofty. Feel like a beer?' He was holding two beers, claiming one was for a mate, who'd disappeared after a police car had turned up. Stumpy had a Harley Davidson and a ginger beard and a short leg. But she drank the beer anyway and rode with him until the fighting started. The old days when they had a club called the Gringos. And got pissed every night and smoked whatever they could get. And got into so much trouble with the—

A young woman came from behind, walking through the park. Heading for the house. May have come from the station. Gave Chook a glance. Probably thought she was a man because of the Harley Davidson. Carried a slim satchel like a solicitor's brief, maybe not. Didn't look old enough to be doing law. But you never knew. Could have been eighteen, maybe nineteen. Crossed the street and opened the front gate. Walked up to the front door, high heels clicking on the tiles. Produced a key, turned it. Slipped in, turning back to close the door. Then the porch light went off.

That was it. No-one else was expected.

They'd been waiting for the girl.

Chook gave them ten minutes. Time enough for her to freshen up, the women to serve the food. The girl would come back and take her place at the dining room table and—

Something squawked overhead, fluttered for a moment, then settled down—a bat in the night. Hundreds of them in the Botatic Gardens across the river.

It was time.

She got up, chained the bike to a tree and walked across the street. It was dark now; the moon was down and no birds sang. The city had closed in upon itself, restless, carrying the weight of another day. It would have to continue, endlessly. To what end?

She opened the front gate, quietly not a squeak.

Walked up two worn steps, bluestone. Above the door was a fanlight. A sort of ventilator made of glass, hinged so that you could wind it out using the long cotton cord inside. To get air as well as daylight in the hot summers of a hundred years ago.

She pressed the bell button. Something like a tinny alarm-clock rattled inside. Very old, amazing that it still worked.

Someone inside said, 'Who could that be?'

Footsteps approached. Not actual steps, but distinct impressions. One, two, three...

The door opened. A young man stood there, looking surprised.

'Hullo?'

'Mr Medich?'

'Yes?'

'Is this the house of Mr Medich?'

'Yes.'

'I met him last Tuesday, outside a school in New South Wales.'

The young man glanced back, uncertain.

'Tell him Mrs Becker is here.'

'Mrs Becker?'

'Anna Becker. I said I'd contact him, if I heard anything.'

'Anything?'

'About his son. Branko, he said.'

'Branko?'

'I think I know what happened to him.'

'Oh, we're about to sit at the table and—'

He looked frightened, began to shut the door. She pushed her way in, using her full weight. She hit him, not with a fist but an open hand, flattening him against a wall. Plates and pictures rattled.

'Where is he, sonny?'

'Who are you?'

'I just told you.'

She walked past him, past the living room. A light was on but no-one in there. A table lamp on a cabinet, yellowish light. The kind you get from a vellum lampshade. Then the dining room. An old woman was holding a serving dish, about to place it on a cork mat. On a beautifully polished table, set for six.

The woman looked up, startled.

'Where is Mr Medich?'

'Medich?'

'He lives here.'

'Josep? Josep? Not here.'

'Don't lie to me.' Chook pulled out the Colt, held it to her ear. The woman jumped back, but Chook had her by an arm—not squeezing, but firm enough.

'Tell him to be here in fifteen seconds.'

The old woman dropped the dish, just an inch or two onto the table. Crockery lid rattled. Lovely smell, some kind of stew, possibly goulash. Lovely smell of paprika.

She screamed or shouted or gasped. 'Ivanka? Ivanka? You get Josep, quick!'

A middle-aged woman poked her nose in, saw the gun and screamed. Then ran off.

They waited. Old footsteps shuffled along the carpet, a man grunting something. He spoke another language. Shuffled in, dragging a leg, no doubt swollen.

It was Medich.

Last Tuesday, in the car outside the little school, he'd seemed to be old, not in the best of health. Obvious now that his health was bad. He'd reached that stage in life where hope no longer exists. Emphysema in his lungs, bloated limbs and swollen joints. In the five days since they'd met, his eyes seemed to have sunk, like abandoned fruit on a tree. Worn out, wasted, bloated with fluid, phlegm, and all the unwanted juices of the human body. Likely a high level of uric acid, high blood pressure—Josep Medich probably had the lot. Lucky he was not dead. He shuffled closer, staring with baleful eyes. He'd had a premonition, as soon as he heard the first scream. Someone or something had turned up.

'Come in, Mr Medich,' Chook said.

He stopped, still staring at Chook, then tottered, puzzled. Apparently she was sitting in his chair. A high chair, high backed and carved wooden arms. Quite plain, nothing fancy. At the head of the table, the master of the house.

'Sit down, Mr Medich.'

The old man blinked, as if he'd been wakened from a doze.

'What this?' He peered at her. 'Police lady? Why you come?'

'Yeah, I used to be a cop. Sit down, Mr Medich.'

'Why you come?'

'Just sit down, so we can have a little chat.'

'Chat? What for to chat?'

'Business.'

He shuffled closer, the young man guiding him.

'What kind business?'

'Serious business.'

'Serious? I dunno any business with you.'

'Sit down, anywhere you like.'

He shuffled again, looking hurt. Maybe because she'd taken his chair. The young man pulled out another for him beside Chook, carefully helping him in. Then sat on her other side. Waiting, his eyes darting.

'This is your son, Mr Medich?' Chook asked.

'Son? No, he, he is—'

'Gran'son,' the old lady said.

'Grandson, is he?' She looked around. 'Anyone else?'

They didn't seem to understand.

'Anyone else in the family?'

The boy looked about to answer, but hesitated.

'I'm asking you, anyone else?'

The boy said, 'Two brothers.'

'And where do they live?'

'They don't live here, not enough room.'

'Where do they live?

They clammed up. Chook tapped the table with the Colt. 'I'm asking you—where do your brothers live?'

The mother said, 'They live with their uncle—'

She was about to continue, but the old woman had shaken her head at her.

'Where?'

'I don't know.' She was lying, you could see it. Lying to protect them.

'What are their names?'

The boy said, 'Ivan and Marko.'

'Ivan and Marko? And how old are Ivan and Marko.'

The woman looked at her own mother, the old lady—lined, blotched, cranky, hateful. The old lady said, 'They big boys, they soldiers.'

'Soldiers? They're in the Army?'

The boy said, 'Croatian Army.'

Chook was surprised. 'Of course.'

It had hit her, the realisation. They were big brothers and they were either in Croatia or back home now. The war against the Serbs had ended last year, but the hatred persisted. They might be seasoned fighters. So, where were they now?

'You're gonna get these big brothers to deal with me?' No answer. She tapped the table again. 'That's exactly what I want them to do.'

Someone started to cry; it might have been the girl.

'I'll let them fire first. I have a right to defend myself. So, I kill them. You understand?'

She slapped the table. Crockery and cutlery jumped. 'Understand?'

They all flinched, except the old man. He was past caring.

She looked at each of them in turn. 'If any one of you tries to get help—' She waved the Colt. 'I'll blow his or her brains out.'

Reluctantly, they sat.

'We had a little talk up north, Mr Medich, eh? An interesting talk?'

The old man nodded with his eyes, not much more than a blink.

'I forgot to tell you something. You know what it was?'

He tried to reply, but failed.

'You said you were looking for your son, Branko. Is that right?'

He nodded, faintly.

'I should have told you then. He came looking for a man, seven years ago. The man's name was Alfredo Scarafini. You know that name?'

Medich shook, not so much his head as his whole body.

'He came with a gun—a .32 Browning automatic. With a silencer. Did you know that?' Another shake. 'He killed Alfredo Scarafini in the house of Mr Becker. Did you know that?'

He shook his head.

Chook watched him for a while. She smiled, not a smile so much as an acknowledgement. 'You didn't know what your own son used to do? What sort of a father are you?'

The women gasped.

The young man looked worried. Glanced at his grandmother and then his mother and then his sister. Or, maybe she was his wife. He seemed to be asking, What the hell is going on? Perhaps he was learning for the first time how his crazy brother made his money. The women gazed and watched, hands clasped on laps. Hoping that somehow they'd get out of this.

Something had gone wrong, very wrong.

'He was paid to kill Mr Scarafini. Did you know that?'

Medich blinked, his eyes hurting badly.

'In Canberra, he'd already killed a police officer, Anna Politis, known as Polly. You know anything about that?'

No answer again. 'She was trying to protect a lady, Mrs Evelyn Crowley. Heard of her?'

Medich was staring, as though watching a nightmare unfold— one filled with things he'd never imagined doing in his life, yet happening right before his eyes.

'Then your son killed Mrs Crowley.'

One of the women gasped out loud.

'Branko?' Medich said.

'Yeah, Branko Medich, a hired gun. He'd already killed a man in some spaghetti joint in Carlton a year before that. Walked right in and shot him while dining with two men from Griffith. Then took off on a bicycle, a big red Honda dirt bike, shouting, "Hi-ho, Silver!"'

Someone cried out, a foreign word filled with pain.

'He took money for killing people, didn't he? That was your son.'

'No!' someone said, quite clearly.

'Who paid him to do that?'

They looked at each other. The old lady was defiant, but her daughter and granddaughter began to sniffle. As for her grandson, his eyes were popping out of his head.

'Who sent him? Did you?' No reply. Chook tapped the table with the Colt. 'I'm talking to you, old man.'

'Dunno,' he said.

'You dunno? Your son kills people for a living and you don't know who is paying him?'

Medich tried to speak, but nothing came out. He looked bad, bad in the face, a hand to his chest. He began to cough.

'Did you tell him to go up to Canberra and kill two women?'

The mother and daughter gasped, but the old lady said nothing. Sat up straight and tight and angry. Her dinner getting cold.

'No, no, I never tell him do that thing.'

'Who told him? Did someone ring you first? Tell you he had a job for your son? Very urgent?'

'No, no—'

'Someone with a lot of money?'

'No, no, not me. Somebody, he ring me, message for Branko. My son, Branko.'

'What name?'

'Oh, I —'

'What name?'

'Oh, oh, oh—' He began to choke, slowly toppling forward. Hands clasped on his lap. But he raised them very slowly, perhaps to pray.

'Was it Salvatore Pisano? Eh?'

His eyes closed, then he began to say something over and over softly, perhaps pleading not with Chook but with God. For mercy? Or for a quick clean death?

'Papa,' his daughter was saying, reaching for him.

'Did he say his name was Salvatore? Did he sound like an Italian?'

Medic nodded. 'Yes.'

'Pisano wanted Branko?'

'Yes.'

'He spoke to you?'

'Yes, he say he want for to speak Branko.'

'Did he speak to Branko?'

'He tell me tell Branko he gotta call him, urgent.'

'Telephone him? When? At night?'

'Night, yes, after we finish dinner. The phone, it goes. I answer. No, Ivanka she take it and she come to me, you know? She say man want to talk Branko, urgent. So I get up from table and I say hullo. And he say he got contact Branko, quick.'

'Did he sound like an Italian?'

Medich nodded. His voice was coming like a big whisper. Like the wind blowing through an open window in a storm.

'And I say, Branko he out. He say, Where is he? I don't want him talk to Pisano, that Italian bastard. He Mafia, I know. Big man Mafia, I know. He want for to talk Branko something bad, I know.'

'About killing someone?'

Medich nodded, his eyes down. 'Yairs,' he said.

'What did you do?'

'Ring his friends, many friends. I tell all them Pisano want to talk him.'

'Why did you do that? Pisano wanted him to do something bad.'

It took him some time to get the words out, his mind and tongue struggling.

'Because, how you say? I got ob—'

He struggled, the word would not come.

Someone at the table said a word Chook did not catch. May have been in a foreign language.

'Obligation,' Medich said, worn out now.

'Obligation? You had an obligation to the Mafia?'

'Yes, obligation.'

'What sort of obligation?'

'I have for to pay him.'

'Pay him back?'

'Yairs,' he said.

'You got into trouble? You needed money? No-one would help you? Not the bank? So, you went to Pisano? The Mafia boss in Melbourne? Of all people?'

Medich nodded. He looked exhausted, more by shame than emphysema.

'And Pisano found Branko and told him to get on a plane to Canberra?'

He nodded. 'I think, I dunno.'

'And he got on the plane. He took a small Browning pistol?'

'Maybe, yes.'

'Where did he get the pistol?'

'I dunno. Somebody he know, maybe.'

'And he killed Anna Politis and Evelyn Crowley?'

'Yairs.'

'Two women in Canberra. Anna Politis was a cop. Did you know that?'

'I hear 'bout that, yes.'

'How did you hear about it?'

'I ask him when he come back. I say, You go to Canberra and you do what he say?'

'He just smile. He smile like big man. I tell him he do bad thing, plenty bad. The police, they to come. He smile again. You kill police lady, I say to him.'

'What'd he say to that?'

'He jus' laugh.'

'He laughed? He killed a police woman and he laughed?'

The old man nodded, eyes closed. Looked about to get down and ask for mercy, not for himself but for his son.

Chook was about to say she and Polly were great friends. In fact, she had loved Polly. They had shared a flat, shared a bed. But she didn't get a chance. Then old man was rambling now. Rambling and mumbling, almost weeping. Something about concrete.

'What was that?'

'Say he no gonna shovel concrete shit no more.'

She was absently tapping the table with the Colt. 'What then?'

'He just walk out. Get on Honda bike, go off. He wave goodbye. He say, Hi ho, Silver!'

'Hi-ho, silver? Just like that?'

'Yairs.'

'And three months later, he does another job, doesn't he?'

Medich nodded.

'He killed Alfredo Scarafini—in my house, near my daughter's school. You've been there, haven't you? Watching her? Thinking of abducting her?'

Chook looked at each one in turn. Each looked away. The old lady's face was sour with hate. It was a raddled face.

'You know what happened then, Mr Medich?'

No answer.

'I killed him,' she said.

Chook waited, watching each one. She raised the Colt, playing with it loosely. Making a silent statement: This is the very gun I used to kill Branko Medich.

They watched it.

She tapped the table lightly, respectfully. It was a lovely old table, deeply brown, perhaps maple. Beautifully polished with loving care over the years. This house had a good, homely atmosphere. The kind of atmosphere she had never known. The serving dish was still steaming, and the scent was gorgeous.

'Yeah, I shot him dead. This is the very gun I used.'

She waved it, immediately realizing that she'd made a mistake. It was not police issue, it was private. She'd been on vacation when she's used it on the kid, as they called him. Maybe someone could work that out. She'd been on a personal mission. If the Federal Police worked that out, she'd be in big trouble. But the Medich family would not give her away. Their son was a professional killer. The disgrace if that got out.

'I was in the Federal Police then. I'd traced him up from Melbourne. To Griffith. You know Griffith? Someone said he'd been there but had left. He was following Alfredo Scarafini, Mrs Crowley's brother. Where had Alfredo gone? I asked myself. To see Harry Becker. Why? To cadge money out him, so he could clear out, right out of Australia. Why? Some people wanted Alfredo dead. Why? Like his beautiful sister, he knew too much about what was happening at the Royal Bank. Anyway, when I arrived at Harry's house, your son had already killed Alfredo, three shots in the guts. Then he was going to kill Harry. Are you following me, Mr Medich?'

The old man nodded, head still down. Resting on his folded hands on the table.

'Harry was now a witness to a murder, wasn't he? Your son had to get rid of him too, didn't he? He wasn't fast enough. I shot him. Shot him in the head, one clean shot. That's all it took. Not much blood, just a few drops on the carpet.'

The girl was crying, sobbing.

'I was a police officer at the time.'

Chook let that sink in.

'I had to do my duty. You can understand that, can't you?' None answered. 'Now Harry Becker is my husband.'

The middle-aged woman, who must have been the mother of the boy and girl, began to sing to herself. A wordless song of woe.

'And—' She made them wait. 'And the father of my daughter, who attends the little school you were watching.'

She glared at Medich.

'You were going to snatch her, weren't you?'

'No, no, I do nothing like that!'

'You were going to kill her, weren't you? For revenge?'

The women gasped. Medich tried to gasp but it it sounded more like choking.

'I never do thing like that!'

'Never?'

Medich began to moan.

'Let me say one simple thing, old man. You touch my girl, I kill you. Understand what I am saying?'

He nodded, shuddering.

'I'll spread your guts around.'

The mother and daughter began to cry.

Not the old lady. She must have known all along about her grandson, Branko. Or guessed what he was up to. Maybe she'd even encouraged him to get into a 'profession' where the money was good and the work easy. Maybe she came from some place in Europe where killing was a noble way of dealing with people who broke the rules.

Chook had one more question. 'You are a fat man, Mr Medich. Everyone says a fat man called the hit. The big man who paid?'

He looked up at her. His eyes tearful. 'Fat Man?'

He thought about it. He was going to shake his head, but the old woman cut in. 'Oh—'

'You know him?'

'Nekrasoff,' she said.

Chook was surprised.

'You know Nekrasoff? How do you know Nekrasoff?'

Medich gulped, then spoke.

'Oh, he do job for Pisano.'

'What kind of job?'

No-one answered immediately. At first they were not going to talk, then the grandson spoke. 'Maybe,' he said.

'Maybe what?'

'Maybe he is the Fat Man you mean.'

'You know Nekrasoff?'

'We have met him.'

'Where did you meet him?'

'In a restaurant, at a table.'

'What club was that?'

'The Croatian Club in Footscray. I can show you.'

'Show me what?'

'If I go to the next room—'

'Why?'

'To get a photo.'

'You have a photo of Nekrasoff?'

'In an album.'

She raised the Colt. 'If this is some trick—'

'No trick,' the boy said. He stood straight, waiting. In his fear there was something brave about him. Brave and good. No tricks about him.

Chook nodded. 'Get it.'

He went out. They looked at each other, maybe expecting rescue or some development. If he was calling someone on a phone, a hand over it, a door closed, she'd kill the old man. But one thing was sure. They would not be calling the police.

The grandson returned holding an album. 'Here,' he said.

He spoke well, had a good voice, educated.

Opened it where he'd placed a thumb and showed Chook. It was a candid snapshot taken at a party. Maybe in a restaurant, or a club. There were tables and people behind them. The shot featured diners. Medich was easily recognisable and two of the women, then Nekrasoff. He looked like Medich, except he had a cruel little nose and eyes even smaller. And bad teeth, gaps between them. Some sort of spectacles sat on his tiny nose. He had a moustache, but not as big as had been supposed. He did not look a lot like the Nekrasoff in photos she'd seen years ago. When she was with the Federal Police. This man was more like a fat German plutocrat in Nazi times. His smile so big almost all his finer features, if he'd ever had any, had disappeared. All that was left was a huge beaming mouth, wide open. And a tuft of hair in the centre of his forehead, or just back from the centre. In a neat little curl.

The flash from the camera must have reflected off his glasses; they shone so much you could hardly make out his eyes, only two tiny dots behind the lenses. If this was the real Nekrasoff, he was a fat nobody who made a comfortable living out of killing people—or arranging for others to do it. He looked like a happy man, the type you'd want to know if you had a serious problem.

'The Croatian Club, you said? Is he a member?'

'No, we took him.'

'You took a Russian assassin?'

The boy said, 'He's Ukrainian, he said.'

She bridled. 'He's not Ukrainian! He's a Russian born in the Ukraine. A fucking invader, like the rest of them!'

They watched her, waiting.

'Where can I find him?'

They shrugged.

'Where does he hang out?'

'Maybe the Russian Club.'

'Where is that?'

'In Fitzroy, I think,' the boy said.

His sister offered: 'He could be at the Troika Bar.'

'And where's that?'

'Little Lonsdale Street, just past William Street, I think.'

'He might not be in the country,' the boy said. 'He comes and goes.'

They said nothing more. Chook stood up. The chair did not scrape. Good carpet on the floor, Axminster. Deep blue, like the waters of the Adriatic. The blue went with a top shot of the city of Dubrovnik hanging on the wall behind the old man at the other end. It was a famous shot of a famous city, a tourist favourite.

Medich had dried his eyes.

'You said he called you?' Chook asked.

He didn't seem to hear.

'What is his number?'

He shook his head.

'You must have his number? What number have you got?'

'No, no, I try call him. They say he not there now.'

'Who says this? What's the address?'

'I dunno, I dunno. He give number, not give address.'

'Well, where is he?'

Threw up his arms, hopelessly. 'I dunno. Nobody tell me where he live.'

'Then you'd better find out.'

Medich looked like he'd prefer to lie down and die.

'I dunno, I dunno.'

The boy said, 'We'll find it, don't you worry.'

She hesitated. If Nekrasoff really did move around, change his address often, leave the country then come back, they may be right. They'd have to wait for him to call them.

'Okay, okay.'

She got up, shouldered the Colt. Felt around in a pocket, found a card. Dropped it on the table.

'You hear something, call me at this number.'

She began to leave, but paused.

'You'd better be telling the truth.' No-one spoke. She made for the front door but turned back. 'I'm sorry it turned out this way,' she said. 'Maybe you couldn't do anything about it.'

'What happen?' the old woman snapped.

'What do you mean?'

'What happen?'

'Happened? To Branko? To his body? He had a decent funeral,' Chook said. 'It was cremated, with great respect.'

'Where?'

'Does it matter?'

Medich got to his feet. Stumbled and hit a chair, had to hang onto another. His grandson grabbed him.

'I tell you,' he said, 'I sorry. Don't want my boy do bad thing.'

'It's too late, Josep. As Lady Macbeth said, What's done is done and can't be undone.'

'Who you say? What Lady?'

'It doesn't matter now.'

Chook went to the front door, turned the lock. The old man followed. All others too. 'I'll let myself out.'

'I say thank you for telling.' Medich said.

He was holding out a hand. Chook was surprised. His grandson was holding him.

'Maybe someday—' he said.

'Yeah,' she said.

Then let herself out, sideways. One hand close to the Colt now under her jacket. Just in case. She spent a night in Melbourne, looking for this man named Nekrasoff, who may or may not have been the Fat Man. Went from place to place, but she did not find him.

Nekrasoff was no more than a name and a face.

Next morning, she rode back home.

▲

CHAPTER 6

'So, what are you going to do?' he asked her. It was now Monday morning. They were sitting on the eastern verandah, having breakfast in the shade. It was a fair sort of day, neither hot nor cool. And the breeze was gentle, coming from the south-east, off the mountains. She was eating the toast he had made for her. Thick grainy bread, two days old, but still tasted fresh. One thoughtful bite at a time. Looking away at the hills. Then at her horse, Viento, her head above the gate past the barn, looking at her. She was thinking what a beautiful horse. She would ride this morning, after she'd taken Roberta to school. Viento needed it. A mare with a male name in Spanish. Next to her stood Pixie, small by comparison. Wendy had groomed both horses on Saturday afternoon but had exercised only Pixie.

She finished chewing, swallowed the last of the coffee.

'I'm gonna find Nekrasoff,' she said.

'Yeah? And then what?'

'I'll ask him if he blew up this house. Did he hire those two turkeys down in Henty? Did he send Branko Medich to Canberra to kill Evelyn? All sorts of things.'

'And if he did?'

'I'll kill him.'

'And if he didn't?'

'I'll still kill him.'

'Jesus, Anna—'

'He deserves it.'

'You can't go around killing people, no matter how bad they are!'

'Why not? Men like him are immune from the law. He fools them every time.'

'No court would agree with you.'

'That's the point, isn't it?'

'Isn't what?'

She did not answer.

Becker was disappointed. It would never end, he knew. She would kill and then someone would try to kill her. Or kill him. Or worse still, snatch Roberta. And what then? They'd kill her. From their point of view, they'd have to. She would be able to identify them. She was old enough. The girl would be six at the end of the month.

'And how would you find Nekrasoff?'

'I have that photo.'

'Did you show it around in Melbourne?'

'Yeah, I tried all the Russian joints, but no-one knew him—or they said they didn't.'

'You think they were lying?'

'I think they have a good reason to lie.'

'So, what happens now?'

Chook shrugged. She was still looking at Viento. The horse was looking back at her, occasionally flicking her ears, looking away and then back at Chook, patiently waiting for her to the make the first move.

'I have a feeling someone is going to ring me,' she said.

She was quite right. When she returned after dropping Robbie at school and collecting a few essentials at the local store, like milk and bread, Becker had a message for her.

'It was a guy called Ivan.'

'Ivan?'

'Said he was Medich's son. Said he was sorry he hadn't been there when you called. Said he could have helped.'

'Why?'

'He said Nekrasoff was in Melbourne, but he did not know exactly where at present. But he's going to find out.'

'He's Medich's son?'

'That's what he said. Apparently, there are two older sons. They don't live with their parents.'

'So, why do the grandchildren live with the old people and the sons do not?'

'Maybe they're married, with kids.'

'Yeah, maybe. Did he leave a number?'

'No, said he'd call again, when he had a location.'

She put the groceries on the kitchen bench, slowly, one item at a time.

'This sounds too good to be true.'

'You think it's a trap?'

'I'm not sure, Harry.'

'It sounds genuine to me.'

'If it's a trap, it would sound genuine, wouldn't it?'

'You said yesterday they owed a lot of money to Nekrasoff. Maybe they're thinking if you get rid of him, they'll be free of debt.'

'Maybe, maybe…'

She put down a carton of eggs. They'd have scrambled eggs and bacon on toast for lunch. They should have their own fowls, perhaps a dozen. They'd have to build a pen for them under the trees by the creek. A high fence to keep out the foxes. And the goannas. Goannas liked to steal eggs. That would be her next project, after she dealt with the Fat Man, one way or another.

Depending upon how things turned out.

Nothing happened for a few days. Chook waited, always listening for the phone. It was the line phone. Apparently, Ivan, if it really was Ivan—if there was an Ivan Medich at all, and she was pretty suspicious—it seemed that he did not have her mobile number. Which she thought strange, because she'd left it with the old man and the grandson.

It seemed that someone wanted her to be in the house when the call came.

As a result, she did not do the run to and from school each day. Becker did that, worried because Chook was going to do something stupid—a woman who would not let it go. She was made like that. Perhaps, he thought, Ukrainians were like that. Or perhaps, the other side of her, the Tartar side. Nothing could be satisfied according to written law. In the final analysis, everything had to be settled according to the unwritten.

Roberta loved Chook. No-one had had the heart to tell her Chook was not her mother, but her stepmother. No-one had told her that her real mother had been killed following a terrible blast right under the floor of the old timber-framed building. Had blown out one side, blown Robyn off the verandah, to crash, nearly nine months pregnant, onto a path, hitting her head on rock. But had lived long enough for the doctors at Wagga Wagga Base Hospital to save the baby. Most likely, she would not understand, if she knew. Big Mummy, she called Anastacia. *I love you, big Mummy. Pick me up?*

No, no, you are far too old to be picked up. You must use your own legs, so that you grow up with good legs, she'd say. *Legs are for walking and running and dancing and jumping for joy. Mummy*, the girl would say, *pick me up and make me jump right up to the sky! Like a rocket!*

Always, Chook gave in, laughing. She'd lift the girl, making her scream with delight, as she'd soared her up into the trees.

Like a Saturn rocket taking off at Cape Canaveral: T minus five, four, three, two, one—lift-off! We have lift-off! Excited, the girl would want Chook to lift her like a big rocket, going to Mars. When she grew up, she said, she was going to be a space girl and go to Mars.

Sometimes, Becker wondered what would become of her, a smart girl like that. Although nominally in first grade, she listened to and answered questions Nerida Larkin put to the second-graders in the same room. She was, the teacher had confided, well ahead of the second-graders. And so: 'This is not official yet, but your girl may be going straight to third-grade first thing next year. When she will still be six.'

He was proud of Roberta—a kind, funny, honest, enthusiastic girl. She should go far. If not to Mars, then to some place where clever girls were given the chance, not so much to be clever, but...

He had two other daughters, he knew. His own flesh and blood. Chesney and Kat, short for Ekaterina. He didn't know what had happened to them. They had been placed in a children's home somewhere in the western suburbs of Sydney, probably until their mother came out of jail, where she'd been committed for having carried ten-thousand dollars' worth of Indian hemp onto a commuter aircraft about to fly to Sydney. Money she'd stolen from him. He'd been pretty mad at her at the time. She deserved what she got, three years in the clink. Or, was it two and a half? He couldn't remember now. But what of the two girls? They would be two or three years older by now. What future did they have with a mother like that? Brainless but as reptilian as a goanna, or a snake, or something that stared out from under bushes at twilight, looking for an opportunity.

That brought him back to Chook's idea—the poultry run under the trees. He'd been working on it, almost completed the fence. Now all he had to do was build a small but cosy shelter where they could roost up on poles for the night, away from the rain. And anything else that might come calling in the night.

He was thinking that when he heard the phone. It was the line phone, on a small table by a window. Everyone except Roberta had a mobile phone.

'Hullo?'

A slight pause, puzzled. 'Who is that, please?'

'Who are you?'

'I am Ivan. I called on Monday.'

'Yeah, I recognise your voice.'

'Is the lady there, please?'

'Which lady is that?'

'The one they call Anastacia.'

'Anastacia? She is not here.'

'Oh, I see.' A long pause now. Maybe a hand over the mouthpiece.

Actually, she was there, but in the bathroom. He waited, anxious to hear the voice again. Make up his mind about it. Chook had been sceptical, suspecting a set-up.

'Can I get her to call you?'

'Oh, no—'

Again, Becker sensed that a hand had been placed over the mouthpiece. Maybe reporting to someone in the background. To whom? Medich? Maybe someone in the family? Maybe not. Maybe Nekrasoff.

'It is fine,' the man said. 'I will call back some time. When'll she come home, please?'

'Maybe half an hour.'

'Oh, thank you, sir. Yes, I call again. Maybe half hour.'

The line went dead. Chook was at the door.

'Who was that?'

'Your friend, Ivan.'

'Anything?'

'Nothing. He'll call in about half an hour. I said you were not here.'

'I heard that.'

She went to a window, pulled a curtain aside.

'You think he may have been out there?'

She did not answer. 'I don't like this,' she said.

Chook went to their bedroom and opened a drawer, took out the Colt. Picked up the magazine, slipped it in. Felt it go click. Pulled back the slide, popped one round up into the chamber. Ten rounds, ready to go.

'Jesus,' Becker said.

'Maybe someone is watching the place.'

He followed her to the front door. She opened it a few inches.

'You think they want to get at you when no-one else is here?'

'Could be.'

She opened the door wider, sneaked out. Looking each way. Particularly at the big pepper tree and beyond, at the grevilleas along the front fence. Crept out, crouching. Reducing the target size. Got as far as the front gate, peeped out. Opened the gate, slipped out, still crouching. Perhaps to jump back at once.

There was nothing or no-one that could arouse suspicion. No parked car, none speeding away in a hurry. Chook found the dogs lounging in the shade by the stables. Grabbed Nutty's collar, tugged him to the creek. 'Come on, sniff him out!' she urged. The dog wagged his tail, confused.

'Go, on, stupid, use your nose!'

He walked around, mainly in circles, puzzled. Had no idea what she wanted.

'Go on, find him!'

She wanted Nutty to go off up the creek, hunt any intruder—someone who might be hiding up there, possibly watching through binoculars. But the stupid dog was more interested in play. He was the best kind of children's dog in the district. Roberta adored him, hugged him, kissed him. Much to Chook's disgust, telling her not to kiss dogs, but Roberta didn't understand. When she had no-one to play with, Nutty was her best friend.

It was no use trying to get Blue to hunt out anyone. He was a cattle dog, bred never to leave the camp. Never to wander. Always stay with the cattle and the boss.

Chook checked every nook and corner, fearing a shot, but none came. She went back to the house. Becker was waiting at the back door.

'Nothing?' he asked.

She did not answer.

That afternoon, they heard heavy clumping on the front verandah. Not really man-sized heavy, but vigorous and decisive. Becker was about to go to the door to check when they heard a key being inserted in the lock. They waited. The door opened.

In walked Terry.

'G'day,' he said. 'Anything happened?'

CHAPTER 7

It happened on Saturday, a week after the first call. Terry was about to go back to Wagga to stay with his grandmother, Muriel. When they told him what was going on, he was intrigued. They wanted him to stay, keep an eye on things. He was all for it.

Terry and his mates had walked from Perisher Valley to the top of Mount Kosciusko, a distance of nine kilometres, and then walked back. No cars were allowed up there at the top of Australia. When they'd reached the top, they'd looked around, amazed. Everything from there was downhill. Even Mount Townsend, they could look down on it next door. And the hills and valleys and peaks and ranges and the summery haze like smoke. Not real smoke but moisture in the still, chill, alpine air. They'd made it to the top.

'What the hell?' he said.

'We have trouble,' Becker said.

Suddenly, he felt a matey sort of fondness for his stepson. Terry was now a young man. Young but reliable. You could depend upon him in a crisis. If there was any crisis at all. They had to be careful. Someone could come while Stacey was away. That's where Terry would come in. He'd have to take one of the night watches, with the two dogs loose and listening.

'Who the hell is this guy?'

'He crept in a back door and shot a police officer, a friend of Stacey's.'

'Christ!'

'In Canberra, years ago.'

'You're kidding?'

'And crept out again.'

'Just like that?'

'Yeah, just like that.'

Becker was giving him the short version, a very short version. There was no need for the boy to know the whole details. He'd probably run for his life, or die defending his sister. Half-sister, that is. Young Roberta. They impressed on him the need to be alert and stay at the farm for a while. 'Until this thing is over,' Becker said.

'So, you think he wants to kill Stacey too?'

'Yeah, that's about it.'

They had it worked out. They'd make it simple and true for as far as it went.

She was sitting on the divan, watching Becker give it to him. The bare facts, and the menace. She was holding a beer, waiting for the oven to go *ping*! She'd prepared a simple Ukrainian dish, *golubtsi*, traditional cabbage rolls, stuffed with minced meat and rice and topped with sour cream.

Becker was drinking a beer. So was the boy, a small one. Probably not his first, but the first at home. He had done the finals exams at school. Done them in October. Just waiting around for the results. He'd not been outstanding academically. More of an action man than a student. Probably smart enough to get into the Army as a rifleman. He was mad about rifles. Terry Sheldrake was fairly tall and thin, not much flesh yet on his bones. But he was energetic, and springy and fearless. Quite mad at times, Becker thought. But he was all for action, any sort of challenge. He'd made it to the top of Mount Kosciusko. There was not much more than that to conquer. After that The Rock would be a cinch. He was going to run up and down The Rock once a week. To get fit for the Army. The Rock rose more than one-thousand feet above the plains and had a general inclination of some thirty degrees. The usual time taken to walk to the top over rocky ground was two and a half hours. He was going to do it in one and a half hours. Should be a piece of cake.

'That's why I want you to stay here for the time being,' Becker said.'

'You think they might have a go at us?'

'Who knows. You can handle the Winchester, Terry. You'd better get out there and do some practice tomorrow morning.'

'Yeah, sure.'

'Heard anything from the Army?'

'No, well, yeah, just an acknowledgement. They said there wouldn't be another recruitment until March.'

'Three or four months to wait, eh?'

'Yeah, well—'

'What are you going to do till then?'

'Maybe get a job in Wagga.'

'Perhaps Wendy can get you something with old Tommy.'

'Yeah, maybe.'

'Or, she knows someone who needs a young bloke for Christmas. Or, perhaps something—'

The phone rang.

They snapped to attention, even while seated. Went rigid, waiting. It rang and rang.

Chook put down her beer and went to it, carefully. Reaching for it and not reaching for it. They watched her hand sneaking out to the phone. Then she lifted it.

'Hullo?' she said.

Roberta came out of her room. She'd been watching a children's show on TV. Watched only the instructional programs, and could tell you all about the icebergs crashing into the sea off the coast of Alaska. She'd be able to tell everyone at school on Monday all about icebergs.

Becker raised a finger. 'Shush,' he said. And pointed. Roberta understood. You didn't talk when Mummy was on the phone.

They stood or sat, waiting. She was listening.

'Yeah, I am Anastacia. Some people call me Stacey.'

More listening.

'Where is he?' she asked.

She listened some more.

'So, you don't know where he is?'

Chook looked at Becker, raised her eyes to the ceiling. Exasperated, or perhaps overdoing it. She could act up if she wanted, but normally was as straight as a die. No fuss nor foolery with her. What she said was what you got. She could express her contempt at times. Especially when anxious.

'Don't mess me around. Either you do know where he is or you don't.'

The guy on the other end was getting agitated, they could hear. Not quite hear the words, but the tone—a tiny protesting buzz. Trying to make a deal and getting nowhere.

'Why should I come down there? What? I said, why should I come all the way to Melbourne, when you can't produce the bastard?'

She caught herself and looked at Roberta, then shrugged apologetically at Becker.

She went on snarling. 'Where exactly in St Kilda? That place is full of tourists and dozies and dolls and molls and drunks and shysters and freaks half-bombed out of their brains. He doesn't sound the sort of guy who'd live in a sleazy dump like St Kilda. What?'

She repeated most of what she heard for Becker's benefit.

'He called you? Demanding his money? What? Yeah, well, that's your fucking problem—' She caught herself, grimacing. Terry grinned and reached over, so that he drew the girl in and put a hand over her ears and pulled her against him in a big hug. She was delighted. She could take any number of hugs and kisses.

Chook was getting mad, as mad as a wet hen, as the saying used to go. 'Now, listen, and listen good. Here's what's going to happen. Next time he rings— What? Now, shut up and listen good or I'm gonna come down there and rearrange your face. Are you listening?'

No sounds from the phone. Maybe the line had gone dead.

'Are you there? Okay, this is what's going to happen. Next time he rings, tell him you've got the money. What? Shut up and listen, will you? Next time, tell him you've got the dough and he'd better come over and get it. No, no, tell him your father will not hand it over without seeing him. He wants to shake his hand. He wants to do it the old way. With a handshake, one good man to another. Understand? You get that?'

She listened, fuming. Or, perhaps simply steaming.

'Okay, you then ring me and tell me what's going on. Understand? If he agrees to come to your place, I want at least four hours' notice. You understand that? Four frigging fours and I'll be there. And he'll walk in and you then leave things to me. Okay? You've got that?'

More talking, distantly. A tinkling in a tingling sort of distance.

'Okay, that's the deal. You set him up and I'll— What? For Christ sake, I won't do that there. I'll march him off somewhere and make sure he has a nasty accident. Understand? And another thing, if you try to mess me around, I'll take you apart. Even your own mother won't be able to put you together again. Got that?'

She listened for another two or three seconds, then put down the phone fast. Angrily, but pleased.

She went to Roberta. Picked her up and kissed her.

The little girl was worried.

'Mummy, you said something naughty.'

'Oh, God, darling, did I? I'm sorry. I was upset.'

'You said shut up.'

'Did I?'

'Nerida said you should never say that.'

'She's quite right. I apologise. Do you know what apologise means?'

'When you do something wrong, and you say you did wrong.'

'Yes, that's about it.'

She stood like that, holding the girl, her face pressed to her own. Thinking: It was going to happen. And when it did, she would not apologise. Never in a million years.

Next day, Sunday, the call came again. A few minutes before lunch.

She spoke quietly this time, without raising her voice. Without anger and without swearing. Most circumspect. She listened for a while, then finally, said: 'I'll be there about seven.'

That was about the time she'd arrived last visit.

She got ready by three o'clock and then said goodbye. She kissed Roberta, who wanted to know where she was going. Then she kissed Terry, wished him well. Finally, Becker.

She did not kiss him but pressed against him, head to toe. It was a gesture—part farewell, part surrender, part something else. She was dressed for the part—skin-tight jeans, a loose leather jacket, and heavy motorcycle boots. Freed her hair before donning her helmet. It was almost white now. Snow white.

All in all, she looked striking.

Said she'd be all right, in the breeze, the rush of air, even if it were warm. But the sun would go down in a few hours, the temperature would drop. She was not wearing a holster, but had the Colt in the right hand pocket of the heavy jacket. Then, she'd got on the Harley and waved to them at the gate. And was gone, westward again, to the turnoff, then southward along Henty Road. And on into what remained of the day.

Becker had implored her not to go, but she was unrelenting.

'No need to worry,' she'd said, attempting a smile. But the smile didn't quite land.

'Goodbye, Mummy!'

Now, she was alone. She had been alone all her life, until she met Harry Becker. Being alone wasn't a bad state—it depended on what you wanted out of life. A good time or a better time. One in which you did what had to be done.

She was going to meet the Fat Man.

One of them was going to die.

CHAPTER 8

She arrived about fifteen minutes early. The sun was setting behind church spires and tall Cocos Island palms, silhouetted against electrical gear atop double poles, transformers, and substations. In the distance loomed a skyscraper—the tip of urbanisation in a flat world of history, refuse and refuge. It was the end of a dry, dreary day. Nothing to do but go home, thank the sun for being considerate. Getting down and out of sight. Deserting the scene before the shootout.

The road traffic was fairly active for a Sunday evening.

She parked the Harley a few houses away and walked past the house. It looked unchanged—not a hint of a welcoming party. The front door was closed. No lights were visible. Not in the house anyway. No sign of the big, black Ford. A utility truck was parked in front of the house. On the side was one big word: Medich. And a phone number.

Nothing moved, except a bird squawking in a thick bush next door, a bush with tiny white flowers. A lilli-pilli perhaps. The bird sounded hot, thirsty and near exhaustion.

A few bushes down the left-hand side. It was a narrow block of land, so that the gap between the house and the fence on the left side was about four feet, the minimum distance in Melbourne when that house was built. There was a deep, cool, earthy smell. A shady place. But not exactly a secret place.

She stood in front of the house, inspecting. Considering.

A boy was walking toward her, wheeling a bike along the foot-path. He looked about sixteen. She walked up to meet him.

'Got a flat?'

'Yeah,' he said, 'an' no friggin' pump.'

'What happened to the pump?'

'Some bastard went and nicked it.' His whole world seemed to have collapsed.

'No pump is going to fix a flat.'

'Yeah,' he said.

'Want to earn a tenner?'

'Yeah?'

She pulled out a ten-spot. Waved it at him. 'Got a watch?'

There was something on a wrist.

'Yeah,' he said.

'Does it go?'

'More or less.

'All you have to do is wait two minutes, then go up to that door there—'

'That one next door?'

'That's the one. Go up to the door and knock, good and loud and definite. Nothing piss weak, like a girl. But hard and sharp, but respectful, like someone important has arrived.

'Like the police?'

'Not that important, only like the local vicar. Or the tax collector.'

'What then?'

'You walk off. With your bike.'

'Yeah?'

'Is this a trick or something?'

'Not a trick, not even a treat.'

'Yeah?'

'What do you think?'

'All right.'

'Okay, here's the tenner. Remember, two minutes.'

'This better be all right.'

'No worries, mate.'

The boy took the money and waited, watching his watch.

Chook climbed the brick fence under the flowering tree—not a big tree, more like a big bush, perhaps ten feet high. Then she went along the left side of the house in its snugly thickening shade. Creeping from bush to bush, ducking her head below windows. Even getting right down in a squatting sort of creep. Or she'd shuffle on her haunches. Until she made it to the back door. It was unlocked. It opened easily, not a squeak. She waited. From the back she heard the knock. The boy was right on time. She opened the door a few more inches, listened. Something had happened in the house. Someone had moved quickly, perhaps sat up or got up or walked a few steps. Then a voice.

'She's here!'

Then a silence full of words you cannot hear. Perhaps grimaces and hand signals. She opened the back door enough, slipped in. It was a kitchen. To one side was, by the smell of it, a laundry. Old laundries had that smell, of zinc and sink, caustic soda, soap and Persil. She stood in the kitchen to one side, behind a cupboard. Cups hung on brass hooks. Something squeaked ahead, like a loose floorboard. She would have to avoid that. Have to guess where it was.

Peeking around the cupboard, she saw it was old, made of unpainted deal wood, scrubbed clean. It smelt of sand soap—the best for cleaning deal.

Nothing rattled.

She listened.

A man said, 'You goin'?'

No answer, but there must have been a nod or a wave.

Someone went to the front door. A hall light switched on, inside the door. No lights in the other rooms, she thought. But then one in a side room, perhaps the dining room, came on too. She saw a figure. No, two figures. One at the door, the other much nearer, looking out from a room, perhaps the dining room. There was a sundown glow in the fanlight above the front door, not much. Then the front door opened. She got a clearer picture now. The man near to her, the one peeping out of a side room, was holding something in his right hand. The hand was down, the whole arm down. As the front door opened, the arm moved. It moved behind the man's right leg. And in the hand was a weapon, a flat automatic. More than that, it was fitted with a silencer.

Chook ducked back.

'No-one here,' the man at the door said.

'What?'

'Not a fuckin' soul.'

'Then who bloody knocked?'

'Dunno, must've been some kid havin' a lark.'

'It ain't the time for larks. Not with the sun down.'

'What's the fuckin' sun got to do with it?'

'They'd be home havin' dinner.'

'Who'd be home?'

'Kids playin' games.'

'You're sure?'

'Go and have a look out front.'

'What for?'

'See if she's comin'.'

'What fuckin' good'll that do? You want me to go out and wave her down or kiss her arse or what?'

'Close the door, then.'

'I'll have a quick gander.'

The man at the front door went out. Wandered about a bit, perhaps peered over the fence. Looked up and down.

When he came back, began to say, 'Nah, nothin' anywhere, no sign of—'

He stopped, surprised. His brother was standing with his hands behind his head, fingers interlocked. Like they had to do, when the Serbs surrounded them during the troubles. When the Serbs were carrying out ethnic cleansing. That's when the brothers had fled back to Melbourne to join Father Josep. Get some work laying concrete. Building paths, walls, even houses, bricklaying. Doing stucco work. Anything that needed cement. It had been hard, but it had been worth it. Until that stupid kid, Branko, had gone mad and started killing people, just for the money. Like a fucking Serb conscript. Like they'd done at the ancient city of Vukovar. Like when they slaughtered eight-thousand Bosniaks at Srebrenitsa. The fucking United Nations standing by, watching.

It had been a hard life. The memories were worse than the struggles.

'What are you doin'?'

The man with his hands behind his head indicated with his eyes.

The tall woman stepped out, long hair glowing. Holding two handguns. They knew something about handguns. They used them in the war now past, but the hate would never pass. In one band was something like a Colt. They could see the hammer. Pulled back, ready. In the other hand was the German Walther they were going to use to kill her. And keep it quiet too.

'What the hell?'

'Come in,' she said. 'And close the door. Turn on that light over there.'

She indicated a switch on a wall. An old switch with a brass casing on top of the porcelain base. It was an old house and nothing much in it had changed since the war. Since the old people had arrived in the early fifties. Having escaped Tito and his Communist gang. As refugees. And worked hard and made some money and had some children, and eventually had bought a house. An old house, but a good house. One of which you could be proud.

He closed the front door slowly.

'And this is Marko, eh?'

She poked the Colt at the base of his skull. He had not known she was there until he'd felt the hard steel. And sniffed the burnt propellant. It had been carefully cleaned and oiled, but you can never get rid of that distinctive smell, oil and burnt propellant.

'Now, were is Nekrasoff?'

The one at the door was Ivan. She recognised his voice.

'We dunno. We was makin' sure he didn't try nothin'.'

'You expect me to believe that?'

'No, no, lady, we contact him. He say he be here now.'

'You were to tell him you'd killed me and he had to see the body? Wasn't that it?'

'Yeah, yeah, that's what we said. He's a bastard.'

'And he was gonna cancel your debt?'

'Yeah, yeah, that's what we said on the phone.'

'You were going to kill me for real, weren't you? Show him a dead body, full of holes? That was it, eh?'

'No, no, we wanta get rid of him.'

'By getting rid of me?'

'Ah, you know, lady, we don't mean for you any harm.'

'You want me dead? Because I killed your evil little shit of a brother called Branko? Because it was a shame on your family. A woman killing your young brother? And humiliating your old man in front of his family. You couldn't take that, could you—'

Marko swung around fast.

Tried to knock her down. Knock out the Colt. But not fast enough. Chook had already anticipated. Simply took the blow, at the same time firing the Walther. There was no sound except a gasping sort of cough. Fumes blowing out sideways. Silencers do not silence, they suppress. The bullet went straight through the man, came out the front, almost hit his young brother, Ivan. Who stood there, astonished. Marko tottered in the soft personal light. Began to faint, more with shock than injury. Staggered a few steps, then fell.

Chook went to Ivan. 'Where's Nekrasoff?'

'I don't know, I don't know!'

'Try again.'

'I don't know, I don't know!'

'So, how were you going to convince him you could pay off your debt?'

'Ah, we—we phone him.'

'What's his number?'

'Ah, dunno.'

'You'd better remember fast.'

'Ah, Marko—he's got the number.'

'Where? Where's he got it?'

'I don't know, maybe in his pocket, in his shirt or his wallet or maybe—'

'Roll him over!'

'Eh?'

'Search him!'

'No, he's dying'.'

'You'll join him if you don't find that number.'

'Ah, he's all over blood.'

She kicked him. 'Do it!'

'Ah, ah, I dunno.'

Ivan tried to roll the man over. Marko was older, much older. Maybe aged forty-five or more. He was still breathing. And popeyed, unbelieving anything could go so wrong.

'Find that number!'

'I can't, I can't! I don't know where he put it.'

'Ask him?'

'Eh?'

'Go on, ask him!'

He said something, unintelligible to Chook. Maybe in a foreign language. The wounded man tried to speak. He was lying on his side, a hand down, perhaps trying to stem the flow. But he was weak. His eyes were closing now. Opening and closing, opening and closing. Tongue sticking out.

'He's gonna die!'

'You should have thought of that. Whose idea was it?'

'Eh?'

'Who thought up the trick? Killing me? Paying off Nekrasoff that way?'

'Marko, he did. Papa say don't do it, she very brave. She kill you, she kill everyone. Whole family for what Branko do.'

'He was right, your father. He's not a bad old man. I was sorry for him. Now he's got to come home to this. Where is everyone?'

'They go out—to church, to club.'

'The Croatian club?'

Ivan nodded.

'They're gonna get a surprise, aren't they?'

'Oh, ah—'

He began to cry. His big brother was dying. Marko looked as though he was lying on a bed of hard and unsympathetic nails. The pain, the pain.

He sighed, his body collapsing too. Everything shutting down.

Ivan began to cry, shaking his brother. Repeating something in that strange language, over and over. Maybe calling to him to come back.

'Now, you listen,' she said. 'You ring me, with the number. Don't ring Nekrasoff. Got it?'

'What'm I gonna do?'

'You heard me, get that number and call me. Don't say a word to the cops about this. Bury him somewhere, up in the hills or in an old quarry. Get rid of him.'

Ivan was whining to himself. 'What I tell *Sisa*? *Dadda*? All the family?'

'Tell 'em you had an accident. Playing around with guns is not healthy. You shot him in the back. Didn't know it was loaded.'

She kicked him. 'Understand?'

He gasped or moaned, perhaps affirmatively.

Then lay down beside his brother, holding him, singing to him.

It was the kind of singing that always brings back the dead.

Not necessarily the flesh and blood dead.

▲

CHAPTER 9

A week later he called again. He had the number, he said. 'You've got the number?' she said. She was not asking but challenging him. You could not rely on a lot of creeps with bad English to get anything right. From their point of view, the only justice is what is best for the family. But he had a surprise for her.

'What?' she said. 'You had a funeral? You had an undertaker? What did the undertaker say? How did you explain the holes— one in his back, one in his guts? What about the police? Did you inform the police? If you play around with guns and shoot your brother, you have to tell the police.'

Chook was saying all this more for the police or anyone else who might be listening. A family like this was sure to attract police attention now and then. She went on snarling into the phone. The voice on the other end was trying to explain, but she cut him off.

'You know a good undertaker? He won't talk? Jesus, you have to report a death. So does he. Do you want the police calling? Are you out of your mind? If you did that, you've got to do it legit. You understand what I'm saying? Strictly by the book. I don't care what the family thinks or feels or prefers or anything else. You brainless dickhead, you're making a big mistake. Understand?'

Ivan was silent for a long time. Or, to put it another way, he was not silent but he did not use words. She could hear him on the other end—breathing, snorting and sniffling and probably wiping his eyes and ears and mouth and every other thing that could weep in a dumb ox of a plasterer. A man who smeared sloppy cement across brick walls and tried to make them look new again, and smart. And worth a packet to someone who'd been hoping real estate was the answer to his dreams. Inflation, someone once said, was the secret of success in real estate. You've got to keep the inflation going, if you're gonna make a pile.

Finally, he got around to controlling himself enough to speak: 'I got the number.'

'How do you know it's the correct number?'

'It's a St Kilda number.'

'St Kilda? In Melbourne? Those phone exchanges cover large areas.'

'It must be St Kilda.'

'Why must it be?'

'Cos Marko saw him there.'

'He did? When was that?'

'Once he was down there to have a drink at that hotel, you know.'

'What hotel?'

'The famous one, on the corner.'

'What corner?'

'Where they all go. Because of the fights an' girls an' the band and—'

'You mean the George? In Fitzroy Street?'

'Yeah, that's the one.'

'He saw Nekrasoff in that bloodhouse?'

'Eh? No, not in it. No, Marko came out an' saw Nekrasoff standin' on a corner. Under a light.'

'Standing on a corner? Doing what?'

'Nothin', just standin' there and lookin' at the crowd, goin' every which way, you know? It was Friday night.'

'When was this?'

'Ah, three or four months ago.'

'What'd Marko do?'

'Nothin', he just watched him.'

'How long?'

'I dunno, maybe three or four minutes. I dunno.'

'What did Neckrasoff do?'

'Ah, well, he just walked off.'

'Walked off where?'

'Down the street to Ackland.'

'Ackland Street?'

'Yeah, that's right.'

'What did Nekrasoff do in Ackland street?'

'Just walked along, lookin' at the crowd. It was busy. Friday night, it's always busy.

'Yeah, I know.'

'Then he went in a shop.'

'In Ackland Street?'

'Yeah.'

'Where the trams stop and wait?'

'Yeah.'

'What kind of shop?'

'Ah, that cheese shop. You can get any cheese you like there. We always get some for *sisa*. For the cookin'. When we down that way.'

'Yeah. So, Marko breezed up and had a look at him? In the shop? Buying cheese?'

'Yeah.'

'What happened then?'

'He wait a while and see him come out.'

'With his cheese?'

'Yeah, under his arm.'

'And what then?'

'He walked off.'

'Nekrasoff walked off? With the cheese? Where did he walk?'

'Off along Ackland Street.'

'Heading toward Elwood? In the night?'

'Was followin' some girls, arm in arm.'

'What kind of girls?'

'Street girls, you see 'em on every corner, Friday nights. Saturday too.'

'Did he speak to the girls?'

'Nah, they went in a house.'

'What kind of house?'

'You know.'

'Yeah, I know. Where did he go then? Into a house?'

'No, no, Marko couldn't see. Had to wait while a big truck went by, sprayin' water. For to clean up, you know? When he see again, Nekrasoff's gone.'

'Gone? You mean disappeared? Into the night?'

'Yeah, jus' gone.'

This was something, she knew. Nekrasoff haunted St Kilda. At night too. If necessary, she'd go down there, look around for him. He followed whores, so they probably knew him. Knew where he lived.

'All right, what's that number you found?'

Ivan read it out slowly, as if every number was a story in itself.

Yes, it was a genuine St Kilda number. Chook used to know people in that area many years ago, when she rode with the Gringos. When she was young and stupid. But that phone exchange served other suburbs. For example, Elwood and North Brighton. Perhaps Balaklava, Ripponlea, Elsternwick too.

It sounded genuine.

'Where did you find this number?'

'Marko, he had it in his drawer, under his shirts.'

'He kept a number like that in a drawer under his shirts?'

'Yeah, *Sisa* ask him what for that number for and he say, "To settle debt."'

'Who is *Sisa*?'

'*Sisa*? That mean sister.'

'Which one is your sister?'

'My sister? Elena.'

'Elena? Is she the one who does the cooking?'

'Yeah, that's right.'

'And does not speak?'

'Yeah, she no speaks.'

Chook was going to ask why she did not speak, but it did not matter.

'And what did sister say?'

'She say what debt? And he tell her we owe that man, Nekrasoff, much of money.'

'How much?'

'Twenty-seven, twenty-eight thousand. She cry out, you know. She nearly fall down dead.'

'Did he say what they were gonna do about the debt?'

'He say he gonna kill somebody.'

'He said that? Kill someone?'

'Everything be okay.'

'So he got a gun? A Walther with silencer? What then?'

'You know what we do.'

'I know only what I know. You killed your brother.'

'No, no, I no kill him!'

'Yes, you did. You told me.'

She had to be careful. A fool like Ivan Medich could make a mess of everything. She had to steer him, or else everything could end up on the rocks.

'You got a gun and you shot him in the back.'

'No, no, he get the gun—'

'And you messed around with it and you shot him. By accident. That's what you told me when I arrived.'

'Ah, no, I dunno what for to do.'

She thought that was enough. Anyone listening would get the right idea.

'What about the number?'

He took a long time responding. 'For Telephone? I got it here.'

'What is it?' She had a pen poised.

He read it out slowly, like a man who was not too literate in the English language or any language, even Croatian. She wrote it down carefully. Even read it back to him.

He said, 'Yes.'

'That's it?'

'Yes.'

'Have you rung it lately?'

'I don't want talk that man. I hate him. All that trouble he give us.'

'Don't give me a sob story.'

Chook understood their quandary. They take money from a criminal to do a job, kill someone or kidnap a little girl or whatever. Then they chicken out, spend it on clearing debts. There was some sort of tragedy in all this. This could have been a good family once upon a time. No doubt it had been. They had a pride in their house and themselves and friends and their job and their former nation. They could have been something, but they were not. She spoke slowly and carefully, more for any potential listeners' benefit than for this dickhead on the other end of the line.

'Listen to me carefully. If you warn Nekrasoff, I'll come down there and break your guts for you. Nekrasoff has been trying for years to kill me. I don't like that. I took two bullets, one on a shoulder and another in my back and ribs. It went right through my left lung. I don't feel too good some days. Are you listening?'

Ivan did not reply, but she could hear him breathing. It was a lost sort of breathing. The kind you wish you didn't have to breathe, because it kept you alive. And, at this point in a life that should have been better, you wonder whether it might be better to stop breathing altogether. Get it over with.

'You are going to the police. You're going to tell 'em what happened. You accidentally shot your brother. He died, you got a shonky undertaker down a back street in Footscray or wherever to bury him, no doubt at half price and no questions asked. You are very sorry for what you've done, but that's life. Accidents happen. You got that?'

'Yes, I got.'

'Make it your next call. Don't worry, you won't go to jail. All you'll get will be a fine or just a rap over the knuckles for not reporting a death. And the undertaker likewise. It's no big deal. You can tell the court you didn't know you had to report a death. Play the ignorant peasant from Croatia. Tell the judge you had a bad time in Croatia, the fucking Serbs killing people and dumping them in ditches, and you'd seen that. You'll have the court crying.'

Ivan didn't speak, his breathing was bad.

'You got that?'

She didn't wait for his response. Hung up and turned to Becker.

'He says it's the correct number.'

Terry was there too. He'd been out riding with her in the morning. Other than that, he had been hanging around, doing some shooting and working in the stables and the paddocks. It had been a quiet day compared with Friday, when a cow had gone mad.

With the help of Blue, they'd rounded up ten cows intended for the market. He knew exactly what to do, nip their heels and get them to head for the truck. The driver had a prod. He'd got four on board, when the fifth went mad. He'd prodded it, but it had overreacted. Had run around bellowing. Charged Blue and Nutty, who'd bolted for their lives. Nutty went on barking like mad, but Blue had just stood back, watching. He'd seen this sort of thing before. Then it had headed for Becker and Terry, who dodged behind the truck. Then the cow went for the driver. He had to jump over a fence. Then she had rushed about, still bellowing before heading for a fence. Tried to jump over, but failed. She was caught in the wires. They tried to get her off the fence, the two dogs barking like mad. She'd caught her legs in it, kicking frantically, breaking wires. If she'd got out, she would have rushed onto the highway. God knows what would have happened then. A big smash with a big truck possibly. Or, a worse smash with a small car, spinning out of control, rolling over and over. Doors flying open. Humans spilling out, splayed across the bitumen.

Becker threw his keys at Terry. 'Get the rifle! For God's sake, get the rifle quick!'

The boy ran at full speed, returning with the rifle and fitting the clip as he moved. Standing back about thirty yards, he took aim.

The cow was still thrashing and struggling, her bloodied legs tangled in the wires, her udders caught in the mess.

And he'd shot her in the head.

They'd waited. She went on struggling. Not a good shot.

He moved closer, twenty yards now, and tried again. Still, the cow spasmed, her movements slowing but not stopping.

Finally, Terry walked to within ten yards and fired directly into her brain.

The cow collapsed in a heap, shuddering as life left her.

Everyone was shocked. These things happen on a farm. Thank God Roberta was at school. She would have been horrified. They feared the day they'd have to tell her where the cattle went. What would happen to them.

So, they finished the loading and the truck went off to the saleyards.

Now they had to get her off the fence. Becker called a local man with a front-end loader that arrived inside half an hour. They cut the fence and her off. Becker was going to bury her, but the contractor said, 'Why don't you sell her to the abattoir?'

'This one's dead,' Becker protested.

'Doesn't matter,' the contractor replied. 'Dead or alive, they'll still take 'em.'

Becker agreed. The contractor called a mate with a truck, and they loaded the carcass. In exchange for the cow, they waived their service fees.

A bit of excitement for the day. And one more reason why farmers need rifles.

Later, they repaired the fence—a tricky job. The Cyclone wire was curled, springy, and dangerous. One snapback could take out a person's eye.

'Are you going to ring it?' Becker asked.

'Ring what?'

'This number he gave you?'

She thought about it.

'I don't know. I'd like to ring it and hear him pick it up and say hullo or whatever he says. I'd listen for a while, maybe doing some heavy breathing to make him wonder who's on the line. I'd let him say it again. I'd listen to him, this bastard named Nekrasoff, who's tried to kill me more than once. Actually killed others, including Robyn and her father, Robert. All for a price. Then I'd like to say: This is Anastacia Babchuk, I know where you are, Nekrasoff. And

I'm coming for you. A few minutes later he would not be there. He'd clear out, running to his next refuge. So, what's the point?'

'Can't the number be traced?'

'Yeah, it can.'

'The police?'

'They can trace any number, even silent numbers.'

'You know anyone back in the Federal Police?'

'Yeah, but they'd be suspicious.'

'Suspicious?'

'Of me, with my reputation.'

'Yeah, I suppose. What about the local cops?'

'I'm not sure they like me.'

They were mooching around the yards, everyone listening. It was close to lunch time.

'I think you have one or two admirers there, Stacey.'

'Yeah? Who?'

'That new cop, what's his name? The American?'

'Yeah?'

'He was here a few days ago. Checking on us, he said. Because of the black car at the school. I said we hadn't seen it since he called last time.'

'Considerate of him.'

'He wanted to know how you were. I said you were out of town at present. He started to tell me what wonderful stories he's heard about you. How you were the fastest gun in Australia. He was impressed by the number you'd killed. I said it was only two. And the last one was Palfreyman and that was a mistake. But you were acting under orders and you were pretty cut up about it. Would not wish to talk about it. I gave him the usual line about every cop hating to kill anyone, even under orders.'

'Really?'

'I think he has a crush on you. To him, you're probably some figure out of the old wild west. Maybe his idea of Annie Oakley.'

'Yeah?'

'Maybe if you fed him a few lines, he might be able to get the address for you?'

She smiled. 'Harry, I love you!'

'Of course, he might feel he can't do a thing like that, even for a former cop.'

'He might not, I agree.'

'Or, he might ask Jack if that's right.'

'That would arouse suspicion.'

'So, there you are. That guy, Tex—'

'Dex,' she said. 'His name is Dexter C. Grass.'

'Seagrass?'

'No, just Grass.'

'Okay, then. Maybe you could have a drink with him at the Hovell one day after work?'

Chook thought about it.

'Why don't we invite him to lunch?'

▲

CHAPTER 10

Next time he called, bashful and gawky, they asked him if he'd like to pause for lunch. He was delighted—astonished, you might say. Could not believe his ears. Nor his eyes, being invited to lunch by the famous Anastacia Becker. Dexter arrived, cap in hand, when he called the next day. All spruced up, his hair slicked back, hands washed clean back at the station. He knocked at the front door, which opened at his touch.

Terry stood there.

'Ah, g'day,' he said. 'You'd be Dexter?'

'Yayah, well, yayer, I am, I reckon. That's what they call me. I gayss I'm here all in one piece and ready to meet with you folks, if the invitation still stands.'

'I reckon so. Come on it.'

So, he went in. Becker met him and asked him how things were going and if he were allowed to drink while on duty? Becker had a mint julep ready mixed in a big cut-glass jug on a silver dish on the cabinet in the living room. It was a real mint julep, except that there was no whiskey. They had to add that for themselves. They'd chosen it because, apart from straight bourbon, they couldn't think of any drink an American cop might prefer.

Of course, they used Jack Daniel's, which any expert will tell you isn't bourbon since it isn't made in Bourbon County, Tennessee. So Becker, Anastacia, and Terry had inauthentic mint juleps, while Dexter had one without whiskey—being on duty and all.

Still, his eyes lingered on the Jack Daniel's bottle. They had Jameson as well, but Irish whiskey didn't seem right for a mint julep.

They sat down pretty well right away, because Dexter had to watch the time.

Anastacia had made a big pork pie, served with a heap of American salad. When Dexter asked how she made an American salad, she replied. 'We chopped up an American.'

He laughed so hard he almost choked while chewing. But he couldn't shake the suspicion that there was an ulterior motive behind this hospitality.

Which, of course, there was.

She got pretty quickly to the point, stressing that he shouldn't believe everything she heard about her, especially coming from his workmates. For example, that she had set up that varmint named Graham Shafter by taunting him, challenging him to draw. And he'd got so mad he had to draw on her, but she was a lot faster. And had filled him with a lot of hot lead before he could hit the floor in the famous Bar None Saloon in the main street of Wagga Wagga.

'It's all lies,' she said firmly. 'I didn't beat him to the draw. He'd already drawn—a shotgun, would you believe. A sawn-off pump-action with five in the magazine.'

She leaned closer, her voice lowering. 'And any story about me being as cool as ice under fire? Pure fiction. I was scared stiff.'

'You were?' he said, chewing. Accidentally, he had dripped tomato chutney, on his pants, while listening goggle-eyed and trying to eat at the same time.

'I was nearly pissing myself,' she said. 'As a matter of fact, I *was*. It was dribbling down one leg. Inside, of course. I could feel it creeping down, like an ant or a spider or a skink. It reached my knee and kept going. I thought any second now, it's gonna trickle onto my boot and spread all over the barroom floor. And everyone standin' around or huddled in corners would see what it was, and start laughing. And saying to themselves, Hey, she's scared shitless. And they say she's tough! That's what got me worried. I didn't want anyone laughin' at me. Not when I was trying to make out I was the fastest gun in the west. That is, the west in Australia, which starts just a few miles west of the Great Divide. Or, west of Bondi Beach to some lazy, sunburnt, lotus eaters with nothing to think about, except where they're going to get their next buck or next shag. That's what this country is now, Dexter. You think you've got it bad back in the States, but we've got it, probably worse. Money and sex, you know? That's all they think about. It ain't Christian, is it?'

He was fascinated.

'You're durned right, ma'am.'

'Anyway, I wasn't worried about any damned two-bit psycho, who didn't like women in any shape or form. And I wasn't out for revenge.'

'You weren't?' He was chewing, wide eyed.

'Not at all. Mind you, I had to keep an eye on that sawn-off he was holdin'. It kept drooping, like his dick in the old days when I used to know it. And he couldn't get it up and had all the girls laughing. That's what was wrong with old Shaft. He couldn't get it up unless, you know—' She dropped her voice, glancing at Terry, who was all ears. 'Unless you gave him special treatment. If you know what I mean?'

'Yayer?'

'And another thing, Dexter—'

She dropped her voice again, leaning a little closer. His table manners the worst she'd ever seen. Eating with the fork in the right hand. And dropping bits of salad. And chewing with his mouth open. All ears, he was.

'I was so scared I thought he was going to kneecap me. That gun was drooping lower and lower. I didn't mind so much having my guts shot out, if that had to happen, because I wouldn't know too much about it for more than ten seconds. But—and here is the point, Dexter—if there's one thing I fear most in my life it is being knee-capped. I'd rather be dead. I mean, how is a girl to get down on her knees to pray to the Lord above, if she don't have no knees?'

'You're durned right, ma'am.'

'Yes,' she said, chewing too.

'So, you had to shoot him?'

'Yep, straight through the heart.'

'Just one shot?'

'That's all. I don't like to waste lead. You have to account for every round, when you're a cop. As you probably know.'

'You're durned right.'

'So, Dexter, I'd be obliged if you'd straighten out those guys back at headquarters. Most of them did not witness the event. Except Max, he was there. He was in at the kill.'

'Yayah, he told me. He said he was so scared, creepin' along that damned wall up to this crazy guy, he nearly befouled his own britches.' Dexter looked around, realizing too late he shouldn't have said such a thing at the lunch table. But the others didn't mind. Befouled was polite enough for lunch.

'Yeah, that's true,' she said. 'Have some more salad, Dexter?'

'Oh, hell, no.' He laughed. 'Hey, I've done gone and etten all that salad. You know, back in the States, we start with the salad.'

'I should have given you a separate plate.'

'Ah, that's just fine. Gee, I'm really grateful for the opportunity to sit down with you folks and—'

Words failed him. He was so happy he couldn't speak. He swallowed and tried, but nothing came out. His eyes were full of blue birds. This was it. This was why he had come to Australia.

They said folks down under were okay, real neighbourly. There ain't no crime, nothing serious, anyway. No mass shootings in schools and cinemas and no great drug problem, because they had no borders—just ocean. Indeed, there was not much for a cop to do in Australia. And the girls were gorgeous, all stark naked or next to stark naked on every beach and on some beaches fully stark. Cos you couldn't go onto the beach unless you *were* stark naked. You could be fined, if you were wearing a stitch.

So, he came to Sydney on spec. And applied for a job. After all, he had been three years with the LAPD, until they realised he was wanted back in Tulsa for misappropriation of eight-hundred dollars belonging to a sheriff, would you believe? The cops in Sydney took one look at him. Everyone said he sounded and acted like that guy in the old TV show, *Gunsmoke*. The one who had a limp and was always sweeping outside the sheriff's office and saying, Yes, sir, Mr Dillon! That convinced them he was authentic. So they said, 'Okay, you're in!' And gave him a badge. And sent him to Wagga Wagga, of all places.

He'd had to get out of the States.

He couldn't take in any longer—after his father had told him what had happened in the Marines when he was a kid. This was back in the late sixties in Vietnam. This patrol was making its way through the jungle, when one shot came out of a village. Only one rifle shot. It got the sergeant in the butt. The lieutenant, whose name was Sharpley, said, 'That's it!' So he got on the phone and called up for backup. Well, the artillery sent down a storm of fire. Blew the village to pieces. When they walked in, M16s and M60s at the ready, they couldn't find one living *thang*, except a dog with a shattered leg. Everyone in the place was dead. So, that, Dexter said, when his aged father had told him that story a few years ago back in Oklahoma, it was the end for him. He had to get out of a goddamned nation full of gun-crazy yahoos. When the U.S. Marines would blast a whole village, cos some foul-mouthed sergeant got shot in the butt…

They left it at that, more or less. After lunch, when they were having coffee and Dexter was saying that he had to leave soon, get back on the highway, Anastacia said, 'Dexter, have you ever heard of a guy who calls himself Akim Nekrasoff?'

'Hell, no, ma'am. Don't reckon I'd forget a name like that.'

So, quickly and intimately, she told him the story of Nekrasoff.

If they could catch him, they could score one of the biggest busts in history. A man who organised hits. A coward, who never got blood on his own hands. Got weaklings and derelicts and drug-soaked dozies and bad cops to do the jobs for him. Dexter was astonished. He didn't know Australia was anything like that.

Hell, that was why he'd left Oklahoma—and the States, and democracy as it was practiced back home. He'd seen it firsthand, cops back in Tulsa getting gunned down in drive-byes while eating Big Macs in their vehicles. That sort of thang. He'd seen it with his own eyes.

'All we need to know,' she said, 'is who owns a certain phone number.'

'You mean, you have a number but no address?'

'That's about it.'

'Hey, we can get information like that from the phone companies.'

'I know, but it's illegal to give it to anyone outside the police.'

'You ain't a cop no more?'

'Not since I took a couple of slugs from that guy.'

'This guy, Nekrasoff?'

'Uh-huh, the very one.'

'Hell, eh?'

'Hell is right. If we had that address, we could nail this guy. If he's at home, that is.'

'Where do you think he is? By the number?'

'Somewhere in Melbourne, maybe.'

'Hey, that's ay interstate job. The Federal officers can git that for you.'

'Ah, no, I don't want to involve them.'

'You don't?'

'No,' she said, softly with a tickling edge of despair. 'It's personal.'

'Personal business?'

'Yeah, personal.'

Dexter's eyes lit up. Fairly shone with the thrill of the chase.

'Ma'am? You got that number? On you right now?'

'Right here in my hip pocket.'

CHAPTER 11

She sat in the rental car and watched the house across the canal. The address was in Elwood. It made sense. Ivan Medich might well have seen Nekrasoff walking around in St Kilda. That's where the nearest shops were. Not that they were all that classy in St Kilda. A hundred years ago, it would have been a desirable seaside suburb, where you could bring your family on weekends for a swim or walk on the beach or stroll on the pier and have lunch. Or go for a boat ride, in a steam launch, tooting and steaming and smoking, flags waving. Everyone waving from the long jetty. From the shore. Enthusiastic, excited. Men wearing straw boaters and girls with bows on white blouses and button-up shoes.

Now it was full of tourists and permanent residents in hotels and boarding houses and houses of doubtful character. Perhaps a few nice houses remained from before the First World War—old seaside mansions along Marine Parade or nearby. Mansions built by wealthy builders, city lawyers, or retired graziers from the bush.

But walk up to one now, and you might find it converted into a boutique hotel. Press the doorbell, and a receptionist in a long red gown might welcome you, take your credit card, and lead you to your room. The room might feature silken beds, gold-coloured bedposts, red walls, and golden curtains—possibly a mirror on the ceiling. Inside, you might find a girl who looked barely out of school or a PhD student making ends meet. Or maybe just a luxuriant cat with long fur and enormous whiskers, blinking at you as if to say, She won't be long. She's getting ready. Especially for you.

But that wasn't where Nekrasoff lived.

The house was across the Elwood Canal, on a gloomy but respectable street lined with cavernous trees. It wasn't in St Kilda but in Elwood—a surprise.

It was dusk now, the sky a cobalt blue, with one or two bright stars twinkling above. Streetlights flickered on. Chook had picked up a map from the hire-car place in South Yarra, where she'd checked into a motel and left the Harley. Now, she sat on the St Kilda side of the canal, watching the house.

It was early in December 2002. The day had been hot, and the night lingered with residual warmth. The sooner she got out of this, got back to the motel, got out of her jacket, the better. Have a nice cold drink.

In the dusky house, a light switched on. Someone moved behind a curtain, just a shadow. Then it was gone, and the light went off.

The house was fine-looking, a sprawling Federation-era design with huge brick verandahs. Built on reclaimed swamp, it dated back to the hopeful years between Federation and the horrors of the First World War. The house embodied that era: terracotta tiles, tall red-brick chimneys, and a spiral staircase leading to a tower with views of Port Phillip Bay—when the trees were young, and neighbours far apart. Moulded windows and wide, welcoming doors. To lead you into a hallway of comfortable wealth. Where there was sure to be, on one side, a silver dish on which you might drop your card to show you had called. And drop your gloves if well received. Pick up your card and clear put, if you were not.

There must be some mistake, she thought.

Although, perhaps Nekrasoff had made a lot of money over the years. Not only in murder but possibly sound investments. A new car dealership or hotel, perhaps a string of brothels. Nekrasoff may have had social pretensions, like most thugs and shifty sharpers and standover men and dealers in all kinds of substances.

A few windows lit up. A shape moved behind one—a figure, setting a table or taking a book from a shelf?

Chook hesitated. Either Ivan Medich had gotten the wrong number, or this was another trap. She stepped out of the rental car and crossed the bridge. Tired of the whole business. Nekrasoff was a killer. No doubt he hated her, not because anyone was paying him now. He'd tried at least three times to kill her and failed. It was a matter of professional pride. He had to kill her. If he didn't, he'd never be accepted into Melbourne society. He was a man of property in a city of relentless nobodies.

She got out of the car and walked across a bridge.

The canal was old and dirty and smelt bad the way canals do. Stale and yet somehow full of hope. She reached the street on the other side, walked under the trees and into their darkness. And reached the house.

Studied it closely. Checking all ways of escape.

She didn't have a silencer and she would not buy one. That would raise suspicion. She didn't know what had happened to the one Marko Medich had screwed to the pistol he was going to use to kill her. But that was their problem. Marko was dead. And that dim-witted Ivan was probably at home crying his eyes out, or in jail charged with the murder of his brother—while the family waited to see what would happen.

The police. The ambulance. The gravedigger. The coroner.

Everything had gone wrong.

She opened the front gate and listened. It didn't squeak. There might be a dog. If there were, it did not appear. Perhaps confined to the backyard.

Took a few steps. Went up a stone paved path. Noticed what looked like dahlias each side. Somewhere in the warm night, a rose. No doubt more than one. There were a few tea-trees to one side and something dense and dark like an elm on the other side. Big thick leaves, like five-pointed dinner plates.

She walked up a cobbled path, came to three steps. Slate steps, worn but not worn out. Light spilled from the windows and the leaded-glass panels on each side of the heavy front door. It was a white door or an off-white door. There was a knocker. But also to one side was an old bell pull.

She pulled it. The bell tinkled inside.

Nothing happened for a while, then a bolt moved in a lock and quietly the door opened, a chain across. You had to be careful if you lived in a place like this. So close to the riff-raff of St Kilda's fetid streets.

'Yes?' a voice said.

One old eye appeared in a crack, plus a wisp of white hair. And perhaps a wisp of white eyebrow. All above a taut and tight chain.

'Mr Nekrasoff?'

'Yes?'

'Mr Akim Nekrasoff?'

'Yes?'

'Could I have a word, please?'

'Who is it, please?'

'My name is Babchuk, Anastacia Babchuk.' There was no reply. 'Did you hear me?'

'What name?'

'Babchuk. You know that name?'

'Babchuk? Is that a Russian name?'

'It is for some people, Ukrainian for others.'

'Babchuk? I'm sorry, I don't know anyone of that name.'

'Could I speak to you for a moment?'

'Well, I don't know—'The old man looked back inquiringly.

'Do you have someone in there, a member of the family?'

'Oh, yes, I think. Yes, my son.'

'Could I speak to him?'

'You wish to speak to my son?'His breathing was weak, crotchety.

'Just a few minutes, please.'

'Oh, oh, we don't normally—don't normally have visitors at this time of night. We were about to sit down.'

'I'm sorry. Could I speak to your son? Just speak to him, at the door?'

'Oh, I don't know. At the door?'

'At the door, yes. If he's available, just a minute.'

He looked back again. She could see the back of his head, then an old grey eye again. Then the back of his head. A dithery old man. Scrawny but clean.

'I'm looking for a man named Akim Nekrasoff.'

'Nekrasoff? Oh, we don't know anyone named—what's' that? Oh, yes, yes. If you say so. My son says it's all right. What? Yes, all right.'

The chain rattled, the door opened.

The old man stepped back. Behind him was another, middle aged. Not fat at all. Rather, he was tall and slim and wore a white cotton jacket over black pants. Also a black tie over a white shirt. And black shoes. Looked like a waiter about to serve dinner. Or, someone you might have seen an an old film about incarceration in a very expensive Swiss hospital.

In his left hand was a small Beretta.

On his face was an expression of indifferent surprise. An eyebrow raised.

He didn't fire. Probably knew all about her. Knew how fast she was. Knew the Beretta was just a pop gun, no match for her Colt .38.

She stepped in, smiling.

'Mr Nekrasoff? I thought you were much heavier.'

The black eyebrow went up, disdainfully.

'We refer to you as the Fat Man,' she added.

He said nothing.

'I thought we should talk.'

'Talk?' he said.

'Man to man, if you like.'

'Man to man? Some say you are a woman.'

'I am sometimes, then sometimes I'm not.'

'What are you doing?' he said.

His was a softly modulated voice, like an actor's.

'What am I doing? You can see what I am doing. Thought I'd drop in and see how you are?' She leaned back against the heavy door, heard it click shut.

'What do you think you are doing?'

'What do I think I'm doing? I'm looking for a man called Nekrasoff.'

'We don't know anyone of that name.'

'What is your name?'

'My name?'

'That's what I said.'

The tall dark man thought about it. His cheeks were sunken and his hair was thick.

'No-one of that name lives here.'

'You've never heard the name?'

He did not reply. Chook had walked up a few steps.

'Someone in Cremorne said he lived here.'

'Cremorne?'

He spoke as if he had never heard of it.

'Across town, between Richmond and the river.'

'In this house?'

'This very house.'

He thought about this too. 'Who said so?'

'A guy named Medich.'

'Medich?'

'Ivan Medich.'

'Medich?'

'You know anyone of that name?'

'What name?'

'Medich? Medich? I don't think we know any person of that name, do we, Father?'

Chook had had enough. 'It don't matter all that much.'

The man in black and white still thought about it. His jaws seemed to be working. Something had happened in his life, you could see. He did not know what to do. But one thing was sure. There would be no dinner tonight.

She pulled out the Colt and fired.

Hit him in the middle of his thin chest.

He went down slowly and easily, still holding the Beretta. Went down on one side in a half-hearted spiral until he hit the floor, where he curled up like some vast and repulsive insect. They watched as the life went out of his eyes. Strangely they remained open, as if relieved. As if he'd known it would end this way—someone walking in the door and asking for Nekrasoff. Somehow, he seemed grateful.

The old man cried out, frightened. Not much more than a squeal.

'It's all right,' Chook said.

She secured the Colt, went to Nekrasoff. Checked his pulse. He was lying on his side, as if listening for sounds down below, down in the cellar. These old houses always had cellars. Long before refrigeration.

Took out a tissue and gently prised the Beretta from his grasp. Then stood up, pointed it at the door and fired twice. Splintery holes appeared in the solid oak.

The old man shook, hands going to his face, his eyes. Frightened.

She dropped the pistol by the body and went to him.

'You'd better sit here for a while.'

Got him to a chair. It was beautifully carved, scratched in a few places but highly polished. Well worn, possibly well-loved many years ago. A telephone sat on a small table beside it. It was the place where you sat and did your phoning, back in the days when you had to buzz the exchange and give a number. Beside the phone was a small framed photograph. It showed a woman among a small crowd. They were looking at her, but she was looking past them. As if amazed. Not looking at the photographer, but at space. As if she had been released from something dark. Some sort of building. Just the end of a wall and a doorway. A name on a wall, a few words in a foreign language. She was young but not a big child. Just a woman in a long dark coat. Her white face was shining, as if she'd never believed that this would happen.

Reminded Anastacia of pictures you sometimes saw with historical articles about people being released from camps after the war. The Europeans and their wars. And their millions of deaths. In those days, Europe was a continent of death.

Anastacia dialled 000 and asked for the police.

She waited, humming a little tune to herself as she waited. It might have been a Russian lullaby.

'Police,' a man said.

'I want to report a death,' she said.

While they waited for the first car to arrive, she talked to the old man.

He was hard to follow. Tried often to speak but suddenly, in mid-sentence, he'd give out one lonely howl, like a frightened dog. Then he'd resume as if nothing much had happened. Gave bits and pieces of a life. First Poland, then Russia under Stalin and the labour camps and finally the escape—via Crimea and Turkey and Port Said. Where they'd picked up a P & O boat bound for Australia, loaded with English migrants wearing socks and sandals and playing Housie before an electric fire that looked like a cosy fire in a grate, but wasn't. And unwanted children out of Liverpool. In short pants and short skirts, looking like they were being abducted from a place they could never call home. Orphans from the Blitz.

Every now and then, the old man would get up and go to a door, try the handle.

'Are they coming? Are they coming?'

He was that kind of old man, who needed help.

Chook tried to get him away, but he would not leave. He'd bend his head, lean with his forehead on the door. Moan a little, and say a word over and over so softly that it was like the wind talking to itself in its own secret language.

At last she separated him from the door and led him to a chair.

'Why does your son wear a white jacket?' Chook asked.

'Jacket?'

'He is wearing a white jacket.'

'Is he?'

He leaned forward, peered

'Dinner,' he said. 'He always wears a jacket.'

'You were about to eat?'

'Yes, to eat.'

'He prepares dinner? Each night?'

'Oh, yes, he's quite a capable boy.'

'He cooks?'

'Oh, yes.'
'So, there is no lady in the house?'
'Oh, yes, she is here. She's confined.'
'Confined?'
'To bed.'
'I see.'
'Is that your wife there, in that photo?'
'What?'
'This one here beside the phone?'
'What?' He had to twist to see. 'That is Natalia.'
'Where was it taken?'
'What's that?'
'Where was the photo taken?'
He had to twist again. 'When they released her.'
'She was in a camp?'
'Yes, she was in Plaszov. The Russians were coming. They took me, made me march back with them.'
'The Germans took you back?'
'Yes, into Germany.'
'They left her behind?'
'In Plaszov. The Russians, you know, they released her.'
'And you went back for her? After the war?'
'To Warsaw. They had taken her to Warsaw.'
'Then you came to Australia?'
'Australia?' He did not seem to know where he was. 'Yes, to Australia. That was a long time ago, wasn't it?'
'Yes.'
Anastacia thought she heard a car door slam.
'What is your name?'
'What's that?'
'Your name? Your son said it was not Nekrasoff.'
'My name? You want my name?'

'If you don't mind.'

'Medvedev.'

'Medvedev? That's a Ukrainian name.'

The old man didn't seem to understand. She pointed at herself.

'I am Ukrainian.'

The old man stared at her, wide-eyed. Seemed to have difficulty putting two simple facts together, Medvedev and Ukraine.

'What's your son's name? His first name?'

'His first name? Oh, Nicholas.'

'Nicholas Medvedev?'

Someone knocked on the front door, heavily.

'Did he ever use the name Nekrasoff?'

'Nekrasoff?'

The old man simply stared at her.

She let them in.

The two officers listened to her story. The senior was short and tired and his eyes looked as though he'd seen enough crime for one day.

'Anyone else here?'

'I think there's a woman.'

'Yeah? Where?'

'In a bedroom.'

'Yeah?'

'I think you'll find a key on him.' She pointed at the body.

'Yeah?'

When they walked in, she was lying on the bed, not in it. Natalia Medvedev had been like that for some weeks, dressed in a night-gown and lace cap. She looked very peaceful, although somewhat shrunken and desiccated. Parts of her body were missing.

'Christ, what a stink,' one of them said.

'Who did this?' the other said.

The old man had followed them to the door. He looked at his wife with unseeing eyes.

Another car arrived, including a sergeant. He went to the old man.

'What happened, sir?'

The old man did not answer.

'Who shot him?'

'I did,' Chook said, 'after he took two shots at me.'

'Is that right, sir?'

Again, no answer.

The sergeant went into the bedroom, took one look and came out. Went to the old man on the chair.

'What is your name, sir? Can you give me your name?'

He seemed to have fallen into a deep hole of bewilderment. His eyes were closed. He spoke, but it was barely a whisper.

'*Moy syn sdelal neskol'ko uzhasnykh veshchey.*'

'What did he say?'

'It's Russian,' Chook said.

'You speak Russian?'

'Very badly.'

'What does it mean?'

'My son has done some terrible things.'

CHAPTER 12

He sure had. Years ago he'd faked a collision between a truck and a car in Melbourne. The Federal Police had considered this, when they were trying to find Akim Nekrasoff, but nothing had come of it. As we now know, Nekrasoff did not exist. After searching the place in Elwood they found a lot of incriminating stuff, including a photo of the driver of the car. It was a woman, who had a frock shop in Chapel Street, Prahran. Medvedev fancied himself a ladies' man. Either they adored him or he fell into silent, simmering rage against the whole female sex.

The lady car-driver had been married.

She'd dated the handsome Russian—a prince, no less. At least that's what he'd claimed. An *emigré*, although a bit late for an *emigré* from the Russian Revolution. He was born in Melbourne soon after the Second World war, the son of a lecturer at Melbourne University, who claimed to be descended from a member of the Russian royal family.

The woman, though impressed, resisted him. She refused to disgrace herself—she was unhappily married but unwilling to commit adultery. Enraged, he raped her. She was horrified, vowing to go to the police. But she didn't. Her husband, a state parliamentarian, would have been outraged—not because of the assault on his wife but the scandal. He'd divorce her, take the children.

You know the story.

The woman kept saying she was going to the police without actually doing so. That had got on Medvedev's nerves so much he decided to get rid of her. At that time, instead of being a wealthy *emigré's* son in Elwood, he was driving for IPEC or one of those parcel companies that flit like butterflies around cities at high speed, or at least they advertise same-day service. No sweat. That was his job.

He decided to silence her.

Waited for her as she left the shop in Chapel Street. When she was coming along Orrong Road, Windsor, he came out of a side street full pelt and whacked her, from the right. It was perfectly timed. He must have rehearsed it over and over. Anyway, she was crushed, like an eggshell, as they say. He had all the excuses in the world. He was late with his deliveries. Another vehicle was right behind him, tail-gating. He was watching the other car in his rear mirror and didn't see the stop light. He'd smashed into the old Alvis saloon at sixty miles per hour. A terrible mess, glass shattered everywhere. Her car rolled over multiple times, careening into a pole and then a parked car. The impact was devastating; the Alvis's steering wheel crushed her chest, breaking her ribs. Blood covered the scene by the time the ambulance arrived.

Lucky for him, no-one associated him with her. She had not told a soul.

And that's how Nicholas Medvedev got his start, almost twenty years ago. After that he killed two tarts, young women, separately. They wandered the streets at night and did it up against walls or behind private hedges or even at the back of Luna Park, or the *Palais de dance* in St Kilda. Disgusting bitches, he would say to himself, walking away.

So, that's how it had begun.

Nicholas began to earn fairly steady money, doing odd jobs such as intimidating people who were slow to pay up. So that, when his father, a noted scholar of Pushkin, Lermantoff, Gogol and other Russian pioneers, had to retire—because of his intolerant attitude toward his students and his ranting delivery—Nicholas was able to come to the rescue. The family left their brick cottage in Caulfield and moved into the atmospheric old house by the canal in Elwood. Gradually his fame spread.

One day, while eating tortellini and mascarpone-topped prunes at Gianelli's bistro in Carlton, a thickset man sat at his table, uninvited.

The man folded his arms, leaned forward on his elbows, and locked eyes with Nicholas. His own eyes were small and penetrating, giving off the unsettling air of someone pretending to be an old friend. Nicholas had never seen the man before.

The man had a droopy, slightly unkempt moustache, which Nicholas noted with distaste.

'You look like somebody, my friend,' the stranger said.

Nicholas raised an eyebrow. It was always the right eyebrow. 'Oh, really?'

'I think maybe you might be Nicco Caspari.'

'Nicco Caspari?'

'From Castellammare.'

'Castellammare?'

'Castellammare di Stabia. You know, near Napoli?'

'I don't think I'm familiar with such a place.'

'Where they make the big ships?'

'What makes you think that?'

'You look like Nicco. Maybe you work like Nicco?'

'Why would I work like Nicco?'

'He fix some problem now and then.'

'Oh, yes?'

Nicholas was intrigued. This sounded like business.

'Everybody say Nicco good man.'

'I'm afraid you seem to have confused me with someone else.'

'No, my friend, you be like Nicco. Maybe his brother. Everybody say you got disguise. They say you good what you do.'

'Good at what?'

'Fixin' ship, she come in for rust or hole or broken rivet or what you know ships get warning and got to be fix up before you take her out again.'

'A welder, you mean?'

The stranger had smiled.

'Nicco do a good job for me a year or two here since. You know what I mean?'

'What sort of ship do you have in mind?'

The stranger leaned a little closer, his arms now tightly folded. His murky eyes wide with secrecy. 'You see man over my lef' shoulder? He's a drink soup. He's a got a napkin to his neck and dribblin' soup. Nice red soup.'

Nicholas spotted him. He was indeed dribbling soup, red soup. He was sitting at a table with another man and two women.

'That man, he Ritzi Carbone.'

'I don't think I know the gentleman.'

'Maybe you like for to fix his ship?'

'What's wrong with his ship?'

'He got too many leaks, you know what I mean?'

'Really?'

'Maybe you good welder?'

'Maybe I am. I'd really need to know a bit more.'

So that's how it had begun, the relationship with the Mafia.

The stranger's name was Salvatore Pisano.

The job was easy enough. All he had to do was walk into Gianelli's one day and pop this guy called Carbone, who, it seems, had recently been released on bail from Barwon super-max. Everyone had thought that very strange, because Ritzi had been in custody awaiting trial for the killing of Mario Scotto at the Victoria Markets last year. Which had upset some people, particularly Pisano, who was running things in Victoria at that time. It sounded a good job. The pay was good, fifty grand on the knocker. And another fifty grand to come. This was attractive money. Nicholas did not doubt that he'd be paid. If there was one thing he admired about the Mafia, it was that they kept their promises. In this case it was a branch of the Mafia, the Society of Honourable Men. A most honourable society indeed. Besides, he was going to need that sort of money to pay off the mortgage on the Elwood place. His father was on a meagre pension, just enough for the weekly groceries. And his dear mother, half mad when the Red Army had rescued her from the Polish camp at the end of the war, would need special care. She tended to wander off, along the canal, calling.

Nicholas didn't want to get his own hands dirty, so he had to think of a sub-contractor. Someone simple. Someone disposable.

On Swan Street one day a commotion caught his attention. A young man—or perhaps a youth, a scoundrel, or a ruffian—had been knocked off his bike by an old Daimler driven by an elderly gentleman man with a hooked nose like a judge. The argument went on for a full minute, while a tram was approaching. Nicholas loved trams. Usually fell into conversation with at least one interesting person each trip.

The Daimler man had offered the kid five dollars as compensation.

The boy had thrown it back at him.

'Take your fuckin' fiver!' he said. 'What about my bike? You've fuckin' ruined it!'

'I really am sorry,' said the gentleman, 'but I must be off.'

And off he'd driven, leaving the urchin fuming.

Nicholas had strolled up: 'You handled that rather well, I thought.'

'Eh?'

'Completely in the right according to the law.'

'I'm gonna sue 'im! I got his number.'

'I don't like your chances, my friend,' Nicholas had said. 'That was Mr Justice Bellwether.'

'Bellwether?'

'He's a judge.'

'A fuckin' judge?'

'Now retired, lives in Hawthorn, by the river.'

'Ah, shit!'

'You can't beat the law,' Nicholas had said. 'It's a pity about the bike.'

'What am I gonna do? I've got to get t'work.'

'What do you do?'

'Work for the old man, spreadin' cement or concrete on buildin' sites. Startin' the fire on cold days. Makin' the tea or coffee, emptyin' the shit can or—'

The wretched creature looked to be at his wits' end.

'How would you like a new bike?'

'What sort of bike?'

'Perhaps a motor bike.'

'A new motor bike?'

'What sort would you like?'

'A big, red, Honda dirt bike.'

'How much do they cost?'

'Ah, ten, twelve, thirteen thou, I reckon.'

'Not impossible, if you were to be interested in a little proposition—'

'What sort of proposition?'

And that's how Nicolas Medvedev got into cahoots with the Mafia. He was now in the big time. Until that bitch on her Harley Davidson had begun to give him trouble. Had tracked him down. And finished him off. He'd not resisted. He'd drawn a Berretta on her, but had not tried to kill her. He knew he was a monster. He sickened himself. He firmly believed in Fate. If you were fated to be killed by a woman who rode a big black motor-bike, there was nothing you could do about it. That's why he'd fired off two shots, carelessly. Not intending to kill her, but to get her to kill him. He was sick of it, sick of it all. He was a monster, he knew it. No point in denying it, especially to himself. He'd loved his mother so much that he'd had to eat her.

By midnight, the police had thoroughly searched the house in Elwood. Inside a locked large cupboard, they found not only clothing and theatrical gear but also a collection of prosthetics. The most striking piece was a false pregnancy belly, designed to make a slim woman look pregnant or a thin man appear portly.

Chook arrived home at lunchtime next day, tired and pestered by itchy eyes. She'd been at St Kilda police station in Chapel Street until midnight, telling her side of the story. After some initial scepticism, they eventually came around to believing her. The more they learned about Medvedev from their own files, the more convinced were the State police that he was a sweetly, possibly effeminate, depraved monster. Who prowled the world looking for people in need.

It was broken sleep, wondering whether she'd done the right thing. She'd deliberately hunted down a man and killed him. Not given him a chance. On the other hand, he hadn't given his victims a chance. She had eventually dozed off, to be woken next morning by someone banging on her door a few minutes before eight.

She opened it, bleary-eyed, only to be blinded by a camera flash.

A reporter shouted: 'Ms Babchuk, how does a Federal Police officer end up involved in this kind of affair?'

'I'm not a Federal officer,' she snapped, slamming the door shut.

Anastacia quickly packed her things and left, shoving her way through the throng of journalists like a beleaguered Hollywood starlet.

CHAPTER 13

When she told Becker, he exploded. He stormed and stamped around the room, shouting almost voicelessly. There was no need to keep his voice down. It was a Thursday and Roberta was at school. But he was a polite man. Even as a police constable, he'd never shouted at anyone. Never lost his temper, not seriously anyway. Tried to hold it back now. Couldn't believe she would do such a violent thing—killing a man in cold blood. Over the years he'd got used to her violence. It had always seemed to be justified as self-defence or at least a righteous sort of reaction to something repulsive. But this, this was blatant murder for the sake of murder.

She liked to tell people she was a Mongol, which she was not. Or probably not. She was a Tartar driven from some place east of the Caspian Sea by the Golden Horde. From Turkmenistan and all points east. That was long ago. Her story was part of the ancestry that people invented for themselves, like saying you are descended from the Vikings. Another fine body of men who liked to murder, rape and pillage. All over the world. Those were the good old days.

'Yes,' she had said, drinking whiskey and soda on an empty stomach. 'I must be Mongol. I kill people. I like to kill people. That's why I behave the way I do.'

Maybe she was Mongol, in part at least. Maybe some Tartar woman way back in her ancestry had not been able to run fast enough, when Genghis Khan and his mob of horsemen had turned up in Turkmenistan. Her eyes were not round, but slitted. Not puffy slitted. Which makes you wonder.

Becker was enraged. 'Christ, Chook—'

She shook, about to snap back at him, but could not. She loved him too much. Also, he was perfectly correct. She had done a terrible thing, had deliberately executed Medvedev. Smack in his chest. She should not have done it. Couldn't resist the temptation. It was in her blood. She was that kind. You hurt me, I hurt you. Understand?

'Christ, Chook.' He repeated it deliberately, she knew. He was extremely angry. 'Do you want to go to jail? By God, you certainly deserve it!'

'I'm sorry,' she said.

'You're sorry? I don't think you are. You seem to get joy out of it. God stuff me dead, you're going to bring disaster down upon us, the way you are going.'

She was sitting on the sofa, holding the whisky. The glass was slowly tipping, about to spill. She sensed it but did nothing about. Let it spill.

'At least, he won't menace us anymore. He won't take Robbie.'

That stopped him.

In some ways, he agreed with her. He could understand that a woman—as strong and fast and ruthless as Anastacia—would want to destroy anyone and that menaced her child. Not a child of her body, but more precious to her than any child of her own could be, because he had given Roberta to her. Proof of his love, trust, and admiration for her. A smart cop who'd taken two bullets ordered by a madman—one who, if she had not acted, would have tried again.

Becker was still storming around the room.

'You've got to let the police handle people like that. You are not God Almighty. You don't decide who lives and who dies.'

'I kill the bad ones—only the very bad.'

He was calming down. 'Ah, God, I hope that is the end of it.'

'I hope so too, d—'

She'd been about to say 'darling' but stopped.

She had failed. Her husband was outraged. She finished the whiskey in one gulp and stood. 'Do you want me to leave?'

He did not answer.

She walked out, strode out. Went to her room, their room, but changed her mind. Instead, she went to Terry's room, flopped on the single bed. And cried. It was the end, she knew. She had ruined everything.

Anastacia lay face down, her face buried in the pillow, not moving. Nothing happened. Distantly, she heard birds by the creek. Galahs wheeling and screeching before they settled in the trees. Now and then one of the heifers bellowed. Nutty barked at something. She wondered if it were a snake. She should go out and check, but did not. She couldn't show her face. She waited, listening for Becker's footsteps as the dog stopped. The wind came up, probably raising an eddy of dust, perhaps a willy-willy. Summer was coming in and the land was dry. The school would shut for the long summer break tomorrow, Friday. There would be a breakup ceremony, perhaps a concert. She had done nothing about it. She should have volunteered, but had not. Certain that, if she had offered her services, they would have been refused. Politely refused. Anastacia was notorious. Anything could happen with her around—and usually did. She was bad luck.

A footstep, he was in the room. She recognised it by his breathing. He had a particular way of holding his breath when upset—or relieved, or puzzled. Like constrained or measured breathing, such as an opera singer or a horn player in a big orchestra. One who knew the value of breathing in certain ways. One way meant one thing and another meant something quite different. Such as, *I'm sorry my dear*, whereas the other could mean, *Pack your bags and get out.*

This time, she wasn't sure.

He sat on the edge of the single bed, barely an inch or two to spare. Placed a hand on her hip, letting it rest there for a moment, then patted her gently.

'I am sorry,' he said.

She turned quickly, looked up at him, surprised.

'I won't do it again,' she said.

He did not argue. He was not even looking at her, but out the door towards the laundry—the only separate room on the western side of the house.

'I promise,' she added.

Still, he did not look at her but left his hand on her, rubbing it slightly. She was still in her jeans and had not taken off her boots.

'I know you have had a bad life,' he said. 'I know you hurt still. I understand you want to get even with those who've hurt you. But you take it too far. You can't go around killing people, no matter how horrible the things they do. One day you will be caught. You will go to prison. And where will we be? What would happen to Robbie? She needs a mother. You are a very good mother. She loves you. You encourage her. Help her with her homework, explain things very carefully. You are a good teacher.'

She rolled over, looking up at him, surprised.

'I admire you greatly, Anna,' he said.

It was one of the names he used for her. Anastacia always seemed too long and formal and Stacey never quite suited her—it felt too ordinary. And Chook she detested. She knew that when he called her Anna, something significant had happened. Perhaps a critical turning point.

'Harry—' she began.

He didn't answer but kneaded her hip gently, like rubbing out a bruise.

'What would you like to do for Christmas?' he asked.

She was so surprised she could not immediately think of an answer.

'We might go to a beach,' he suggested, still without looking at her.

She watched him. He was both angry and yet not angry. She was Anastacia, and that was that.

'What about the farm?' she asked.

'Maybe I can get someone to look after it for a week. Or,' he added, 'you and the children go away.'

'By ourselves? No, never!'

She put her arms around his neck. 'I would never leave you, Harry.'

He shrugged, pulled a face. Slightly embarrassed.

'Because I love you,' she added.

'Hell, Anna—'

'I really and truly love you.'

He leaned down and snuggled her. She burst into tears.

'I really do, Harry. You have given me all this. I never thought any man would want me.'

He kissed her on the lips.

'Now, I have everything I don't deserve.'

'You are worth it.'

'I will never do such a thing again!'

'Okay,' he said.

'Do you believe me?'

He nodded but didn't believe it. Killing was built into her genes. She should have been a soldier girl, fighting for her country. Dying for her country. She was that kind of woman. Anastacia had come out of history, a mythical woman. Not quite human, but some sort of creature that belonged to story books and tales told around the campfires on the lonely plains at night. The horses whinnying unseen.

'No,' she said, 'let us stay here. We are farmers, we have to look after the stock.'

'We could send them all to the yards.'

'Sell them? Oh, God, no. That would be so awful. The children would cry.' She shuddered. 'No, no, we'll make do here. We can have them all on Christmas Day. I'll arrange it. We'll get everyone, we'll have a splendid luncheon on the eastern verandah, out of the sun.'

'The last time we did that the house blew up.'

She laughed. 'That was when we were on the western side.' She patted him on a shoulder. 'No, no, no-one will hurt us. They've all gone now. All the bad people.'

'Yeah, okay, but any time you want to get away, have a break—'

'I don't want a break, Harry. Who would want a break from heaven?'

He had to laugh. She sounded corny, the kind of remark only a woman would make. It sounded like words from a crappy old Hollywood movie, in garish Technicolour.

She laughed too, chuckling rather than laughing. And rubbing his shoulder. Then she took his hand and placed it between her legs. He was surprised, but she was smiling in a way both happy and hurt. As if being happy was the most painful hurt of all.

'Let's do it, Harry.'

'On Terry's bed?'

She laughed outright this time. 'It's a bit too small, isn't it? Come on,' she said. 'Let's get to bed.'

So, they went into the main bedroom, holding hands. As she walked, she was pressing against him, her head against his. Breathing, saying, 'Oh, oh, oh…'

'What's the matter with you?'

'Oh, I think I'm going to come just thinking about it.'

He laughed and she laughed and stripped quickly, headed for the *ensuite* bathroom.

'Where are you going?'

'I'm going to have a shower first.'

'I should too.'

She looked back. 'Come on, let's have one together.'

So they got under the shower. It was cool, delightfully refreshing. She laughed as they did it under the shower or up against a wall. He was giving it to her and she was chuckling with her head back, mouth open, drinking the water. And giving herself to him, again and again and again. When they finished, they came out and reached for towels and were drying each other, when they heard knocking. Nutty was barking. He was not at the front, but had the best ears and nose in the business.

'Oh, God,' he said.

'Don't answer it, Harry.'

'Oh, I—'

'Pretend we're not at home. Or, out in the paddocks.'

He was pulling on clothes. Barefooted, he went to the door.

Opened it, slowly. It could be anyone. He opened the door. At first, he thought no-one was there. Then he caught an edge of something, a uniform. The big red Holden was standing outside the gate, on which the sign said: *Nil Desperandum.*

It was Dexter.

'Heck, sorry to bust in on you folks this way,' he said.

'What's the matter?'

Dexter didn't seem willing to answer. Becker stepped out a few inches, then saw Max Kruger standing back and to one side.

'What is it, Max?'

He looked embarrassed.

'We've had a request from the State police in Melbourne,' he said.

'What about?'

Anastacia had appeared behind Becker.

'Yeah, well, mate,' Max said. 'This old bloke in Melbourne says Stacey murdered his son yesterday.'

'What?'

'Reckons she fired first.'

CHAPTER 14

She pushed Becker aside, stepping forward, almost naked. Wearing nothing more than a long shirt and a pair of knickers.

'What? What did you say?'

'Yeah, well, Stacey—' Max said, clearly embarrassed. 'Jack asked us to tell you.'

She was ropeable. 'He sent you out here to tell me that?'

'Ah, no, mate, we were on our way back from a job in Lockhart.'

'What the hell does he want with me?'

'Only a chat, I reckon. I mean, there's probably nothing in it. But you see, he didn't know you'd been involved in anything down in Melbourne. Maybe he just wants to know what the hell is going on.'

'Why didn't someone in Melbourne phone me?'

'I dunno, mate. I mean, Dexter and me, we're just the messenger boys. That's right, isn't it, Dex?'

'You're durned right.'

'Christ, what do those idiots down in Melbourne think they're doing? I mean, I spent three hours with them last night, giving my story. I signed a statement. A guy in Melbourne tried to kill me, two shots. I shot him, one shot, he died. What don't they understand about that?'

Max wriggled a bit. He'd not taken off his cap, but Dexter had.

The Okie was jigging around, doing his absent-minded square dancing again. His feet going like mad on the verandah boards. A sort of boot dancing. And screwing up his bottom lip, and looking away at nothing. She wondered whether Dexter had a brain. He acted like a wind-up dancing doll. He could speak, but only in stock phrases, like: *Excuse me, ma'am?* when you said something he didn't understand.

'Murdered his son? That demented critter says that?'

'That's what he says.'

'That old guy was away in fairy land. He'd left his wife in a room by herself, dead for weeks. They were eating bits of her, for Christ sakes.'

Max blanched. 'I don't know anything about that.'

Anna sighed.

'Ah, Jesus, I had a bad night last night, and worse this morning, when some fat-arsed cop set the press onto me. I've just got back after a bad drive. I've just had a drink with my husband. Now some dickhead in Melbourne thinks there might be something in it? Just because some old bird, straight out of cuckoo land, says I killed his son.'

'Murdered his son, they say.'

I killed him, but I did not murder him. He was taking shots at me. What was I supposed to do? Stand still and let him?' She stopped fuming. 'Let me put something on.'

Dexter chatted all the way into Wagga Wagga. Complained all the way about Victorian police having no consideration for a lady just tryin' to git herself some rest.

'Dexter, you know what we call Victorians up here?'

'Ma'am?'

'Mexicans.'

'Mexicans?'

'They come from south of the border.'

He laughed so much, he couldn't steer straight. He laughed the rest of the way.

They got there without any trouble. No-one looked at them, even when they arrived at the Wagga Wagga police station in Sturt Street. A handsome old building of biscuit-brown bricks, although not all that old. Built in 1927 and gracious and simple and well balanced for an unpretentious official building. White window trim, white arch over the main entrance, well-trimmed lawns and a flag flying, the flag of New South Wales. You hardly ever see it now. Blue like the national flag but instead of the Southern Cross there was a coat of arms. No-one ever looked at the coat or arms, but that did not matter. It was a connection with the past, the colonial past, the historical past. When the only defence for miles around were six mounted troopers in white jodhpurs and blue jackets and caps and long rifles, the kind that might or might not have brought down a bull kangaroo or a bushranger or a tribe of attacking blacks on some lonely station like *Nil Desperandum*. A distinctive post-colonial pride in what was ours. Chook always felt happy when she went in there. It was like coming home.

The duty sergeant gave them a nod. Jack was free.

They walked into his office behind the front desk. He rose. Or almost rose—used his hands to push off the desk in an act of courtesy, but he didn't fully stand. She strode in, sat before him, and said, 'What the hell's going on, Jack?'

He wasn't free at all. Two men sat in the corners, leaning back the way senior officers do, legs crossed—or not quite crossed but loosely cocked. Making a statement: Now, let's get this straight from the outset. We ask the questions, okay?

Jack nodded to Max, who retreated, closing the door behind him.

Dexter had wanted to linger, clearly wanting to eavesdrop.

He was obsessed with Anastasia. But Max indicated to him to get out of there. Dexter had not stopped chatting all the way in. First, about some case in Oklahoma, where he had to bring in an oil worker, who had gone mad and set fire to a well and the pumping gear and the whole damned kit and caboodle. He'd followed that guy for seven days. All over the Eastern Wichita Mountains and even up Elk Mountain, the ruggedest durned piece of rock in the whole of Oklahoma. Then he lost him. Until at last he got him. And where was that? Back at the same rig, among the clean-up crew. Faking it, pretendin' he didn't have nothin' whatever to do with any durned fire in any durned oil well in Tulsa. The guy was crazy, Dexter said. He asked him why he'd come back to the rig? To clean it up and get it pumping again, he'd said. Why the hell? *So Ah could burn the dang thing down again*, the crazy guy had said. He'd given Dexter a whole lot of trouble, all for nothing. One of his workmates had spotted the guy, even though his face was covered with grease. And had already called the local cops. So Dexter had got himself a bundle of trouble and grief and overtime for nothing. For which he was not paid. And that was another reason why he'd quit Oklahoma.

But there was something worrying about Dexter. He'd begun checking out facts about her, not behind her back but to her face. Wanted to know her entire life story. Maybe there was no harm in it; maybe he was just a simple farm boy from Oklahoma. Maybe he was thinking of writing a book about her. Make a few dollars on the American market. She'd discouraged him, especially after he'd asked about Harry and his experiences in Sydney at Kings Cross.

Jack closed the door. 'You know Brett Feeny?'

'I've seen him around.'

'And Ted Whitton?'

'I don't think so.'

'Chief Inspector. Said he'd like to sit in and listen.'

She'd heard about him.

Whitton had recently replaced the man who'd interviewed her after she'd shot that repulsive little maggot, Shaft, or Shafter, or Schaaf. Whacked him with a Glock 22 in the front bar of the William Hovell six or seven years ago. That man, Chief Inspector Alan Kesey Knowles, had broken down when she'd told him what Shaft had done to her with a broken broom handle. How time flies, she was thinking. The past was running through her brain like a high-speed train going backwards.

'To what?'

'Pardon?'

'Listen to what?'

'Oh, nothing serious. As Max might have explained, we've had a message from the Victorian police. They said you were interviewed yesterday at St Kilda Police Station and made a statement about the death of a man known as Nicholas Medvedev.'

'Get to the point, Jack.'

'They have taken a statement from another man, Anatoli Medvedev, who claims to be the father of the dead man. He says you deliberately killed his son.'

She sighed. 'Jack, do we have to go through this again?'

'I'm sorry?'

'We went through such a procedure right here in this building— When was it? Seven years ago? After I shafted that spectacular piece of male shit called Graham Shafter? Who I killed in self-defence. Remember?'

'I remember it well.'

'And what came of it?'

He looked a bit put out. 'Well, nothing came of it. It was decided that you had shot the fellow in self-defence.'

'And that's the position this time.'

Feeny interceded. 'You're saying you shot this man, Medvedev, in self-defence?'

'That's what I said in the statement I signed. Don't you have a copy?'

'They didn't send a copy.'

'They should have.'

'Well, they did not, Stacey, only a message.'

'And what did the message say?'

Jack Jackson reached for a piece of paper.

'Mr Medvedev senior has stated on interview that he saw you shoot to death the said Nicholas Medvedev with a pistol you had carried on your person. That this action was unprovoked… Where is it? That Medvedev was not armed and that he was not in any way attacking you. That…that you shot him in the chest without any warning, and…Then you fired into the front door, twice. And what else? Yes, you then rang the police. Well, that's about the lot. Here, you can keep this copy.' He floated it to her. She picked it up. It was nothing but a lot of words. She didn't bother to read them except the last line or two.

'They also want a rundown on me?'

'Yeah, I've drafted something. You can have a look at.'

He floated another piece toward her.

She glanced at it. Her eyes fell on some words by chance: '…brave and efficient and intelligent at all times.' She smiled: 'How sweet of you, Jack.' She meant it. Really liked him, as good and straight a cop as you'd meet in a long day's walk. Glad he'd made it to the top, station sergeant. There was a bit more about her service as a Federal Police officer, including her time in Wagga Wagga, concentrating on organised crime. A sergeant, she'd retired in 1998 after being shot twice by local persons believed to have been paid by a man known as Nekrasoff. And so on…

'That's nice, Jack. I'll frame it.'

He almost smiled. Feeny said: 'So, what's your response to the allegations made to the Victorian police by this person, Medvedev senior?'

'He is crazy.'

'Crazy?'

'Crazy in the way old people get, imagining things.'

'You deny you deliberately killed his son?'

'Of course.'

'Why did you shoot him?'

'He was holding a pistol.'

'Did he threaten you?'

'Not at first.'

'What do you mean by that?'

'He held it fancifully, like he was toying with it. Playing a shady sort of character who might or might not kill you at any moment—just for the fun of it.'

'You mean unbalanced?'

'I've never known exactly what that expression means. Unbalanced in what respect?'

'Of unsound mind.'

'That did occur to me.'

'Did you ask him to put down the weapon?'

'I did, more than once.'

'He didn't?'

'He moved like he was going to put it away in a pocket.'

'He was wearing a coat?'

She could see where the questions were going. They were checking her. Testing her for any inconsistencies. She was tired, but not all that tired.

'A white coat, like a waiter. I think they were about to sit down to dinner. I could smell food. One room was set for dinner.'

'So what happened then?'

'He decided to kill me.'

They were both surprised. Whitton looked puzzled, but said nothing. He was one of those men who think that his presence is enough. He was a big man in a big suit, the coat unbuttoned. Not exactly fat but stout. Thumbs hooked in his belt—a smart belt with some sort of embossed design. Chook couldn't quite make it out. But there was something else: a thin leather tag peeking out fron under his coat. It was soft, apparently attached to a button on the inside of his pants. He was wearing braces. What the Americans call suspenders. In fact he was wearing both braces and a belt. Harry Becker had once told her about a man who wore braces and a belt. It was a big leather belt with a big brass buckle. Which could be used for—

'How would you know what he'd decided?' Feeny asked.

'By watching his eyes.'

'You know when a man is going to pull the trigger?'

'Yes.'

'How?'

Chook took her time answering. Let her pose gather itself. Eyes tightened, head moved forward but only an inch or two. Face relaxed and went into a sort of careless mood. As if all this was not happening.

'Look at my eyes. Am I going to kill you?'

'I don't think so,' Fenny said.

'And now?'

'What do you mean?'

'Look in my eyes.' He had to force himself. 'Am I going to kill you now?'

Feeny was startled. His whole body tightened. The chief too. Something he did not understand was happening.

'I don't know,' Feeny said uneasily, telling himself it was all an act. But his body was telling him something else. She really did intend to kill him, but intending is not a crime.

The chief spoke at last. 'You knew he was going to shoot?'

'Yes.'

'So you shot him first?'

'Nope, he shot at me. Twice.'

They waited.

'And missed,' she added.

'Missed twice?'

'That's what I said.'

Feeny coughed politely, a hand to his mouth, a loose fist really. He was a smart dresser, she'd noticed. Very expensive shoes. A bit of a dandy.

'But why did you decide to shoot him? I mean, he had missed you twice.'

'He'd missed me twice, because he did not care.'

'Why wouldn't he care?'

'He'd fired in my direction, rather than at me.'

'You mean he deliberately missed you?'

'Not exactly. He did not care whether he hit me or missed me.'

'Why would he do that?'

'Maybe he thought his time was up.'

'Why would he think that?'

'When I told him my name was Becker, he said he knew all about me.'

'Knew all about your reputation? As a marksman?'

'Something like that.'

'You mean he was provoking you to shoot him? Kill him?'

She nodded, her eyes hurting now. Wanted to close them and go to sleep.

'I thought, Third time unlucky.'

'He might deliberately shoot at you next time?'

'Yeah, so I shot him.'

'In the chest?'

'Correct.'

'You deliberately shot him in the chest?'

'Yes, I did.'

'To kill him?'

'Why not? He was holding a gun on me.'

'I believe you are a sharpshooter. People say you never miss.'

'Do they?'

'Why didn't you disable him?'

She sighed. She'd been doing too much thinking in the last twenty-four hours.

'Have you ever killed a man, Inspector?'

'Never.'

The big man smiled faintly. A polite smirk, accompanied by raised eyebrows.

She saw it. 'You ever been shot, Chief Inspector?'

He did not answer.

Feeny jumped in with another question. He seemed eager to know: What it was like, killing a man and getting away with it.

'So you made certain it was instant death?'

'Not necessarily. The brain is still alive. It takes about five minutes for the brain to die after the heart stops.'

'So, why would Mr Medvedev Senior say he saw you deliberately shoot his son?'

'Well, I did, didn't I? I had to.'

'But he says his son was not armed then.'

'Does he? The old man is very vague.'

'Demented you mean?'

'More than that.'

'In what way?'

'Did they tell you about the bedroom?'

'The bedroom?'

Both men looked at Jack. He didn't know what she was talking about.

So, she told them about the bedroom. They were sick, listening. The old man did not know his wife had been dead behind a door in the same house for weeks. The stench was awful. He must have smelt it, even though the door was locked. Yet he thought his wife was still alive. He had never once asked to see her. He accepted what his son told him.

'I see,' Whitton said.

Chook stared at him. There was something odd about Whitton, but she couldn't think what it was. 'Now,' she said, 'I'm going home to get some rest.'

'You didn't sleep well last night?'

His words had an edge of mock sympathy. He reminded her of someone, but she was too tired to think. Someone who wore braces to hold his pants up. And a belt to beat the living daylights out of anyone who gave him any trouble.

'I saw that body,' she said, 'and what he'd done to it.'

▲

CHAPTER 15

She slept most of the way home. Jack had said he'd get Dexter to take her. She'd protested, saying she'd get a taxi. Couldn't take any more of Dexter. Thought again that Dexter was secretly gathering stories from her—a woman faster than greased lightning. There was a big market for gunfire in the country he'd come from. Where folks would fight to the death to protect their constitutional right to kill each other. Yes, sir, there was sure to be a market. Maybe a whole book with pictures—perhaps herself posing with a Winchester in one hand and a Colt .38 in the other. And a Glock 22 between her teeth. Yes, siree. She would never do such a pose, but these days you never knew what could be done with a computer and a bit of imagination.

Max drove her home. They didn't say a word, until she sensed that patrol car was slowing. They crossed the creek and were nosing in toward the gate. She sat up, eyes open.

'Thanks, Max.' She smiled sat him. She really liked Max, a real trouper. He'd do anything for you. She patted him on a hand. She thought of kissing him on a cheek, but he would have jumped a mile.

'You know who he is?' he said out of the blue.

'Who who is?' She almost yawned.

'The big bloke, with the braces and the belt.'

'I was wondering.'

'Whitford,' he said.

'Whitford? I thought his name was Whitton.'

'He changed it.'

'Why did he change it?'

'Because the name Whitford around here wouldn't have made any friends for him, so I heard. Nor anywhere else he's been.'

'Whitford?'

'He was at Kings Cross years ago.'

'Yes,' she said, remembering. The man with the braces and the belt.

'And got killed.'

'So he did.'

'By another cop,' Max said.

'Yeah? What other cop?'

'One he worked with in Sydney. Killed him with a spade, on the sand. Out at La Perouse, they reckon.'

'Really?'

'And who is this guy with the braces and the belt?'

'His son.'

'Yeah? How do you know all this?'

'Jack told me one evening over a beer.'

'And how does Jack know this?'

'Jack had to work with him.'

'Here? In Wagga? When?'

'Ah, it could have been more than twenty years ago, when Jack was a one-striper.'

'Jack doesn't like him?'

Max sat at the wheel, thinking about it.

'He was a bastard, Jack said. A first-rate bastard of a sergeant. Used to beat blokes with his belt. Any suspects he could get his hands on. A heavy belt with a big fat brass buckle. Then kick 'em when they were down. Anyone who gave him any trouble.'

'Christ, one of those?'

'A fuckin' brute, Jack said.' Max checked himself. 'Sorry, that just came out.'

'I say that at home. Harry's chipped me about it. I have to stop swearing—because of Robbie.'

'She's a beautiful girl.'

'And thrilled with herself. She learnt yesterday she's going straight up into third class.'

'Yeah?'

'And she's still only six and a few months.'

She opened the door, a few inches. 'Something happened? Between Jack and Whitford?'

'Yeah.'

'Want to talk about it?'

'Ah, no, better not.'

'I'll tell Harry. He was in Whitford's squad.'

'He was?' Max was surprised, a bit anxious.

'He didn't kill Whitford.'

'Who was it?'

'Better to keep that quiet. Don't mention that to Harry. That you know about Whitford, I mean.'

'I won't.'

'Thanks, Max.' She leaned over and kissed him on a cheek. 'For the lift,' she said. 'For everything, in fact.'

'Ah, gee, that's nothing, Stacey.'

'Anna,' she said.

'Eh?'

'I'm Anna now.'

'Yeah?'

She smiled, got out and looked back.

'Anna Becker,' she said, 'Mrs Anna Becker. No more Bab*chook*,' she added.

The front door opened before she'd reached the verandah. Becker came out. Followed by Nutty, who wanted to jump all over her.

'How did it go?'

'Okay, I think.'

'Who was there?'

'Oh—' She stepped onto the verandah and walked up to him at the door and kissed him on a cheek. 'Oh, only Jack and Brett Feeny and a bloke with a name you know.'

He stood aside, as she went in.

'Who was that?'

'Whitford.'

He jumped, then closed the door. Nutty had come in too. So, he opened the door and told Nutty to clear out. Which he did, resentfully.

'Whitford?'

'Yeah, except he did not use that name now. He calls himself Whitton.'

'Whitton?'

'Apparently he doesn't use his father's name.'

'Whitton?'

'Max told me on the way home. Well, at the gate, really.'

'And how does Max know about Whitford?'

'Jack told him. It seems that Whitford was here as a sergeant some years ago.'

'Yeah, he was. He told me once he never had any trouble in Wagga.'

'Because of his belt?'

'That's right. He was a brutal man. He got me, he dragged me into what they were doing at the Cross.'

She put an arm around him. 'Don't talk about it. What are we going to have for dinner?'

'Oh, we've got some frozen stuff. I'll cook.'

'Where is Miss Wonderful?'

'Watching a spacecraft on Mars. And saying, Wow, golly, gee and Oh my God!'

'Where did she pick that up?'

'Everyone says, *Oh, my God!* these days. Haven't you noticed?'

She walked into Roberta's room. The girl jumped up and ran to her.

'Hullo, darling. You're on Mars?'

'Mummy, Nerida said people are going to Mars one day.'

'Really? I think I heard that too.'

'When they go, do you think I will be old enough?'

'When are they going?'

'In twenty twenty-three.'

'As far away as that? Well, I don't think they take just anyone. You have to do a lot of training.'

'What kind of training?'

'Jumping up and down in space and that sort of thing. Without gravity, and when they get to Mars there's no water. So you'd have to take a whole lot of water, not to mention food.'

'It would be wonderful, wouldn't it?'

'Yes, if you like dust, red dust.'

Becker appeared at the door with a glass in hand.

'Whiskey?'

'Oh, lovely. Just what I need.'

'Still tired?'

'Yeah, I went to sleep in Max's car on the way home.'

They went into the sitting room. She sat, took a sip. 'You know, darling, I kissed him.'

'You kissed Max?'

'On the cheek.'

'Yeah? How did he react?'

'Startled. Oh, God, it's good to be home. You know, he is the only other man I have ever kissed.'

'Really?'

'Yes, the second. I must be changing. I must be changing into a real woman. I liked to kiss him, because I like him. He's a good friend.'

He sat beside her with a beer.

Roberta stood at the end of the couch, a hand on its arm. Watching her mother. Her gaze was so intense that, if you looked closely, you could see her lips moving, silently copying Anna's speech, every word. She understood immediately everything she heard. Or, if not, she asked.

'Mummy, Mr Zsabo has a telescope.'

Mr Zsabo was the teacher of fifth and sixth grade. He was a Hungarian, who'd been in Australia a long time, arriving after the uprising of 1956. He was not married and appeared to be a cold and humourless man. But he had a telescope.

'He said we can come and look through it. He was telling us all about Mars. He said Mars is getting closer and it's amazing how big it is at night if you look. And he said you can see the rings of Saturn, even the titchy witchy moon called Io.'

'Io? Is that a moon of Mars?'

'No, a moon of Jupiter and you can see it crossing the face of Jupiter.'

Chook did not answer; she was staring at Roberta, listening and not listening. She was tired but awake enough to wonder.

'You are a very clever girl, Robbie."

The girl smiled. 'If I really, really tried, do you think I could go to Mars? On a spaceship?'

'When is it, again?'

'In twenty twenty-three.'

'You will be a big grown-up girl by then. You will have to decide.'

'Will I?'

'The bigger you become, the more things you have to decide.'

The girl watched her mother, waiting for her to speak again. Anna was half asleep. Suddenly, Roberta jumped about without going anywhere. And beamed.

'I love you, Mummy!'

'Have you finished with the TV?'

'Oh, yes!'

She ran back to her room.

Becker was listening to her, singing.

'When are we going to tell her?' he asked.

'Tell her what?'

'That you are not.'

'Oh, that? God, I dread the day,'

'She'll hear, you know. Everyone around here knows about Robyn.'

'I dread the day.'

'I'm sure she will take it in her stride.'

'Yeah, I think so too.'

'What are we going to give her for Christmas?'

'I don't know yet.'

'How about a telescope?'

They ate early, frozen whiting and potato chips and salad, much of which Roberta put together. Then, after finishing a glass of red, Anna went to bed. It was Friday, so Roberta stayed out of bed longer than normal. They watched a long documentary about trees, narrated by David Attenborough on TV. In one shot, he stood in the hollow bowl of a giant Mountain Ash in a rain forest in East Gippsland. Saying, or at least implying, that this tree was possibly the tallest in the world. And, as he did, the camera pulled back and back and back, so that Attenborough shrank down to the size of an ant. While the tree went up and up and up, until they got the highest twigs and leaves into the frame. Three hundred and fifty feet high, it was estimated. Roberta was open-mouthed. *Gosh*, she said, *gosh*...

Later, after the girl had gone to bed, Becker sat in the living room, slowly sipping a second red, so slowly that even after half an hour there was still a little in the glass.

He'd been thinking about Whitford and those days at the Cross. And how it had all gone wrong, the graft and the protection and the cold indifference to crime and fixing of deals with smelly dealers and the unfortunates trapped there. Cheap runts in flash coats and hair-dos and cars, with fast money. And the pimps and thieves and standover men and the grafters buying influence with the help of Whitford and his mates.

Every time Becker had tried to get out of it, Whitford failed to approve a transfer. There was always an excuse: a staff shortage, a fault Whitford had discovered, Becker's supposed unsuitability for the role he wanted, or his alleged unreliability. Sometimes Whitford hinted Becker was a suspected accomplice of certain known criminals. Every possible excuse for keeping him under control. Under his big fat thumb.

It had got so bad that Becker had had to get out one way or the other. He'd decided to go to the top and spill the beans on Whitford. But he had not gotten that far. That's when he'd been shot—to shut him up.

Then, later, after Becker had moved to Canberra, he failed to appear at the Royal Commission inquiry into the NSW police. He hadn't told Mr Justice Wood what had happened. He'd been afraid. He was an afraid sort of man. Being everyone's mate did not protect you from a bullet. Thinking about it now, he was surprised he'd made it this far. If it had not been for Evelyn Crowley and her generosity...

When he went to bed, he crept in quietly. Even lifted the bed-clothes carefully not to disturb her. She was breathing evenly. As he slid in beside her, she stirred. He thought she was about to waken, but she reached for him anywhere she could reach him. Then she moved backwards, snuggling into him. And she sighed, almost yawned, then seemed to settle down again. He put an arm under her head, so that she now lay in his arms with her head on his left shoulder. And breathed again regularly, half awake.

He thought about them for a while. How he had first met her. In a police car in Canberra, although it seemed she'd been with him in a hospital, getting him into some clothes. Not his own clothes, they'd been cut off by the nurses. Then they'd driven him up Northbourne Avenue, a chatty brunette and a tall blonde who seldom said anything, heading for a safe house. Where he and Evelyn were to be held overnight. In the morning they were to be at the airport at six, to be flown away. No-one knew where, not even the pilot until after take-off. So that no-one could follow them.

And yet, they had failed.

At Evelyn's funeral Chook had said: *If you ever feel like a beer, Harry—* He'd not taken up the invitation. He'd rejected her. Now, she was asleep in his arms. She was his wife, his third wife. He was tied to her, bound hand and foot. She'd saved his life, when the Medich kid was about to kill him. But she was a dangerous woman. She killed people who did her wrong. Yet, he needed her to protect him and, more importantly, to protect his daughter. He was married to a killer. He didn't know how he could ever get out of it. Probably not until death did them part.

She stirred, turning slightly and rubbing her nose.

'Hullo, darling,' she said.

'You should be asleep.'

'I was, and I feel better now.'

'Then go back to sleep.'

'Oh, I'll go back when I'm ready. Tell me a story.'

'What story?'

'Oh—' she yawned. 'Any old story.'

Her right hand had been had been on his thigh, but not now. Instead, it had risen and her fingers had slipped up his left arm. Now they were creeping across the shoulder to his ear, like ipsy-wipsy spider. Her breathing paused. It always paused before she spoke, when she was like this—in bed and comfortable and inquisitive.

'Tell me about Whitford,' she said.

CHAPTER 16

They had Christmas. Just about everybody was there—at least everyone they considered close enough. Anika and Hank from next door, Muriel, Wendy, and Terry were all present. Even Rosemary and April came along. If you don't remember them, Rosemary O'Hare—better known as Rose—was the woman who'd nursed, cared for, and companioned and cleaned up after Iris Becker during her last years. Iris had lived on for three or four more, a victim of dementia. Not even Rose's devoted care could save her. Eventually, she became so far gone that she had to be moved to the Mary Potter Nursing Home.

Iris never fully understood that she was in the care of the dreaded nuns. If she had realised, she might have screamed her head off. As a child, she had been a vivacious student but a poor scholar, more inclined to mischief than paying attention in class. Her parents sent her to a Catholic school, hoping the extra discipline would help. It did not. The nuns, she feared, would have dragged her screaming down to hell. Ironically, she died under their care, though these modern nuns didn't wear habits—only small gold crosses pinned to their lapels.

Rose had taken a job at Mary Potter to stay close to Iris, so Iris saw her nearly every day. Rose was especially appreciated for her willingness to handle tasks others avoided, such as laying out the deceased or washing them. Rose didn't mind. To her, death was just another part of life. Dying was like being born again—with a different mother.

Becker had visited Iris once a month at Mary Potter. He'd sit beside her and watch, sorry and regretful. She did not know him. All she could say, when she spoke to him at all, was: 'I don't know you, I don't know you, go away!' In her last days—in fact, the last time he saw her alive—she suddenly said: 'I didn't mean it.' Said it over and over. 'Didn't mean what, Mum?' he'd asked. She didn't seem to be aware of him. Lying there with the last few working part of her brain trying to answer.

'Mum? Didn't mean what?'

'Col?' she said. 'Col? Col? Col?' She was calling to his father.

'What is it, Mum?'

She did not answer. Aunt Erica from Uranquinty was there too, with flowers. Erica always brought flowers. Iris was too far gone by then to notice.

'She means it,' Erica said.

'Means what?'

'She didn't mean it.'

'Didn't mean what?'

Erica was trembling. 'She said something to him, when he told her he was going to Vietnam—again.'

'Said what?'

Erica's face screwed itself up like a rag doll.

'I hope you never come back!'

Becker was stunned. He'd never realised it was so bad.

'She said that? To him? When he was about to go off to Vietnam?'

'On the last day, at the airport. When they were boarding. I was there. He leaned forward to kiss her, but she said it. And wouldn't let him kiss her.'

'She said that to a man going off to war?'

'Yes.'

The two Brinsley girls had been opposites. Erica was quietly spoken. Always in awe of her big sister, the chatty one. Who got all the attention at school and after. Iris working in the William Hovell, as a barmaid. Every man making eyes at her, in hope. But she'd accepted only one, a corporal as he was then. An Army man with permanency. Their mother had told them both: Always select a steady man with a steady income, like a policeman or an Army man.

Whereas Erica had accepted Alec Jolley in Uranquinty, when it had become apparent that no other man was interested, steady or otherwise. He had a farm but never had enough money, so he had to do odd jobs for other farmers in the district, like driving a truck or clearing stumps with gelignite or a spot of shearing in season. Alec Jolly was a cousin of Knacker Barnes, who had that garage in Fitzmaurice Street, where he used to beat that kid, Barry. Because he was born stupid and never could get anything right.

'She said that? To a man going off to war?'

'Yes,' she whispered.

'Oh, God, no.'

'And he didn't come back,' she whispered. Into a handkerchief, small, embroidered, her initials in one corner.

'That's what got at her?'

'Yes, dear, that's what made her what she was.'

'Mad?'

'In her own way. Your mother was different after that. Her wish had come true.'

'They found him,' he said.

'Found Colin?'

'In a swamp, the Cong. Two shots into his head. One came out an eye.'

Erica gasped. 'Oh, Harry, how do you know that?'

'A man told me.'

'A soldier?'

He shrugged. 'No, a journalist.'

'A journalist?'

'Philip McNevin, now editor of the *Bulletin*.'

'The Wagga Bulletin?'

The correct name was *The Riverina Bulletin*, but that didn't matter.

'Yes.'

'How did he know?'

'He was a correspondent. He was on the chopper when they brought him in, his body.'

They looked at her lying on the bed.

'To Nui Dat,' he added.

She was so thin that if she'd lain flat, the bed would have swallowed her whole. Not even her head showing. His mother had had fine reddish brown hair. Like his moustache. He didn't have one now, not since he'd married Anastacia. She would have laughed or, if not laughed, at least teased him about it, a health freak like her. Then kissed him.

Colin Becker had not been a Catholic. If anything, he was Lutheran, being descended from the German farmers who'd come up river from South Australia more than a century ago, looking for better land. They'd settled between Albury and Henty.

Erica said: 'I've always feared the day I'd have to tell you, Harry.'

'It's all right,' he said.

That's why Rose was at the farm on this Christmas Day in the year 2002 for lunch. Along with her dumpy but pleasant-enough daughter, April—better known as Prilly.

Roberta was delighted. She also had her big sister, Wendy, who was eighteen now and had finished high school. And her grandmother, Muriel. As well as big brother Terry. So it was a family gathering. Although Rose was not a member of the family, Becker greeted her as if she were. He'd even allowed her to stay on in the house on Docker Street, down by the Lagoon, rent-free. Half a house it was, a three-bedroom weatherboard in fairly good condition, the owner, a retired postmaster and his wife, occupying the other half. Where Rose had cared for Iris all those years. But since her death, he'd not had the heart to tell Rose he would no longer pay the rent.

So, the day came. They had lunch out on the eastern verandah, out of the sun. And ate and talked and laughed and when it came to opening the presents, Anna had gasped and jumped, astonished.

'A computer? My God, Harry, what are you going to do with a computer?'

'Thought I'd get used to one again.'

They unpacked it, a small laptop. Roberta was fascinated, delighted.

'It's like the one at school!'

'Would you like to use it?'

'I can use it already.'

'Did Mr Szabo teach you?'

'Uh hum.'

George Szabo taught the two senior classes. They all watched as Hank set it up.

'Where are you going to plug it in?' Anastacia asked.

'It has a battery.'

'Really?'

Hank got it working. They all gasped as the screen came to life. Roberta cheered.

He typed something. Magically, words appeared on the screen: *Happy Christmas everybody!* Roberta was jumping around.

'Can I do that?'

'You sit here, young lady.'

Hank was going to tell her where to place her hands, but she knew already.

'What are you going to write?'

She thought for a moment. 'Hmmm, I think—'

Becker and Anna stood back, watching. Roberta was still thinking.

'Let me show you where to put your fingers,' Hank said.

'I know, I know!'

Anna said to Becker: 'You really got it for her, didn't you?'

'Well, she can use it too. I'll help her. Look, Anna, I'm not pushing her. They have a computer at school, but only one for sixty kids. She doesn't get a chance to use it.'

'Yes, but a computer at her age?'

'It won't do any harm.'

'Oh, I know you adore her, so do I, but—'

'But what?'

Anna leaned against a post, arms folded. 'Oh, I don't know…'

Roberta called: 'Mummy, I can do it!'

They crept back, surprised. Hank was smiling in his broad Dutch way. Anika was shaking with anticipation.

'Look,' the girl said. 'I know where to put my fingers!'

They crept up, looked over her shoulder.

Roberta smiled, impishly because it was going to be fun. She placed her fingers correctly on the middle line. Then, one at a time, one finger after the other, each finger hopping up and down like a jack in the box, she typed: 'Thank you, Uncle Hank.'

They were amazed.

Then she typed: 'Merry Christmas everybody.'

Everyone was cheering.

At first they didn't hear the front door, but Nutty did. He went racing through the house, barking. He was excited or afraid. Perhaps a bit of both.

'I'll get it,' Anna said.

She followed him and opened it.

Chief Inspector Edward Whitton stood there.

Dexter stood to one side, cap in hand, both embarrassed and ashamed. And wriggling. Not exactly doing a square dance today, but some sort of mortified two-step. Not so much with his feet or boots or whatever, but with his eyes. His dusty little eyes. There was something odd about Dexter. He was not quite all there. Not in the sense of being mentally defective, but that he did not quite add up. Anastacia had just begun to wonder if he'd ever been a cop in L.A. or in Oklahoma. He was more like a man who had played a cop in a lot of movies. But just as quickly she dismissed the idea. After all, the State police would have checked him out. Or, had they?

'What do you want?'

'Your husband at home?'

'Why?'

'Is he or is he not?'

'What do you want?'

'To speak to him, that's all.'

'About what?'

'Are you gonna get him or do I have to get a warrant?'

She stared at him a long time.

'If you think you are going to give us trouble on a day like this—'

'Go and get him, will you?'

She looked around. A town car stood outside the gate.

'Wait here.'

She closed the door tight, even locked it. Went to Becker, told him. He left the party, puzzled. 'What the hell does he want on a day like this?'

'That's what I asked him.'

He went to the front door, opened it.

'Henry Brinsley Becker?'

'That's me.'

'Known as Harry Becker?'

'Right again.'

'You're coming with me to town.'

'Why?'

'So, we can talk about the murder of Richard Oswald Whitford in Sydney on the—'

The day went blank, then fuzzy. Becker's heart jumped or sank or fluttered.

'What the hell?'

It was hard to hear.

'You want to come quietly?'

He didn't know what to do. Chook nodded to him.

So, he went with them, just a few steps. But she called.

'Hey, you!'

Whitton tried to ignore her. But he had to look back, so he could smile at her. Smile in triumph. Chook was leaning against the door frame, still smiling. She was not wearing the Colt today. Instead, she was dressed in a loose cotton shirt, a flowing skirt, and clunky sandals. She looked cute, like a model in a new-season frock in a glossy magazine. Leaning against a rock at a seaside and smiling into space. And the sea air. While the guy behind the camera shoots her fifty times from all angles until he gets The Shot. The money shot.

'You won't get away with this, Fatso!'

'Yeah? What are you going to do about it, little girl?'

'What am I going to do about it?'

She waited while he took another two or three steps, glancing back.

'Ask Jack what I'm gonna do about it,' she said.

'Jack? Jack Jackson? Yeah?' He laughed or tried to laugh. He had a stupid laugh.

She watched them, still smiling. It was now suddenly clear, all the questions. It had been a set-up from the start. Very clever in a roundabout way, but ham-fisted.

'Get off this property,' she called. 'And take your little pimp with you!'

Dexter jumped back. Her scorn hit him. He backed off, protesting: 'Ma'am, ma'am, I didn't know a durned thang about this—'

The door opened wider behind her. Terry came out, Wendy holding Roberta back.

'What's happened?' Wendy asked.

'They're taking your fa—' She'd almost said 'father.' Harry was not her father. 'They're taking Harry. To town, to talk to him.'

'What about?'

'Some copper who worked in Kings Cross, a long time ago.'

'Was Harry mixed up with him?'

'Yeah, he was.'

'Did he do anything bad?'

'Harry? Not as bad as Tricky Dickie Whitford.'

'Who?'

They watched the patrol car depart. Terry said: 'What are you going to do?'

She said nothing for a while. 'I'm going to kill him.'

'Kill him? Really?'

They stood there, thinking. The boy began to shake.

'They'll jail you, Anna.'

'No, they won't'
The day had changed. He was afraid to ask, but he did.
'Why?'
'I won't have to use bullets.'

She walked straight into the police station dressed for battle. Wearing a jacket, flapping a little with the rhythm of her gait. You could see the butt of the Colt. The man behind the desk was a senior constable, Bob Allen. He could see the bulge. He went white with fear. She was gonna kill someone. Perhaps wipe them all out, only four men on duty. She waved him down, even winked at him. Everything would be fine. Where do I find Chief Inspector Whitton? she asked. He was going to say, First floor, first on your left at the top. But he couldn't. He'd gone dry. Did you hear what I said? she said. He nodded. Watched her bound up the stairs.

Then Allen dashed into the sergeant's office: 'Christ, she's here!'

The duty sergeant was Des O'Grady. 'What do you mean? I thought Christ was a man?'

'No, no, that woman, Anastacia. She's gone up the stairs looking for him.'

'Looking for who?'

'Whitton.'

'Anastacia Becker is looking for the chief?'

'Yeah, and she's loaded.'

'Carrying a weapon?'

'Yeah, I saw it.'

'In her hand?'

'No, under her jacket.'

Both listened, heard no explosion upstairs.

'Where is everybody? Where's Dexter?'

'He went out again. I think he's sitting in his car. Cryin', I think.'

'What about?'

'I dunno.'

'Shit, I've got only six men on duty today for the whole of the district. All unmarried men because of Christmas, except me.'

'Inspector Feeny's here, Sarge.'

'Feeny? He's not on duty today.'

'He just walked in a few minutes ago.'

'What do you mean he just walked in?'

'Didn't look at me or anyone else.'

'Where did he go?'

'Straight upstairs.'

'To Whitton's office?'

'Where are y'goin', Sarge?'

'Upstairs.'

O'Grady crept up. A few yards from the door, he could hear voices. No shouting or screaming of abuse or anything else. No gunfire. Quite calm, deadly calm. Like any Christmas Day afternoon.

He knocked on the door.

Whitton yelled from inside: 'Yeah?'

Allen opened the door. Everything looked okay inside, even friendly as if they were having a quiet chat.

'Yeah?' Whitton said.

'Everything in order, sir?'

'Of course everything's— Where's that damned Yank? I told him to stand outside the door.'

'He's out in his car, sir.'

'You mean on patrol?'

'No, he's just sittin' there, in it.'

'Why?'

'I dunno, sir.'

'Well, go and bring him in!'

'Bob Allen has gone out to get him.'

'Shit, well, you stand there, outside the door. Just in case.'

O'Grady was going to ask, *In case of what?* But didn't. He pulled out his phone and called Allen and told him to find Dexter and get him up there A.S.A.P.

'He's in his car, Sarge, but he won't come in.'

'Why won't he?'

'I don't know. I can't understand him. He won't look at me. He's just sitting behind the wheel, talking to himself.'

'What's he saying?'

'I don't know. He's just mumbling to himself.'

'Mumbling?'

'About Mrs Becker.'

'What about Mrs Becker?'

'Says she's gonna kill him.'

Anastacia didn't look as though she was going to kill anyone.

She was leaning back, one arm over the back of a chair, the other hand on or near her chest. Speaking slowly in meaning-ful phrases. So that everyone understood. Feeny was seated beside Whitton, casually dressed as though he'd been hauled in from a charming party by the river. Open-necked shirt, a cravat on a hot day like this. Perfectly polished shoes. Legs not crossed this time. Incomprehension in his eyes.

'So,' she said, 'here's the deal, Fatso.'

Whitton flinched.

He was about to protest, but must have thought better of it. He was a heavy breather. Even as a kid he'd always breathed through his nose, so that everyone knew he was present. He was both watching her and not watching her, like a man confronted by a strange dog which may or may not go for your legs.

'You will release my husband immediately. You will apologise to him for the trouble and embarrassment you have caused. You will drop all charges against him. Then you will get the hell out of Wagga. Run for your life. Because, if you don't—'

'You're gonna drive me out of Wagga?'

'Not personally.'

'You'll never do that, you stupid bitch.'

'Quite right. *You* will drive *yourself* out of town in the middle of the night, hoping nobody sees you. Now, as I was saying, if you do not agree to these terms, I'll call you out in public.'

'You'll what?'

'Call you out.'

'Call me out?' Whitton laughed. 'A gun-crazy bitch like you? What if I don't have a gun? How are you gonna kill me and hope to get away with it this time?'

'I won't need a gun. I'll just call you out, telling the crowd what a piece of shit you are, just like your father. I know the whole story.'

'What story?'

'The one Harry told me. He was a young cop in King's Cross. One night he was called to a ruckus in a side street. Three Chinese were fighting. A man and a woman were trying to drag a young woman back into a brothel. She was yelling and crying. This went on some time, people standing around, laughing. The woman had a phone, trying to call someone. Harry got the girl away from them, put her in his car, and was about to take her to the station when Dickie Whitford arrived. You know that name, Dickie Whitford? He told Harry to let her go. Harry was astonished, but he could do nothing about it. Had to watch as they dragged the girl back into the brothel. Why? Because your arsehole of a father was being paid to protect the filth, wasn't he?

The filth who promise young women work in Australia, but stick them in brothels instead. That's rape, Fatso. Understand?'

'What?'

'Your old man was an accessory to rape.'

Whitton was gasping. His face was white, a fat hand to his fat chest.

'No,' he said.

'Yes!'

'No—'

Whitton was trying to peer at her.

But his eyes looked like they wanted to get out this place. They could not. This woman was calling him out. And a senior officer was present, an inspector, taking this all in. And smiling, like a cat that's just swallowed the cream.

Whitton's face had gone both white and red at once.

'He was a good man,' he declared, 'a good cop. He got results!'

'He was shit, and you know it. Why? Because you're shit yourself, aren't you? Daddy's little boy. You're another fucking Dickie Whitford, aren't you? That's why you dress the same way, isn't it? With the braces and the big fat belt with the big metal buckle? Not to hold your pants up, is it, Fatso?'

'Ah, Jesus—'

'Going to flog someone, are you? Straighten 'em out? Like your old man?'

'What?'

'Your old man once boasted that he never had any trouble in Wagga. You ever hear him say that, Ted? He knew how to use that belt and buckle, didn't he?'

'What?'

'My husband once saw him smash a man's face with that belt. Smashed his teeth, sent one eye flying? He ever tell you about that, Ted?'

'Ah, shit, I don't have to listen to this.'

'You can read about that in the *Bulletin* tomorrow?'

'What?'

'Along with your picture. On the front page.'

Whitton couldn't speak. His eyes had closed, he was struggling to breathe.

'Did he ever belt you? Eh?'

His face was now ashen grey. In a way, she was sorry. She knew what it was like to have the shit beaten out of you.

'You all right, Ted?'

He nodded, eyes still closed.

'Now, here's the deal. You're out of town by midnight or you're reading all about your arsehole of a father in the *Bulletin* tomorrow.'

Whitton looked sick. One hand to his chest, the other fumbling for something in a drawer.

'What've you got in there?'

'P-pills,' Whitton said.

She pulled out the Colt. 'Take your hand out real slow.' He did so, holding a small bottle. 'Now shake it.'

He did so. It rattled. Feeny had jumped away.

'Want your mate to open it for you?'

Shook his head. Got the bottle open. Tipped out one, shakily found his mouth. His face had gone white.

'You want water?'

Shook his head. Popped it in under his tongue, angina. She felt sorry for him. Her mother had suffered angina for years before she died. That was a long ago.

'You listening, Ted?'

He nodded, panting like he'd run a mile.

She waited, Feeny waited. Trying not to smile, but you can't keep a good smile down.

'You want to go home, think about it? You've got until midnight.'

Whitton did not answer. Looked like he was going to pass out in his chair.

They waited some more. A gentle knock on the door, tentative. Feeny got up, opened it a crack. Brief muttering. Feeny said 'thanks', closed the door, sat again. Said nothing.

They waited a full minute. Whitton's breathing improved.

Suddenly he said: 'He killed him.'

'Who killed who?'

'Your bloody husband.'

'Harry killed your father?'

'Yeah.'

'Harry Becker did not do that.'

'He did.'

'How do you know?'

'Torrence told me.'

'Torrence told you?'

'Yeah.'

She laughed.

'You know who was driving Dickie's car that night? At the Cross? Torrence, Vincent Torrence. He's the one who killed your father. Probably the only good thing he did in his whole life.'

'Said Becker did it,' Whitton muttered.

'Who said? Torrence said? When was that?'

'Coupla days later. Was down in Wollongong at the time. When I heard—' Whitton was gasping badly.

'You want another pill, Ted? Nitro, is it?'

Shook his head. Tried to sit up straight. Opened his eyes, looked at her. Tried to focus. At last: 'When I heard, I came up—'

'Up to Sydney?'

'Yeah, an' asked around. Everyone who worked with 'im. No-one'd say. Maybe they didn't know. I dunno.'

'And you asked Torrence, of all people?'

'Eh?'

'That little creep? Fast on his feet, wasn't he? He used to screw stupid women for their money.'

'Eh?'

'Go on. What did he say?'

'Harry Becker hit him with a spade, razor sharp. Brand new. Left it lyin' on the sand.'

'Why would Harry kill your father?'

'Ah, someone took a shot at him. One night, outside his place.'

'Your father arranged that?'

'Eh? Nah, I asked 'im back then. I looked 'im in the eyes and said, "Did you try to kill Harry Becker?"'

'What did he say?'

'What do you think?'

'That's what he said? What do you think, son?'

Whitton didn't answer.

'And what did *you* think?'

'Eh? Ah, he wouldn't do a thing like that, my own father. Everyone said he'd been a great cop, the only one who could handle the cokeheads and meatheads and arseholes you have to deal with every day.'

'Maybe someone decided he was an embarrassment.'

'Eh?'

'Dickie had been called to appear before the Wood Royal Commission. They had him on tape doing deals in cars.'

'Eh?'

'Maybe someone up top feared Dickie'd roll over? Talk to the judge? You know what I mean?'

'Nah, he never would.'

'Never what?'

'Talk, he wasn't a grass.'

Chook studied him for a few seconds. 'How are you feeling, Ted?'

'Ah, Christ—'

She returned the Colt. Feeney had relaxed. He was sitting back, arms folded snow, knees crossed. A mad sort of surprise on his pretty face. Almost laughing now.

'Vince Torrence killed your father, Ted. He told Harry.'

Whitton did not answer, but his breathing was improving. So was his face. For a while there it was going grey.

'And you didn't believe him?'

'I don't know what to believe. That's what I'm trying to find out, aren't I?'

'That's why you brought Harry in?'

'Yeah, more or less.'

'To grill him? All by yourself? On Christmas Day? With no-one on duty? No-one to see? Except your little pal here?'

Feeny stopped smiling. He had bright, shiny eyes.

'So, what's it going to be, Ted? Are we going to be friends? Or do I have to run you out of town with your tail between your legs?'

Whitton straightened up, looked at her, then at Feeny, then back at her. About to speak, but didn't get the chance. A rapid knock on the door this time.

'What?' he snapped. Then shouted: 'Clear off! I'm busy!'

The door opened. Jack Jackson was standing there. O'Grady behind him. Jackson was a senior sergeant, not listed for duty that day.

'What's happened?' He was very angry.

Whitton was exhausted. 'What are you doin' here?'

'I was called in.'

'Who the hell called you in?'

'Des O'Grady.'

'What? Why?' Whitton wriggled in his chair, tried to sit up.

'What's going on, sir?'

'What d'yer mean? We're just havin' a private chat.'

Jackson looked from one to the other. 'You've got a man in a cell. That's Harry Becker.'

'Yeah? Well, let him out.'

'Release him?'

'That's what I said.'

'Why is he in a cell?'

Whitton tried to rise, but fell back.

'I told you, just for a chat.'

'You don't stick a man in a cell just for a chat, sir.'

'He was bein' held on suspicion.'

'Suspicion of what?'

'I was waitin' until Inspector Feeny got 'ere. Thought he might do a bunk if—'

Jackson walked right in. He was in a bad mood. 'Do you understand the gravity of what you have done, sir?'

'Gravity?'

'You told him he was under arrest for the murder of your father.'

'Ah, that was only a holdin' charge to get 'im talkin'.'

'You don't arrest someone you think has killed your own father, sir. You can't be involved personally!'

'Ah, shit, I dunno.'

Whitton's colour had returned, but he still looked beaten.

Anastacia intervened. 'He's not feeling too good, Jack. Go easy on him.'

'I'll have to report this.'

'Who to?' Whitton asked.

'The super.'

'Ah, Jesus, he's probably sleepin' off his Christmas puddin'.'

'It's worse than that, sir.'

They all waited—Feeny, Whitton, O'Grady and Anastacia.

'What d'you mean?'

'Dexter has disappeared.'

'Dexter? That brainless Yank? I thought he was sittin' out there in his car?'

'Bob Allen went out again. He wasn't there.'

'Where?'

'In his car,' Jackson said. 'He didn't come into the station.'

'Then, where is he?'

'We don't know, sir.'

'What about his weapon?'

'Locked in the glove box.'

'And the keys?'

'In the ignition.'

Whitton was really surprised.

'He leaves the keys in a car with a gun in the box? Which anyone can open?'

Jackson didn't answer. Whitton managed to stand. They all stood up. Feeney looked like he'd just come out of a live theatre, where he'd seen a madcap comedy.

'And he just clears off?'

'Maybe he's just gone for a walk.'

'Why would he do that?'

'He left a note, in the car.'

'Eh? What's it say?' Jackson didn't answer. 'What's the bloody note say?'

'I think you should read it yourself, sir.'

CHAPTER 18

Anastacia felt pretty bad. She should *not* have called Dexter a little pimp. That was a bad word, probably more so to an American than to an Australian, where among children and few adults it meant a tattle-tit, a tell-tale, perhaps someone who talks about you behind your back. But it could also mean whoremaster. Which she'd never intended. She'd thought Whitton was using Dexter to get information about Harry Becker and his experiences of Dickie Whitford at Kings Cross back in the old days. Whitton *had* been doing that, but Dexter hadn't realised he was being used. He'd happened to say in passing to Whitton that he'd been to lunch with the Beckers and it was a great house and they sure were neighbourly people.

Whitton's ears had pricked up.

Because that sleek rat, Vincent or Vincenzo Torrence or Torrenza, had said Becker had killed his father. There was no supporting evidence. Whitton knew he could never have got justice on the word of a devious two-timer like Torrence. For seven years, he'd held off, simmering. Then one day, Dexter had said—or at least implied—that he was on friendly terms with Harry Becker and his notorious wife, Anastacia. The woman who called out low-life and, if in the mood, shot them down. Or, so word around town had it.

When last seen, Dexter had been thumbing a ride on the Sturt Highway, going west.

He was not in uniform. They'd found it when they busted into his room in Hadley's Family Hotel, a small hotel in the old part of town by the river in Fitzmaurice Street, just around the corner from the cathedral. His uniform had been neatly folded and placed on a chair. Everything else had gone. He'd paid for his accommodation and said to Mrs Hadley that he would be out of there soon. He'd meant out of Wagga. She'd been puzzled, never having heard anyone say they wanted to be quit of Wagga. It was a cheap hotel but spotlessly clean, having about it an air of old-fashioned dignity. Definitely not a boozer and not a bloodhouse like the Hovell on Friday nights. A family hotel, where you were treated like one of the family, as long as you made no noise and didn't bring in any loose women at night.

Dexter had been standing at the turnoff to Lockhart, an old kitbag at his feet. But it was not clear whether he was going to Lockhart or was bound along the highway, past Narrandera, past Hay, past Balranald, and past just about everything else before you hit the saltbush country. Where nothing much survives, except the sheep and rabbits and kangaroos and galahs.

The truck driver who picked him up said he looked like he'd had bad news, such as a death in the family. As conversational as any well-mannered man, who didn't want to tell you anything about himself. He revealed nothing, not his name or destination or hopes for a job or any sort of purpose in life in the whole trip. The driver had thought he came from Texas. Occasionally, he would comment upon some feature as they passed it. Seemed to be very conscious of windmills. All he would say now and then was: 'They got a lot of those dang windmills in Texas, the same dang kind. Steel, sticking up on the flat and colourless land into the flat and colourless and rainless and bird-less sky.'

Then after another ten miles or so, he'd said: 'This sure does look like Texas, way out haya.'

The truck driver eventually dropped him off at the Caltex station in Balranald. Dexter bought a muesli bar while the truck filled up, and they parted with the usual traveller's pleasantries. The rig was going north, to Ivanhoe. Or, some big sheep station close to Ivanhoe. As it pulled away, the driver caught sight of Dexter in his rear-view mirror. Standing under the Caltex price sign, silhouetted against the emptiness of an outback town at night. A stray dog was squatted before him, watching him eat the muesli bar.

That was the last anyone saw of him.

His note, addressed to no-one in particular, was almost poetic.

I thought I had finally found the perfect woman. Her name was Anastacia Becker. She invited me to lunch. I have never met such a gracious woman, such a noble woman. She was like something out of the old stories about gods, warriors, and dragons. She was perfect.

When she asked me to get a street address for her, I was blessed. Nothing like that had ever happened to me before. Then the big boss, Mr Whitton, told me to dig up information on Harry Becker. I thought it was strange, but he gave me a nod and said—or at least implied—that it wouldn't hurt my career.

So, I started asking around and told Mr Whitton what I'd found: Becker had been at Kings Cross when Sergeant Whitford was there, and something bad had happened. No-one would tell me what, but it seemed Whitford might or might not have tried to kill Becker. And Becker might or might not have harboured bitterness about it. Then Whitton asked me if Becker ever talked about revenge. Revenge for what? I asked. Revenge for someone taking a shot at him, he said. Did Becker ever say he was going to kill Sergeant Whitford?

I said I'd never heard anything like that. Whitton called me a useless little bastard. That hurt.

Dexter went on to describe how Whitton had later asked him to drive him out to the Becker place. Dexter had obliged, unwittingly participating in Whitton's vendetta.

Dexter ended his note with:

I ain't no pimp. I would never harm Anastacia or Harry or their beautiful little girl or anyone. My world is crying itself to sleep now, but I can't sleep. I've had a bad time. I've got to get out of it. I tried to write this all down in my vehicle, but my hand shook so badly I could hardly manage…

That's about where his scribbling had ended. It was a frantic note. Written too fast, lots a misspellings and not much punctuation, certainly with few full stops. So that his scribbling ran on and on, all the way to illegibility. At one or two points, there had been stains—perhaps the salt of bitter tears, as they say.

They guessed that when Bob Allen had gone down and tapped Dexter on the window of the car parked out front, and said, 'Whitton wants you upstairs, now!' Dexter had assumed the big man was gonna tear a strip off him. He'd had a few whippin's in his life. He could take one from a man like Whitton, if he had to—a big, hard, ugly, brute of a man. Who wore braces and a leather belt with brass buckle. Everyone sniggered why. But he could not take it from Anastacia. He'd seen her go up the front steps, push through the door like she meant business. He was not going to sit there or stand there before Whitton, watching with her bright-blue eyes that made you feel you were nothing but clear plate glass. No, sir.

In some ways, Dexter had been pure, even if he had jilted a girl back in Oklahoma and decamped with eight-hundred US dollars. Maybe the girl had scared him. Maybe he wasn't made out for marriage. Even if he was not a real cop, but some conman who'd done walk-on parts in Hollywood, or something like that, he was a romantic. An American romantic. One of those who, bred in or near or influenced for family reasons or by the passion of some primitive teacher early in life, believed in good humans. Especially good female humans. Who saw and were perfectly sure that they saw with open eyes a good woman everywhere, if only passing by. Such as a woman holding a baby by a broken-down truck on a road to the Joachim Valley looking for work in the Great Depression. She was and somehow stood for something that was or should have been in the American soul. It was the inner story of Man since the colonial days, the frontier days. The hopeful days, when things were so bad they could only get better. On the other hand, any Australian romantic will tell you that, when things are that bad, they can only get worse.

She shook. It was a short sharp sob without tears.

'I killed him, didn't I?'

'We don't know that he's dead.'

'As good as dead.'

Jack Jackson phoned the superintendent at home and told him. The super listened silently, except for an occasional hiccup. He was given to hiccups, especially when he'd had too much Christmas pudding. Then he said, *I'll be right in.* He'd arrived within fifteen minutes. First, he called in Jack Jackson and O'Grady and finally Bob Allen. Then he called in Whitton. And closed the door. Twenty minutes later Whitton came out, went to his room, wrote a letter, and signed it. Put it in an envelope, sealed it with a lick of spit. Downstairs, they were worried he might shoot himself. Such disgrace, it had never occurred in the Wagga Wagga Police Station as far as anyone could remember. He had called on Allen and handed him the letter. Then handed in his old Smith & Wesson.

He put on his hat. It was one of those pork-pie hats actors used to wear in such old TV shows called *Homicide* and *Cop Shop*, quite natty on actors, being especially made to fit. Whitton was pretty well bald all over. It sat on his head like a real pork pie; interesting but out of place. At the main door, to the amazement of two women and a child, who'd only then walked in, he turned and said under his breath, 'To hell with the lot of you!'

Then walked out.

He was out in the harsh light when they thought he said something else. They did not hear through the glass doors, closing.

'What did he say?' Grady said.

'Didn't catch it,' Jackson said.

One of the women stepped forward.

'Excuse me,' she said. 'I think he said, I'll be back.'

Every day between Christmas and New Year's Day Roberta practised on the laptop, so that she got faster and faster. One day, close to New Year's Day she said: 'Daddy, I can type anything now.'

'I know you can.'

'I can even type with my eyes shut.'

'Can you really?'

'Yes, just watch me.' She typed: 'The quick brown fox jumps over the lazy dog.'

'You typed that? With all your fingers on the keys?'

'Yes!'

'You can touch type?'

'Yes, I can feel the keys. I don't need to see.'

She shut her eyes and did it again. 'There!'

'You must have been peeping?'

'No, no, no, Daddy I don't have to see!'

'Oh, I don't see how you could—'

'Yes I can. You stand behind me and put your hands over my eyes!'

'Really?'

He did that. Her fingers flew again. Out came the words, but they were different: 'Now is the time for all good men to come to the party.'

'That one too?'

'Daddy?'

'Yeah?'

'Uncle Hank said if you go online, you can send messages to your friends. If they have a computer too.'

'Uncle Hank said that?'

'Yes, and he said you can see all sorts of interesting programs online. He showed me on his computer. We saw *Gorillas in the Mist* with a nice lady who was talking to them. They're big and black and got shiny black faces, like shoes, so shiny. And you can click on Wikipedia.'

'Wikipedia?'

'That's what tells you everything you want to know, when you do your homework.'

'My God, what next?'

Each Saturday morning, they'd drive into Wagga, do their shopping and leave Roberta with her grandmother, who was teaching her Latin. It was an arrangement. Muriel loved Roberta, adored her. Next day, Wendy would drive her back to the farm and spend a few hours riding and grooming Pixie. Then drive back to Muriel, in the little wooden house in Railway Street. Where you could sit on your back verandah and watch the go trains passing by. Any day, any hour.

Then they'd return to *Nil Desperandum*. Becker was driving. The Nissan nosed in off the highway and stopped. Normally, if he were driving, she'd get out and open the gate.

'Anna?'

'What?'

She'd been far away. Staring at the house without seeing it. Her eyes had changed. Instead of their electric blue they were blue-grey, and steely.

'What is it?' he asked.

'I'm not sure,' she said, and got out.

'You didn't kill him,' he said.

She didn't answer. Opened the gate wide, almost ceremoniously, gently and exactly, so that the gate was at a perfect right-angle to the fence. Or, if not, it looked right. Anastacia was a perfectionist. As far as she went, she was perfect. But, she was worried.

In fact, she felt rotten.

He drove through and waited for her. She waved him on. It was only fifty yards down to the house. Much too close to a busy highway. The noise at night was bad. The trucks, the big trucks grinding on and on to the end of the world. She following on foot, head down. When she was in that mood, speech had no words. He drove around the house to the kitchen door, began unloading. Slowly, waiting for her.

She came straight through the house like something military, the back door flying. He handed her a Woolworths bag. She took it but did not move.

'What's the matter?'

'I'm gonna tell her,' she said.

'Tell her? Tell Robbie? Tell her what?'

'I'm not her mother.'

'Yeah?'

'And another thing, I'm gonna find Dexter.'

Becker couldn't believe his ears.

'You're gonna find Dexter?'

'And apologise.'

That evening they sat her down before dinner and said Anna had something to tell her. The girl simply sat and waited like waiting for a movie to start in the cinemas on Fitzmaurice Street, to which she went on some Saturday afternoons with Muriel and Wendy. Smile, jaunty with anticipation.

'You have always believed that I am your mother, haven't you?'

The girl nodded, wide eyed. Something big was coming.

'In fact, I am not your mother, not the one who gave birth to you.'

She nodded, curious.

'Your real mother, the one who gave birth to you, was named Robyn. She was married to Daddy. She lived here on this farm. And she was very happy here. But, unfortunately, she died.'

They waited, watching for her reaction.

None so far, just immense curiosity.

'This sometimes happens. A lady gets pregnant and she gets bigger and bigger and she is very happy, because she is going to have a beautiful baby. But sometimes the baby dies, in childbirth.'

Roberta looked shocked, but said nothing. She could have been watching butterflies on television.

'But, in your case, your mummy, Robyn, died. And you lived.'

'Oh?'

'So Daddy lost a beautiful lady but gained a beautiful girl.'

She smiled, modestly.

'And she has grown up to be a very smart young lady.'

A bigger smile.

'So, I am not your mother. My name is Anna, which sounds like Nanna, doesn't it?

'Uh huh.'

'So if you want to talk to Nanna about it, she would be happy to tell you all about Robyn, because Robyn was her daughter.'

'Uh huh!'

'And she might give you a photograph of your beautiful mother.'

She almost clapped her hands.

'I think she has lots.'

'But, if you like, you can call me Mummy. Just for fun.'

She thought about it. 'I like Anna.'

'You do? Well, you can call me Anna as much as you like. Understand?'

'Uh huh.'

'What do you think about that?'

At first she said nothing, just thought about it. Screwing up her face.

'What will you tell the kids at school?'

The smile broke. 'Hah!'

'What's funny about that?'

'I'm going to tell them I'm a freak.'

'A freak?'

'I've got two mummies! And I bet they haven't!'

As for Dexter, she tried but never did find him. A highway patrol man remembered speaking to a man with an American accent on board a B-double freighter on the Sturt highway west of Mildura. The man was telling a story about a woman he'd met in Wagga Wagga. She was the fastest gun on earth. It had been proved she was the fastest, because she'd been caught on camera firing on an indoor range. Now, as you may know, movie film rolls at twenty-four frames a second. The film showed her pull out a Glock pistol and smoke spurt from the barrel. That took only ten frames, which means she could draw and fire in ten twenty-fourths of a second or just under half a second. This was all news to Anastacia. No-one, she swore, had ever filmed her shooting. But it could have happened while she was working out on the police firing range in Canberra when she was a young Federal cop. When she was getting her speed up. But she did not remember. Seemed to be a product of Dexter's imagination.

Then she heard of him in Adelaide. The police had pulled him up for peddling raffle tickets door to door. He said he was working fo the Church of Latter Saints, but they knew nothing of him. By the time the cops had called on the hotel where he was staying, he had flitted. Next they heard of a fracas on the Eyre Highway, which runs from Port Augusta to Norseman, Western Australia. Apparently he was showing passersby the ruins of the old telegraph station at Eucla. He was tapping out messages on a makeshift Morse-code transmitter. Somehow the machine, covered with dust, would chatter back at him. One tourist, a large man in a Hawaiian shirt, accused Dexter of being a fraud. Which led to a fight, which spread, Easterners against Westerners.

No-one knew how he did it, nor cared very much. It was worth the five dollars' entrance fee to hear him conversing with his mother in Palm Springs, Arizona. As everyone knows, Palm Springs is not in Arizona. Someone wrote to the West Australian Minister of Tourism and complained that he was a trickster. The cops called at the old telegraph relay station, but found nothing. Not even the Morse code apparatus.

There had been no further sightings of Dexter.

There was a news report from Gladstone on the far west coast that someone had been caught selling tickets to see the wreck of the old Dutch ship, Batavia. There was no wreck to be seen. But apparently that was someone else named Walter Seagrass junior.

In the latest development, the Wagga Wagga police received a letter from the L.A.P.D. pension fund. Believing that it may offer a clue, Jack Jackson opened the letter. It was brief and officious. Dexter must prove by the end of the year that he was dead. Otherwise he would forfeit any benefit owed to him. It did not say which year.

▲

CHAPTER 19

They were fishing at the river on Australia Day when the call came. It was Hank: 'Your place—it's on fire!'

'Christ,' Becker said.

Hank was an excitable Dutchman. 'The trees along the creek! The creek, the trees? On the trees? Yes,' Hank shouted. 'I have called the brigade and they're on their way. It's so big, Harry, I can't get in there and fight it. Not on my own!'

'Christ,' Becker said again. 'Is it near the house yet?'

'No, no, about half way across the paddock!'

They jumped to their feet, packed up and raced off home, the whole family. Just him and Anastacia and Roberta and Wendy and Terry.

They were at the end of the lane exactly opposite the lane between their property and the van der Bruggen wheat farm. The lane ran straight to the river. A dirt road, it led past several other farms in good condition. The soil on the north side of the highway at that point was better than the soil on the south side, and worth a lot more to buy. Rich grazing land, more friable, more moisture. Often flooded in spring. Still holding out well, some paddocks green, or greenish.

A popular fishing spot. A fireplace and a sort of shelter, made of twisted poles with a makeshift frame on top, bearing cut branches with plenty of leaves. The leaves had soon died and dropped off.

They were going to have lunch under it, but there was no time for that. They had to get back pretty quick.

It had been a beautiful morning at the river. Hats pulled low against the sun, they'd lounged by the meandering water. The Murrumbidgee wasn't the largest river in Australia, but it was a friendly one—its winding course seemed to embrace the land. Kingfishers darted, ducks flapped noisily into flight, and the breeze carried the smell of water and eucalyptus. If seen from above, the river's loops and curves would make the journey between two points stretch eight miles where the direct distance was only one.

A great thrill before lunch.

Already, three or four tinnies had puttered past with one or two on board, waving. And holding up a catch or two. But out of nowhere had appeared a big launch heading down river, a canvas awning on top and a big outboard at the back. You could hire such boats at some river towns. There were a few in Wagga, or along the river tied up at private jetties. Owned by big squatters. This one looked like one of those fishing launches, capable of putting to sea, chasing marlin. Real Zane Grey stuff. In the Murrumbidgee, there was nothing bigger than the Murray cod, a relative of the grouper. A big cod could weigh up to one hundred pounds. A big feast, if you could catch one. The people on board didn't seem to be interested in fishing. They were having a good time. Waved and held up glasses of whatever they were drinking. And shouting: 'How's the fishing?' And: 'What a beautiful day!' And a large woman, who had a good voice, sang a few lines: *Cruising Down the River on a Sunday Afternoon...*'

They got back in five minutes—not actually back to the house, but near enough. They could see what Hank had meant.

Fire was coming along the creek from the south.

Blazing in the tree tops. Not roaring along; the wind was not all that strong. But strong enough to wipe out the swathe of eucalypts each side. Not to mention the wattles and ferns and occasionally escaped fruit tree.

Smoke was billowing into the blue sky, drifting over the highway and onwards until it dissipated into the warm and excited air. It was a hot day, a dry day. A Sunday, like the woman on the fishing boat had sung. It was the last Sunday of January 2003. A week ago, fire had swept through the western suburbs of Canberra, destroying almost five-hundred houses, horrifying. But that firestorm was driven by a tornado. This was not a tornado, nothing much more than a moderate southerly.

They drove in, leaving the Nissan at the front with the gate wide open for a quick getaway if need be. A few minutes later, the rural brigade arrived with only four men and young girl on one truck. So they got to work, all of them. The fire was burning about four-hundred yards from the house. Working its way downstream. Leaping from tree to tree, from crown to crown. Like a demon hungry for eucalypts. Hardly touching the grass and undergrowth. The heat hot enough to vaporize the sap. It caught and burst in the air, as the fire leapt to another crown.

It was that kind of fire. You could not stop it. All they could say or surmise was that it would not reach the house. The very last eucalypt in the line of trees was at least fifty yards from the house. No fire could leap that far. But burning leaves and twigs could drift. Other trees were near the house—peppercorn trees young and old, and a few citrus trees and flower beds and herbs, but nothing likely to burn.

No water in the creek, no more than a dribble and a few pools. So they waited. It was watch and act, that was the chief's order. No point in wetting the house at this stage. It would soon dry off in the heat and the wind. The roof was green-grey Colorbond and the frame was steel to defeat any adventurous termites. The stumps were brick. Only the cladding and the flooring were timber. Except the stained timber in the ceiling above the living and dining area.

The brigade truck was not big.

Not a massive Mercedes, but a converted Mack truck with a tank on top and a locker at the back for tools and helmets and uniforms and respirators and strap-on air bottles. It was a four-door, so it could hold six crew. When the tank on the truck was empty, they would have to take water from the underground tank, roof water. There was an electric pump, but it fed the troughs in the yards. The fire was heading straight for the yards. They lowered a hose into the underground tank and started up the truck's engine, set the revolutions at fast idle and waited.

The crew consisted of the fire chief and four men and the girl. She wore overalls and a baseball cap, but behind her ears were two golden braids, coiled. Her name was Liesel Eckhardt and she went to Wagga Wagga High.

It became hot, searing hot. Intermittently, black as well as flaming and scorching twigs and bracken and leaves came down, so that they had to put on helmets and protective glasses. And wave and blow the ashes away from their faces.

The fire came closer and closer. One tree after another.

One crown would go *whoosh*! Then the blaze would subside until, suddenly, another crown would explode.

The creek was not only a creek, but a shelter in summer. Some cows had tried to stay downstream, the smoke getting into their eyes, stinging. Gradually, all cattle departed, heading to the north-eastern corner by the highway, half a mile away, where there was no smoke. The weaners following the heifers.

The four men waited for the fire. Two more men joined them.

Through the smoke they could see figures in the lane. Ralph Buchsbaum and two of his sons, waiting to fight the fire if it got away, raced across the paddock toward them. But, it did not. It stuck to the trees, working its way closer and closer to Becker's house. For a moment, he thought perhaps Buchsbaum had started the fire. Not far from the top fence. The creek came through the neighbour's field, his wheat field. There were few trees up there. And the wheat had been cut in November.

No reason to think Buchsbaum had started it, accidentally or deliberately.

Apart from the customary wave and greeting if passing, Buchsbaum and his wife did not bother with him and Anastacia. They had been at the house when it had blown up, on Becker's birthday. The day Robyn had died in hospital. Minutes after Roberta had been born.

All sorts of rumours had gone around. That Becker was the target, because someone in Sydney had wanted to get rid of him. Or, that the tall woman was some sort of law unto herself. A sharp operator, who went around picking fights. Not the type you could be friendly with. Not exactly a homebody, making cakes and running the school canteen. She'd been a sergeant of police and still carried a weapon. Everyone talked about her.

One wild idea was that Chook had placed the bomb, so that she could get rid of Robyn and take her place. Get hold of *Nil Desperandum*. In effect, Harry Becker and his new wife had been sent to Coventry. Treated with respect, but never invited to a neighbour's home.

The horses were all right.

They'd been nibbling or standing in the shade of the trees. But now they'd moved out with the cattle, to the far corner.

The dogs had disappeared. Nutty was hiding under a peppercorn tree against the western fence, while Blue was in the eastern verandah in the shade, watching the cattle and the horses. Didn't seem to be in the least concerned by the smoke.

When they arrived, Becker told Anastacia to keep the children inside, close every door and window and start packing clothes ready for a quick evacuation. She had done all of that. She'd wanted to come out and help, but he'd told her to get back inside with the children. Ordinarily, she didn't take orders from anyone, but she did from him. It was his farm.

Anastacia and Roberta and Wendy watched from behind Terry's bedroom window. He was outside, trying to be useful but not making much impression. Trying to chat up the girl, the chief's daughter, Liesel Eckhardt, a pretty blonde with golden braids hanging down. Roberta was standing on a chair at a window and crying. Wendy was sad and fortitudinous, Anastacia was suspicious.

The fire was close now, blazing twigs and leaves floating onto the roof.

The chief said, 'Dat's it!'

He waved to his daughter. She turned a valve. The driver revved up the motor. Water burst out. The chief began hosing hot spots, wherever he could see smoke on the Colorbond. Terry came back to Becker.

'Hell, how could a fire start here?'

'Deliberately,' Becker said.

'Who'd start it? In the grass?'

'There's no grass to burn. I'm feeding from the bin. And watering from the bore.'

Terry looked around.

'Just as well you harvested in time,' he said.

It was an obvious sort of remark, but he had to say something. He was watching the girl, hoping she'd say something. She did not. She was not even looking at him.

The maize paddock was bare, except for thousands of stalks and leaves. The harvest had been completed last week. Early for maize, but just as well he'd sown early, taking a chance back in September that the earth would be warm enough. He'd had a feeling he was going to need feed in summer. The maize hadn't been as high as he'd have liked and its quality not first-grade, but it was a crop. Normally, maize needs three to four months to grow if you are going to send it to market. But at only two to three months, it was good enough for stock.

'The cows don't like it,' Terry said. He meant the smoke.

'No, nor do I,' Becker said.

The chief came over. 'What you sink, Harry?' He was a German migrant, who'd come to Australia from Hamburg aged six with his family on a Boeing 707 back in the sixties.

'What would start a fire like that on a day like this?'

'Could be anysing, you know? A bit of broken glass in the grass at the right angle to the sun.'

'There's nothing up there,' he said.

'Might be some dry old branch rubbin' up against another. It does happen, you know? Like se blackfellers wis a fire stick. Rubbin' se stick fast in seir hands. Makin' a spark, you know?'

Hank van der Bruggen came up. 'Didn't see it till I came out to look at something,' he said. 'It was big alight by then.'

'Just as well you did, Hank.'

They watched some more. Two cars turned up, other members of the brigade. Now they had fourteen or fifteen ready to fight it, if need be. But Becker was pretty sure it would not take the house. Not even scorch it.

The fire was closer now, not far from the barn.

They began to spray the barn for no good reason other than that the flames were now close enough to lick it. But the conflagration was burning the last eucalypts in the arboreal swathe. They sprayed and sprayed the roof and the walls and held off the fire. They ran short of water and had to drop a hose down into the underground tank, refilled the truck's tank and continued fighting. They were not really achieving anything.

The tank held ten-thousand gallons.

The fire was dying.

Bits of burning sticks and small branches blew toward the crew, so that they had to put on all their protective gear. They were pretty well fireproofed. Two men working the hose were wearing compressed-air bottles. They got a lot of water onto the barn and the fences and stockyards, although not necessarily required. Not a stick of timber among the lot.

Eventually, the fire subsided. Just a few smouldering branches, twigs, and stumps. No significant damage. The eucalypts would recover. In a few months, they'd be sprouting again.

Anastacia came outside. 'I suppose you gentlemen could use a beer?'

They all had a beer, except for the girl. She was sitting on the edge of the back verandah. Had pulled off the cap and was fiddling with her hair. Her father was talking to Hank and two other men.

Anna asked. 'Liesel?'

'Just anything, thank you.'

'Ginger ale?'

'Yes, fine.'

Terry sat beside her. 'Liesel?'

'Hmmm?'

'You want to do anything? Sometime?'

'Like?'

'Go for a walk or ride a horse. We have two, both quiet, a mare and a filly.'

'We have a horse,' she said.

He tried again. 'You want to go to town some day?'

'And?'

'See a movie or something?'

She studied him sideways, still fiddling with her hair. One of the coils was coming loose. She went out with her father every time the brigade went out. The ginger beer appeared before her eyes.

'Oh, thank you, Mrs Becker.'

'Anna, please.'

She turned to Terry, a smile on her lips, but no smile in her eyes. She had deep-blue eyes, penetrating eyes like Anna's. Unblinking.

'Like what?' she said.

'Eh?'

'What do you mean by something?'

'Ah, well, anything you want to do.'

'Anything?'

'Yeah, well, maybe go for a swim or row a boat on the river?'

'You have a boat?'

'No, but I know a kid who does.'

'Who?'

'Craig Aitchison. You know him?'

'I know him. He once put his hand up under my skirt.'

'Did he? Oh, gosh, I'm sorry.'

He was searching for more words, when she spoke again.

'He has a boat?'

'A fishing boat, it's his Dad's.'

'A tinny, you mean?'

'Yeah, well, you could call it that.'

His heart sank. This beautiful girl would not be seen dead in a tinny. Just an aluminium twelve-footer with a pop-pop motor on the back. And smelling of dead fish.

He was getting nowhere fast, he knew.

She said nothing for a moment. Left hand still fiddling with her hair, trying to push it back behind an ear. Her head turned slightly, so that she was both looking at him and not looking at him.

'I suppose you have heard about my mother?'

His heart sank. He'd made a bad mistake, he knew. 'No,' he said, but he had heard.

'She drowned in a tinny.'

'Oh, I'm sorry.'

Greta Eckhardt had fallen in and for some reason had drowned, although she could have hung onto the side, hauled herself back in. But she had not.

He stared at her, at the same time trying not to stare. She was beautiful, even with black smudges here and there. Only sixteen and an orphan. Only herself and her father.

'You have a black stuff on your nose.' He couldn't think of anything more intelligent to say.

'It'll wash off. It always does.'

She sipped ginger ale, thoughtfully. He watched as she swallowed, watched her throat move as the ale went down. Down and down.

'We could feed the ducks,' she said. 'At the Lagoon.'

He was astonished. 'Gee, that'd be great.'

'If Dad'd let me.'

▲

CHAPTER 20

They talked about it after everyone else had gone. Hank was the last to leave. Anika had arrived to see how it was going and to look at the damage and to get Hank to come home. There was nothing more he could do, and she sensed that Anastacia—being Anastacia—would want to talk about what to do next. And if she knew Anastacia, there would be trouble—big trouble for someone.

Hank and Hermann Eckhardt had not been convinced the fire had been deliberately lit. Becker, however, thought it too coincidental that a fire would break out at the very of the creek when they were away. Then make its way down the whole belt of trees and wipe out all the shade and beauty of the beloved creek on a day, when the wind was blowing in exactly the right direction to do just that. They had left it at that and Anika had dragged Hank home. He tended to go on and on forever, apologising for not seeing the fire sooner and not having been able to fight it alone.

Then Wendy went home and took Terry with her.

He would have preferred to stay and try to be of some use. And chat some more with Liesel Eckhardt, but she'd gone home with the fire truck. He had nothing much else to do while waiting to hear from the Army. He would be eighteen in March, but no-one in uniform had yet knocked on his door and said, 'I'm from the Army and we want you for a soldier.'

He was disheartened.

He had to be a soldier, even if he died in the effort.

They were sitting on the back verandah, drinking cold beer and looking at the blackened trees.

'Who do you think did it?' Anna asked.

'Maybe Buchsbaum.'

'Ralph?'

'He's been at me again. Seems to think I owe him something.'

'What?'

'Money.'

'Why?'

'Reckons he was doing well until I came here.'

'He's hit by the drought, lots of people are.'

'He can't pay his mortgage. Reckons the bank is threatening him.'

'To foreclose?'

'He did not say that.'

'What did he want you to do?'

'Solve his problems, it seems.'

'With money? You are not responsible for his problems.'

'Seems to think I have a lot of money and he has none. And that's not fair.'

Anastacia thought about it. 'He would not go that far, light a fire to drive you out or make you pay up.'

'I don't know.'

'What if he'd been caught? His problems would be much worse.'

Becker was not convinced. 'There's something about him.'

'What?'

'Resentment, deep down resentment.'

'Some people are like that,' she said. They thought about it for a while. 'Who else, then?'

'Maybe Whitton.'

'Whitton. Burn us out? Wouldn't that be too obvious?'

'Not to a man mad with anger. Taking him down like that, in front of Feeny, taunting him. Everyone will know about it, laughing at him. The big, fat turkey.'

'I was showing him what would happen.'

'A man like that, the son of a brutal bastard.'

'That doesn't mean he's a brutal bastard, Harry. I think he's a misguided man, very sensitive about his father. He couldn't live with that history. That's why he'd changed his name. Deep down, I think, he's a good man.'

'Beating the shit out of people? Who didn't do what he wanted?'

'How do you know Ted does that?'

'He wears that belt.'

'That's all for show.'

'Showing people who's boss?'

'Yeah, well, Harry, as you know, being a cop is tough. It's not the job so much as the arseholes you have to deal with.'

He thought about it. Maybe she was right, maybe he was paranoid. He'd been like that ever since Whitford had tried to kill him in Sydney. And he'd remained like that, expecting a someone to finish the job.

Maybe Anna was right. It had probably been a natural fire. They were lucky that someone years ago had ensured that there were no eucalypts near the house.

Roberta came out. 'Mummy?'

'What is it, precious girl?'

'Is the fire all out?'

'All except a few puffs here and there. Daddy is going to go up and piss on them.'

'What do you mean?'

'Oh, God, that just slipped out.'

'What is piss?'

'Well, piss is wee-wee.'

'Wee-wee?'

'Yes, wee-wee, what comes out of your whizzy.'

'Ha! Mummy, you are silly.'

'Why?'

'Daddy couldn't put out a fire with his whizzy.'

'Why couldn't he?'

'Because he doesn't have a whizzy.'

'Really? What makes you think that?'

'He's got a dingle-dangle.'

'Has he?'

'You said that's his dingle-dangle.'

'Did I? Well, he can use his dingle-dangle to put out the fire.'

The girl laughed, wriggling. 'Mummy?'

'Hmmm?'

'Would you read me a story?'

'No, *you* must read the stories.'

'I don't know all the words.'

'Look them up in your dictionary.'

'I can't.'

'Why can't you?'

'I don't know how they are spelled.'

'They are spelled in your dictionary.'

'If I don't know how to spell them, how can I look them up?'

She was a rational sort of girl. Everything had to add up, fit together, like the universe. If it didn't, she was not interested.

'Mummy, do we go back to school tomorrow?'

'No, it's a holiday tomorrow, Monday.'

'Do we go back next day?'

'No, the teachers go back then. To get themselves organised.'

'When do we go back?'

'Not till Wednesday.'

'Oh, I want to go back to school.'

'Why don't you look up something on the computer?'

It had been six weeks of summer vacation. She really was bored. Trying to keep a bright girl amused was often beyond even Anastacia's devotion. She would take her to town each few days to help with the shopping, see a movie, perhaps a concert, call on Muriel, have lunch with Wendy at Thos. Thomkins and Son. Always pleased to see her little sister. And sometimes dropping in on Rose and her daughter April, together to play in a park or swim at the beach.

Roberta yawned. 'Oh…'

'Why don't you have a little nap, darling?'

'Mmm…'

She dawdled off.

Becker was still watching the occasional puffs of smoke. The wind had died right down now. Nutty was barking at something up the hill.

'A snake,' Becker said. 'He's found a snake.'

'The fire would have flushed them out.'

He stood up. 'I'd better get rid of it.'

'Don't let it bite you.'

He did not answer.

'And take a bucket of water with you.'

'Why?'

'To piss on the fire.'

Becker reached Nutty, still dancing around. Whatever it was, it had made a run for it, but Nutty had cut it off. The thing crept and crawled. Then it went behind the barn. Nutty went after it. Becker too disappeared behind the barn.

Anna got up, went to the end of the verandah. Still, she couldn't see. Stepped out, walked toward the creek. Then Becker reappeared, waving dismissively. He meant it was not a snake. Possibly a blue-tongued lizard, she thought, or even a goanna. He went on up the creek carrying a bucket, while Nutty still worried it, whatever it was. Scooped up more water, went along the creek up the hill, now and then kicking at burnt debris, or dribbling water onto it, or both. Going up and up the hill, which is not a real hill but a plain, gradually rising to the south and south-east. Now and then he was out of sight.

He was about two-hundred yards up the creek, when he heard her calling.

'Harry? Harry?'

He yelled back. 'What?'

'Harry!'

'What is it?'

'Where is Robbie? I can't find her!'

He dropped the bucket and ran back.

Ran all the way, rushing to her. Anna was back in the house. He found her.

'What? Where is she?'

'I don't know! I don't know! I went to her room. She's not there!'

'Have you looked—'

'I've looked in every room!'

'Has she gone out front? She's tending to wander now—'

He grasped her. 'Is she in the barn?'

'No, no, I would have seen her go there!'

'At the front gate?'

They ran around the house, he one way, she the other. Met out front. No sign of her.

'She may be hiding,' Anna said.

'Under the house?'

'No, no, that's locked.'

He ran to the front gate, while she searched the trees and bushes. Opened the gate, dashed out, looking up and down the highway. Saw nothing. Not a little figure, not a figure of any size. A few cars were passing. And a caravan, disappearing westward. Two trucks were approaching from the east. What looked like a bus coming from the west. Nothing unusual. He scanned the fields around, particularly opposite. Again nothing. Ran toward the creek. Roberta might have found her way into the tunnel under the bridge. Where there was a little cool water, cool shade. They'd warned her not to go under the bridge. Snakes could be there.

Anna came out of the house, called to him. 'Any sign?'

'No,' he said, despairing. The child had vanished.

'Maybe she thought she'd visit Hank and Anika,' he said.

'That's nearly a mile,' she said. 'Anyway, she would not have gone on the road. I've told her never to go on the road. It's dangerous.'

'Look next door,' he said.

He meant the cornfield. The crop had been harvested before Christmas. Only stumps remained, the roots. It was in effect bare, but there were a few dips and rises here and there. And a few broken stalks, what the harvester had knocked down rather than cut.

Anna went that way, westward into the cornfield without corn and he went eastward along the road, glancing around. Trying to spot her walking across a paddock, among the cows. Perhaps she had headed for the far gate that opened onto the lane, but there was nothing to obscure her. It was open country, dry pasture and then, on the other side of the lane, Hank's wheat field, but that had been harvested two months ago. Nothing to see but stalks, stubble. No sign of movement.

No sign of Roberta.

He pulled out his phone and called Hank, told him what had happened.

In the distance, he could see Hank and Anika come out of their house, look around, then at him. Not waving, but puzzled. They circled the house, he went one way and she the other.

Hank called back. 'Still no sign of her here.'

Becker was bamboozled.

He looked at the cornfield next door. It had belonged to old Bert Henchke, cranky old Bert. He'd died and left it to the Salvation Army, which had sold it to Becker, who grew corn there, not so much to sell but to save as stockfeed. Chopped up and stored in the big silo out back. Just in case of drought. Which they were now in. The maize had been cut before Christmas. The field was bare, but strewn with the wide and tumbled debris of harvest. Stumps and roots and broken sticks and leaves galore. The cornfield was large, a square mile. A small girl could be lying in the furrows and ruts and clods and stalks and leaves. There was no reason why she would have wandered into that wasteland, not on a day like this, hot and dry and glary, but they had to look.

They spread out. Stumbling on bits of rubbish from Bert's old garbage dump, looked everywhere. He called to Anna.

'Anything?'

She shook her head. 'Nothing.'

'If she's in here—' He ran a hand through his hair. It was thick now and going grey. He was afraid. 'If she is here, she'd be obvious. If she's fallen over—'

'If she's been bitten by a snake,' Anna said.

They called each way again. 'Robbie!'

No answer.

'If she'd been bitten by a snake, she'd be crying.'

'Not if she'd been out for some time.'

'How long is it? How long before you noticed—'

'Fifteen to twenty minutes, before I found her gone.'

'How long now?'

'Thirty, forty minutes.'

Becker looked stricken. 'If she's been bitten—'

His phone buzzed. It was Hank again.

'We have looked everywhere, Harry. She can't be here. I mean the dogs, they would have heard her, seen her, sniffed her.'

'Yeah, yeah.'

'No sign your end?'

'No, no.'

'You think you should call the police?'

'Yes, I will.'

'Where are you now? I can't see you?'

'In the cornfield, but no sign of her.'

'We will come over, all of us. We have John and Melonie and their kids. Why don't you call Hermie? Maybe he can get some of the boys back again.'

'Yeah, yeah, I'll do that.'

That's what happened, although young Liesel was not with them this time.

Pretty soon they had about a dozen searching the cornfield, starting from the near side of the field and then gradually working westward. Found nothing, got about half way when Becker said, 'That's it!'

'Where are you going, Harry?'

'I'm gonna call the police.'

Twenty minutes later, a patrol car arrived.

A new guy was at the wheel, plus Des O'Grady. They searched everywhere again, but to no avail. Several times O'Grady called back to base. They wanted to use a chopper, but it was difficult to secure one on a Sunday.

It was now a few minutes past six, but still light enough. The hot fields were sleepy.

A chopper turned up late in the day, inspected fields but saw nothing suspicious. Searched houses and paddocks and creeks. It went up and down the highway. Another police vehicle arrived, this time with two dogs. German Shepherds. Not exactly bloodhounds, but dogs trained to hunt up persons lost in the bush. At the sight of them, Nutty fled for his life, but Blue stood his ground and growled. The dogs were given items of her clothing to sniff, but they too failed. Did trace a scent to the front gate, but not surprising. She often went to the gate with Anna to collect mail. But never went onto the road by herself. The dogs sniffed around the gate and the gravel and bitumen for a few yards, but nothing positive. If she had been taken, she must have been carried. No trace of Roberta. A six-year-old girl had vanished. Six years and five months.

Anna felt sick; she cried. Becker held her as they talked to the police. The chopper went back to Wagga. So did the dogs. The sun had reached the horizon, it was now close to eight o'clock, eastern summer time.

'We've done everything we can,' O'Grady said.

'Yeah, thanks, Greg.'

'We've already put out an all-points bulletin.'

Becker did not feel like talking. Each word seemed to fail.

O'Grady hesitated, hands on his hips.

'You suspect anyone, Harry?'

'No,' he said.

'I hear you had some trouble with the Italians in Griffith?'

'That was six or seven years ago.'

'Or, that business in Melbourne? I hear that bloke was a real creep.'

'He's dead.'

'Someone close to him?'

'There was only an old man. He's in his dotage.'

'What about Whitton? I heard he's been suspended.'

'That would be too obvious, wouldn't it?'

'Some men bear serious grudges, Harry.'

The sun was now down. O'Grady's young driver came up.

'Feeny will be here in a few minutes,' he said. 'And Max Kruger.'

'What happens now?' Becker asked. Anna had said nothing. She looked ashamed.

'We're going back, but Feeny will go through it with you again. He'll also outline what we've done so far. Max is going to stay the night.'

'Good.'

That's what happened. Nothing else happened, no developments, no news.

Feeny went through the whole story, making his own notes. Particularly played on the confrontation with Whitford, but gave no opinion on how Whitford could have been involved. He was that kind of officer. Never had an opinion. Gathered the facts as far as he thought he could and let someone else draw a conclusion. That way, he could never make a mistake. He went back to Wagga with the first crew. Max Kruger stayed on. He would stay all night if necessary.

Anna said nothing, but she did make sandwiches and did heat soup and brewed more coffee. Max was drinking the soup slowly, almost reverentially. As if it were special, made by Anastacia.

They sat and waited and did not speak.

Occasionally, Max's phone spat and spluttered the way police radios do, clicking on and clicking off, suddenly and intrusively. Much too loud.

Then, about a quarter to nine, Anastacia had suddenly stood up and said, 'Call me if anything happens.' And went to the first bedroom. She was exhausted. A few minutes later, a phone rang. Not hers, not Max's, not Becker's raucous police equipment. It was the house phone, the line phone.

Becker went to it, but Max signalled. Put out a hand, took it.

'Who is this, please?' he said.

'This is a friend. Tell Becker to lay off, if he ever wants to see his kid again.'

'Yeah? Who is this?'

There was a short, smoky sort of laugh. A hissy laugh. Then a lot of breath, perhaps deliberate.

'You want to know who this is?'

'That's right. Who is this?'

'They call me the Fat Man.'

CHAPTER 21

When Becker told Anna, she went into a sort of shock. Lay on their bed, one hand covering her eyes, speechless. Did not move, except for a twitching of the fingers. Glanced at him and then away. Nothing happened for a few seconds. Time ticked along unhappily. Then she said, 'I thought there was something strange.'

'Strange?' he asked.

'About the fire.'

'What's the fire got to do with it?'

'It was a diversion, wasn't it? To get us outside.'

'But,' he said, 'we weren't all outside. You stayed inside with her, and Wendy was there too. Terry was coming and going.'

She lay back again, fingers twitching over her eyes. He waited, but she didn't speak.

'Anna? Anna?'

She was guarded, then she did: 'They couldn't get to her during the fire. Wendy was inside, so was I much of the time.'

He had to agree.

'But, in the afternoon, the late afternoon, they could. Wendy and Terry had gone and we were both outside. On the back verandah.'

'How would they know where we were?'

'With binoculars,' she said. 'They could see who was outside. All they had to do was wait until she was in her room then come in the front door.'

Yes, he thought, the front door had been unlocked. Her surmise was possible, but difficult to achieve. Snatching a child from her room, while her parents were outside, chatting.

'Who do you think it was?' he asked.

'He said the Fat Man.'

'Yeah, so he said to Max.'

'Was it the Fat Man? I killed a fat man in Melbourne. He turned out to be a thin man with a lot of theatrical gear. He was psychotic.'

Becker studied her. He was holding her free hand, but she was not responding, not squeezing back. As though she had withdrawn into herself. He tried to look deep into her eyes, not so much to see what she was thinking, but what she was feeling. With a woman like Anastacia, he knew, terrible things could happen.

'You think the thin man was not the Fat Man?

'Could be,' she said.

'The thin man was only pretending to be the Fat Man?'

She did not answer. She may, however, have shrugged noncommittally.

'So that the Fat Man now has to do his own work?'

She didn't answer. He could be very wrong, he knew.

'Yeah, it could be.' Then he thought: 'How would anyone know about the Fat Man?' He was speculating, more for his own benefit than for hers.

She spoke. 'They sent me on a false trail, didn't they?'

'Who?'

'Those Medich bastards in Melbourne. Gave me the wrong number.'

'To that house in Elwood? You said that crazy guy was the right man. He knew all about what had happened.'

'Yeah, but maybe someone had told him.'

'You mean someone used that bloke—' He couldn't think of the name.

'Medvedev,' she said. 'Used him as a front. So we wouldn't know who was the real Fat Man.'

'I don't know what to think.'

'I'm gonna go down there and beat it out of them.'

'The Croat family?'

'That bastard, Ivan. He led me astray.'

'You think he really knows who the Fat Man is?'

'They borrowed money from him. They must know where he is.'

Becker straightened up. 'Oh, Christ, Anna, please, don't do anything bad.'

'What's bad about burning shit?'

He sat back, horrified.

'God, no, dear. You can't do that again. Your father's gone. He's out of the country. He hasn't come back.'

Apart from a postcard to say he'd arrived, Anastacia had heard nothing from Victor Babchuk. He was in the Ukraine or he was not in the Ukraine. She had a feeling that soon after he'd arrived in Odessa—after he'd looked around, revisited the scenes of his childhood, the shootings and immolations, he'd been satisfied, relived the past—he'd set fire to himself. That's how he'd have wanted to go—a man who'd once worked in a crematorium. Becker shook her.

'Look, Anna, the message was addressed to me. It said, *Tell Becker to lay off if he ever wants to see his kid again.* Lay off what? Have I done anything lately that could upset someone? I haven't had anything to do with the Italians for five or six years.'

'It's not the Italians,' she said.

'And Whitton, he wouldn't be game. People are watching him, his own people.'

'It's not Whitton,' she said. 'It's someone else.'

'How do you know?'

'Someone much closer.'

'Ah, hell, who could that be?'

'Robbie did not scream.'

'Perhaps, they gagged her or had a hand over her mouth or—'

'She would have struggled, tried to cry out. I would have heard her.'

'Or, maybe they chloroformed her in her sleep?'

He shuddered at the thought.

Anna's expression had not changed. She was staring into space. Or, not staring into space but at some object or person or spectre *in* space four or five feet from her eyes. Maybe confronting it, examining it. Something she both saw and did not see, because it was not there. But it was; she could see it. The thing was a few feet away from her. It was at the front door and the door was opening, and she began to see—

Max knocked. Quietly, respectfully. Stuck his head in. The room was in darkness, the only illumination coming from the hall light. Except there was no hall. Anna glanced at Max. This time Becker could see her eyes clearly. They were not blue but a desolated sort of grey. It was like looking into a bleak land, not covered by ice or snow, but as barren as death itself.

'Excuse me,' Max said. 'They got a trace.'

Immediately after the caller had hung up, Max had called a Telstra operator and asked for a trace. It took a long time. Finally, they got it.

'The call was made from a payphone in Kew.'

'Kew, in Melbourne?'

'Yeah.'

'That's near Burnley,' she said.

'You think it's the Croats down there?' Becker asked.

'Could be,' she said.

'Excuse me,' Max said, 'what's this about Croats? Aren't they people from Europe?'

'Yeah, I was trying to find a certain Fat Man years ago. They gave me an address in Elwood. So I went there.'

'I heard you shot him?'

'He shot at me first. Anyway—'

Anna pushed herself up, sat on the edge. Remained like that for a minute, thinking and not thinking. She'd exhausted herself waiting for news. Now she had the news, she felt wrecked.

Becker said to Max, 'Get the Melbourne police to go to the house in Burnley.'

'No, no,' she said, 'they won't find anything. Those people will lie their heads off. Maybe they don't know anything about this caper. Kidnapping? Oh, God, the poor girl, she must be scared to death.'

'She's a brave little girl,' Becker said.

Anna stood up. 'If they touch her—'

Becker persisted, 'Get the Melbourne police to go there, Max. Even if they don't have her, they might know who has.'

'Yeah, right. What's the full address?'

Anna gave it to him, slowly, carefully.

Becker was holding her, but she was not responding. Not actually rejecting him, but not needing him. He knew what that meant. She was a very angry female. She would deal with this matter in her own way, the old way.

They waited around for two hours. The call came a few minutes before eleven that night. Listened for a couple of minutes, then said, 'Yeah' or 'Yeah?' and 'Okay' and finally 'Thanks for trying.'

'Who was that?' Becker asked.

He and Anna were sitting on the sofa. She was lying against him, sort of in his arms. She was not asleep. Could not sleep, waiting to find out.

'That was Police Operations,' Max said. 'They've had a report from Melbourne. The C.I.B. people went to that address in Cremorne, marched in with a warrant. Found nothing. No sign of any girl. The people there—'

'Medich?'

'Yeah, Medich, that's right. They seemed to be telling the truth, according to the guy who led the raid, Inspector Redlich. In his opinion they were genuinely startled, when the police burst in. They searched everywhere. Waved a few weapons around, gave them a lecture on the punishment for kidnapping. Even mentioned the Fat Man. They looked scared at first but would say nothing. When Redlich pressed them on that, they admitted they did know of a fat man, but had never met him. They had given his phone number to you, Anna. Swore they didn't know anything about any girl or any kidnapping or anything bad.'

'They were telling the truth?'

'Redlich thought so.'

'Ah, Christ,' Becker said.

'I'm sorry,' Max said.

'Thanks for trying, mate.'

Anna sat up. 'It's all part of a set-up, isn't it?'

'What do you mean?'

'The phone box in Kew. That's to make us believe the Medich family have something to do with the abduction. Make us think she's in Melbourne.'

'But what about the demand that Harry lay off? Why Harry?'

'That's to make us think that Whitton is behind it. Lay off the charge of false arrest, false incarceration, and the rest. If he drops the charges, she will be returned.'

Becker almost laughed. 'Even Whitton wouldn't do anything so blatant.'

'No, but someone thinks he *is* stupid and therefore can be framed.'

'But he'd have to be completely irrational, fuming with anger and resentment. Because you humiliated him in front of Feeny. A big fat bully like him. Some people can't take humiliation. But is he like that?'

'There's only one way to find out,' she said.

Anna stretched like a cat, rolled her shoulders and neck and head and eased the physical pain. She stood up.

'Let's go and ask him, have a look at him. Tell him that, if he is responsible, he will have a short and very unhappy life.'

'Jesus, Anna,' Max said. 'You can't take the law in to your own hands.'

'I don't have to kill him.'

'What do you mean?'

'He'll kill himself, when he realises there's no way out.'

Becker stood up too. 'Don't do that, Anna. You just said he's not responsible.'

'Yes, well, we're all responsible, aren't we?'

'What do you mean by that?'

She did not answer. 'I'm going to bed,' she said. And did so.

Max waited until midnight, hoping for another call. But there was not. Nothing happened. No news, no more ideas on who could be responsible. Max said he could get someone to take over from midnight, but Becker declined. He'd look after things. He had a weapon, the old Smith & Wesson, and the Winchester if needed, but that was unlikely. No-one was going to attack them, not at the farm.

So, he went to bed too. He got in beside her and put and arm about her. She was lying on a side, facing away. He knew she was not asleep.

'Anna,' he said. She did not respond. 'Dear,' he said. She seemed to respond momentarily to the endearment. Perhaps surprised that he could feel anything but fear for her, for them both. Their child was missing, presumably kidnapped. There was always the chance that she was not abducted at all, but someone was making it look like a kidnapping. 'Darling,' he said. She rolled back against him, now almost flat on her back, her face dimly clear. Her eyes open.

She reached back and found and held a hand.

They lay like that for a while. Eventually, her grip loosened. He was sure she had fallen asleep.

When Anna slept, she often breathed so deeply it sounded like climbing up a steep hill, perhaps a mountain. Perhaps Everest. Her chest heaved, her body heaved. It was both taut and yet flexible, getting ready. Her body was alive, not with exhaustion but with endurance. She was built for endurance, an athlete. Not a track athlete but a fight athlete. She exercised by fighting against the unbeatable.

She would prevail, he knew. But he did not yet know how.

When he awoke, light was bright behind the curtains. He reached out, but she was not in the bed. He looked around, no sign of her. He listened, no sound from the bathroom, nor from the kitchen. If Nutty heard anyone in the kitchen, he would whimper at the back door. But he was not. If she had driven away or had ridden on the Harley Davidson, he would have heard her. The dogs would have barked, at least Nutty would.

Maybe she had gone for an early morning walk—by the creek or across the eastern paddock to inspect the cattle. More likely, she would have saddled up Viento and gone for a ride, perhaps along the country lanes. She would return.

He got up, dressed, and looked outside. He walked around the verandahs—north, south, east, and west—but saw no sign of her. Peering at the stables, he noted that both horses were there. They stuck their heads out, peering at him, expecting oats, or at least a carrot each. But no sign of Anna.

'Where is she?' he said to them. 'Viento, where is she? Did she go walking? Which way did she go?'

The horses simply pricked up their ears. Nutty appeared, ears pricked too, but neither gave any answers. Becker walked up the creek a little way, expecting that she might be inspecting the fire damage. There was nothing.

He walked down to the bridge, and peered under. Again nothing.

Returning to the barn, he noticed the two cars parked under the carport. Normally, the Harley was parked in front of the BMW, being the shorter of the two vehicles. But the Harley was gone.

Becker went back to the house, disappointed. She must have wheeled it out and then down the highway to a spot out of hearing. Blue would have slept through such a manoeuvre. Nutty would not. He had very good hearing, instantly alert. Such an affectionate dog, he would have gone to the front gate with her, his tongue out. Delighted to see her so early in the morning, hoping for a biscuit. Or, at least a pat on the head.

'Oh, hell,' he said. 'Anna, please don't do it.'

He returned to the house. She always kept the Colt in a lockable drawer by her side of the bed. That too was gone.

CHAPTER 22

Becker had just finished breakfast when she returned. Surprised, he went out the back door and waited for the Harley to come right around the house, heading back to the garage. Or to wherever she was going to park it. She didn't look at him as she came around the corner and stopped outside the door. Dismounted, lifted the helmet and came in. She looked thoughtful, maybe trying to work something out. He did not go down to greet her, unsure that she was in a greetable mood.

Normally, Anna would never leave the Harley leaning safely on its metal foot stand. To do that would have been to entice someone like Terry to get on it and pretend he was riding it. He'd been suggesting that she let him ride it.

'You don't have a licence,' she'd said.

'Just around the farm,' he'd suggested. 'Round up some cattle.'

She had not committed herself, but there had been a discussion. Should she give him the bike or not? Perhaps on his eighteenth birthday. She would be sorry to see it go. Also, she might yet have a use for it. Good use.

'What happened?' he asked.

'I went to see Ted.'

'Ted Whitton?'

'Had a thought. You were sound asleep, so I let you sleep.'

'You could have left a note, Anna.'

'Yeah, I know.'

She came up the steps and stood next to him. Did not embrace him or kiss him or even look directly at him as she took off the jacket. The Colt hung there, under her left shoulder.

'Any coffee left?'

'Yes, but I'll have to heat it.'

She led the way in. He followed like a pet dog, wondering what she would do.

'You want to tell me about it?'

'I don't know whether I can trust him.'

'Ted Whitton? Why did you go to see him?'

'To do a deal.'

They were in the kitchen. He put on the coffee pot, the plunger type. Poured a mug and then heated it in the microwave. It might boil over, so he stood close as she leaned against the bench.

'And?'

'I had an idea. I'd been thinking about it, even in my dreams. I woke about dawn with it running through my head. It could be them.'

'Who?'

'The Mafia.'

'I thought we agreed that they would not be interested so long after events in Griffith. They've been lying low since all that bad publicity with Angelina.'

'I was thinking of the other Mafia—the people in Melbourne.'

'Yeah?'

She did not elaborate. Looked tired. Probably hadn't had much sleep. They'd both had a terrible shock. She seemed to have taken it worse than he. Robyn's baby, untimely snatched from her mother's womb. Who'd said that? He thought they'd read about it in school, but that was many years ago. More than twenty-five now.

The microwave bell went *ding*!

The mug had not boiled over. He took it out and found a spoon. 'You want sugar?'

Normally, she had only one teaspoonful, but this time she said: 'One and a half.'

Must have felt a need for energy.

'Get much sleep last night?' he asked. It was a silly question. Obviously she had not, but he had to say something.

If she were going to say why she'd been to see Ted Whitton, she'd tell him in her own good time. She stood at the bench, a hand on it, leaning against it, drinking. Wearing the usual gear when on the bike—shirt, jeans, big boots with leather straps. The way she'd been dressed, when he'd seen her get on her bike in Wagga Wagga outside the William Hovell Hotel late one day back in 1996. She'd let her hair down before putting on the helmet. She'd had to do that. A bun or knot or pony tail wouldn't have fitted under the helmet. She'd caught him looking, had kissed him. Then had reached across and said: 'Don't wait up for me.' And ridden off into the late afternoon and the oncoming night, heading for Melbourne.

He had a feeling that it was going to be something like that again.

'I asked him who he knew in Melbourne,' she said suddenly.

Becker was surprised. He was right. There was a Melbourne angle to it. Normally, he was not too intuitive. Women, he believed, were able to read your mind. Also, they could converse effectively without using words, just body language. Also, they were highly inquisitive, loved sticking their noses into other people's business.

'Why did you leave so early? It must have been soon after six.'

'Ten past six. I couldn't sleep once I'd woken.'

'You had no breakfast?'

'That's okay. I'll have something after I shower.'

'You went into his house?'

'Yeah, if I'd rung the bell, he most likely wouldn't have admitted me. And I did not wish to state my reasons by shouting in the street. Anyway, he does not have a house. It's a flat. Pink brick on Docker Street. Garish in the morning light.'

'How did you get in?'

'I broke in.'

'Jesus—' He almost said 'Jesus, Chook,' but caught himself.

'So what? He's in no position to complain, is he?'

'What did he say?'

'*Jesus!* Just like you. Then he said, "What do you want?" Quite aggressively, I thought. A little chat, I said. What about? My daughter. "Your daughter? The one that's gone missin'?" he said. I don't know anythin' about your friggin' daughter. "You've heard something about her?" I said. Only what Feeny told me, he said. All right, Ted, I said. I made him turn around. Look at me, look in my eyes, I said. Just like they say in the tough-guy movies. What for? he said. He was heading for the refrigerator. I thought he was reaching for orange juice or milk, but he took out a can of Vic. Why? he said. I want you to tell me, did you take my daughter? What? he said. Take your daughter? Me? Are you bloody well mad? I'm plenty mad, I said. I couldn't think of anything more original. Look in my eyes, I said again. Stand still, don't move, look at me. Tell me the truth. He looked at me. It must have hurt him, but he did it. He pulled the ring off the beer can and said, "Why would I take your kid? I'm in enough trouble already." Some people would say you have plenty of motive, I said. Humiliation and all that. That's what the police are thinking right now. You are the number-one suspect. You want that on your back as well, Ted?'

She paused, took another swig of coffee. Took a long time to resume.

'"I did not take your kid," he said.'

'"Employed another?" I asked. "For instance, the Fat Man?"'

'"What Fat Man?" he said.'

'"He's been around for some time, since before your time. He's a professional. He kills people for a price. Quite expensive, so it seems. Sure you haven't heard of him?"'

'"I don't know what you're talkin' about."'

'"Maybe you called the Fat Man, Ted? Asked around and found him. Offered him a little job. Snatch a kid, easy enough for man with talents like his, eh?"'

'"Ah, shit," he said.'

'Easy enough, eh? Why'd you do it, Ted?"

'"I didn't take your kid," he said.

'I looked at him for a while. If I thought you did it, I said, I'd kill you. You'd die very slowly. You'll wake up screaming in the night. But no-one will hear you. You'll be taped up and bound. And you'll see a fire going in an old oven somewhere, maybe an abandoned factory. Maybe a brick kiln. You understand?'

Becker could take it no longer. He thumped the table. A plate rattled. His coffee mug bounced.

'Ah, God, Anna, you must stop this! You're behaving like your father.'

She drank the last drop. Shrugged, stood up straight.

'I had to shake him up a bit. He began to go to water. Said he was sorry he'd ever done anything. I thought he meant he'd taken her. But he meant getting Dexter to spy on us. He was trying to get closure, he said. Closure on his old man's death. Head chopped off by some creep like Torrence. It's a sad world, isn't it, Harry? Everyone wants closure, finish. I suppose I would want it too. My idea of closure would be different. I'd want to close the door on whoever did it, close the furnace door.'

'Christ,' Becker said.

He was being stupid, he knew. Christ had nothing to do with it. Could do nothing about it. He'd been unable to stop the Romans stringing him up on a cross. Except pray. This woman, Anastacia Babchuck, did not believe in the power of prayer. She believed in action. Like the Mongols thundering across the *steppes* of central Asia. On their horses, all the way to the Ukraine. Cutting down anyone who resisted. All for what? The joy of conquest. Plus, the smell of blood.

She began to walk off. He followed her, talking.

'What did he say?'

'Changed his tune, suddenly. Agreed to make some calls if we dropped the charges. I said okay, but not until he'd come up with something valuable. Something that'd identify the Fat Man.'

'He agreed to that?'

'He's an old-fashioned copper, tough enough. No doubt he carries a lot of I.O.Us. Every bad cop does.'

'You think he knows the right people in Melbourne?'

She had gone to the main bedroom, had taken off the holster.

'If he doesn't, he'd better find a few quick. Even if he has to pay them.'

'Why would he do that?'

She took out the Colt. He thought she was going to point it, but she did not. She took it in her right hand by the barrel, not the grip. Checked the safety. Then used it like a club, slowly.

'You're gonna hit him?'

'No, I hit him *then*, on the spot. Kneecapped him, smashed the patella. To make an impression,' she added.

'Oh, no, no—'

She put a hand on him.

'Trust me, Harry. I know what I'm doing.'

Later, after she had slept for three hours, they were having lunch. An early lunch. She was quite bright by then, relaxed, gentle, surprisingly unconcerned.

'You look chirpy,' he said.

She nodded, eating left-over moussaka he'd heated. Greek dishes were her latest experiment. Anastacia was a trier. If he didn't like one dish, she'd try another.

'Our daughter is still missing,' he said.

'I know.'

'What can we do about it?'

'We draw out the crabs.'

'What does that mean?'

'We offer a bait?'

'Who to?'

'Those who have her.'

'Who has her?'

'Quite possibly someone near at hand.'

'Who would that be?'

'I think she knew the person who abducted her. That would explain why she did not cry out.'

'Someone we know? That's horrible, Anna.'

'Someone who has a problem.'

'You mean a debt? They have not asked for money.'

'You don't have to ask for money to make money.'

'What do you mean?'

She did not answer.

Becker chewed slowly, watching her. She was remarkably relaxed, even offhand.

'Who's behind it, Anna?'

She did not answer at first, still eating. 'Of course, it could be those people in Melbourne.'

'You mean that Pisano family? The big boss in Melbourne? The one you visited in the hospice?'

She nodded. 'Yes.'

'And you dispatched him.'

'I helped him on his way.'

'They called you Mr Groves, didn't they?'

'That's right.'

'And now you think they are taking their revenge on Mr Groves?'

'It's quite possible.'

Becker frowned. 'That was six years ago. Why would that family wait so long?'

'The old lady,' she said, finishing the moussaka and salad. Strangely, in the circumstances, she was eating quite heartily.

'What about her?'

'She died, some weeks ago.'

'Did she?'

'Yes, I looked her up on the computer last night. Found a death notice in *The Age*.'

'You were up that late?'

'She was terrified of me. I shook her up a bit. Told her I'd come back and kill her if she lied to me. She fainted at one stage. I left her. Found Pisano was in the *Relais* rest home.'

'And you went there and choked him.'

'She believed what I'd said. Frightened I'd come back and choke her to death. I did not, but that wouldn't have mattered. She would have told her sons not to retaliate. Not while she lived.'

'And now she's dead?'

Anna nodded. 'Uh-huh.'

'You think the sons have decided there's no restraint?'

'Why shouldn't they? They'd want revenge. But they've probably heard I don't give in to threats. They will not take me on personally. So—'

'They hire a hitman? The Fat Man?'

'It looks like it.'

'Why would he take on this contract?'

'He's been trying to kill me for years. First with the bomb under the old house, then with the two drongos with the rifle. Of course, I may be wrong.'

'But why would they be doing this for Whitton? Why would they even know about Whitton? They said lay off, but did not name anyone.'

'I'm still thinking about that.'

He thought about it too. It was a reasonable theory. They grab the girl. Threaten to kill her if he does not lay off. Lay off what? They did not say. Lay off Whitton? Yes, of course. How ingenious. It's made to look as though Whitton is behind the kidnapping. Clever. You had to admire some criminal minds. It was a pity they weren't put to better use, like saving the planet from over-population or climate change, rising seas, starvation. The scientists had been warning for years, but the politicians were interested only in growth and money. Look how much we're gonna make out of boosting the population. Everyone is going to be happy. Making a motza.

'And then what? What happens to Robbie?'

'After I've been assassinated, she miraculously reappears.'

'Really?'

'At a police station or a hospital, left on the door steps. A car seen speeding away.'

'They don't need her any longer?'

'That's it.'

'But she will have seen them. She could identify them.'

'Perhaps the one who grabbed her, but not the others. She would be hooded. Locked in a room. There's one good thing about the Mafia.'

'What's that?'

'They don't kill children.'

Becker chewed an apricot from the bowl on the table. Apricots were in season now, but they didn't last long. Peculiar fruit, the apricot—its season and life both fleeting. One day, you could bite into a hard, sour one from the market. Two or three days later, it would be sweet and juicy. A few days more, and it would turn mushy and rot. A short, sweet life, much like the human one if you thought about it.

'So what are you going to do? Go to Melbourne and find the old lady's sons? Beat them up? How does that find Robbie?'

'Probably it would not be a good idea. They'd deny everything. And try to kill me, if they have the brainpower to beat a Colt .38.'

'So?'

'So what?'

'How are you going to do it? Without getting yourself killed?'

'It's quite easy. All we have to do is draw the crabs, as I said.'

'And how do you do that?'

'Offer the Fat Man a contract.'

'To do what?'

'To kill me.'

'What?'

Becker almost collapsed. His brain began to fold down, protectively. Swooned but caught himself. Had to hold on. He'd bitten on the apricot stone, hard and sharp. Possibly had broken a tooth.

'What did you say?'

'Offer the Fat Man a contract.'

'To kill you? Are you crazy, Anna?'

'Not entirely. It's a bit risky, I know.'

'God help us, what are you saying? Who is going to do this? I mean, you can't offer the Fat Man any contract, because you don't know who he is.'

'Yes, but I know where Whitton is—and he will make the offer.'

Becker looked at her, dazed, confused. She was mad, he was sure. So reckless, so confident of herself that she must come a great cropper. The daring young woman on the flying trapeze. He'd heard of crazy Russians, playing Russian roulette and all that, but the Ukies must be crazier.

'You're going to get Whitton to contact the Fat Man and ask him to kill you?'

'Yes.'

'And how is Whitton going to pay this?'

'Oh, we will provide the money.'

'We will? Our money?'

'Yes, if you don't mind.'

'How much will this cost?'

'Possibly a hundred thousand dollars.'

'God almighty, Anna, you are mad. Really and truly mad. Things could go horribly wrong. Whitton might betray you, tell the Fat Man it's a trap.'

'Oh, he won't do that.'

'Why not?'

'Because I'll tell him we've taken out a contract on him too. If anything happens to me, he will be killed.'

Becker was astounded. He could not believe she was serious. This must be her idea of a joke. She must have lost her mind.

'Why on earth would the Fat Man reveal himself to Whitton? These negotiations are usually made anonymously, by phone or mail. There is no personal contact. The client is not given any details that could identify or locate the assassin.'

'He will reveal himself to me.'

'Who? The Fat Man?'

She nodded. 'When he tries to kill me.'

Becker was beginning to pass out. He was married ot a mad woman.

She nudged him. 'Darling, it is quite safe. I assure you. There will be police everywhere.'

'The hitman will expect that.'

'Not too close. Look, Harry, we have to do this. For Robbie, don't we? You know that, don't you?'

He knew she was right, but he hung his head unhappily. He feared both would be killed. Perhaps all would be killed—he, she, and their darling daughter, Roberta. He felt like crying. It had been a wonderful life so far. If he'd never met Evelyn Crowley, none of this would have happened. On the other hand, if he had *not* met her, it wouldn't have been a wonderful life. He picked up another apricot and absently began to eat it.

'You are insane, Anna. You can't always win. The odds are stacked against you.'

'I don't play games, Harry. You should know that.'

He sighed, closed his eyes, chewing. She reached out.

'Harry?'

'What is it now?'

She smirked, her eyes flickering with mischief.

'Are you going to eat *all* those apricots?'

▲

CHAPTER 23

That afternoon, Anna went to Wagga Wagga and checked on Whitton. He'd been admitted to the Base Hospital, so she went there, found him in a room by himself, full of resentment and self-pity. Even before she reached the room, she could hear him complaining like the overgrown baby he was. A nurse was checking his blood pressure and trying to soothe his bad temper without success. Twisting and turning, obviously trying to ease the pain in his left knee. The nurse was saying she'd get him some Panadeine. But it was all a facade, anyone could see. This big cry-baby was carrying on because some bitch of a woman had kneecapped him. But he could tell no-one. If he'd told the hospital staff, they'd call the police. Who'd want to know *why* the bitch had kneecapped him?

Anna strode in and said quite brightly, 'How are you, Ted? Heard you had a nasty fall? In the bathroom, on the tiles was it? God, that must have hurt?'

He glared at her, the bitch herself. Laughing at him without actually laughing. He was astonished. She was back again.

The nurse had turned, smiling.

'Ah,' she said, 'you have a friend?'

Whitton scowled at her. 'For Christsake, piss off, will you, love? And get that stuff A.S.A.P.'

She jumped, about to protest, but Anna got in first.

'Just ignore him. He's an old copper. And he drinks too much. His vocabulary is limited. Never got past sixth grade, did you, Ted? How is he?'

'He's been to X-ray and we've bound his knee. There's nothing the surgeons can do. The patella will mend itself if he keeps still. He may be able to walk in a few days, if he's careful. But he'll need crutches.'

'Jesus,' Whitton said.

'You'd better do as he says,' Anna said. The nurse scooted off, her nose in the air. She had rarely encountered such a belligerent patient.

Anna stood beside him, a hand on his strapped knee. Gave it a friendly squeeze.

He jumped, frightened.

'Stop whingeing and pay attention,' she said. 'Otherwise I really will make you squeal.'

He stared at her, stupefied. Things rarely went the way he wanted. Often they conspired against him, thought up plans to bring him down. Whitton was naturally suspicious, like the dumb ox he was. Here he was again. Someone was trying to destroy him. Not exactly this bitch of a woman, who'd hit him. She was a straight talker. She didn't say one thing and mean another, like some people he knew. He was always trying to get ahead of them. Lately he'd not been fast enough. He was getting old, he knew. Fifty-four but still a long way from retirement. Too proud to go out early, try his luck elsewhere. Didn't like his chances. If this bitch believed he had kidnapped her kid, she'd kill him.

She knew how to kill you and get away with it.

And she carried a Colt .38.

People had been trying to get it away from her for years. Every time they tried, she'd go to court and tells a sob story about how she's been sexually abused as a teenager, shot at by some nutter called the Fat Man, who no-one had ever seen. And been blown up and threatened with death more times than you could count on your fingers. And what happens? The piss-weak magistrates burst into tears every time. And tell her she can keep her copy of the classic Colt, introduced way back in 1911. Saying she had a right to defend herself.

Anna tapped his knee again.

'Anyone been to see you, Ted?'

'Yeah, one or two.'

'Who was that?'

'Feeny and that bastard Carrick.'

'Sergeant Carrick?'

'Yeah, the bastard.'

'You don't like him?'

Carrick was Feeny's offsider. They tried to work as a team. Carrick was a tough cop, a man of few words. Believed in the old adage: Hit 'em first, then ask questions. The type who was sure to have an unpleasant habit. In his case, spit on the ground while talking to you. Just missing your foot by an inch or so each time. Telling you something. Cranky Carrick, he was called. Anna didn't know his given name, if he had one. The type of man who didn't need a Christian name. There was nothing Christian about him. As for Feeny, he was a smooth operator, with a twinkle in his eyes. Who never said the wrong thing and wrote perfect reports. His clean-up rate was good indeed, more than eighty percent. If Feeny said you were guilty, you probably were. He was a polished sort of cop, who wore top of the range off-the-peg suits. And had a warm, friendly smile. Popular with the ladies too.

'And Feeny?'

'And?'

'That little ponce, he's after my job.'

'You're sure you're not a bit paranoid, Ted?'

'I've had my eye on him for a while.'

'After your job, eh?'

The nurse came back with two pills in a paper cup on a stainless steel dish. She held the dish like a waiter in a posh hotel, very efficient. Did not look into Whitton's eyes. Kept her head up, nose in the air.

'Here is your Panadeine, Mr Whitton.' Put the paper cup on the chest of drawers beside the bed, and a glass of water. Then, spinning on a heel, was off again on her squeaky shoes.

'You've heard the speculation?' Anna asked.

'About me? Yeah.'

He was sullen now. Lying back so heavily he seemed about to sink into the pillows and disappear.

'It's those first few words, isn't it?'

'Yeah,' he said.

'They told you, Tell Becker to lay off. Lay off what?'

'Yeah,' he said.

'You're up against four charges, including wrongful incarceration. Plus, conducting an official inquiry into a matter involving yourself.'

'Eh?'

'Investigating the murder of your own father.'

'Ah, shut up, will you?'

'Lay off the charges against you, eh?'

'Yeah,' he said again. He was wincing.

'It sounds like the man on the phone wanted the charges against you dropped, doesn't it?'

'Yeah, the bastard.'

'You know what that looks like, Ted?'

'Yeah, I know.'

'Like you kidnapped Robbie to make Harry drop the charges.'

He didn't say 'Yeah' this time. Just looked at her directly, his lips closed, red. He had a small mouth in a plump face, a blood-red face. Pressure going up again. Someone had set him up, he knew. It sure did look bad. Everyone in the force knew about his father. What he did to those who gave him any trouble. A blight on the force, Dickie Whitford.

He looked away. Fear written all over his face.

'I don't believe you did it, Ted—'

'Thanks.'

'Got any ideas?'

He didn't answer. Some sense of fair play hung around him. She changed the line of questioning.

'What did Feeny say when he was here?'

'More or less what you said.'

'People at the station were thinking it was you, the Fat Man?'

He did not answer. His eyes had closed.

'Did Feeny say who he thinks could have done this job?'

Whitton was going to deny it, but changed his mind. 'Yeah, that's what he was trying to say. That I'm the prime suspect. Then he mentioned my old man.'

'Implying, Like father, like son, eh?'

'Yeah, the bastard.'

'He didn't actually say it?'

'He wouldn't dare, would he?'

'You don't like him, do you?'

'That devious little fuckwit.'

She tut-tutted. 'Language, Ted. You're in a hospital.'

'Been after my job since the day I arrived.'

'Would he have the money to hire a snatcher?'

'I dunno, I dunno.'

'Someone set you up, Ted.'

He rubbed his head. His eyes had almost disappeared down their own holes of despair. 'Ah, shit, what the hell have I done to deserve this?'

Anna still stood, a hand on his bad knee. She believed him. He was a piece of work but—as Palfreyman had said to Becker one night in Canberra—there was good shit and there was bad shit. He, Palfreyman, had started off as good shit, but was stupid. Then he became bad shit, a cop on morphine. This man, Whitton, was bad shit. He was born into it, but he wanted to do better. He might never be good shit as good cops go, but he was trying.

She put a hand on a shoulder. He was surprised, perhaps afraid she was going to hit him again. Just for the hell of it.

Instead, she patted him.

'Hang in there, Ted. Let me know if you think of anything.'

Then she was gone.

The nurse came back. 'You haven't taken your Panadeine,' she said.

When Anna returned, she found nothing had changed. Except that there was a young female constable in uniform sitting beside the phone, the line phone. Beside it was a tape recorder, and beside the recorder a pair of headphones. Her name was Daisy Cornford and she was very new, a probationary constable. No stripes on her shoulders. No gun on her hip. At sight of Anastacia, she shot to her feet. Like a girl in school when the headmistress walks in.

Max Kruger was there too. No-one had called.

'Very strange,' she said.

It was now about half past three on the second day.

Anna took off her jacket. Not wearing a holster, the Colt was in her bag. Unlike her to carry a handbag, but she did have one. A dark-blue thing that clashed with her eyes. That did not matter. Anna Becker was not clothes-conscious. Never worried whether this would go with that. Had a few dresses, one or two pretty items. She could dress up, but what was the point? No man was going to date a woman over six feet tall. Wore what he could drive in, work around the house and farm in, pick up her daughter from school in, talk to cops in. Whatever would be free and open and accessible. Free to get the Colt out and fire in less than one second. No snags, no hesitation. But, she did look odd with a handbag. As for personal accoutrements, she carried no more than the average man. Money, keys, a couple of tissues, but no cosmetics.

As she'd put the bag down on a table, the phone rang.

Daisy grabbed her headphones, switched on the recorder.

Anna picked up the phone.

'Hullo?'

'Mummy?'

She jumped. 'Robbie? Robbie? Where are you?'

No reply. Anna sure that the girl was being restrained, perhaps with a hand hovering over her mouth. Roberta spoke again: 'Mummy? I'm all right.'

'Thank God, darling. Where are you?'

Again, no sound. Nothing but the sound of silence, in which you are sure you can hear something but cannot make it out.

'Mummy? I had dinner last night and breakfast this morning. And I have some books to read. I can watch television and—' Another sound blackout.

'Robbie?'

She had to wait, seconds ticked by. Someone, she was sure, was coaching the girl.

'Robbie?'

'Mummy, if you promise not to do anything—'

'No, we won't do anything.'

Another blank spot.

'Mummy, N—' Anna was sure she was going to say a name. The girl spoke again, but seemed to be away from the phone. Someone else was holding it to an ear.

'Mummy, please say you won't do anything.'

'Yes, all right, I agree, we won't do anything.'

Another pause and muffled sound.

'Mummy, say you won't do anything.'

'I can hear you, darling. Yes, I agree—' She looked back at Becker. 'Daddy agrees too, don't you, Daddy? Yes, he nodded, yes. What's that?' She was sure she could hear whispering. Couldn't make it out. 'We will not proceed against you in court—' She was addressing the person, apparently a woman. 'We will not take action against you. Please let her go! Where can we pick her up?'

'Mummy—'

The line went dead. It was purring.

The probationary said: 'I got it all.'

Outside, they could hear Max Kruger speaking to someone. He'd been speaking throughout, trying to get a trace. No doubt the caller had realised the police would be doing exactly that. If it were a woman, she'd hung up just in time.

They waited. Max came back, taking only a few steps, a hand to one ear, his phone to the other. Came right in, walking sideways, head down.

'Yeah?' he was saying. He looked up at them. 'They got a trace, but only so far.'

'Where?' Becker asked.

'Definitely New South.'

'Where in New South?'

'Not in Sydney, not in Canberra, not in Wagga Wagga.'

'Not here?'

'It was a mobile call. They can't pin that down to an exact site.'

'But they can pin it down to the last tower used.'

'Yeah, they're trying to do that.'

They waited. Anna went to Becker, collapsed against him. 'At least she is alive.'

He held her. She was exhausted. Shuddering in short waves. 'If they'd killed her—'

'Don't speak like that.'

Max Kruger was leaning against a door frame, the one leading from the living room onto the western side verandah. The house had four doors, front and back and each side. A house with verandahs all around needed so many doors. In fine weather, you could open up the whole house, not so much for fresh air but for the freedom of being both in and out of a house at the same time. Openness, a homely comfort.

'Where?' Max said. Suddenly straightening up, even kicking the door in surprise.

'Jingara? Jingara?'

He looked at them. They were staring at him.

'I see,' he said. 'Yeah, we did. We recorded it. Thank you for your help.'

He shut down the mobile he held.

'On the Old Man Creek-Jingara Road,' he said. 'The last transmitter.'

'That's right behind us, on a hill,' Anna said. 'I've seen it when out riding.'

'So the caller is somewhere near us?'

'Not necessarily. That tower will be on a hill. It could pick up a signal from anywhere within twenty miles.

They waited again.

Nothing happened. The sun was going down. Anna got up and began to do something about dinner. She thought of soup, canned soup. She had some, held against eventualities. The house had no other cooking method than electric. Got out pea and ham soup and some toast and cheese and tomatoes and mushrooms on toast. Sunlight shot through the doorway and windows on the western side. About to burst with gold. They knew she was coming home. They were waiting for a call from the police, to say she had been picked up at some obvious spot in full view of the public, like a church or shop or post office. But no call came.

They waited and waited.

Nutty sat up suddenly. Pricked his ears. He had the best ears in the business. Big ears for a small to middling dog. He looked about, expecting something, but sat down again.

Vehicles on the highway. Fifty yards to the gate, so that the slow woosh and rattle and thud of vehicular business went on and on, night and day. Frequently, he heard things that came to nothing. As much as he tried to make something of them.

Nutty crouched again, his head on his paws. Then he sat up, all ears.

The front door opened.

Roberta stepped inside. "Mummy, I'm sorry.'

Anna rushed forward and swept her up.

'Nerida said to tell you she's sorry too.'

▲

CHAPTER 24

Max and Constable Cornford immediately left for the house, abandoning their gear in their rush. It was the closest lead they had. When they arrived, the house was empty. Nerida Larkin had packed her bags and fled. She had been packing before she rang, her bags ready to flee. Roberta said Nerida had brought her back. By car. Had told her to go inside. Then driven on eastward, but that *didn't* mean she was headed for Wagga. There were all sorts of unpaved backroads, where she might dodge and divert and leave false clues. Maybe she was heading for Melbourne. Maybe not. The clue about Melbourne came when the line phone rang again. This time Becker picked it up. It was Ted Whitton.

'About your missing kid,' he said.

'She's back home,' Becker said.

'Yeah, I heard. Well, I've been thinkin'. That bastard, Feeny, has a girlfriend.'

'Who?'

'Nerida Larkin, she lives out your way.'

'Yeah, she's the one who snatched her. She came to the house and asked for us, but Roberta said we were out back. Nerida grabbed the girl and drove off in her car.'

'Ah, Christ, I'm sorry,' Whitton said.

'Max Kruger and the young constable went after her.'

'Have they caught her?'

'No, Max just called. She's fled.'

'Where?'

'No-one knows.'

'Ah, Christ, she's a teacher at that school. Been there a year or so.'

'How do you know her?'

'How do I know her? That shameless little tart? Went around to Feeny's place one day. Wanted to know why the hell he'd not reported for work. Pressed the door bell, no reaction. Had a look through a window. She was on top of him, bangin' away like mad. Rang the bloody bell again, nothin' happened. So, I kicked the door in. Went in and dragged her off him. Gave him a clip in the ear, stark naked he was. Didn't have a dick to bless himself with. No wonder she had to do all the work. Tore a strip off him. Gave it to the young sheila too. She started cryin'. Said she was goin' to call the police. I am the bloody police, I said. Started howlin' buckets of tears. Had to give her a smack on the backside to settle her down. Told him to get into his strides and get in the frigging car. If he ever did that again, I'd have him for dereliction of duty. He's hated me ever since.'

'That's why he did it? They cooked it up between them?'

'Nah, it goes back further than that.'

Becker waited for an explanation but none came.

'Anything else?'

'Nah, don't think so.'

'You think it's as simple as that?'

'What?'

'Someone starts a fire on my property on a day when the fire will blow towards the house. It can't go anywhere else, there's nothing else to burn but the trees along the creek. Then someone snatches my daughter on the same day. Then someone rings and says they've got her and threaten to kill her. That sounds more complicated than simple revenge by some police officer and his girl sprung by you, isn't it?'

Whitton groaned. 'Suppose you could look at it that way.'

'I am looking at it that way. Why pretend to be the Fat Man?'

'I dunno. Who is this friggin' Fat Man, anyway?'

'We thought it was a skinny bloke down in Melbourne. But it looks like that nutter was pretending to be the Fat Man. Maybe he was working with the Fat Man. We don't know.'

'I don't know either. I haven't had anything to do with this so-called Fat Man.'

'Maybe he *is* connected with this in some way?'

'How would I know?'

'Use your great big copper's brain while lying there and think about it.'

'Ah, shit, mate, I thought you might have had some sort of a change of heart.'

'Why?'

'I'm tryin' to help you.'

'Help me? Christ, Whitton, you've given me enough grief. Your fucking father hired a gun to kill me. Had me thrown out of the force. I didn't get a disability pension, and I still have a hole in my shoulder. You want me to pity you? Pity Anna didn't finish you off.'

Becker hung up.

He turned around. She was standing right behind him, arms folded.

'He's not that bad, Harry. Your father was a soldier, but his father was a thug. You were lucky, he wasn't.'

Becker calmed down. 'How is she doing?'

'Getting dressed. She's had a shower and smells sweet and lovely, just like her mother. Now, she's getting herself organised for tomorrow.'

'You mean Robyn?'

'Yes, like Robyn. I hope she grows up like Robyn.'

'Not like her hard-faced stepmother, eh?'

'I didn't mean that.'

'I wouldn't want any girl to grow up like me.'

Roberta came out of her room.

'Hullo? How are you feeling now?'

'Oh, I'm all right, Daddy.'

'Do you want me to tell you a story?'

'What kind of story?'

'One about a beautiful lady who had a little girl.'

'What little girl?'

After dinner, the phone rang.

It was the duty sergeant at Wagga Wagga police station. They hadn't been able to find Miss Larkin, and Inspector Feeny had disappeared as well.

'Thank you for letting me know,' Becker said, hanging up.

He was still not sure it was as simple as that, two lovers who'd been humiliated by Whitton. Abducting a child, making it look as though he had done it.

That did not ring true.

They had dinner, watched the news, and talked to Roberta without pressing her for information. Dismissed the whole episode as a game. Miss Larkin had been trying to give her a special treat before school restarted—something to liven things up. Third grade was going to be harder, and she might've thought Roberta needed more preparation. Big surprises were part of schooling, just like in real life.

She'd already accepted the truth—that Anna wasn't her mother. Her real mother, a beautiful lady with curly brown hair, had died in childbirth. Sometimes even the best of women don't survive childbirth, though it's rare. Another kind lady—who now had white hair—had agreed to be her mother so she wouldn't grow up unhappy and could have a good life, full of surprises.

As the story ended, the girl gazed up at her stepmother. 'Is that a true story?'

'Yes, darling. It's a perfectly true story.'

She said, 'I love true stories. They are the best.'

They went to bed. But soon after ten, the phone rang. Becker picked it up.

'I've had another idea,' Whitton said.

'Yeah? It'd better be good.'

'That woman that calls herself Nerida Larkin—'

'Yeah?'

'Had to look her up some time ago—'

'So?'

'She was married once, to a bloke called Larkin.'

'What was her maiden name?'

'Medich, Nerida Medich.'

When Becker told Anna, she thought about it without comment.

'Did you hear me?'

No response.

'She must be one of the family. The old man must have been trying to get her to snatch our girl. That's why he was hanging around for days.'

'Yeah?'

'But she refused, until she gave way under pressure. Grabbed her while no one was looking.'

At last Anna spoke. 'That's your theory?'

'What's wrong with it?'

'It might have been the other way around.'

$\blacktriangle$

CHAPTER 25

It was lunchtime in Melbourne. The streets of Cremorne were not too busy for a Tuesday. Anna Babchuk waited until certain someone was at home. The old lady had come out and checked the mail box and had gone back inside. Then at last Nerida Larkin arrived by car. A small red car she'd often seen parked at the school—the little school where Roberta had to go. Anna had taken the girl to school that morning before heading to Melbourne. She could have put Roberta on the school bus, but the girl may have been uncertain on her first day of the school year with a new teacher. She didn't want Roberta to feel uncertain. They'd done their best to convince her it had been only a little game played by her Nerida.

She'd called Becker and told him where she was, and asked him to pick her up from school at three. It was now about one o'clock. It was hot in the muggy, oppressive, almost dusty, dry and stuffy sense of Melbourne summers. Not pleasant at all. The place had the usual urban smell of humans and smoke and breath and dry earth and hot bitumen. Even a sense of an electric current in the air. It looked dark to the south-west, perhaps something building up over Geelong. She'd left home without telling Becker what she was going to do. If she'd told him, he would have tried to stop her. But she was that kind of woman, driven and determined. And she'd taken the BMW rather than the Nissan, because it had a boot and the Nissan did not. The Nissan was a big hatchback.

She knocked on the front door and waited.

There are some old houses in which you can sense movement. Even old red-brown brick houses like this, squeezed between paling fences overgrown by bushes.

Although she didn't hear anything, she knew someone was coming to the door.

A bolt moved, the door began to open.

It had slid only one or two inches, when Anna burst in. Threw someone against a wall.

She walked in, closed the door quietly.

The grandson was sprawled on the floor, astonished.

He was gasping, trying to find words. He did not need them. Instantly recognised her.

'Ah, ah, ah, ah—'

Anna kicked him. 'Where's your sister?'

'What? What?'

'Where's your fuckin' sister?'

'Ivanka? Ivanka? I dunno, she's not here.'

'I don't mean Ivanka. I met her, she's your little sister. Where's big sister? Where's Nerida?'

He gaped at her, still not rising. He'd made an effort to push himself up on an elbow, but he wasn't going to get up. His eyes rolled as though he couldn't make sense of anything. He couldn't think fast enough.

'Nerida? She's not my sister.'

'What is she, then?'

'My aunt.'

'Your aunt? She's pretty young to be your aunt, isn't she?'

'She's mother's little sister.'

'Where is she? Do I have to break your neck?'

'Nerida?' he said, or squawked.

A voice came from the back. 'What is it?'

'Ah, hell, ah, God, it's her!'

'What?'

'It's her! She's come and she's gonna—'

'Who's come?'

Nerida Larkin came out of a rear room, perhaps the kitchen. Wiping her hands. On a tea towel. She looked puzzled, even annoyed.

Then she saw the intruder.

Her face drained of colour. She gasped, or froze, fear-stricken, unable to think fast enough to escape. Tried to flee, out the back door, screaming. But did not make it. Anna caught her by the hair and hauled her back. Slammed her up against a wall. Things clattered to the floor: a cast-iron pot stand, a spice tray, a barometer or thermometer. Anna barely noticed.

Shoved her against the wall, made her bones rattle, her teeth too.

'Talk,' she said. 'Why did you take my daughter?'

Nerida Medich was in her late twenties. Perhaps close to thirty. Trying to scream, but Anna had her by the throat with one hand. In the other was the Colt.

'You see this? You see this? Now talk or I'll splatter your brains around your fucking mother's nice, clean kitchen.'

The woman was gurgling, choking. Anna eased the grip on her throat. She tried to scream. All that came out was a dry hiss. Shock in her eyes. She began to cry.

'Tears won't help you now, you little bitch.'

'Please, please!'

'Why did you do it?'

'Please, I didn't want to!'

'Don't give me that shit! You stole my girl. You scared the wits out of her.'

'No, no, I didn't want to do it!'

'You're going to jail for a long time.'

She wailed: 'You said you wouldn't do anything!'

'I've changed my mind. You stole my child!'

'No, no, no, please—'

She was blubbering now, dribbling onto Anna's hand at her throat.

'Why did you do it?' Nothing but gasping and wheezing. 'You want me to smash your teeth?'

Nerida Medich wailed. Couldn't control herself. Hands to her face, trying to hide. But peeping out between fingers. Anna looked to one side. The boy had appeared, holding a vase. A clay vase, spun on a wheel by hand. Green-grey with a few black smears. The kind you could fill with lilies. Make a beautiful display.

'Put it down,' she said. 'Or I'll shoot it out of your hand.'

He put it down. The old lady was at the kitchen door, hiding and yet peeping. Just an edge of her face. Popeyed, horrified. Saying, What is it? What has she done? Voicelessly, her eyes said it.

'Come on!' Anna kicked the teacher. No more than a poke with a foot.

'Please,' she said, 'I d-didn't want to.'

'Why did you do it?'

'He said we-we had to.'

'Who said?'

Her whole body shuddered. It rattled in a sort of wave that began in her legs, moved up to her guts, then rose to her shoulders and finally filled her eyes.

'If you don't tell me, I'm gonna have to break something.'

Anna stamped on the woman's left foot, hard. Possibly broke one or two metatarsals. She was wearing high-heeled sandals, it being hot outside.

Screamed under Anna's hand. Spluttering this time.

Anna took it away a fraction. 'Now talk.'

'I—'

'What?'

'I—I—'

'I, I what?'

'I didn't want to d-do it. He said we had to.'

'Who said? Feeny? Was that it? Your boyfriend? A smart, little cop with the pretty smile and the five-hundred-dollar suit? Looking sharp, always on top of the situation? That the one who told you?'

She did not answer.

'How did it begin? Who thought it up?'

She shook her head, mouth open wide. But could not get it out.

Then began speaking about something else.

'I used to say t-to him, She's such a l-lovely girl. I wish she were mine.'

'And?'

'He said, Why don't you t-take her?'

'And what did you say?'

'I said I'd love t-to but I couldn't. She's not my girl.'

'And what then?'

'One day, he said he was going to t-take her and p-pin it on Whitton.'

'Because Whitton had caught you two in bed, when he should have been on duty?'

She nodded, whispering. 'Yes.'

'And gave him a tongue-lashing?'

'Yes.'

'So he thought he'd get his revenge?'

'Yes.'

'And he suggested you take my girl? Snatch her, when we were all out back watching the fire? Or the damage?'

'No, no, I went there to say goodbye. To say goodbye to her. She c-came to the door. I just wanted to t-tell you I was leaving. That I'd have to go away. I knew I couldn't t-take it any longer. Wrote to Nora Hopkins and said I was g-going back to Melbourne. I left it under her door, so she'd g-get it first thing tomorrow. I mean today. Tuesday, isn't it? They go back today, the staff. The kids tomorrow, yes. I w-was very sorry about leaving her in the— the lurch, no teacher for the F-Firsts and S-Seconds.'

'Robbie came to the door?'

She nodded, gulping. 'I asked her where y-you were.'

'And?'

'S-Said you were out the back. Looking at the fire.'

'The fire was out by that time.'

'Was it? I could still see sm-smoke. Or, I *had* seen some smoke, from my place. At the village.'

'What then?'

'Oh, I said I had to g-go away and I'd never see her again. And, and—'

'And what?'

'She came out and hugged me and s-said, Don't go!'

Nerida was shaking now, shuddering. Hands to her face.

'I bent down and gave her a big cuddle. I could not help it. Just t-took her by the hand and said, Would you l-like to come to my place? Get ready for th-third grade? She nodded and said Yes.'

'So you took her?'

'Yes, I couldn't stop. She was hugging me and asking me not to go. She said she loved me. That got me, I could not stop.'

'She went with you willingly?'

'Yes.'

'To your house?'

'Yes.'

'Did you hurt her?'

'Hurt her? God, no! Never would I hurt her! I loved her. She's so beautiful, not only to look at. She's so-s bright. Has the mental age of a t-ten-year-old.'

'Who said?'

'The sch-school psychologist. He came, he tested all the kids. Oh, God, I'm so sorry!'

Anna softened.

'Have you ever had a child?'

'What?

'Have you ever given birth?'

'What? No, no, no, I—'

Anna shook her. 'The truth!'

'Uh, huh, I, I—'

'Tell me!'

The woman began to break down. 'Yes, yes—'

'When was that?'

Began crying. 'On, oh, nineteen—'

'You had a child at nineteen? And how old are you now?'

'T-Twenty—' she said.

'Only twenty?'

'Twenty-nine!'

Anna stepped back, one hand still on her.

'It was a girl, wasn't it? What happened to her?'

'What?' She was wide-eyed, still gasping.

'What happened to your baby?'

'I, I—'

'The baby? Do you still have her?'

She shook her head.

'What happened?'

The woman at the kitchen door, stepped out. 'Nerida, Nerida!'

Anna shook her. 'Tell me, what happened to your baby?'

'I can't, I can't!'

'Did she die?'

The woman, who must have been her mother: '*Nemoj joj reci! Nemoj joj reci!*'

'What did she say?'

'Don't tell her!'

'Why not tell me?'

'I can't tell you.'

'Did she die? Is that it?'

The teacher sobbed.

'She did? Is that why you stole Robbie?'

No reply. Anna was beginning to understand.

'Why did the baby die? How did it die?'

Nerida Larkin began to slip again. Anna jerked her back up.

'Tell me!'

'Because—'

'Because what?'

Because I—'

'Because you what? Tell me!'

Nerida was gurgling now, unable to speak.

A voice came from nowhere. 'She threw her in the river.'

It was the boy, now on his feet. Anna turned. 'What did you say?'

'She killed her own baby.'

'Why?'

'She wasn't married.'

Now it was becoming clear. 'What river?'

'The Yarra. At the end of the street.'

She loosened her grip. Stood back, lowered the Colt.

'Depression?' she asked.

The teacher gasped. Said something again in Croatian, hands to her face. The old lady said nothing. Nerida Larkin nodded, wiping her own face with her hands.

'Did you go to prison?'

She didn't answer. The boy said: 'She was found to be of unsound mind.'

'I see.'

Anna stood back. All seemed to be clear now. A woman who'd drowned her own child, had spontaneously taken another. Could not resist, presumably. Robbie being so smart. Not a pretty girl, but good, obedient. Loved her teacher, who was going to leave her. Going back to Melbourne.

It was understandable now.

'You have caused us great distress, you know.'

'I know. I'm sorry.'

'I don't forgive you but I know how you must have felt.'

That seemed to be it.

'Thank you for telling me.'

Nerida had pulled out a handkerchief, blew her nose. Went on talking, to Anna's surprise.

'I d-didn't want to do it. But he said we had to d-do it. I said, Why? He said because someone's r-riding my back.'

'Whitford? Was riding his back?"

'N-no, someone else.'

'Who was riding his back?'

'Oh, I—'

Shook her, gently this time. 'Who?'

'Oh, God, no.'

'Was it Carrick?'

'Carrick?'

'Sergeant Carrick, did he put you up to this? Carrick doesn't like Whitton, does he? Did he set Whitton up?'

'Carrick? What? I don't know.'

'You must know something?'

She was gulping air. 'Oh, God, what have I done?'

'What do you mean?'

'He was pushing me to d-do it.'

'Feeny was pushing you?'

'Yes.'

'That doesn't make sense. Why go to such lengths to hurt Whitton? What had Whitton done to him? I mean that caper in bed? What about that? You two got a good smacking. He whacked you on your backside, didn't he?'

'We were trying to make a child! Don't you see? We were trying and trying—'

'And it wasn't working? So what? That doesn't justify taking a child.'

She sighed. All the air went out of her.

'It's the other man.'

'What man?'

'I don't know. He calls him the Fat Man.'

'The Fat Man? What do you mean?'

'He knows all about it.'

'The Fat Man knows all about what?'

'That Brett did something bad some time ago. Years ago.'

'What did he do?'

'I can't tell you, I just can't!'

'What fat man? You mean Whitton? He's a fat man?'

'No, no!'

Anna raised the Colt. 'Tell me, you little bitch!'

'Please don't hit me!'

Larkin began to blubber again. Anna stood back, looked at the grandson and the two women. The old lady was peeping well out now. Kept on glancing at her grandson and saying: *What is she saying? What is she saying?* In some foreign language, her face showing her words.

The boy didn't reply.

'Why did you decide to return Roberta?'

'Oh, no—'

'Why?' Anna shook her again. At the same time put away the Colt.

She went weak again. 'He said—'

'He said what?'

'I can't tell you, I can't tell you!'

'You should be in jail, you stupid bitch!' She shook her. 'Understand?'

Then it hit Anna. 'You were going to kill her?'

The teacher began to howl, like a mad woman confined for her own good. Anna let her fall slowly, folding up on the floor.

'He said you'd have to kill her? Because she could identify you?'

'Yes, yes—'

'That disgusting little creep!'

'I couldn't do it! I packed up and drove her back, left her at the gate.'

'You dumped her there?'

'She knew the way. She's a capable girl. Not upset, Anna, I swear it.'

'You kidnapped her and you thought of killing her?'

'No, no, I never did. I never did, I swear it! I could never do such a thing.'

'Get up!'

Anna kicked her, not really hard. She howled and howled and slid again. Anna let her slide. She lay, curled up against the wall. It was a gulping sort of howl.

'Who is the Fat Man?'

'What?'

'You said the Fat Man said you had to do it.'

'No, no—'

'What fat man are you talking about?'

'I don't know. He lived in Elwood—'

Anna stepped back. Glanced at the grandson and the old lady, shocked by what they'd seen. What they'd heard. Anna leaned down, both hands on her knees.

'That arsehole is dead. I killed him. Don't you read the papers?'

The woman sobbed and shook her head.

'I know—'

'Don't lie to me. What particular fat man are you talking about?'

'I don't know, I don't know!'

The grandson spoke. 'He's another man.'

Anna turned on him. 'What other man? Have you seen this other man?'

'No, never, but Ivan has seen him.'

'Ivan knows him? Ivan knows him?'

The boy nodded. He was more than a boy, twenty at least. Looked like he might grow up to be a decent sort of man one day.

'Where's your grandfather today? Where's Ivan?'

'They're doing a job. In Balwyn.'

'Laying concrete?'

'Yes, all day.'

'You!' she said to him. 'Get on the phone and tell Ivan to be here in fifteen minutes or his witless sister is dead. She won't be real dead, but she'll wish she was. Don't think of calling the cops. Not yet. Got that?'

He faltered.

'And speak English. You hear me?'

He went to the wall phone. She heard him calling. Mentioned Ivan by name. They waited a long time. Several times the boy had to call and to get good reception.

'He's on Canterbury Road now.'

'Tell him if he's not here in fifteen minutes, I'm gonna drag her down to the nearest cop shop. By the fucking hair!'

The message was relayed.

They waited some more. It took twenty minutes.

The front door opened. Ivan dashed in, followed by the old man. Painfully awkward in his walk. Josep Medich was in a bad way. Seemed to be on his last legs. Anna Becker was leaning against a wall, holding the Colt again, but with both hands. Down by her knees, as if about to unclip it. Or whatever. No-one knew.

The old lady cried, ran to her husband.

'What are you doing?' Ivan shouted. 'What are you doing? Haven't you done enough to this family. You killed my brother—'

'Shut up, you want the police to hear what she's done?'

Ivan went to his sister. 'What's this woman done to you?'

Nerida could not speak. The grandson began to explain in Croatian. Anna snapped: 'Tell him in English.'

'She took a girl in Wagga.'

'Not Wagga,' Anna said. 'A little village outside Wagga. From a house on a farm, our farm. My daughter, our daughter. My husband gave her to me. This slobbering bitch took her away. They were goin' to kill her.'

'What?'

'He was going to kill her—'

'What? Who was gonna kill who?'

'Her boyfriend, but she would not do it. She returned the girl.'

'What?'

'That's your sister, a kidnapper?'

Ivan was horrified. 'Ah, no, no, Nerida, what you done?'

'It's true,' she said from the floor.

She was sitting up now, rubbing her face again. Looked like a broken tree, something hit by lightning. Cracked and sorrowful, a wasted sort of woman.

'And she says the Fat Man was behind it.'

'Fat Man? What Fat Man?'

'Not the one in Elwood. That was a neat trick, wasn't it? You sent me to the wrong man. That maggot was working for the Fat Man. Or, if not, he was trying to copy him.'

'I got nothing to do with any that. That the number he give me.'

'Yeah? Tell him, Nerida. Tell him what Feeny said they had to do.'

The teacher began to speak in Croatian.

Anna was going to interrupt, but she could see that Nerida was telling the truth. Could tell by her brother's face. Eyes bulging and hands going to his guts. Looked like he was going to vomit. Slowly he got down beside her, put out a hand, touched her on a shoulder, tenderly.

Ivan began to weep. It was more like keening than weeping.

'*Nerida, Nerida, moja mala sestra, sto si ucinio?*'

He was speaking Croatian, but that did not matter.

▲

CHAPTER 26

All the way home, she worried about it. If Ivan had been telling the truth, how was the Fat Man involved? That is, assuming he even existed. Maybe he was now dead but, for some reason, people think he still exists. Maybe there is another one, who likes to imitate him. Calls himself the Fat Man and does jobs, paid or unpaid. Like killing people. Medvedev probably began as an offsider for the Fat Man, doing small jobs and running messages for him. Not surprising that Ivan would think Medvedev was the Fat Man. But Medvedev was dead, so there must be someone else. After all, there was no doubt about it. Max Kruger had heard him on the phone. Max had asked: 'Who is this?' The caller had laughed and said: 'They call me the Fat Man.'

According to Max, the voice sounded like that of an older man—heavy, perhaps fat—a croaky kind of voice, smoky, menacing. The kind that gives you the creeps when you hear it. Was it real? Or was it put on by someone close to the scene? If the Fat Man was real, how did he come to control the whole affair? Why had Nerida Medich claimed that the Fat Man told Feeny he had to do it? What did the Fat Man have on Feeny?

Nerida had hinted that Feeny had done something long ago. And it was so bad that if anyone knew about it, he'd be finished—disgraced not only as a cop, but as a person. Yet Nerida didn't seem to know what it was.

What the hell was going on?

Anna was driving along the Goulburn Valley Highway, which would link her to the Newell Highway after crossing the border. She'd already noticed that a police car was lingering behind her. Maybe the cops were calling in her number plate. She was not speeding, not driving carelessly or dangerously or was in any way a menace to anyone on the road. Only a few minutes ago, she'd passed through Shepparton. Not far to go to the river and the State border.

She would cross at Tocumwal, then cut through Jerilderie and Lockhart to get home. All going well, she should be there by six o'clock.

Then a siren blared.

Flashing lights lit up her rear-view mirror. Anna slowed down casually and respectfully.

She'd been a cop for thirteen years, including a motor cop for two or three years, with the Federal police in Canberra. She was sympathetic. They had a hard life with little thanks, the traffic boys. And the long highway patrols were the pits. You could be chasing someone for hours, no time for a decent piss. And in the end what do you get? You could pull up a suspect vehicle, it may be only bald tyres. You walk up to the driver, smiling or trying to smile, because you never know what to expect. When someone sticks out a shooter and pops you.

Full in the face. It doesn't happen often, but it does happen.

She pulled over and waited.

A man with two stripes on his shoulders approached. His hand hovered near his sidearm, not resting on it but close enough.

'Good afternoon,' he said.

'Good afternoon, officer.'

'Would you step outside the vehicle, please?'

'Would I step outside?'

'That's what I said.'

'What's going on?'

'Please step outside the vehicle and I'll tell you.'

Anna checked the mirror again. A young bloke was still in the car, the driver, grinning. She opened the door and stepped out, leaned against the B.M.W.

'Step away from the vehicle, please.'

'What's going on?'

'Are you the owner of this vehicle?'

'My husband is the owner, but I drive it now and then.'

'Have you just come from Shepparton?'

'From Melbourne. Stopped in Shep for a piss. On my way home.'

'Where to?'

'A little farm not far outside Wagga Wagga. It's in New South Wales.'

'I know where it is, madam. Let me see your licence.'

'Is it my driving?'

'Please show me your licence.'

She got it out, showed t.

'Anastacia—' he read.

'Babchuk,' she said. 'That's what it says.'

'Is that your name?'

'It used to be, but I got married five years ago. Now I'm Anna Becker.'

He handed it back. She handed over another document, folded too small for a wallet. Showing years of wear and tear.

'What's this?'

'A permit.'

He was surprised. 'You carry a weapon?'

She opened her jacket, showed him the Colt. He edged back a few inches.

'Why are you carrying a firearm?'

'Because I never know when some scumbag will try to whack me. Perhaps someone dressed like a cop.'

'Yeah?'

He stepped back a few more inches, tempted to go for his weapon. His young partner had seen it. He got out of the patrol car, stood at the ready.

'What's this all about, officer?'

'We've had report of someone being pushed into a car in Shepparton. Into the boot, in fact. According to our information, this is the car. The number checks.'

'Someone saw me stick a woman in the boot? Of this car?'

'According to the witness, back in Shepparton.'

'Quite right. I did that.'

'You what?'

'Stuck her in the boot. She's my prisoner.'

'Your prisoner?'

'Yeah, she kidnapped a child aged six. She and her boyfriend. He wanted to kill the child, but she couldn't do it. She dropped the girl at our farm gate and pissed off. All the way to Melbourne. I followed her, arrested her, and now I'm taking her back to Wagga to charge her.'

'You what?'

'Are you hard of hearing, officer?'

'What?'

This was getting serious. His pal unfolded his arms, put a hand on his own piece, and stepped forward slowly, anxiously. Anything could happen to a cop on these lonely, outback roads. It was not lonely at all. Vehicles were flashing by at the rate of one or two each ten seconds. Every time a giant rig went by, the B.M.W shook a little. Making Anna shake along with it. It was as though the road was playing a game with her. Pushing her, and running away laughing.

'You arrested her? And put her in boot?'

'You want to have a look?'

Anna walked past him to the rear of the car, pulled out her keys, and opened the boot. Inside, Nerida lay curled up, fists at her throat, eyes wide and defensively startled.

'Jesus,' he said.

'This is Nerida Medich, a teacher at a little school near us. She cleared out yesterday. She's confessed.'

'Confessed?'

'To kidnapping.'

'Whose child did she kidnap?'

'Mine.'

'You're the mother?'

'Stepmother, aren't I, Nerida?'

She nodded jerkily.

'And you abducted my daughter, Roberta, didn't you?'

She burst into tears. Very few left, but she managed.

'They were going to kill her, weren't they, Nerida?'

The teacher howled.

The officer was amazed. 'She was going to kill your daughter?'

'Yes, at first, then she got cold feet.'

She called out: 'I wouldn't do it! I wouldn't do it!'

'What's her name?'

'She calls herself Nerida Larkin but she's Nerida Medich, aren't you? She pissed off to her family home in Cremorne.'

'Cremorne? In Melbourne? Is that right, miss? What street?'

She would not answer, so Anna told him. He wrote that down.

'Do you admit to the charge? Kidnapping?'

She shuddered, said something unintelligible. But she nodded.

'Why have you got her in the boot?'

'To stop her escaping. Or fighting with me while I'm driving. Or jumping out at speed.'

The senior man was worried. 'That's illegal, incarcerating a person like that. Also, it must be hot in there?'

'What would you do in the circumstances? Lend me your cuffs. I'll send them back, I promise.'

He sighed. 'What about this alleged boyfriend?'

By this time, his partner had sauntered up. Stepped forward, peeped in the boot.

Anna sighed. 'Ah, that's where it gets interesting, doesn't it, Nerida?'

The prisoner did not answer, defeated.

'His name is Brett Feeny.'

'So, what's he do?'

'He's a cop, isn't he, Nerida?'

She did not answer.

'A cop?'

'Yes, an inspector of police.'

'Christ Almighty!'

'What's your name, mate? Bob? Jim?'

'Angus.'

'Got another name?'

'Lethbridge.'

'Lethbridge? Well, Angus Lethbridge, I'd appreciate it if you and your people back at base did *not* contact Wagga Wagga to check on any of this for a while. You see, this bloke may be on duty, or hanging around. Waiting for news about Nerida here. He might do a bunk.'

The cop stared at her, clearly uncomfortable. His young partner was enjoying this. Looked too young to be carrying a gun.

'You can't arrest a woman and take her across the border.'

'She's agreed.'

'She's agreed?'

'That's what I just said.'

'If she's agreed, why do you need to arrest her?'

'Because she's a criminal, that's why.'

'Who says she's a criminal?'

'I say.'

The two-striper was not convinced.

'I'll have to talk to someone about this.'

He got out his phone, walked away and chatted.

The young bloke grinned at her. He had a happy face, inquisitive.

'What's your name?' he asked.

'What's yours, sonny?'

'Rory.'

'Rory? I knew it'd be something like that. How long have you been in?'

'Ah, four or five months. Since I finished college.'

'Still on probation, eh?'

'Yeah.'

'Still exciting, is it?'

'Ah, yeah, terrific. Gee, nothin' like bein' a cop, is there?'

She did not answer. A huge rig loomed up. All the way to Brisbane and points north. She blinked as the wind hit her. Then watched it go lumbering on in the late afternoon and the limitless distance.

The boy cop was still grinning at her, wide-eyed this time.

'You're Anastacia, aren't you?'

'How'd you work that out?'

'Tall, hard and fast and a mad blonde, they say. White hair.'

'Who says?'

'Blokes at work. Reckon you're a legend.'

'A legend?'

'Hey, you're the one that shot that geezer in that hotel in—where was it?'

'Wagga?'

'Yeah, that's it.' He studied her nervously. 'How was it?'

Anna did not answer. Every bonehead she met wanted to know: What was it like to kill a man? In an Aussie pub? Everyone looking? How did you feel about that? She just leaned against the car. Nerida was silent. Seemed to have gone to sleep. It must have been uncomfortable in there. The BMW did have a soft mat in the boot, but it would have been a rough ride nonetheless.

'Hey, Anastacia,' the boy said, 'has anybody called you out? You know, challenged you?'

'For Christ's sake—'

'Yeah, well, someone must be tempted?'

'Just shut up, right?'

'Only askin'.'

'Stop asking or I'll have to hit you.'

'Gee, sorry.'

They watched the traffic go by. A campervan came up. The idiots inside waved at them. The boy cop waved back. Then he got something out of a shirt pocket.

'Anastacia?'

He was holding out a notebook and ballpoint. 'Could I have your autograph?'

'Just piss off,' she said.

It took three more minutes. Anna was fed up. It was well after four and she was sick of the exhaust fumes. The senior man came back.

'You can go,' he said. 'But we have to see you to the border. And you can't carry your prisoner in the boot. We can, however, provide you with an escort.'

'You mean prisoner escort?'

'That's right.'

'Not sonny boy here?'

'Is there a problem?'

'He wants my autograph.'

'Yeah, well, you are famous, you know. A hot shot with a Glock, so they say.'

'How do you know?'

'They had to ring Melbourne.'

'What did Melbourne say?'

'To give you all possible assistance. And not to call you Chook.'

It took another hour to cross the river, go through Jerilderie and then Lockhart. As they approached the farm, she thought of dropping in for a few words with Becker, but that would not have been a good idea. She couldn't leave the little bitch outside in the car. She might well jump out, run away. Even worse, throw herself under a passing truck. If she took her to the house, Robbie would know or sense she was there. Or outside on the verandah. That would be be bad. Robbie believed in Nerida Larkin—as she was known. Loved her. Probably still believed it had all been a big surprise, sleeping over with her teacher. No, she decided to drive on to Wagga. She did, however, call Becker and tell him what she was doing.

'Has anything happened?' she asked.

'No, nothing. She's done her homework. With the aid of *Wikipedia*.'

'Goodness, she can manage *Wikipedia*?'

'With a little help from Hank.'

'Really? How was her first day?'

'Good, but she was a bit disappointed. She called her new teacher "Gay." And got a cold reprimand. She has to address her as Mrs Phillips.'

'The poor girl. Gay Phillips is a bit stuffy, but I think she knows her job. Give her a big hug for me. I'm going straight on to Wagga. I'll drop Miss Medich there. This may take some time.'

'Okay, honey.'

'I'm not honey any more. I'm going white.'

'You'll soon be an old lady.'

'Oh, God, don't say that.'

She was getting on in years, she knew. Next birthday she would be forty. She didn't know what she would do then. Colour her hair or stay white, as white and cold and bare and blizzardly as a Siberian winter.

When she reached the outskirts, she changed her mind. If she walked in with a prisoner, there could be trouble. Unfriendly trouble. She was not now a sworn officer. Did not have a warrant, either a card or badge. So she rang Whitton, told him the story.

'You abducted a woman from another State? You can't do that without a court order.'

'I didn't abduct her. She agreed to come. The cops we met agreed to let her go.'

'I don't know how you're going to get away with this.'

'I don't care about that. Who is the custody sergeant tonight?'

It was now approaching seven o'clock and her stomach was hurting. She hadn't eaten since breakfast. The sun had set but the western sky was lit up like a carnival.

'Tonight? Wednesday? I dunno. I'm suspended, you know.'

'Could you find out and ring me back?'

He did, but reluctantly.

'Carrick?' she said. 'What's he doing on the desk? He's a detective.'

'Someone's sick, they reckon.'

'Can you meet me there?'

'Why?'

'I may have trouble with Carrick. He can be difficult. He might refuse to take her into custody. I think he's too close to Feeny.'

'Yeah, I think so too.'

She waited outside the station on Sturt Street until Whitton arrived on foot, still limping. His knee still bound. Limping with the aid of a stick, but making good time. He lived only a few blocks away on Docker Street. Had told everyone he'd busted the patella when he slipped in his bathroom, getting out of the shower. Didn't look too cranky, but friendly despite the hobbling pain. Even glad to see her.

'Any problems?' he asked.

'Nothing serious. Let's get her inside.'

They got Nerida Larkin out of the B.M.W, each taking her by an arm. She could barely walk. She dragged her feet, head hung down. Hair long and messy. She had cried so much she had hollow, tear-burnt eyes. Did not bother to look where she was walking, so they had to lift her up each step. Took her through the glass doors, led her up to the charge desk. Carrick was waiting for them.

'I'm arresting this woman for the crime of kidnapping,' Whitton said.

Carrick's face did not change. No body language or any other form of expression, except that his eyes lit up. Like the eyes of a dog on seeing a cat in the distance.

'You're suspended,' Carrick said.

'No longer,' Anna said. 'All charges against Inspector Whitton have been dropped.'

'Who by?'

'My husband.'

Carrick glared at them both, then nodded at the captive.

'Who is this?'

'Nerida Medich, also known as Nerida Larkin. Teacher resident in the village of Old Man Creek. I'm charging her with the kidnapping of a child, Roberta Becker, on the twenty-sixth day of January this year.'

'Yeah?'

'Australia Day, remember?'

Carrick did not answer.

'Where is Inspector Feeny?'

'Feeny?'

'Yeah, Inspector Feeny. Have you heard anything of him?'

'Heard *from* him, you mean?'

'What?'

'No-one's seen Feeny since late this afternoon.'

'What happened?'

'Sittin' in his office, workin' away on a case file, when he received a call.'

'A phone call?'

'Yeah.'

'And?'

'Just sat there for a while, starin' at nothing, thinkin' I suppose.

'Yeah?'

'Went in to speak to him about somethin', but didn't hear me at first. Then he woke up and said, *What?* I told him. He just stared at me a long time.'

'Still thinking?'

Carrick nodded. 'I said, You all right, sir?' He said, *Yes, yes,* a couple of times. A few minutes later he walked out.'

'Just walked out?'

'Yeah.'

'Didn't say where he was going?'

'No.'

'Jesus,' Whitton said.

Anna intervened, 'Exactly what time did he receive this call?'
'Why?'
Whitton said, 'Just answer the question, sergeant.'
'I don't know. Maybe a quarter past four, maybe twenty past.'
Anna had a sinking feeling. The Victorian cops had phoned Melbourne just after four. When the senior constable had said they'd been told to escort her to the border, she'd flipped open her watch once again, noted the time: nine minutes past four. Someone had phoned Feeny, tipped him off. Probably someone in Melbourne.
'Did anyone check on the call, the number? The area?' she asked.
'Me? Check on him? I've got no authority to check on a senior officer.'
Whitton said. 'Take this young woman into custody and get on with the paper work.'
It took another ten minutes. Carrick wanted to know every detail. 'This is irregular, Chief Inspector.'
'Are you questioning my judgement, Sergeant?'
Carrick read her rights to Larkin then called someone on a phone. A young female probationary came out. It was the pretty one who'd sat by the recorder at the farm, waiting for the call that eventually came through from the Fat Man. Or was it really the Fat Man? She flashed a smile at Anna. Daisy? Yes, that was her name, Daisy Cornford.
'Take this prisoner next door,' he said.
'To the cells?'
'Yeah, lock her in.'
'Yes, sir.'
'Make sure she gets some food,' Whitton said, more to Carrick than Daisy. 'And a doctor. I want a medical report. Tonight,' he added. 'She don't look too good. And another thing—' This more

to Daisy than to Carrick. 'Tell the turnkeys not to let her have anything she could use for a noose. Understand?'

'They're not stupid,' Carrick said.

'Are you tryin' to tell me something, Sergeant?'

Carrick did not answer. You could feel the tension.

Whitton said to Daisy, 'Go on, love, off with her, hand her over. But check up on her every now and then. Ask her if you can do anything for her.'

'Sir?'

'Just in case she wants to chat. Get her confidence without actually asking, understand? Do not take notes, keep it all in your head. You know what I'm saying?'

'Yes, sir, I do.'

'Off with you now, lass.'

'Thank you, sir.'

Daisy led her to the cells, located between the old police station and the courthouse.

Nerida Medich said nothing. She looked like something fished up from hell. Maybe she was thinking things must get worse. Maybe she was thinking of topping herself.

Carrick was unhappy. 'You want a probationary constable to interrogate a prisoner? In her cell? Without a lawyer present? A bit sneaky, ain't it, sir?'

'Got a problem with that, sergeant?'

Carrick went rigid, but didn't answer.

'I want an all-points search done for Inspector Feeny,' Whitton said.

'You want him brought in?'

'That's exactly what I'm saying.'

'You're gonna arrest a senior officer?'

'Not arrest him. He's deserted his post. Just find him.'

Carrick stared at him as if he were hard of hearing—or pretending to be.

'Got a problem with that too, sergeant?'

Anna was tired and painfully hungry. 'Need me anymore, Ted?'

'No, mate. I'll find him, wherever he is.'

She drove home thinking: Someone in Melbourne had tipped off Feeny. One of the Medich family? Ivan Medich's distress had seemed to be genuine: Oh, Nerida, what have you done? What had *she* done? Not: What have *we* done? Or was it someone else in Melbourne? The police? They'd been called by the Shepparton police. They'd been told that the notorious gunfighter, Anastacia Babchuk, had plunged into Victoria, snatched a felon from her home and was dragging her back to New South Wales—apparently with the consent of someone up high. Who knew about her down there? Who knew her well enough to warn the boys on the road not to call her Chook?

There had been an incident at St Kilda Police Station, when they'd taken her in after she'd shot Medvedev. Just routine. Anna had had no argument with that. She'd felt quite relaxed. Everything had gone well. With one exception.

At first she'd been intervened by two detectives, an inspector and a sergeant. The sergeant was a little bastard, liked picking at her. Liked telling his superior all about her. Seemed to have read up on the shoot-out at the William Hovell. He'd said, Where's your Glock tonight? You gonner give us an exhibition? That sort of thing. The inspector told him to shut up. Five minutes later he was at it again. She'd set up people so she could kill 'em and claim self-defence. The inspector told him again to stop it, but he was soon doing it again. Is that what you did tonight in Elwood? The inspector had jumped up and dragged him outside. Told him he was jeopardising the whole fucking interrogation. Still the little terrier couldn't let it alone. Quite distinctly she heard him say:

'All right then, but don't call her Chook. She'll cut y'down. Quick as look at yer!'

The senior man had come back with a different offsider. What happened to your little friend? Chook had asked. The inspector had said: 'You won't have to worry about him again.' She smiled again to herself. That little creep had done her a favour, intimidated a witness. No wonder his boss had been angry.

What the hell was his name?

Shan-something? Shand? No. Shannon? No. Shannahan? No…

She drove home in the last light of the day. The carnival in the west was over. One by one the little stars came out to play.

＾

CHAPTER 27

They searched everywhere but did not find Feeny. He'd had a few hours' start. When they'd broken into his flat in Turvey Park, it was clear he'd left in a hurry. Not all that much of a hurry, because he'd packed clothes and he'd gone through drawers, pulling out this and that, throwing aside much of it. Probably looking for documents, films, anything incriminating. May have spent as much as an hour getting what he needed. Which way he went, no-one knew. They put out a call to all cars and stations, but no-one spotted him. By seven o'clock, he could have been in Melbourne or almost to Sydney or at least halfway to Brisbane. If he were connected to the Fat Man, he'd be in or near Melbourne. But that was just a guess.

Ted Whitton phoned each day, giving progress reports, trying to be helpful. He was as friendly as a man like him could be. Even appeared at the farm one day, complete with a bottle of whiskey.

As a peace offering, he said.

By this time, Anna was fairly relaxed with him. But Becker was not. He was still hostile. Wanted to hit him, but that would have been ineffectual. His fist would have bounced off. The atmosphere improved when Roberta appeared. They were on the front verandah when she peeped out. Smiling and saying: 'Hullo, I'm Robbie.'

Whitton grinned at her. 'You're Robbie—the one all the fuss was about?'

She was puzzled. Becker cut in quickly.

'This is Mr Whitton. He thought you were missing. But you were safe, weren't you? You got on well with Nerida, didn't you?'

She came right out. 'Yes, we had fun.'

'So, everything's fine, isn't it?'

Whitton caught on. 'Well, that's all good, eh?'

She looked up at him. 'You are very tall. You are taller than Daddy. I think you are as tall as Mummy. We call her Mummy Long Legs.'

'Yeah? When I was your age, I was quite small. So, every time my mother watered the geraniums, she watered me too.'

She laughed. 'Did you get wet?'

'Yeah, quite wet. But it was all right, because she put fertiliser in it to make me grow, like a beanstalk.'

'*Ha!* Like Jack and the Beanstalk?'

'And so I grew up and up and when I was fifteen or sixteen I had to say to Mum, You've got to stop puttin' all that fertiliser on me, Mum. I'm gettin' too tall. I'll bang my head.'

She laughed again. 'What happened?'

'She wouldn't stop. Went on waterin' me and I got so tall, every time I got to a house I had to dip my head to get inside. If I didn't, I'd bang my head.'

'Is that why you wear a hat?'

'Yeah, exactly. So no-one'll see the bumps and bruises.'

'*Ha!*'

'That's a true story.'

'I love true stories. When I grow up, I'm going to write true stories, like Dell.'

'Dell?'

'Yes, Dell, she works at the newspaper.'

'Deloraine Duffy,' Becker explained.

'Ah, yeah, I know the one.'

'You'd better come in,' Becker said.

So, they went inside. Anastacia joined them and they sampled the whiskey, Johnnie Walker Double Black Label. They had water and ice, while Roberta studied Mr Walker in his top hat on the bottle.

'Why does he have a stick?'

'That's a cane,' Whitton said.

'Why does he have a cane?'

'Why?' They looked at each other. Anna had an idea.

'I think he was a man about town.'

'What do you mean?'

'Well, in olden days, men, who had enough money and didn't have to work, used to be called young men about town. They dressed up like that and they carried a cane.'

'Why?'

'Well, I suppose to show they did not have to work. They were usually smart young men and talked a lot to impressed ladies. They were very courteous and raised their hats to every lady they met in the street and smiled a lot, and sometimes bowed.'

'Like Mr Brett?'

'Mr Brett?'

They all jumped a little.

'That was his name? Brett?'

'Huh-hum.'

'You mean this Mr Brett was at Nerida's house, when you were there? In the afternoon?'

'Yes, Mummy.'

'What did he say to Nerida?'

'They've got dogs looking for her, a chopper too.'

'Oh, hell.'

'You were in the kitchen with them?'

'No, I was in the front room, looking at books. Nerida had lovely pictures, all so shiny. Trains going through the Rocky Mountains.'

'You could read that?'

'No, she was showing me. We were sitting on the floor.'

'When Mr Brett came to the house?'

'Yes,' she said.

'When was that?'

'Mmm, late in the day.'

'What did he say? To you?'

'I waved to you and you didn't wave back.'

'Waved to you where?'

'At the river. He was on the boat.'

'What boat?'

'The one with the lady.'

'I'm sorry, darling, I don't understand. What lady?'

'She was singing.'

'Singing?'

Roberta sang: '*Cruising down the river on a Sunday afternoon…*'

'That lady?'

'Yes, Mummy.

'Did she come with him? To Nerida's house?'

'No, next day.'

They all looked at each other.

'So, getting back to the first day, what did Mr Brett say to Nerida? When he came in?'

'He made her go into the kitchen.'

'Made her?'

'Uh hum. Took her by an arm.'

'What did he say?'

She paused. 'Dirty things.'

'You don't want say dirty things? That's s all right. Mr Ted won't be upset. He's a policeman and he's heard everything.'

'He said: You pinched a fucking kid and now we are really in the shit.'

They were shocked, such words coming out of the mouth of a small child. Roberta was a perfect mimic. She could hear a song just once and immediately repeat it, not missing a word.

'So, darling, what did Nerida do?'

'She cried.'

'And what did Mr Brett say?'

'We can't take her back, you realise that, you stupid bitch?'

'What did she say to that?'

'I couldn't hear. I think she was crying.'

'What did Mr Brett say next?'

'We could take her to Royd.'

'Royd? What did he mean by that?'

'I don't know, Mummy.'

'And what did Nerida say?'

'She just said, I'm sorry, I'm so sorry.'

'Oh, my God, darling—'

'Don't cry, Mummy.'

'What? Oh, oh, I—' Anna gathered her wits. 'What did he mean? Royd who?'

'I don't know. Then he said, *for a picnic.*'

'Perhaps he meant Boyd?'

'Mmm?'

'You were going on a picnic with someone called Royd or Boyd. A man? Or a boy?'

'I don't know.'

Anna thought about it. 'Did you ever see the lady on the boat again?'

Roberta nodded. 'Uh hum.'

'She was there too?'

'Uh hum.'

'On the first day?'

'No, no, the next day.'

Anna said, 'Come here, darling.' The girl went to her. 'Now, you must think very carefully. Will you do that?'

'Yes, Mummy.'

'What did the lady do?'

'Oh, she just had a drink.'

'What time was this?'

'After we had lunch.'

'She came after lunch? Did she say where she came from?'

Roberta shook her head.

'What did the lady say?'

'I was very pretty.'

'Did she say anything else?'

'Oh, we talked about the song. I said we heard her sing the song. And she looked very nice and Terry said, Nice tits. And she smiled and went all—' Roberta rolled her eyes. 'And stuck her tits out.'

'Breasts, darling. You must say breasts.'

'Terry says tits.'

'Terry is a boy. He says coarse things at times.'

'What do you mean, coarse things?'

'I'll tell you some time, but now. Please tell us what did the lady say after that? Did she say anything about you?'

'No, I don't think so. They all had drinks and then she said she had to go.'

'Go where?'

'I don't know, Mummy.'

'Did she come in a car?'

'Yes, it was quite big.'

'Like the Nissan?'
'Hmmm, longer and blue.'
'How much longer?'
'Oh, long like a long car. She said, "Now I might get a new Jag."'
'A Jaguar?'
'Yes, that's a big cat, isn't it? In the jungle?'
'She was talking about money?'
'Sometimes.'
'When exactly?'
'Oh, when they went into the bedroom.'
'Into Nerida's bedroom?'
'Yes.'
'Everyone went into her bedroom?'
'No, only Mr Brett and the fat lady.'
'Fat lady?'
Roberta nodded.
'I see. Where was Nerida?'
'In the kitchen, washing dishes.'
'After lunch? What did she say?'
'She grabbed me and said: I can't do it! I can't do it! Over and over. She was squeezing so tight I started to cry.'
'Can't do what?'
'I don't know. Mr Brett and the lady came out. They were talking.'
'What did they say?'
'Mr Brett said, As much as that? Half a million?'
'And what did the lady say?'
'More if she was a blond. They love blond kids.'
Ted Whitton jumped to his feet, exploding. 'By Christ!' he said.
Roberta was puzzled.
'Why is Mr Ted jumping like that?'
'Oh, he does that, when he's drinking whiskey.'
'Is he allergic?'

'It's the malt in the whiskey.'

'Why is he looking at me like that?'

'Oh, he's not upset with you. It's Mr Walker. He doesn't like dandies, men who wear top hats and bow and scrape. Mr Ted is very conservative.'

'What does conservative mean?'

Anna was holding her own throat, as though she were going to vomit backwards, if that's possible. Becker was on his feet, indicating to Whitton to come outside. They left Anna with the girl.

'Mummy? What's wrong?'

'Come here, lovely girl.'

'Why are you crying?'

Aelete Inside, fuming. 'By Christ, the bastards, I'll get them for this!'

'They were going to sell her?'

'Fuckin' paedophiles.'

'They would have sold her?'

'After they'd finished with her.'

Becker turned white, almost fell off. Whitton had to grab him.

'You all right, mate?'

'Yeah, yeah.'

Whitton shot out a hand. 'Got to get back, mate. I'll let you know. You didn't get a number? By any chance?'

'A number?'

'Of the boat? Registration number?'

'We didn't think of it at the time.'

'We'll find it. And we'll find him.'

Patted Becker on the back. 'Hold on, mate.'

Becker tried to get the world into focus.

'The teacher?' he said. 'Has she told you anything new?'

'A few bits here and there. Never mentioned Feeny.'

'Thanks, Ted.'

'If you hadn't mentioned the picnic…'

They soon found Feeny's car.

One of the locals went down a lane in Yarragundry to do some fishing and saw the car. It was there with one door partly open. No sign of Feeny. Then he spotted clothes on the bank, neatly folded. He called the police, who sent in a team of divers. They searched for hours up and down the river, but found no body. They took casts of tyre tracks at the site, hoping to identify a Jaguar. Someone must have picked up Feeny, taken him somewhere. But they got nowhere with the tyres. Nothing specifically identifiable as Jaguar tracks.

Back at the station, Whitton cornered Des O'Grady. 'Where's that girl? What's her name?'

'Girl?'

'The one whose dad is in Tumut.'

'Probationer Cornford?'

'Yeah, that's the one. What's she doing at present?'

'Twiddling her thumbs in Records, I think.'

'Get her up here, will you? Pronto.'

▲

CHAPTER 28

They found the woman soon enough. Once a big star, she'd been loud, brassy, and celebrated—until her career came crashing down after a conviction for assault. She'd gotten drunk at a party and pulled another woman's hair. When the victim fought back, the singer had removed a shoe and attacked her with its heel. It wasn't quite a stiletto, but it was high and sharp enough to cost the victim an eye. That was the end of the contralto's career.

She was a big woman with, as Terry had noted, big tits. She was handsome in a heavyset way, and no doubt dangerous when angered. Had changed her name more than once. Now she was Carla Verducci. Had a few minor offences to her name: Drunk in a public place, swearing at a police officer, common assault, shoplifting, passing valueless cheques. That sort of thing. When they hauled her into police headquarters in Docklands, she was snaky and snitchy.

Whitton and a female officer went to Melbourne to interview her. She turned out to have more effrontery than Raging Bull and King Kong combined. Ranted and raved with indignation. When asked whether she had said the girl was worth half a million dollars, she looked stunned for a moment. You could see her cunning mind ticking over like a two-bob watch. Then she smiled, all sweetness and light.

'Yes, I had a good look at her. They asked me to look at her, since I'd been in show business. Now I'm in the tourist industry, Pacific cruises and all that. Working the phones to get some trade. I said she was good looking and cute and smart, another Shirley Temple. Remember Shirley Temple? On the good ship Lollipop? You're old enough to remember, ain't you, copper? Little Miss Becker could be a star. She'd be worth millions in Hollywood. But they had to get her quick. Get her a contract. Start on TV. Show business is hard and cruel, even for a six-year-old. One day you're in, next day you're out…'

When Feeny had asked her how much a contract would be worth, she had said that, in her opinion, the girl could be signed up for half a million.

'You're tryin' to tell me that Feeny, a police officer, would be thinking of putting a small girl into movies, making a fortune. How was he going to do that? Especially without her parents knowing?'

'By acting as her manager, darling. Apparently, he wanted out.'

'You expect me to believe that?'

'I don't give a fuck what you believe. I'm no kid-snatcher.'

Whitton had stared at her a long time. The officer with him, a sergeant called Nellie Bligh—not her real name, but everyone in Wagga called her that—later said Whitton seemed to transform into a Mallee bull trying to stare down an Indian cobra. This went on so long that Nellie had said: 'Do you expect us to believe that?'

Verducci snapped back, 'I don't fuckin' care, sweetheart, what you believe. I'm no kid-snatcher!'

Nellie responded: 'Like the school teacher, Miss Medich?'

'That stupid bitch can't keep her hands off other women's kids.'

'Yes, we have been checking on her. She's done it before, hasn't she? And been caught. Every time she tells the same story, doesn't she? Post-natal depression. And she's let off each time.'

'So? What's this got to do with me? I was asked to give an opinion. How would that kid go in show business? With her amazin' memory, she could win prizes on TV. They could start her off in spelling bees, then move her into kids shows. She'd capture a million hearts in no time. She's worth half a million, easy.'

Nellie responded: 'That's what we're interested in. Some of your friends don't seem to be too solvent these days.'

The soprano blew up.

'You can't say a thing like that to me! I'll sue you, sweetheart. My fuckin' friends'll sue you. I've got friends in high places. Big cops too.'

Whitton asked: 'Would any of them be known as the Fat Man?'

'What? What Fat Man?'

He did not answer.

'Do you know, Miss Verducci, that Mr Feeny is now a hunted man?'

'Feeny, that pathetic little ponce? God, what's he been up to now?'

'Attempted abduction.'

'What? Abduction? Of that little sugar plum fairy? With the cute big eyes?

'His accomplice in the said abduction, Miss or Mrs Nerida Larkin, sometimes known by her maiden name of Nerida Medich, is now in custody. And she has provided us with a signed statement. She has accused you of being part of the plot. To sell a child on the market for sexual exploitation. You know what I mean?'

'Sell the kid? Jesus, what next? So what? What's that got to do with me?'

'If true, it will mean a lot to your future.'

Miss Verducci sighed heavily, exhaustedly.

'That pathetic little bimbo? You'd believe her? Oh, for Christ's sake, spare me.'

'You deny you were part of a plot to abduct Miss Becker?'

'Absolutely!'

'And that you intended to take her to some spot, where she was to be abused by a certain type of men?'

'You mean fucking kids? God help us, you spend too much time watching crime stuff on television, Fatso. That crap addles your brains, you know. You should be careful, Fatso.'

Whitton jumped up. Nellie had to grab him.

You could see what she was trying to do. Make Whitton assault her. If he did, anything she'd said would be inadmissible in court.

Ted calmed down, although wheezing a bit.

'Why were you on that boat?' he asked.

'Why was I on that boat? I was on a cruise, sweetheart. We puttered up to Wagga Wagga and then floated down. Cruising down the river on a Sunday afternoon. It was a Sunday, as I recall. I was with some friends. We're all in show business or *were* in show business. I used to do Pacific cruises, you know, after some adverse publicity. All I did was pull some bitch's hair after she said, "Up yours, sweetheart!" at a party. She pulled my hair. I pulled hers. What did I get? Nine-hundred dollars fine, plus court costs and a warning to keep away from her for two years. That little bitch, she ruined my career. What a phoney world, eh? Yeah, show business, sweetheart. Fucking show business.'

'So is pornography,' Whitton said.

After that, they gave up. She refused to cooperate any further. Her story was perfectly plausible. She could have been innocent. Some court might well believe her. It all depended on what Feeny had to say. If they ever found him.

They were standing outside the building, waiting for a taxi. It was late in the day. The skies were dark and it was raining softly. Two lights were approaching, a third on top. Whitton held up a hand. The lights slowed down for them. Nellie opened a door for her. They got in and settled own.

'You know, Ted, she might be telling the truth.'

'And pigs might fly.'

When they got back, no-one had any news of Feeny. The young probationer, Daisy Cornford, had spent hours searching every record, both printed and online, for the word 'Boyd.' Or 'Royd'. Phone books, electoral rolls, police records. There were many people named Boyd but none called Royd. She'd found only one place called Boyd in Australia and that was Boyd Town on Twofold Bay. Not a town but an old inn, once used by whalers. Back when whaling was done out of Eden, also on Twofold Bay. But local inquiries had failed to find any trace of Feeny there.

Early next day, Daisy came to Whitton.

'Excuse me, sir, there's a place—'

'A place?'

'South-west of here, not far. It's at the back of The Rock.'

'A town? Boyd? Never heard of it.'

'Not a town or place or crossing or anything else—'

'So what is it?'

'I think it's the name of a property.'

'You've been through a list of every property in the district?'

'No, sir, but I remembered something.'

'Yeah?'

Whitton sat back, growling habitually. If he had no-one to growl at, he'd growl at himself.

'When I recorded that phone call at the Becker place—'

'When the girl went missing?'

'Yes, sir.'

'Go on.'

'Telstra told Constable Kruger the name of the last tower used.'

'And?'

'It was on a hill south of Old Man.' She meant the village called Old Man Creek.

'Was it?'

'It was designated as Jingara-Old Man-Rock.'

'What's your point, constable?'

'Old Man-Rock means Old Man to The Rock.'

'A back road?'

'Yes, and Jingara was the name of a property.'

'The one the tower was located on?'

'Yes, sir.'

'And?'

'A list of all such tower locations is available on the net.'

'So?'

'One tower is designated Robroyd-Lockhart-Rand.'

'Cripes! Where is it, love?'

'Near Rand.'

'Rand?'

'Yes, sir.

'But where exactly is this Robroyd?'

'The list gives the exact latitude and longitude.'

'It does? By gee—' He jumped up. 'By Jesus, Feeny was born in Lockhart. Why didn't I think of that?' He had pressed a button on a console. 'Carrick?'

'Yes, sir?'

'Get a team together!'

'Where are we going?'

'Fishing.'

'But where?'

'I'll tell you in the car.'

Whitton didn't trust Carrick, a man who kept too much to himself. He turned back to Daisy Cornford. 'Thanks, constable. That was smart. Your father would be proud of you.'

'Thank you, sir.'

'If that bastard is there—'

'Could I go too, sir?'

'Eh? With us? Ah, I dunno. There could be trouble—'

'Dad said never miss an opportunity.'

'Did he? You ever done any shootin'?'

'Only on uncle's farm, sir.'

'Been issued with a weapon?'

'Yes, sir.'

'What is it?'

'A Smith and Wesson, sir.'

'Yeah? Well, strap it on.'

Max Kruger was in one car with two others and Whitton and Carrick and the girl were in the other. They alerted Lockhart police, but did not say where they were going. No-one but Whitton and Daisy knew. They drove first to Lockhart and picked up the local man. Lockhart was a one-man outpost. If you wanted service after hours, you had to ring Wagga. The local officer was Derek Duckworth and he came out dressed in Army fatigues. He was a reservist and must have been on an exercise at Kapooka. Or, was about to go on an exercise and had been told to forget it, the Army can wait. On his left hip was a Glock. In his right hand was a Colt M4 carbine rifle with scope.

'What are we looking for, sir?'

'A transmission tower on or near a road running down to Rand.'

'A tower?'

'Ever heard of a property called Robroyd?'

'Never.'

'Well, that's where we're going. Constable Cornford has the bearings. You lead the way.'

It was on a pleasant sort of hill, not rocky. Lots of farmland all around and a small lake, nothing more than a big pond, in the distance. A few ducks and other waterbirds on it, some fighting. Otherwise, the place was dead quiet. The police cruised around, everyone's eyes on farm houses and farm gates. Except that Whitton's eyes were on Carrick, who was driving. Daisy was in the back seat. They went up and down lanes and around the hill twice. No signpost indicated Robroyd or anything like it.

They'd gone another three or four hundred yards, when Daisy spoke up.

'Excuse me, sir. There must be a track up to the tower. Otherwise, how would service crews reach it?'

'And?'

'The track must go through a property known as Robroyd.'

'You're right, lass!'

So, they went around again. Until she shouted: 'Look, there's a track, sir. It goes right up the hill to the tower!'

They paused. No sign of life, except for a few sheep in a corner near a dam.

'Stop here, sergeant.'

Carrick stopped, looked around.

'Doesn't look like anyone lives here,' he said.

'What about the sheep?'

'They could be a neighbour's.'

Daisy was squinting. 'There's a house or shed or shack up there, sir.'

'Where?'

'In those trees, very small. About three-hundred yards up.'

'I can't see it.'

'It doesn't stand out.'

'You'd think this place'd have a name, if anyone's livin' here.'

Carrick asked, 'Who are you lookin' for?'

Whitton ignored him. 'There's a mail box, on that post. Pretty old and rusty. Can't see any name, though.'

Daisy had another idea. 'Shall I hop out and have a look, sir?'

'Look at what?'

'There might be a name on the box.'

Carrick said, 'This place is abandoned.'

'Let's ask a neighbour.'

Daisy had already hopped out, gone to the box nailed to a post.

She bent down, running a finger over something. The box was a rusted kerosene tin, cut open at both ends. Below it was a piece of half-rotten board. It might have been an inch thick years ago, but now most of it had rotted away. Letters had been cut into the board, and filled with white paint. The first letters had rotted away entirely. Only a few specks of paint still clung to the last few.

'See anything?'

'Ah—'

'There's nothing here,' Carrick said. 'No-one's been here in years.'

'How do you know, sergeant?'

'You can see for yourself.'

'Yeah, well, my eyes aren't what they used to be, but I can see fresh tyre tracks and they don't suggest a Telstra truck made 'em. Those are car tracks.'

'They could have been made by anyone. A council inspector or the owner of the sheep.'

Daisy was still picking away at the board with a fingernail, talking to herself.

'The first two or three letters are missing!' she called.

'What about the last?'

'I estimate seven letters originally.'

'Can you make out any?'

'Not the first four, sir.'

'What about the last three?'

'They look like—' She got right down. '—oyd!'

'It could be Robroyd?'

'Looks like it, sir.'

Whitton said to her: 'Open the gate, constable.'

She did so. The old Cyclone drooped and dragged and tore at the ground in protest, so that she had to push and lift and shove. But she got it open.

'Now,' Whitton said, 'drive up!'

Carrick did not move. The squad car did not move.

'Who are we looking for?' he said.

Whitton did not answer.

Daisy was hesitating, not sure whether she was expected to get back in the car. The second car was waiting behind them.

Whitton said from a window, 'Not you, love. Stay down here. Take cover if necessary.'

'Oh, gosh.'

'I'd better go up,' Carrick said.

'Why?'

'To see if he's there.'

'See if who's there?'

'Inspector Feeny.'

'Did I say his name, sergeant?'

'Jesus, everyone knows you're looking for Feeny.'

Whitton began to get out of the car. 'All right, you drive up there and, if he's there, talk to him. Tell him to come quietly. He's never gonna get away. Not after what he did. And what he was gonna do.'

'What was he gonna do?'

'Sell the girl to the perverts and arseholes and animals that like to shag children.'

'What?'

'And sell the pictures on the internet.'

'What?'

'That's what he'll be charged with.'

Carrick had gone white in the face. 'Jesus, I didn't know he was like that!'

'Not what you thought, eh?'

Whitton was out of the car now. Still Carrick did not move. He looked sick.

'Sergeant Carrick, I'm ordering you to drive up to that shack and see whether Feeny is there. Is that understood?' Carrick did not reply. 'Keep a safe distance. Don't go into the hut. Just indicate yes or no. Got that?'

'Yeah, right.'

'Drive up there slowly, don't take any risks.'

'Yes, sir.'

'And Derek here—' He indicated the man with the rifle. 'He's gonna walk up behind you, behind the car, aren't you, Derek? He's gonna cover you. If anyone gives you any trouble, he's going to hit him. Understand?'

'Yair, all right.'

Whitton slapped the roof again.

'On your way, sergeant!'

Carrick did not answer. It was not clear whether he was afraid. Or suspicious of a trap. Or sickened by what Whitton had just said. He put the car into gear and went up slowly, not much more than a good walking pace.

The marksman was following on foot.

Holding the rifle high, moving with military precision. Making remarkably good time behind the car. Nothing changed ahead. No smoke, no vehicle, nothing to indicate habitation. The shack was decrepit—one of the originals in the area by the look of it. A real pioneer's hut. Just two rooms, a stone chimney at one end, much of it covered by lichen. There could be a shed at the back, an outhouse, a yard. Maybe a car too. Maybe a long, sleek Jaguar, maybe not.

The squad car went on and on, three hundred yards up. It reached the hut. Slowed to a crawl, then stopped uncertainly. At one stage it backed off a few yards. Then went back to its original position. No-one could see what Carrick could see. Nothing happened for half a minute. The marksman came up to the squad car, stood behind it, sighted up.

Carrick got out and called. Seemed to call hullo or is anyone in there? Or something like that. They couldn't hear well. No reply. No-one came out of the hut. Or, no-one that the watchers down below could have seen.

Carrick called again. Still no reply.

Carrick took a few steps from the car, edging this way and that. Crouching, left hand on his weapon. He stopped, as if he had seen something.

Had someone appeared? They did not know. Carrick seemed to be speaking. His mouth opened and shut a few times. He nodded too. Looked back at Duckworth.

He said something to the marksman. Who nodded.

Then he disappeared.

Nothing happened for half a minute. The Army man had positioned himself behind Carrick's car, leaning across the roof, aiming at something. Perhaps a doorway. Carrick did not reappear. Perhaps he'd gone inside the shack.

Nothing happened for half a minute.

The reservist looked at them. Sort of shrugged with his shoulders and the carbine. Then sighted up again.

Then there was one sharp *crack*! Although faint, as if muffled, as if inside.

The marksman looked down at them. Shrugged again, raising his rifle, as if nonplussed. Did not know what had happened.

Then Carrick came out, spoke to him.

The rifleman went into the hut. Or behind it. Not clear what was going on. Carrick simply stood where he was, holding the Glock at his side, down one leg. He was left-handed. With the other hand he wiped his face, perhaps at perspiration. Then glanced at his hand, as if to see. See what?

The second car started up, the one driven by Max Kruger.

'You want me to go up, sir?'

'We'll all go up.'

They got in with Max, even Daisy.

When she'd told her father she was going to join the police, he had said: 'Good, but understand one thing first, lass. You are going to be asked to do some bad things.'

'I know, Dad.'

'And see some bad things.'

'I know, Dad.'

She had to go, if she were ever to make it as a cop.

Whitton said nothing as they drove up.

They stopped behind the first car. Nothing much to see—a small shed at the back, now not much more than bits of rusted iron, cracked and open and dilapidated. And an old outhouse that looked like an original. Some sort of clothesline, but it was rotten and drooping and disintegrating. As they looked, it simply gave way, frayed beyond all hope. No other vehicle was there. So how did Feeny get there? The fresh tyre tracks must have been left by someone who'd dropped him at the shack, then left. Obviously, he had an accomplice. Or, at least a friend, who was trying to look after him.

The Army man came out, shaking his head.

'He had a weapon?' Whitton asked.

No answer.

Whitton looked at Carrick. 'He shot himself?'

Carrick shook his head. 'No, sir.'

'Is he dead?'

'Yeah, he's dead.'

'What happened?'

Carrick was looking away, over the hills in the dusty haze of summer. Up high were thin white clouds like vapour trails looking for some sort of meaningful pattern.

'Carrick, I'm speaking to you.'

'I shot him, sir.'

'You shot Feeny?'

'Yes, sir.'

'Did he have a weapon?'

'No, sir.'

'Did he challenge you?'

'No, sir.'

'Sergeant Carrick, look at me. Why did you shoot him?'

'A piece of filth like that,' he said.

He was shaking so bad he was rigid. His gaze was rigid.

They all went into the shack.

It had two rooms, as they'd thought. One contained an old rusty stretcher bed and a kitchen, a mess room years ago. It was indeed a mess. Old pieces of furniture and bits of fallen timber and yellowed newspapers and empty food cans and an old mackintosh hanging on a nail. A fairly new travelling bag was sitting on two broken chairs. It was unzipped but the lid was down. Even so, it seemed to contain nothing but clothing. Beside it was a satchel. It too was open and they could see, without checking, that a laptop was inside.

Feeny was lying in the debris and dirt.

He lay partly on one side and partly on his back, holding his guts. His eyes were open, but nothing looked out at them.

At first sight they thought he was dead, but his body spasmed. Then it was still. They stood around, staring in the smutty light.

The body spasmed again. He'd been trying to stop the blood. It was still seeping through his fingers, a few inches above the navel. The bullet may have hit the aorta. When that goes, you go too.

They waited.

What seemed to be another spasm began, or they thought it began. No more came. Brett Feeny didn't moan or groan or say any last words. He just stopped living.

No-one thought of calling an ambulance.

They stood around thinking and not thinking. No sound except Whitton's breathing. He was a noisy breather, six feet tall and sixteen stone.

Suddenly he said, 'Leave the room, Constable Cornford.'

She nearly jumped. 'Oh, it's quite all right, sir. Dad said I would see—'

'Senior Constable Kruger?'

'Sir?'

'Escort Constable Cornford to the car she came in. Then come back.'

'Yes, sir.'

At first, she didn't move. Max had to nudge her. Then she obeyed, walking out smartly, arms straight down. Like a toy soldier.

They waited for Max to come back. Whitton was still thinking.

At last, he said, 'What am I going to do? Any ideas?'

He looked at one after the other.

'Anyone?'

Max made a suggestion: 'Perhaps Sergeant Carrick *thought* he had a weapon, sir?'

Ted Whitton gave it some thought. At last he spoke.

'Yeah, it'll have to be something like that.'

Carrick might have deliberately killed Feeny in order to shut him up, but no-one could prove it. Carrick was suspended from duty pending an inquiry, then removed to another post a long way from Wagga Wagga. Separately, Whitton was chastised for his misbehaviour toward Harry Becker, who had already dropped the charges against him. Or, to put it another way, Anna had said he'd dropped the charges, so he had to go along with that. Whitton became a reasonably decent sort of man. Changed his tune, showed consideration for others, including his staff. Went out of his way to be friendly with Anna and Becker.

She tended to be tolerant toward him.

Even thanked him for his pursuit of Feeny. Who, it turned out, belonged to a ring of paedophiles, which distributed photographs of their victims online. Some of the police could not bear to look at the stuff on the laptop. It made them sick. They had to call in a couple of specialists from Sydney, who said they'd seen it all before.

As for that strange woman, Carla Verducci, she was never charged with anything. The police could not disprove her story that she'd been asked to say whether Roberta was a prospective movie star. That she had no other part in the affair. And, there was still the mysterious Fat Man. Was he involved in the whole sordid business of kidnapping Roberta Becker? Was there a real Fat Man or someone pretending to be him? Perhaps the Fat Man was a fat woman? No-one could say.

There was one bright aspect of this episode. Daisy Cornford was visited by the superintendent next day—and congratulated on her contribution. He put a hand on her shoulder, something a male officer should never do to a female member, and said: 'I believe you are responsible for the breakthrough that led to Feeny's location?'

'Yes, sir, I had an idea, you see.'

'Good for you. That's what the force needs, isn't it? People with ideas.'

'Yes, sir.'

'Well done, constable.'

'Thank you, sir.'
'How's your father? Still happy in Tumut?'
'Oh, yes, sir.'
'Remember me to him will, you?'
'Yes, sir, I will.'

Terry the Terrible, as Anna called him, became eighteen in February. On that day, Anna gave him the Harley Davidson. He'd already learned to ride it on the farm and had a licence to ride. Next month he received a letter from the Army. They wanted to see him, have a look at him. He was told to be at the recruiting office in Sydney at 0900 hours on the following Wednesday. He was there almost an hour early. Got the train down the day before. Got into Central about five. Found the Y.M.C.A and had a good night's sleep. Went to bed about nine; slept so well that he was awake about six. One of his mates had applied last year and had turned up ten minutes after the appointed time. Told he was too late. When he'd protested that the train had broken down, he was told the Army does not wait for any man. Nor any train.

Terry arrived about an hour early. The door was locked. He hung around staring at passing buses and people going nowhere, by the looks on their faces. They were all in a hurry and seemed to be thinking of anything but work. Not for him the commercial life. He was going to be a soldier. Suddenly, the door opened. A smart-looking corporal looked out and said, 'Name?'

The interview went badly, at least from his point of view. The corporal asked him a lot of questions about his background. He said his father had died in a motor accident. His stepfather had been in the police, but was now a farmer. His mother, who had also been a police officer, had famously killed a dangerous criminal in a gunfight in—then he realised he was talking about the wrong mother. Any sports? He'd been a footballer, having scored two tries against Junee in the last game last year. In reserve grade.

'Do some running, do you?' asked the non-com.

'Yes, sir, miles and miles, up and down lanes. Even climbed The Rock.'

'The Rock?'

'It's down past Wagga.'

'I know where it is,' the corporal said. 'How long did it take?'

'Ah, well, one and half hours.'

'One and a half hours?'

'Yes, sir. Well, pretty much like that.'

The corporal stiffened a little. 'I was never able to do it under one hour fifty-two,' he said.

Terry's heart sank. He'd be shot for lying to an officer, who wasn't an officer. The corporal was not impressed. 'Honesty never hurt a good soldier, Mr Sheldrake,' he said. 'That will be all. If we like the look of you, you'll be told to come in for a medical and a physical. Psychological too,' he added.

'Psychological?'

'To see whether you have any personality problems, like inaccuracy.'

To his surprise, Terry was accepted. Just what the Army wanted. Smart, silly, boastful, a reckless show-off and an expert with a lever-action Winchester. He'd make a perfect grunt, as the Americans called them.

One day after Roberta turned seven, they were surprised to see a car drive in off the highway and park near the old pepper tree. Perhaps for a little shade. It was a smart car with a Canberra number plate. Two men inside. They saw her watching. Two doors opened, and they got out.

'Mummy? Who are those men?'

Anna came to the window. 'Get back, darling, and call Daddy.'

'Where is he?'

'Talking to Hermie. They're getting ready to sow.'

Harry Becker had been late this year. It had been a cold winter, and maize did not like cold. He'd had to wait until early September to start. Any later and he'd have no hope of getting a second crop in January or February. Especially if it did not rain.

Anna recognised one of them—Breckenshaw. The other man she'd never met, but had seen him on the job in Canberra. His name was Carl Embury, a sergeant then, working in the prime minister's protection detail. He'd shot dead a man outside Parliament House, during a demonstration. The man had been wielding a sword. Embury had gone places since then.

She watched them approach. This, she knew, was the end.

These two men had Nemesis written all over them.

CHAPTER 29

When Becker arrived, the visitors were standing on the front verandah. Anna was leaning against a post, arms folded. The other two seemed pretty awkward about the whole business. Breckenshaw was a self-important sort of man—not so much in stature. Average enough in his own way, trying to be impressive and failing. Anna looked as though about to hit him. Embury was relaxed and less talkative. Smiled as Becker approached. Breckenshaw scowled, as if Becker were interrupting a private conversation.

'What's going on?' he asked.

Breckenshaw opened his mouth to answer, but Anna got in first.

'These two characters say I killed a man.'

Becker didn't jump, cry out, remonstrate. Nor did he leap to her defence. He was that kind of man—phlegmatic. He'd been a cop for twelve years, and after that nothing was new. No matter how bad, he'd seen it all before. Or, if he hadn't seen it, he'd heard about it. Or, failing that, he'd expected something like it to turn up one day. Habitually, he never jumped to conclusions.

He simply said, 'Yeah?'

'Yes,' she said.

The senior man held out a hand. 'Carl Embury,' he said.

'Chief Inspector Embury, from Canberra,' Anna explained. They shook.

'And the other one,' she said, 'is Inspector Breckenshaw, who went to water after I shot Palfreyman dead.'

Breckenshaw tried to protest, but she ignored him.

'Shot him on this little creep's command. Against my better judgement.'

'Yeah?' Becker had heard all about it, but played dumb.

'And he's never stopped blaming me for that whole fucked-up incident.'

Breckenshaw was furious. About to harangue her, but Embury got in first.

'Now, now, we're not here to discuss that matter.'

'She can't be allowed to get away with slander like that!'

'Calm down, understand?'

Breckenshaw sniffed and snuffled, like an outraged terrier.

'What's going on?' Becker asked again.

'Just a minute,' Anna said. The door was ajar; two big brown eyes were peeping.

'Darling? Don't you have homework to do?'

'Who are those men?'

'Only a couple from Canberra. Go to your room and do your homework. Okay?'

'I'm going to Canberra one day.'

'I thought you were going to Mars?'

'I don't think I'd like all that dust.'

'Scram!'

She ran, laughing.

'Aren't you going to invite us in?' Breckenshaw asked.

'Invite a moral defective like you? Why should I?'

Embury almost chuckled. 'Miss Babchuk—' he began.

'Mrs Becker,' she corrected.

'Yes, of course, Mrs Becker. There's been an important development.'

'In what?'

'A certain person has died.'

'Who?'

'A man named Giorgio Adamo. You may have known him as George Adams, when you worked in Canberra.'

'Adams? That piece of shit?'

'Yes, well, he was not the most admirable of men, but he paid the price. Sentenced to life imprisonment for the deaths of—'

'Christine Billings, Tony Russo, Vincent Torrence or Torrenza, and my buddy, Anna Politis!'

'Not Miss Politis.'

'What?'

She knew that was true; Adams had not killed Polly Politis. That was the kid, Branko Medich. And she'd killed Medich, in this very house, eleven years ago. Not in this exact one, but in the one that had stood on the same spot before it was demolished and replaced. Outwardly, they were almost identical.

She played dumb. 'He didn't?'

'No, it was proven that he did not do that.'

'Then who did?'

'That's the reason for this visit.'

Breckenshaw was smiling, oily with satisfaction.

'Well?'

Embury looked around, perhaps checking the door, open a crack.

He was a fairly big man, an amiable sort of man with a flexible face—one that could burst into a clown's face if you dressed him up for a kids' party. And would say 'Boo!' to all the kids, sing silly songs, maybe even break into a goofy dance and trip over his own feet. Courteous to a fault. Looked like the kind you would find running a department store, more than a cop. Or, perhaps an actor, who could change his spots on command.

He would have been in his mid-forties. In his spare time, he did a lot of work for the Salvation Army. His father had been a brigadier in the Army, back when young Carl used to play trumpet in the Army's band, standing on street corners. The girls in purple bonnets singing songs of praise.

'Adams made a confession before he died.'

'In jail?'

'Yes, to a priest.'

'I thought the Catholics never divulged a confession?'

'This priest thought it was his duty to inform the civil authorities, now that the prisoner was dead.'

'Go on.'

'He said the job was done by a young fellow named Medich, Branko Medich.'

'Medich?'

'You know the name?'

'I'm acquainted with certain persons of that name.'

'In Melbourne?'

'Yes, I was pursuing inquiries about a creature known only as the Fat Man, who has persistently tried to kill me.'

'The Fat Man?'

'Yes.'

'Really? To kill you?'

She nodded. 'He nearly succeeded.'

'Really?'

'You want to see my scars?' She began to pull up her shirt.

'No, no, please, that's all right.'

'Why is it all right?'

'Oh, look, I'm sorry, I didn't mean to say—'

'What did you mean to say?'

He wriggled a bit, looked away at the big peppercorn tree. It was bright green despite the drought. They were tough trees, imported from South America. When everything else was dead, that tree would still be there— bright, gnarled and unyieldingly happy.

'As a result, we are looking at that case again.'

'Please get to the point.'

'A motor cycle belonging to Branko Medich was found at this address—'

'Outside the fence up there, by two Aboriginal kids who took it to Wybilonga. This is well known to the State police.'

'Yes, well, it seems strangely coincidental that they found it here.'

'Why?'

'Well, it's more than coincidental, isn't it? Your partner was killed by Medich in Canberra. And the bike he owned subsequently turned up here?'

'So what? Coincidences happen.'

Embury flexed his shoulders, working up to the big question. Breckenshaw was delighted. He was going to get even at last. This bitch had humiliated him at the official inquiry. Accusing him of being a nervous Nellie, who should never have been put in charge of that problem with Palfreyman. She, a sergeant, saying a thing like that. He was a career policeman. He drove a desk in Canberra, doing his job. Since that inquiry, they'd put him in charge of cold cases. To get rid of him, get him out of the way. A humiliation, until he'd come across the case of Branko Medich. The Federal Police had known Medich had killed Ritzi Carbone in Melbourne, but they could not connect him to the killing of Evelyn Crowley and Polly Politis in Canberra. Not until Russo had confessed in hospital, after Adams had shot him in an effort to silence him but failed to kill him. Russo—the driver during the botched hit on Evelyn in which her daughter had been killed—had revealed it all. But that was long ago.

'And then Medich disappeared,' Embury said.

'People do disappear, don't they?'

'Yes, but—'

'But what?'

'A man known as Alfredo Scarafini disappeared at the same time.'

'And so?'

'According to our information, Medich was employed to kill Scarafini.'

'Yeah? Who told you that?'

'I'm not at liberty to say.'

She stared at Embury. Someone had talked. Who? She couldn't place it just yet, but it would come to her. She still had friends in Canberra.

'And Scarafini was last seen in Griffith.'

'So?'

'He told friends he was going to see your husband.'

'Really?'

Becker was startled. His heart was jumping. He wasn't feeling so good these days. Too much hard yacker on the farm. Too much good food. Too much sour cream. He sat on one of the deck chairs out front. They had such chairs on each verandah. They had four verandahs. In his off days, he tended to sit there in a chair and watch the world go by.

'What is it?' Anna asked. 'Harry? What is it?'

'I'm okay,' he said.

Embury pressed on. 'Did he come to this house?'

Becker considered denying it but didn't. Rubbed his head, thinking about it. Ran fingers through his hair, the way old Bert next door used to run his fingers. So that his grizzled hair always looked a fright. Probably hadn't had the motherly love of a comb in many years. Perhaps he was going the same way as Bert.

Blue came around a corner, his nails scratching on the hardwood boards. The dog looked at the group, did not pause or start back at the sight. Came up, rheumy old eyes flicking here and there. Then stood beside Becker. Anna was going to tell him to clear out, but did not get the chance.

'Yes,' Becker said.

'What?' Embury said.

'Yes, he came here.'

Anna was stunned. She hadn't expected this. Everything was about to unravel.

'Harry,' she said, a hand on him.

'Scarafini came here?' Embury asked.

'Yeah, he wanted money.'

'Money?'

'To get away. To America, I think. He was sick.'

'Did you give him money?'

'I would have, if only to get rid of him.'

'Why?'

'He was on the run. From the Mafia. They were going to kill him.'

'Why?'

'He knew too much about what was going on at the bank.'

'The Royal Bank?'

'Yeah. He had a brother named Giancarlo and an uncle named Ennio, small-time crooks down in Melbourne. They had a finger on Dennis Crowley, a big operator at the Royal Bank. Had him laundering Mafia money, sending it to Italy. Suddenly they were big fellas, talking to Mafia bosses. They couldn't keep their mouths shut. Even talked to an undercover cop. You know how it is.'

Embury nodded.

'They were a problem. Uncle Ennio and that blabbermouth Giancarlo were killed.'

'And Alfredo had to get out? Of Melbourne?'

'Yeah.'

'And Mrs Crowley? She knew what her husband was doing?'

'Yeah.'

'You tried to get her out of Canberra? With some help from us?'

'Yeah, in a big hurry, but it failed. I failed.'

'You retired to Wagga?'

Becker didn't answer. He looked bad. Still rubbing his head. His hair was a mess. He was a mess. Anastacia could see that he was going to spill the lot. He was finished with running.

'But Alfredo turned up. Did you give him the money?'

'I would have but this kid arrived. On a bike, looking for him.'

Anna's heart stopped. He was confessing. She didn't know what to do. They were closing in. She was about to be arrested for murder. They would not be able to prove it was murder, unless Harry talked.

'You mean Medich?'

'I didn't know his name then.'

'How did you know his name?'

Becker looked about without seeing anyone. 'Well, as it happened my cousin, Barry Barnes, who was a local cop, told me. Apparently, he checked with the Victorian police and found the name. Of the owner.'

'Of the bike?'

'Yeah.'

'What happened?'

'Medich walked in. While I was talking to Alfredo.'

'Alfredo Scarafini?'

'He had a gun.'

'Medich did?'

'Yeah.'

'What did he do?'

'Well, he talked for a while about how he'd been following Alfredo. All the way from Melbourne. Said someone in Griffith had given him away.'

'Given Alfredo away?'

'Yeah, he said you can't trust no-one, especially a dame. That's why Alfredo had fled Griffith.'

'Then what?'

'He shot him.'

'Medich shot Scarafini?'

'Yes.'

'How many times?'

'Three in the guts.'

'Good God,' Embury said.

Becker sat with his head down, a hand still to his head, scratching. The other hand hung down, almost touched the boards. He looked frightful. It was all over. They could not lie about it any longer. Becker was trying to protect Anna.

'Then what?'

'Well, late that day, I took the body to the river.'

Anna shook him. 'Harry, no, don't say that.'

'Please, Mrs Becker, let him speak.' Embury turned back to Becker. 'Why did you do that?'

'I didn't want anyone to know what had happened. You see, I was married then to a lovely woman. She had two children of her own staying with us. If she'd seen the body, if the police had come, if the children had seen it, or seen the police searching around—'

'They would have been horrified?'

'Yeah, my wife, I mean Robyn, she would have wondered what sort of man she'd—she'd—'

'Married?'

'A good man,' Anna said.

She'd pulled up another chair to sit close, holding him.

'So, you disposed of the body? In the river?'

'Yeah.'

'You carried it in your car?'

'Yeah.'

'Which car was that?'

'The—' For a moment he couldn't think of the name. 'The B.M.W.'

Breckenshaw was grinning with delight. This man, Becker, was going to pieces.

'Yes, but what happened to Medich?'

'Medich? Oh, I—I don't know. He just went off.'

'And left his bike?'

'Yeah, well, I don't know what happened to him.'

'He shot a man dead in your house and then went off without killing you. And abandoned his bike?'

'Yeah, well, he'd shot a woman in bed with me in Canberra, but didn't shoot me. Must have been that kind of guy. He wasn't being paid to shoot me, so—'

They waited.

Anna was watching him, knowing they did not believe a word. He was going to get into serious trouble. Why would Medich leave his bike?

'It is not true,' she said.

'What did you say, Mrs Becker?'

'I said it's all right.'

'Before that, please.'

'I disposed of the body.' Then she added, 'Both bodies.'

'Both?'

'Yes, Medich shot Scarafini. That was before I arrived. I'd been following Medich. You see, Polly Politis was my buddy in Canberra. And that animal Medich had killed her. I went to Melbourne, met up with some old mates, bikies. They knew he'd killed that grape-grower down in Melbourne. Knew where he lived. I went to that joint, but he'd gone—off to Griffith, someone said. Following Alfredo Scarafini. When I got to Griffith he'd cleared out in a hurry.'

'Who'd cleared out?'

'Alfredo, I figured he'd go to Harry to get some money, get out of the country. I came here, to the old house. When I arrived, Medich had already found Alfredo. Had already killed him and was pointing his gun at Harry. He'd even said, "So long, pal." So I shot him.'

'Killed him?'

'Yeah, with one shot.'

'With your service pistol?'

'With my own pistol, a Colt.'

'You had your own pistol, not the standard issue?'

'The standard issue then was a Smith and Wesson. I did not like it. It was old and slow and unreliable. The Colt was even older, but more reliable. And it didn't miss at fifty yards.'

'I see.'

'Then I disposed of both bodies.'

'Where?'

'I will not say.'

'Why not?'

'There are no bodies now.'

'I have to insist, Mrs Becker.'

'And I am telling you you don't need to know.'

'If you have committed a crime—'

'Don't give me a lecture. I shot Medich in the course of duty.'

'That's true,' Becker said. 'She saved my life.'

He'd raised his head now. Felt a little better. Embury's tone had changed. Not so amiable, efficiently quizzical.

'Did you warn Medich, Mrs Becker?'

Harry Becker intervened.

'There was no time. His finger was on the trigger. He'd just said, So long, pal. He meant it. I could see it in his eyes. Everything was going to end. My marriage, my life. And if my wife had walked in, he would have killed her too. Perhaps the children, if they'd heard the shots. All my hopes to make a go of it here—'

'I see.'

'I was going to report it,' Anna said. 'But, when I saw his face— Harry went to a window, the kitchen window in the old house. It's a different layout now, but much the same to look at. He was looking out the window, watching his wife and the children and the dog playing. The dog chasing a ball, the boy falling in the creek, everyone laughing. Everyone happy. He would have lost everything.'

'I see,' Embury said again. He'd folded his arms.

Breckenshaw was worried. Embury should be delighted. Everyone should be delighted. They'd nailed her down at last. She'd killed a man. She'd disposed of two bodies. She'd not informed her superiors. The stupid bitch.

'So I took the bodies in the boot of my car. It was a hire car. A big one, a big boot.'

'Where did you take them?' Breckenshaw asked.

'I've already answered that question.'

She was rubbing Becker's arm and shoulder, both shoulders. Holding him, leaning across. Loving him.

'So,' Embury said, 'you did this to save Mr Becker from the distress that'd follow a police presence? Distress to his wife and family?'

'And seeing the bodies. One on the couch, one on the floor.'

'No-one saw them? None of the family?'

'No-one but Harry and me.'

'Was there any blood?'

'A few drops, on the carpet.' Becker said. 'I told my wife at the time, Robyn. My second wife, you see—'

'Yes, yes.'

'Told her that the old man had had a nose bleed. Nothing serious.'

'She accepted that?'

'Yes.'

'I see.'

Breckenshaw was worried.

'The bike, what did you think you were going to do with the bike?'

Anna answered. 'I left that to Harry to dispose of.'

'But, he did not?'

'He was going to take it to the river, but some kids nicked it.'

She was trying to kiss Becker.

He leaned over and let her. He smiled. She was a good woman, as good as Robyn. He'd always known that what she'd done for him was beyond all obligation. She should have done her duty at the time, reported in. Let the law take its course. But Robyn the Good would have taken it badly. Her children would have been dismayed, revolted. A good marriage destroyed.

Now, he didn't know what to do.

He and Anna were in serious trouble.

Breckenshaw was grinning like the cat that'd swallowed the cream.

That's what Iris Becker used to say used to say when he was a kid. He'd never known what cat it was. They didn't have a cat. Nor did they have a dog. He'd say it would be nice to have a dog, something to play with, take for walks. Go rabbiting. She'd rub her head and say: No, not a dog, all that barking and the cost and the smell. Having to pick up—

For a while Embury said nothing. Hands now in his pockets, thinking.

'I'm sorry,' Anna said, 'but I had to think of the greater good.'

'Yes,' he said. His voice was soft, sure, precise. It was a smooth voice.

They waited. The front door had opened, several inches. Roberta was peeping out, smiling. 'Mummy, I can spell Woolloomooloo backwards!'

'Darling, please, not now!'

The door shut tight.

Embury was still thinking. At last he said: 'Very well.'

They were surprised.

'Thank you for your assistance, both of you. I'm not sure how this will turn out. Not reporting you'd killed someone in the line of duty, Mrs Becker. Disposing of a body, but—'

He was making moves like a man about to depart.

Breckenshaw was puzzled. Things were not going right.

Becker finally raised his head. 'Do you need a written statement?'

'Not at this stage, no— No, I'll talk to someone.'

'Talk?' Breckenshaw said.

'That should be be all for now,' Embury said.

Stepped forward and shook hands quite formally. First with Becker, then with Anna. Almost with a click of the heels. At the same time, winking with both eyes. Not exactly winking, but a friendly sort of squeeze. As if to say, *Trust me*.

'Thank you both for your cooperation, Mr and Mrs Becker.'

He stepped off the verandah briskly, set off for the official car. A sure-footed man, deft. Possibly quite deft on a ballroom floor. Breckenshaw dashed after him, hissing.

'You can't leave it like that!'

'That's all for now,' Embury said to him.

'What? What?'

The sun had shifted; the day was growing hot. He went to the driver's door, opened it. They thought he was going to drive, but he stood by the car, looking back.

'Breckenshaw?' he said.

'What?' The inspector ran this way and that, as though he'd forgotten his hat.

'Get in,' Embury said.

'You want me to drive?'

'Get in the car.'

'What? You can't speak to me like that.'

'Is there a problem?'

Nothing came of the visit.

No-one asked her to come in for an interview. She was not charged. Embury must have had a chat to someone in the Federal Police's legal department. What would stand up in court and what would not? Very little, apparently. Not reporting a death and disposing of a body without notifying the authorities were not hanging offences. More like breaking rules or customs or official procedures than any criminal code. Perhaps her record in the Feds still stood her in good stead. She had been a top sergeant, a really brave and productive field officer. A bit of a tearaway, but not exactly out of control. She should never have resigned. Could have been an inspector by now. Coulda been someone. Maybe a superintendent one day, quoted on television almost every night on how a certain investigation was going. She wasn't, but she was not complaining.

There was a real surprise on another day.

They came home and found the black car standing by the front gate. It was Saturday and they'd left Roberta with Wendy in town.

They pulled up and waited. It was certainly the old Fairlane, the long black box-shaped Ford. Becker got out and opened the gate for the Nissan. At the same time the driver's door of the Ford opened, the young man got out. Looking a bit sheepish. Then the girl appeared on the other side. Both stood still for a moment, as if waiting to be formally received.

'Hullo,' Becker said.

'*Deda* sent us to tell you,' the boy said.

Anna had never heard his name. The girl, she recalled, was Ivanka, no doubt the daughter of Ivan. She and Becker walked over, puzzled.

'*Deda*?' Anna said.

'*Deda*, he is dead now.'

'Your grandfather is dead?'

'Yes,' both sibilated, standing to attention and shamefaced. A soft breeze was wafting the girl's skirt. Both were squinting. Looking into the sun.

'When?'

'Oh, two or three weeks.'

'Josep is dead?' Anna said.

'Yes,' they said. The boy said: 'He wanted to tell you he was sorry.'

'Sorry?'

The girl said: 'For what Nerida did.'

'Oh, that's all over now. The court let her off once again, but with a warning. Never to teach again.'

'She has always been a problem,' the boy said.

'She is your aunt?'

'Yes, she is our *tetka*.'

'How is she?'

'Oh, Nerida is working on the railways now.'

'The railways?'

'At Spencer street.'

'What does she do at Spencer street?'

'Oh, she is a personnel officer.'
'And what do you do?'
'I drive trains.'
'Really? Is that fun?'
He did not answer.
'And you, Ivanka?'
'Oh, I am at university.'
'Melbourne? Doing Law?'
She was surprised. 'How did you know?'
'You walked like a lawyer through the park one night.'
'How does a lawyer walk?'
'Judiciously, especially after dark.'
She giggled.
Anna was impressed. 'Is that expensive? Doing Law?'
'Oh, no—' She glanced at her brother. '*Brat* is paying.'
Anna smiled. 'Is he?'
The girl nodded.
'Would you like to come in? You must have travelled a long way?'
'Thank you, but it is all right,' the boy said. '*Deda* said to take the car, and come to you.'
'Personally,' the girl added.
'It's kind of you to do so. I am sorry that he is dead.'
'No, no, he said he is happy to go.'
'How is your father, Ivanka?'
'Oh, *Otac* is okay.'
'What is he doing now?'
'Oh, he is working for another man, rendering.'
'Rendering walls with cement? Coloured cement?'
'Yes.'
'No hard feelings?'
She hesitated. 'He says you are a *smaj*.'

'A *smaj*? What is that?
'It means dragon.'
'A dragon?'
'Yes, he says no-one can beat you, even Saint George.'
They laughed.

Again they invited them in, but they insisted that they had to return to Melbourne. It was well after lunch.

'You have three or four hours before sunset,' Becker said.

They thought about that.

'The sun has set on *Deda*,' the boy said.

'*Bogda mu dusu prosti*,' the girl sad.

'Tell me, why did Josep wait outside our school?'

The boy and girl glanced at each other. The boy replied awkwardly: 'He told Nerida that she must not take the little girl.'

'Not take?'

'Nerida said the little girl was so beautiful, she would love to have her.'

'So, your grandfather was trying to stop her? Day after day? By waiting outside the school? Reminding her?'

'Yes, every day.'

'That worried him, because of her past history? Stealing children?'

They looked at each other. Perhaps neither had thought of their aunt as a kidnapper.

Anna explained: 'Taking the child of another woman?'

They had no answer to that. Looked at each other dismally. Ivanka spoke again.

'Grandfather said to say the family apologises.'

'We accept.'

They shuffled and looked worse for the experience.

'We will go home now,' the boy said.

'Thank you,' the girl said.

'Have a good trip,' Anna said. 'And thank you for coming.'

They watched as the long black car started up and turned and made its way back toward Wagga. Seemed to be taking the long way around, ignorant of the short cuts through to Tarcutta and also to Culcairn.

It was a hot day, but the old Ford was air-conditioned.

'Did you hear that, Harry? Her brother is paying her fees?'

'What's that?'

'What are you looking at?'

'There's a man. Over there in the lane. Got his hands up, looking.'

'Looking?'

'Through binoculars.'

'I can't see any binoculars.'

'Old Bert said he saw a man doing that, just before the bomb went off.'

'That was years ago.'

'Now he's looking at us, looking at him.'

'Do you recognise him?'

▲

CHAPTER 30

Late that year, Harry Becker received a thick envelope in his mail. Inside was a sheaf of papers—ten pages typewritten. The covering letter was brief:

'You once asked me whether I had ever written anything worth a pinch of shit. I wrote this many years ago, when I worked for the Navy. They sent me to Vietnam to shoot some film on our people trying to do a job there. When I returned, I had ideas of getting out of journalism, setting myself up as a writer. I wrote this story, which was a real story, not what journalists call a story, just a factual report of events. I tried to add to the facts some impressions. What I felt and what the men I met felt, thought about it. Then gave up. I never had it published. Perhaps I realised that you were right. I was nothing more than a hack journalist.'

It was signed, Philip McNiven.

Becker was surprised. McNiven had been the editor of the *The Riverina Bulletin*. And his father, old Angus McNiven, was the managing editor, a family business. Or, more correctly, an independent newspaper. Several of the old families of the district had money in it then. Now, it was just one link in the chain of regional papers owned by a dying media conglomerate.

It was late in the morning. The sun was high. A perfectly still day. The mist had lifted from the big paddock, the one in which the ladies grazed contentedly. Three crows sat on a wire fence, arguing. One flapping its wings. Tumbling off. Then it'd get back up, still squawking. The other two, no doubt its parents, were not impressed. They were not going to teach the stupid kid to fly.

He began to read. The story was perfectly typed, back in those days a rare quality in a journalist, even if he were a naval officer. The pages were high-quality parchment, though fading—not to white, but to an antique sort of gold.

The title was simple enough: *Dust Off*.

They sent him to Vietnam to get some footage on what the Navy was doing there. He flew on a chartered Qantas aircraft to Saigon, caught an Army bus from Tan Son Nhut airport to the Buis, a single officers' billet in downtown Saigon. The Buis may have been smart in the French colonial day, a pale-yellow concrete building, but now it was as sparse and steamy as a public bath-house—nothing exotic or even eastern about it. After he checked in, he walked to the Majestic Hotel, three or four blocks away.

The streets were tumultuous—constant streams of traffic, small Renault taxis, the three-wheeler trucks, tiny Honda motorbikes usually carrying two, often a girl in flowing *ao dai* perched on the pillion. Pushcarts plodded along, old women carried cans of cooked food hanging from long poles. US Army trucks rolled by, loaded with uniformed men clutching M16 carbines at the ready. Pedestrians teemed everywhere.

In 1968 Saigon was a shoddy, stifling place, crammed with ref-ugees from the North. Some sat on the pavements, hands out, begging. And it was dangerous. Beware of pickpockets, he had been warned. Also, beware of people carrying satchels. A girl walking behind you, a student, might be a suicide bomber.

A small Renault taxi crawled beside him, the driver looking at him, saying something. Kramer waved him away. He found the Majestic, then found Hurford in a room upstairs. Hurford was a petty officer photographer. A lot of his time was spent taking still shots of men and their machines to send back to Canberra. To be used as publicity shots in home-town papers.

'How'd you get here, sir?'

'I walked.'

'You walked from the Buis? In uniform?'

'It wasn't far. Thought I'd see the town.'

'Jesus, you could've been shot or kidnapped.'

'It's that bad?'

'Haven't you heard of Tet?'

'That was early in the year.'

'They're still shootin' people. Just the other day a bloke jumped off a bike, ran up to a Yank, and shot him dead in the street.'

'It must be my lucky day.'

'You ought to be careful. This ain't Canberra, you know.' Hurford was a street kid from Marrickville who'd made a living in television with an Bolex movie camera, chasing fire engines, ambulances, and police cars through the streets of Sydney. He'd joined Navy public relations a year ago to see some action. After four months in Vietnam, he hated it.

'If you want to see the sights, take a bus. They're not goin' to bomb their own people.'

'All right, let's see the sights.'

It was still possible to see how Saigon had been years ago, before the French had given up the fight against the Viet Minh. It had wide streets lined with trees, old colonial buildings, flags flying from masts, exclusive mansions behind white railings. The bus wound its way through the Cholon market and along the docks, ships at every berth, the wharves stacked with crates. G.I.s in trucks drove away tons of materiel, guns, shells, napalm, avgas, as well as Campbell's soup, Budweiser beer, baseball bats, condoms—everything an occupying army needed. They returned along a thin street, stopped outside some trees which had once been in a tiny park. There was no grass now, just worn dirt.

'This is the P.X. You want anythin', sir?'

'Yes, shaving cream.'

'You can get anythin' here.'

'I'm not American.'

'It don't matter. Anyone can go in as long as you're not a slope.'

'A what?'

'A slopehead, an Asian.'

They walked through the P.X. It had everything, not just foodstuffs and personal items like shaving cream, but television sets, Hawaiian shirts, sporting goods, pharmaceuticals, booze, and hosiery. It could have been a shopping centre in San Diego or Phoenix or even Montgomery, Alabama. Not a Vietnamese was in sight. G.I.s and marines in fatigues, carbines slung over their shoulders, strolled about, always in pairs, their eyes habitually sweeping. It was war, even here in Montgomery, Alabama. Hurford bought a carton of cigarettes and four pair of stockings.

Kramer was surprised. 'I didn't think you smoked?'

'These're not for me.'

'And the stockings?'

'For a girl I know.'

They walked out of the P.X. 'What now, sir? Want a drink?' Kramer looked at his watch. It was not yet five o'clock but he felt awful. 'I could do with some sleep.'

'You can kip on my bed.'

He flopped on Hurford's bed, the room getting darker and slightly cooler. From somewhere came the smell of a tidal canal, then a man calling in Vietnamese. Distantly, he heard a radio, a woman singing about the red lilies of Hue Palace—far away, in another time…

They spent the next two weeks filming Australians patrolling the perimeter of Nui Dat, tanks sitting in ditches, their guns used as artillery, talking to men eating under canvas, riding around in choppers, doing resupplies in Tai Ninh province, unloading Armalites to emplaced Arvin units, the blades whirring overhead, not stopping for fear the Cong out there in the bush would hit them.

Then a week with R.A.N. helicopter crews at Camp Bear Cat in Bien Hoa Province, home of the U.S. Army 135th Assault Helicopter Company, inserting Filipino troops into suspected V.C. zones, dropping them and getting out fast, then going back when the Filipino major radioed they'd found nothing. The Filipinos never did find anything. Everyone said they wouldn't fight and the Cong knew it.

The 'otherness' of war was sometimes joyful, sometimes disgusting. One night in the mess a young U.S. lieutenant, a slim blond from Virginia who looked as though he wasn't yet out of college, was relating, spluttering Jim Beam in a voice close to hysteria, how his chopper had been flying over a paddy field. The left gunner had called him on the intercom:

'They's a guy down ther-yah a-holdin' somethang, suh.'

'Yeah? So what?'

'I dunno, suh, could be a A.K.47.'

'Yeah, I see 'im, I see 'im good.'

'Permission to open fire, suh?'

'Permission granted.'

The gunner hit the man, blew him away. Later, they went down to take a look. The lieutenant spluttered:

'He was a mess. But what did he have? Nothin' but an itty-bitty stick.'

'You mean you wasted a guy for holding a stick?' someone asked.

'Sho' did.'

'How you feel about that?'

'Don't rightly feel nothin'. That guy had no right to be standin' there holdin' a stick with a Huey hoverin' around. Anyway, he was wearin' black pants.'

'But they all wear black pants.'

'So do the Cong.'

'Why didn't you ask him?'

'Ask him? Ask a gook?'

One night at another American camp, a *frisson* ran through the officers' barracks. 'Hey, you comin' to the picture show, pal?'

'What kind of picture show?'

'A French picture show.' The American was grinning. It was like screwing the whole damn country, a place that was once French.

'You mean dirty pictures?'

'Yeah, yeah, have some laughs.'

He went along with them and some Australians. Pornographic pictures for the troops. Perhaps only the Americans provided such comforts. There was a sort of grandstand made of wooded planks and behind it a projector. In front was a makeshift screen, white in the last light of the day. A few stars were out. Even at night it was hot and dusty. The whole place was dusty, like the back of Bourke in summer. He'd not realised that Vietnam could be so dry in winter. Sweat ran down his legs inside his greens, even though the sun had gone down. He found a seat as someone shouted: 'Okay?'

'Okay!'

The man pressed a switch and the projector rolled. Spotty and scratchy pictures flashed upon the screen. The film must have been made well before the war, the Second World War, possibly even in the twenties. It was a silent black and white, indistinct figures jumped about the screen. A man and two women were on a bed.

Each woman, both dressed, got on top of the man in turn. Then one of them got up on the end of the bed, squatting on her hands and knees. The man got off the bed lifted her skirt and did her from the back, at which the audience cheered. Their cheers had hardly stopped when the flickering images abruptly stopped, as if the film had broken. In all it had run for four or five minutes. There was another such film, not much longer and even drearier. A white woman was on a bed shagging a black man, who looked embarrassed by being filmed. When that film ended, the projectionist shouted: 'That's it, you fuckers! No more!'

Men booed, then rose disappointed. It had all been so brief and sexless that there seemed to have been no point. It was like a tour of Vietnam, one year and then back home they flew. Some went back early, sick, wounded, or dead. Others just got so demoralised they wangled a furlough, then saw to it that they never returned. Kramer walked back to his hutch, ashamed. He had not liked what he had seen. Those men had degraded themselves by being there, and so had he. But something else had degraded them all: the immense, impersonal machine of *realpolitik*. This whole war seemed like one great unfeeling obscenity. In which a man could be wasted just because he held a stick.

Sometimes, flying over Vietnam was scary. Returning by helicopter to Vung Tau one day, Kramer was surprised to see what looked like a thin black line drawn in the sky. The pilot put the machine over on one side, dived and got out fast. Kramer looked at Hurford.

'What was that?'

'Friggin' machine-gun fire.'

'Bullets? Real bullets?'

'Yeah, they just set up these big Chicom machine guns, watch for a chopper comin' in low, then pull the triggers, not aimin' direct at you, but in front, waitin' for you to fly right into that stream of lead. Shit, mate, if that lot'd come up though the floor, it would've chopped our arses to bits. You remember Tony Billings?'

'Yes, I do.'

'That's how they got him. Right through the arse.'

They spent some time in Vung Tau too, talking to Navy pilots, and went out one day to the foothills of the May Tao Mountains. The pilot was a handsome young man with dark curly hair, who looked as though he should be back home doing television commercials.

'What's on, Andy?'

'A dust off.'

'A what?'

'A dust off, a medical evacuation.'

'Someone been hit? An Australian?'

'No, some Yank.'

They took nearly an hour to get to the May Taos, a big V.C. stronghold on the north-eastern border of Phuoc Tuy Province. Below them, the forest grew denser as they hammered their way northward. Looking down on that beautiful country, it was hard to imagine that this was a killing ground, men chewing up men, women, children.

In clumps of trees Kramer could see lines of craters like the holes in a cribbage board, the same distance apart, perfectly placed, where a whole carpet of bombs from a B52 had hit. Nothing in those trees could have survived, not bunkers, not dugouts, not underground tunnels, not even concrete. When the B52s came in from Guam, nothing would escape. With computer-controlled precision, they could hit anything from thirty-thousand feet. The concussive force alone shattered not just eardrums but skulls, minds, and the humanity of anyone nearby.

When they reached the May Taos, it was difficult to see anything. The trees were more than a hundred feet high. The clearing was so narrow that you couldn't put a chopper down there. It would be like sticking a lawn mower down a rabbit burrow. So, they just held it there amid the leafy crowns. The co-pilot that day was a kid named Vidal, a sub-lieutenant. He'd graduated on Hueys only three months ago.

On the intercom, Kramer could hear them talking.

'Just hold it there. Don't take your eyes off the trees.'

'I've got it, sir.'

'Don't look down.'

'I'm not looking.

'Hold the blades about five feet out.'

'What's where they are.'

'Hold it right there.' Andy looked back at the port crewman, who had the winch ready. 'Okay, drop it.'

The harness descended. Hurford leaned over the side, aiming the Bolex straight down. Below, in the broken brush, men in G.I. helmets looked up, their hands reaching for the harness. From the starboard side, Kramer could see them securing it around a man whose arm was in a makeshift splint.

'It's down now. Hold it steady.'

'I am holdin' steady.'

The blades were almost touching the trees ahead. Kramer expected branches to fly off at any moment. One slip and they'd crash onto the Yanks below. The crewman signalled, okay.

'All right, haul him up.'

Soon, a red-headed soldier in a helmet and grubby fatigues came on board, clutching at anything within reach with his free hand. Kramer and the crewman helped him in. The G.I. looked bewildered but grateful.

Andy glanced back. 'Okay?'

'Secure, sir.'

'Let's go.'

Peering down as the Huey lifted, Kramer saw the Americans in the broken brush, hacked out of the jungle. One man with two bars on his helmet was looking up, smiling, saluting in that lazy American way, the palm downward, the elbow not high enough, not good enough for Duntroon, more like a wave than a salute, but complimentary. Kramer tried to talk to the redhead.

'You all right?'

The American nodded.

'Hit your arm?'

'Yeah, the Cong jumped us.'

'Anyone dead?'

He shook his head.

'Where are you from?'

'Omaha, Nebraska, sir.'

'You volunteered for Vietnam?'

'No, sir, they just sent a wire one day sayin' your country needed you.'

'A conscript?'

He nodded. It was almost impossible to talk above the noise. They swung away to the south, heading for Vung Tau, too high now for any machinegun to get them. The American leaned closer. 'You ain't from Stateside, sir?'

'No, Australian.'

He didn't seem to understand.

'Australian.' Kramer had to spell it out.

The G.I. thought about that, then pointed at his bandaged arm. 'Maybe this'll get me back home?'

'Maybe it will.'

The American closed his eyes, seemed to go to sleep. He was hurt, frightened but relieved. Perhaps he was grateful for the broken arm.

On their final day, they did another dust-off. This time it was an Australian. More a retrieval than a medical evacuation. The Da Dung River rose in the Long Hais, then ran across swampy ground. When they arrived, Australians were walking around, FN rifles at the ready. They'd found a body not far from the river, amid clumps of wild bamboo.

The Huey touched down near the men, standing as if the body were still alive. A sergeant approached but said nothing much—perhaps there was nothing to say. It might have been simply 'Good day'.

The huge rotors thudded above, drowning out every other sound.

Four soldiers carried a stretcher towards the chopper, something lying upon it. An arm protruded, lifeless. Bush hat on the dead man's chest.

They came closer, heads down.

Came right up. The crewman reaching out, guiding the stretcher in, two bearers pushing.

Kramer and Hurford had to shift to the port-side gun. Not filming, out of respect. Chaotic noise. The troops looked startled, sombre, and yet resolute, their movements faithful to their duty and their comradeship.

The crewman secured the stretcher so it wouldn't slide as the Huey lifted off. The chopper's rotors clutched at the air.

Kramer stood back, hanging on.

The rotors roared. The soldiers stood back, at a casual sort of attention. One or two saluted. The chopper lifted, thudding and thudding. The bearers looked up as if saying goodbye, respectfully. Faces full of the fatigue and misery and the grim certainties of war.

Kramer tried to see the man, his face, his name.

His body was flecked with bamboo leaves, one or two on his chest, on his neck. His eyes were closed, his face swollen. Waterlogged, his clothes and body. Kramer knew his name would be stitched into his shirt. But couldn't read it, soggy and dark and lifeless.

'What's his name?' he asked the crewman.

The man said something. Kramer couldn't hear above the noise.

He tried again, still too much noise. The chopper was tilting to port as it swung around, going back with the causalities and the debris of war. Everything went to Nui Dat, the Australian forward base.

The crewman hung onto a grab rail, looking out at the endless trees and the gentle rises and falls and the rivers of Vietnam. Then, as the machine straightened up and flew straight and true for home, a listless sun shone on the limpid body.

The sergeant had been lying in shallow water for several days until someone found him, hit by a short blast from an AK-47. Fired with hate and detestation from behind. His neck was open and grisly and wrecked. The last shot had gone through his head, just to finish him off. It had come out through his right eye.

At last the name jumped up from the sodden cloth. It was Becker.

The crewman saw his shock and half-smiled.

'Fuckin' war, eh sir?'

CHAPTER 31

The drought persisted, unrelentingly. Harry Becker planted crops only in late winter now. That meant he had to depend on winter crops for stock fodder. There was no point in planting for a summer crop. It would be too hot. The seed would sprout, but grow only a few inches then dry up, go grey in colour, droop and die. Rain came occasionally, but only in brief bursts, ten or fifteen millimetres at most. The paddocks remained dry, forcing him to hand-feed the cattle. As his stored feed dwindled, he began reducing his herd. By 2006, he was down to just ten Black Angus.

Times were tough. Had he not had such substantial savings, it might have been ruinous for him, Anna, and Roberta. But there was still Evelyn's money—about one and a half million dollars—mostly invested in Royal Bank shares. The dividends, paying around fifteen per cent at the time, earned him $150,000 a year for doing nothing.

He was a frugal man, naturally cautious. Never spent a dollar unless he had to. That's not to say he was mean. Far from it. He really did support himself and wife and Rose O'Hare and her girl in the little half house on Docker Street. Several times he had told himself he'd have to tell Rose she should pay her own way. She was still working at Mary Potter, but it was low pay. Carers got a pittance. Rose was a lovely woman, not very bright but ample in both body and soul. And, when in the mood, she was full of fun. So, he did not tell her.

Roberta was now in High School. Only ten and a half when she began, reputedly the youngest student. Everyone said she'd be the Dux of Wagga Wagga High one day. And a professor soon after that.

Anna adored her. They rode together, not only all over the land, but in the local gymkhana. Roberta was fearless on the jumps, as brave as a charging bull. She was riding Viento now. The mare was not a keen jumper. With some loving encouragement, got used to it. Her big sister, Wendy, had a boyfriend. She was very shy and modest about it. He was keen to marry, but she kept shying away. He was a young grazier from an old colonial property upstream toward Gundagai with a river frontage. Where there was still green feed. It had a famous name, Murra Murra.

One day, Becker met him. He walked into the agency and startled Wendy. She'd been talking to some young galoot in an Anthony Squires sports coat. Leather patches stitched to its elbows. Wearing R.M. Williams boots too. He was plump but not yet fat, and his name was Cudlip. He was startled, as if caught out chatting to a famous man's daughter.

Wendy was embarrassed.

'Oh, this is Adrian,' she said. Almost stuttered. Never addressed Becker as Dad or Harry or any sort of name, as though she didn't know what to call a stepfather.

The squatter's son blushed. His hair was red and his face even redder.

'Oh, ah, how are you, sir,' he said. The poor fellow looked as though he'd just gone twenty-one and didn't know what to do with the rest of his life.

'Well enough,' Becker said. He was in a hurry. Pixie was down with bloat. 'I've got Gifford to have a look at her. He thinks she'll get over it.'

Wendy was relieved. 'He won't have to pierce her?'

'With any luck.'

'Oh, poor Pixie.'

'Bloat, is it, sir?' The young squire ventured to ask.

'That's what I just said.'

'I'll come out,' Wendy said.

'I'll take you, if you like,' the young squire said.

'No, no, no need. Anna's there. Is Tommy about?'

'Oh, he's at the yards. It's Wednesday, you know.'

'Yes, of course.' Stock sales were held every Wednesday, except when they weren't.

'Can I give him a message?'

'Message? Tell him— Oh, no, I'll catch him some other time.'

He reached the door. Young Cudlip was trying to say something, but Harry Becker had disappeared.

Terry had now done three years with the Army. Including a stint with a U.N. peacekeeping unit, then some patrol work in the Solomon Islands, then exercising with the US Marines rehearsing on a beach in Queensland. Which was terrific, he said. This was big time. In the middle of the year, there was a rumour that his battalion was going to Afghanistan. He was enormously excited, raring to get stuck into the Taliban. But Anna and Becker were scared. He was the kind of young idiot who'd give it all he had, only to be blown up by a roadside bomb. Or, walk into an ambush in the hills north of Tarin Kowt.

Hank van der Bruggen was cutting chaff for his milking cow one day when he started feeling unwell. Pain in his chest getting worse. Anika saw him coming to the back door. She opened it for him. He put a foot on the first step, paused, looked up at her, and said: 'The will is in the—'Then fell down dead.

Anika is still on the farm next door. One of her sons, the unmarried one, lives with her now. But the wheat paddock is bare. Things don't look too good for them. They still have the bakery and the tarts and pies and rolls and coffee and chocolates on Baylis Street, just around the corner from the Lagoon.

In August 2007, Roberta had her eleventh birthday. Unlike the mothers at the local school, those of her friends at Wagga Wagga High were quite sociable. Seemed thrilled to be invited to the home of Anastacia Babchuk. Roberta invited six friends to her party. Wendy and Anika were there. So were Rose and Prilly. Terrey was in Queensland, could not get there. They had the party on the back verandah, it being mild and sunny and delicious. Held on a Saturday, just like the day she'd been born. Not a luncheon but a mid-afternoon affair. Lots of cakes made by Anika and ginger beer made by Anna, not expecting anything serious to come of it. But it had tasted good.

'This is fun, Robbie,' one girl said.

'Can we have a ride on your horse?' another asked.

So, they all had a ride on Pixie. Only a walk, Anna's hand on the bridle. Accompanied by Nutty, who hadn't had so much attention in years. All these children to play with.

Becker was standing on the back verandah, holding a post, watching them. Wendy and Anika were in the kitchen, cleaning up.

The gumtrees were in full foliage, proudly defiant. No bushfire was ever gonna get the best of a eucalypt. Nutty was dashing in and out of the creek, dry now except for a pool banked up behind the old weir, built by John Kettle's men to form a washpool for his sheep. That had been long ago, back in the middle of the nineteenth century. Incidentally, one of Roberta's school friends was

Alice Kettle, great great great granddaughter of John Kettle who'd founded *Nil Desperandum* in 1838.

Becker was smiling, watching the children.

It was his daughter's great day, her first big party. And she was the hostess. Anna brought out Viento and walked her around, showing her off. Both horses were so steady, many excited girls wanting to pat them. They were good horses. Friendly, pleased to be horses. Even Blue was on his feet, standing with Becker, watching.

'Now, girls,' Anna said, 'time's up.'

Two parents had arrived to pick up six. Anna was taking Viento to the stables.

'Robbie,' she said, 'put Pixie in her stall, please. It's going to be cold tonight.'

The girl looked at her watch. It was brand-new, her birthday present, stainless-steel and electronic. In a leather case too, like her mother's watch.

'Mummy, can they stay a while?'

'No, no, their transport has arrived.'

They got both horses housed for the night.

Anna walked up to Becker. 'Wow,' she said, 'thank God we don't have six kids.'

'Seven,' he said, 'counting Robbie.'

She began calling the girls. 'Come on, you lot!'

They began to walk up.

It was a lovely day, the sun was low now, flooding the dry and tired and fruitless land with light—long, slanting beams, creeping toward the cattle.

Anna had almost reached Becker, when the bullet hit.

No-one was sure at first that it was a bullet. Becker simply jumped back, clutching his chest, his mouth open as if to cough. A gasp was all they heard. Still holding the post, he began to go down. Took his hand away. It was bloody. His shirt was bloody. It was pumping out fast.

Anna rushed up, grabbed him.

'Get back, get back!' she yelled.

Children screamed, puzzled. Had that been a shot? Even Robbie was not sure and she'd heard enough gunshots in her life. Becker stumbled back, trying to reach a chair. He hit one, it slithered on the boards. Anna stopped it with one hand. He fell into it, a hand again to his chest.

'Oh, God,' she said.

Knelt beside him. Not carrying a weapon. Not with children around.

She looked across the creek, couldn't see anyone.

Nothing different about the backyard trees. The nearest eucalypt was some fifty yards away, but the shot could have come from anywhere.

Roberta cried. 'Mum, Mummy!'

'Get inside,' she said. 'Quick, run!'

The children were transfixed. Wanted to rush to the door, but too frightened. Mr Becker was collapsing, bent over in the chair, a hand grasping. Gasping badly now. Mrs Becker was furious. Looked as though she was going to kill someone. She was so angry.

Still, they did not run.

Wendy ran out, crouching low, trying to round them up. Shooing them. But still they did not move. Just stood about, shocked.

Nutty stood rigid, ears pricked up. Looking back at the trees. He might have heard or seen something. Perhaps someone running.

'Anna—' Becker said again, gasping.

'Harry, no, no, no!'

'I think it was—'

'Who, darling?'

He did not answer.

It was too late. His eyes fluttered for moment, then he keeled over. Dying in her arms.

'Harry, Harry, no! no!'

Anika came out, shouting: 'Quick, in the house! All of you!'

And stamped a foot.

Children came running.

CHAPTER 32

That all happened years ago. Ted Whitton did his best, but could not work it out. It might have been a paid assassination. But who would want to kill Becker? He'd not been involved in anything for many years. Not since that caper out at Griffith with Angelina Cosco. If the Mafia wanted to get rid of anyone, surely it would have been Anastacia. She'd been the one who'd hounded the criminals out there, humiliated them. Showed them who was boss around here. But Griffith had been quiet a long time. An occasional raid on cannabis plantations on the back blocks now and then, but no bodies have been found floating in irrigation canals recently. And gradually, what Cosco had done to his elder daughter, Contessa, had leaked out. The Italian community had been shocked, disgusted. Too many people in the know were now willing to talk to the police. Down in Melbourne, the Pisano family might have harboured a grudge. Again, Anastacia was responsible for knocking off the old man, *il capo dei capi*, not Harry Becker.

It was one of those mysteries without an answer.

Or perhaps there was an answer—one you could never quite get to. Or, now and then in your idle thoughts or as you are dropping off to sleep, you have an idea and think, *That's it, that's the one! That's who did it!*

The police had a theory.

The sniper was a professional, they thought. He'd lain on his stomach behind the trees and sighted up, using a scope. And a bipod, a simple metal stand with two legs on which you can prop a rifle. All good snipers use a bipod. Saves taking the weight on your arms for too long. Keeps the sights rock-steady over a long distance. What was the evidence? Two deep marks in the hard dry dirt. On the eastern side of the creek. They got hold of a standard bipod from a gun shop and checked. They were right. The metal feet matched the marks. And another thing.

There were elbow marks in the dirt behind the bipod marks. And elbow marks, and then boot marks. Sharp marks, the kind made by steel-capped boots.

The sniper had lain there for some time, trying to sight up on Harry Becker through the trees, but having difficulty. The target was moving around, even stepping onto the verandah occasionally, talking to Roberta or Anna or Wendy or Anika or one of the girls from school. It was not until he'd sat with Anna that he was steady enough for a good shot. This was it. This was the shot.

His face was big and sharp in the scope.

At first, he seemed surprised. He must have seen something—sunlight glinting off the scope's lens, perhaps. His expression shifted. First, puzzlement. Then suspicion. Then apprehension. And finally, certainty.

He tried to say something—to Anna or maybe just to himself. Run! Someone's up there, and I think it's a man with a—

Bang!

Too late.

Harry managed a few words before he passed out, his voice fading: '*I think it was*—'

Did he recognise the assassin? Anna is sure he did. But who?

The police measured the distance from the bipod marks to the steel-capped toe marks. Estimated that the sniper was a tall man, possibly over six feet tall. An expert marksman who wore steel caps on his boots.

Everyone thought perhaps he was an Army man. Then thought of Terry, crazy enough to do something stupid. Perhaps he harboured a secret resentment toward his stepfather. Resented the special attention his stepsister, Roberta, was getting. And another thing, she would inherit the farm. But, he was in Afghanistan at that time.

Maybe the killer had no motive at all. Perhaps he killed for the sake of killing. Like shooting ducks. Perhaps he thought nothing of it—it was just another sport.

Wendy finally said Yes to her shy suitor in 2007. She'd not been too keen to marry, but he was persistent. Her grandmother, Muriel Elliott was not enthusiastic. She would not say why, except to say or imply that the Cudlip family were different. Even so, Wendy gave way. It was a big wedding under a magnificent oak tree out front of the grand old homestead at Murra Murra. Everyone, who was anyone in the district, was there.

Roberta, now aged thirteen, was her big sister's flower girl. It was hot and late in the day she went swimming in the cold waters of the Murrumbidgee. Dived off the old wooden jetty where huffing and puffing paddle steamers used to load up with Murra Murra wool. Back in the days when wool was king.

Each time she went to Murra Murra, she'd dive off that jetty.

Until one day, Wendy asked her not to dive, a big Murray cod might get her. Some cods were as big as a man. But that was not the reason at all...

Two years later, Roberta's beloved grandmother died.

Muriel had had several falls, lost her balance. One night in June, she fell. A solid thump, although she was not a solid woman.

Wore a nurse-alarm bracelet. Managed to call an ambulance. Admitted to Wagga Base Hospital only a few blocks away. She'd fractured her pelvis in two places, both hairline. Hard to pick up on an X-ray. Very painful. She'd been in the orthopaedics ward for two weeks, but hadn't recovered enough to return home. Transferred to the rehabilitation ward, where she developed a cough. It became worse. They gave her antibiotics. Muriel became feverish. This went on for weeks. One morning about seven, they rang Wendy to say her grandmother had not survived the night.

Everyone was miserable.

Becker, an undemonstrative sort of man, was shaken. He'd lost a mother, not the real one who had died in mental derangement a few years ago, but Robyn's mother. Two lovely women, as gentle as a morning sunrise.

Terry happened to be at home at the time. Given a twenty-four-hour leave pass.

They gathered at the church. There was a good attendance. Angharad Thomas gave a funeral oration. 'A beautiful lady,' she said. 'We shall never see her like again.' Said it many times. Then took it upon herself to sing, not 'Rock of Ages' or 'Abide with Me' but 'All through the Night.' Her melodic Welsh voice moved everyone to tears.

They sang hymns. And praised the Lord.

Becker and Anna sat beside Wendy and Terry. Behind them sat Rose and April and others who'd known Muriel. Even Dell Kruger. You remember Dell? She was Deloraine Duffy. The gorgeous Dell, as she was known. The best figure in Wagga Wagga, everyone agreed. Married that architect's son, Hedley Devenish. Who'd been on top of a steel-roofed building in an industrial estate, when lightning had struck.

So badly that a man on the ground had said Hedley had lit up, like a man in a black and white negative. An ambulance was called, the police too. Max Kruger was the first there. Got him down on a rope. The ambulance crew worked on him. He was horribly burned. Got him to hospital, but too late. Max had the job of informing the new widow, six months gone.

After that, as they say, one thing led to another. But I digress…

After the funeral, everyone went to the wake in Muriel's little weatherboard house in Station Street. Murra Murra was too far out of town and, anyway, no-one in that family seemed to care a damn about Muriel Elliott. Adrian Cudlip seemed incapable of making a decision, accepting responsibility.

So, that was it, the funeral.

They were riding often now, Anna and Roberta, at the farm.

'Anna, where has Nanna gone?'

'Well, she has gone up into the sky.'

'Where?'

'You can't see her. But she's up there.'

'In the clouds?'

'No, up higher than that.'

'Up in the stars?'

These were childish questions, but they seemed to help.

'Yes, Nanna was a star herself. Now she's at home in the stars.'

'Has she gone to Mars?'

'To Mars?'

'Nanna could be up there on Mars, couldn't she?'

'Oh, I don't think she would go to Mars, not with her chest. It's dry and dusty, no air to breathe.' They trotted on. 'Still determined to get to Mars one day?'

'Oh, yes,' she said. 'Oh, yes!'

Anna leaned across, patted her on a shoulder.

'I think you are going to make it, darling. One way or another.'

CHAPTER 33

Roberta did well at school. Ended up as dux of Wagga Wagga High. One of nineteen in the State with a perfect score in the finals. Began next year at Charles Sturt University when only sixteen and a half. I remember her well. I was teaching economic history at the time, but as an historian not an economist. She sat in the front row, legs crossed, a smart skirt and blouse. Notepad on her knees, pen poised. Expensive shoes I couldn't help noticing, shiny brown leather, high heels. Altogether a well turned out young lady with a very serious gaze. If she blinked once, I did not see it. As I spoke, she took no notes, but did occasionally jot down a few words, presumably reminders of questions to ask or ideas to follow up. I'd heard of her of course, we all had. Apparently the key to her success at school had been her eidetic memory. She was some sort of freak, a student who never forgot whatever she wanted to remember. Otherwise, she was an ordinary sort of girl, amiable, respectful, devoted…

Recently, a few of us gathered for a quiet beer with Jack Jackson, who was retiring. It was his last day on the job. The conversation turned to Anastacia, and then, to our surprise, she walked in. Max Kruger had tipped her off.

Anastacia strode in wearing her usual gear—a loose blue sweatshirt, tight blue pants, and gym boots—moving with the easy confidence she's always had. Her hair now is as white as snow. Sold her share in the gymnasium soon after Harry's death. Had to give it up. Couldn't manage a farm and business in town at the same time. Has to look after Roberta, of course. Devoted to the girl. Looks on herself as her guardian. Ferociously protective.

She breezed up: 'Who's buying?'

'I am,' Max said.

She had a Jack Daniels for Jack's sake. Said she was feeling great. Put an arm about Jack's shoulders and stood with her legs crossed. She was fond of Jack, a good friend over the years. Holding a glass with the other hand, smiling and laughing. Quite a different woman now. Almost a lady, not the head-kicker she used to be. Max Kruger is now a sergeant, has been for a few years. Isn't on the road so much these days. The word going around is that he'll get Jack's job as station sergeant. That would please everyone, he being a decent sort of bloke and always has been.

'Cheers, Jack,' Anna said.

'Cheers,' we all said.

'Ah,' Anna, leaning back. 'Did it really happen?'

'Did what happened?' Max asked.

'Did I really kill a man in this bar all those years ago?'

'According to the papers, you did.' He pointed at the framed press cuttings still on the wall behind them, next to the portrait of William Hovell. The portrait that fell off the wall when Greg Shafter went crashing back against it, full of holes. Blood everywhere.

'You can't believe all you read in the papers,' Jack said.

Everyone laughed, including Bettina. She's still there, but she's the head barman now. And still living with her friend at Lake Albert. The friend is a radiographer at the Base Hospital. They say that, when she puts out the light to go to bed at home, she glows in the dark. But that may be a furphy.

Anastacia leaned back, musing. Perhaps reminiscing, or maybe philosophising—it's something she does more of these days, whether about life in Wagga or the wider world. She began speaking, her voice carrying the weight of reflection.

'What is life?' she asked of no-one in particular.

'It's what you make it,' Jack said. 'That's what they say, don't they?'

She did not seem to agree.

'Life is like a story someone made up out of memories and impulses and wishful thinking and every sort of idea that can float around in your head. Like you're dreaming and someone is telling you a story and you don't believe it, even in your dreams. You know you are dreaming. But someone is saying to you: This is no dream, sweetheart. This is true and it's gonna hurt. You aren't getting out of this. You're inside some sort of story, for which you are at least partly responsible. And if it's not the kind of dream you'd prefer, stop protesting. Crying for help, exclaiming you are being abducted by some fiendish storyteller, who comes in the night and rapes you with facts and fancies, won't help. The story has got you by the tits, or by the tit if you are male, telling you to stop crying for your mother. You're inside a story you can't get out of. That's life, so hang on, here we go. We're goin' for a ride, baby. Yeah, we're goin' for a ride.'

'Gee,' someone said. It must have been me. I'd never heard her so passionate about anything, except getting even.

'That's what it's like, isn't it?' Anna said. 'Life, it's like a fast ride around your own brain. You can't get off. And, although it scares the shit out of you sometimes, you wouldn't have missed the ride for worlds, would you?'

'Eh?' someone said. That too must have been me.

'Yeah,' she said, leaning back and smiling. 'Some ride…'

The William Hovel has changed. Back in her time it was known as the twelfth most violent pub in New South Wales. Since then someone has taken it over and tarted it up, so they now have card games and pinball and karaoke and off-course betting on anything, even flies climbing up a wall. All to the sound of a reggae beat if you're lucky. Or, to the singing of Heddy Haasberg from the West Coast of New Zealand, if you're not. She has her own guitar and pedal drum. Her singing is awful, but that doesn't matter. No-one listens. Also, professional bouncers with small brains and massive biceps and real tattoos at the door, both front and back. Samoans, they call them. As a result, the Hovell has dropped to seventeenth in the State bloodhouse ratings, which is disappointing. The clientele has changed. But it's all right for a beer if you get out before six. Before the tourists walk in.

And they still sell Jack Daniels on the rocks.

As for Terry, he did two tours of duty in Afghanistan and managed to avoid getting himself killed. He's a corporal at Kapooka now, so they see a bit more of him. Could have been a sergeant, he's old enough. But he's still a bit of a tearaway. Never too strong on Army discipline. Never married either. Was stuck on Liesel Eckhardt for a long time. But he was a bit too impulsive for her. Always doing or saying the wrong thing. Didn't know how to handle women.

Recently, I asked Anna whether she'd ever thought of marrying again. Not that I was thinking of proposing. I'd be a bit too old for her. And not much to offer any woman now, certainly not a retired gunfighter like her. She smiled in her own offhand way and said she wanted only one man, but he would never return.

'You don't feel he's still here?' I asked.

'Yes, I do—in my dreams and in my heart. I will love Harry until I die—and perhaps a bit longer.' We were sitting on her front verandah, with Nutty asleep at her feet. Then she asked: 'What did you think of Harry?'

'He was a simple man,' I said, 'but a complete man for all that.'

'Yes,' she said, 'he completed me.'

www.ingramcontent.com/pod-product-compliance
Lightning Source LLC
Chambersburg PA
CBHW040516170726
48295CB00012B/217